THE WHITE SWORD SAGA
BOOK ONE
THE EYE OF EBON

P. PHERSON GREEN

 GOLD DRAGON PUBLISHING

Join the White Sword Saga Newsletter for updates, promotions and exclusive material at the White Sword Sage website: www.thewhiteswordsaga.com
Contact info: **www.pphersongreen.com**

Written by: P. Pherson Green
Edited by: Stephanie Taylor
Cover Art by: Teresa Jenellen

This book is entirely human created content, no AI was used in any portion of this creation
Published by Gold Dragon Publishing, Odenton, MD, USA

ISBN: 979-8-9905328-0-9 - Hardback
ISBN: 979-8-9905328-1-6 - Paperback
ISBN: 979-8-9905328-2-3 - Ebook

LCCN: 2024914984

First Edition: Aug 2024
10 9 8 7 6 5 4 3 2 1

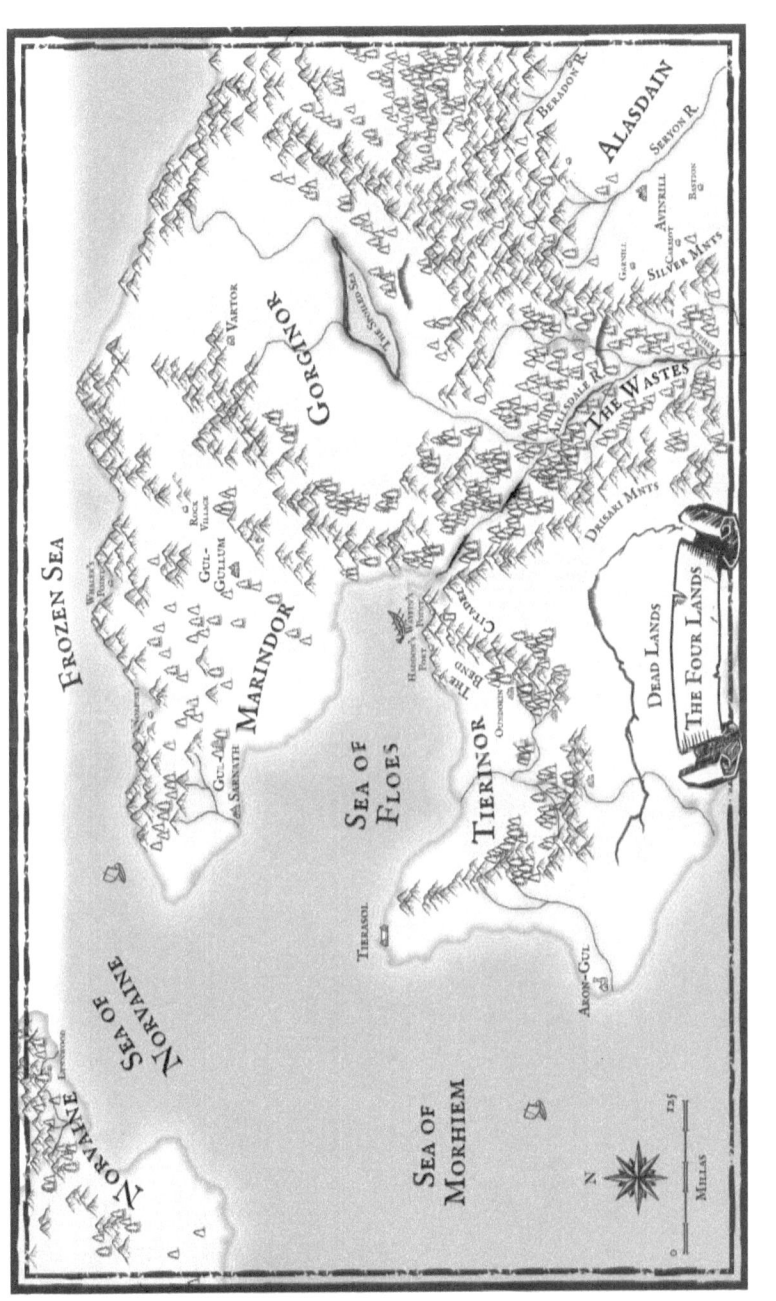

THE EYE OF EBON
PROLOGUE

IN THE DARKNESS of the cavern blood flowed in rapid streams. Dripping from stained garments, and forming into a shallow pool, it fell to the feet of the lone figure who shed it and colored red the dark rock beneath. The figure resembled a man, but was changed; like a Wight he was in his gaunt features and pallid caste. He was not a man, he was of the race of the Allarie, one that should live forever, and would if he were not in the grip of something other than immortality. His right arm hung limply at his side, the flesh of it ripped apart in crude fashion and the shreds peeled away to reveal the bone beneath. Upon the stone before him was the slender shape of a thin dagger, it too covered with the same blood that stained the stone and bore the figure's own bloody hand prints on its haft. In spite of his injury, the gaunt figure seemed unconcerned. He held in his last perfect and bloodstained hand a thick fragment of stone, looking on it with an unnatural lust in his dark and sunken eyes.

"It is prepared," he spoke, his voice raspy, filled with anguish and yet holding the strength of madness in its tone. "The way is well hidden. It awaits you." His breathing was strained and he wheezed with each rise of his sunken chest. "I can do no more." He moaned, and then descended into ranting. "The Priestess…She knew. She ruined me!" He began to weep. He held the fragment to his head and coughed as convulsions wracked his body. Desperation consumed him and he cried out, screaming, "That wretched Priestess brought this upon me!" His sobbing grew and lingered with him, but soon he calmed and seemed to gather strength. Standing, he held the fragment of stone before him.

"What must I do?" he spoke to it.

"Yes," he said. "I know. When you are strong you will come for it."

He turned to face the upward slope of the cavern, and trailing blood from his shredded arm he staggered forward. "The sarcophagus," he said as if resigned. "I will wait in the sarcophagus I made. I will hold it until you are ready."

PART I
TORRENTS OF
NORVAINE

THE NIGHTMARE CONTINUED. Men and wicked creatures with evil faces gloating in the light of a fire. Two sisters screaming, one clinging to the other, but for them there could be no comfort. With rough hands they were separated and then dragged apart. The younger succumbed to their threats, but the older lashed out with gashing nails–she clawed into one.

Words were spoken, foul words she could not understand. A fist rang out her senses. There were screams, her sister cried to be with her but she was dragged away and then she was gone–taken, never to be found again. Left alone, the torment began; bound, she was beaten, trying once to flee, her feet were pierced, disobeying, she was punished. Out on the snow, she was stripped and given to the pleasure of the crowd. Each took their amusement, some with cruel fists, others with exploring hands. She cried at first, but soon she felt nothing at all, soon it was all just a vision of her delirium; one brutal trial after the next.

Surrendered and helpless, she prayed for mercy, prayed to the one god she knew–the one who watched over. And she prayed for justice. It lasted for days, and as she grew numb to their torments, their brutality grew. One carved words into her belly, a foul creature that took joy at her horror, and then another wished to see her burned. A sword was heated with fire, its length made hot enough to melt flesh, and she was tied for her marking–stretched over a load-bearing sled. It touched her and she screamed, but her screaming only brought them mirth; again she was touched, and again they laughed. Her prayers turned to desperate screams. She begged for mercy, and cursed them in her rage. The branding continued, three times, four times, five times her flesh was seared. But then it stopped.

Her bonds were cut, and she was kicked onto the snow. Having had their fill, her tormentors left her for a time. She was meant to die, but death did not come.

As she lay upon the cold white blanket, her voice rose above the winds. She cried out, she wanted deliverance–she was answered: descending from grey skies high above the snowy plain, a creature, first of light, and then becoming a man, glowing with splendor and brilliance, came forth. He held before him a gleaming sword, a silver blade and a golden hilt, and he carried it to her hand. He spoke, not with words, but in a way that was much like a song to which she knew the words–she was to deliver herself.

Her pain gone, she rose, but in her fear, she hesitated. As her tormentors took notice, she grew in rage. They may have fought, she did not know; she did not care. She heard their screams, and saw their desperation. She hated them. The sword in her hands burned with an unconsuming fire, and against it, there was no mercy, only slaughter.

The battle forgotten, she lay in the snow waiting for the end, her thoughts lingering on the one thing she still wished to change– *Nechare*. She struggled to speak the name. It formed on her lips, and she gave it breath. "Nechare," she spoke, and then repeated it again, and again, and again...

SAMIARE PASSED BACK into consciousness. A man carried her.

Then she writhed. Burns at her back flared with new intensity, and blisters rubbed against his arms–she screamed out. She was wrapped in a red cloth. As she moved, she felt again the sword–*the sword*.

"Make way," the man screamed, his boots pounding on a wooden deck, the smell of brine and sour vinegar stale in the air, the chill of winter and the wetness of snow pressing in. Figures moved about.

"Seven Gods," she heard one exclaim.

She struggled to move, to escape his grasp, but he held her tighter and said words to soothe. His motions stopped, he lay her down on a pile of old sacks. She could not be still. She twisted against her pain, turning to her side. The blanket fell open, the sword falling out. Her hand still grasping it.

A woman came next to the man, and looked over her. Bright red hair, and gold mail, she also wore a sword.

"She'll never make it," said the man. "She's too far gone. We should do her a mercy."

"She'll live," said the woman. "You will live..." she said again to her. "I promise."

She turned again, the sword pulled up to her breast, her body exposed, bruises and red marks covered her, pierced feet and carved flesh leaked with red. But the sword,...the sword, it sang to her, and she could barely believe. *Was it over? Had it even happened? Men and the foul creatures like them...twenty or more...Had she slain them all...* And then a new pain, one who was missing. "*Nechare,*" she called out, but they could not understand her. "*Nechare...*"

The man scoffed, the woman crouched down low, touching her face gently, brushing aside the flax of her hair. "We'll get you out of here," she said. "My name is Ruegette. I am from Tierinor, and I promise, you will live."

THE STRANGE GIRL safely aboard their ship, Ruegette stood on the deck of the Tieran vessel as the light of Mirneth's orb drifted towards the western mountains, and the crescent of Meridel, shrouded in the world mist, rose dimly from the east. A cold wind blew, churning the waters and causing the ship to creak. She hated what she had found. She hated that she had come too late, and that she had failed to stop them. The Groll were never gentle, and she had seen too much of what they could do already.

Zarue lumbered over the planks and came to stand next to her. "It's a hard life," he said. "This one we lead. The Wardai never rest, and we always see the worst of it."

She heard his words, but remained sullen. If only she could have learned of the Groll sooner. They were on the seas, and slipped by unknown. They should have known–Tierinor should have known. "She was just a child," she said. "Fifteen summers…"

"It's not your fault," said Zarue.

"I know," said Ruegette. "It's just….And how could she have…"

So many thoughts raced through her head. Twenty were dead on the snow. Both Groll and Morkind. She could read the signs, she knew well her role. They had not fought against each other. They had fought all against one. They had all fought, and they had all lost. The girl held a sword, but the things they had done…she could not have done it. She was too close to death herself. And the sword was ornate, a gold hilt on a silver blade. Where would she get it? Ruegette could not understand it. She saw what was written on her–*Shal mot*. Carved into her flesh in the Durish language of the Groll, they called her 'Groll Whore'.

"I don't know what happened," she said. "But I want her to live."

"You have done a good thing," said Zarue. "But it's out of our hands. We can take her to Tierasol. Let the temple have her. If she lives, it will be some time before she recovers. We won't be there to see it."

Ruegette looked up at him. His dark eyes held the look of so many of the Wardai, not that he held no compassion, but that he had found a way to push it aside. His eyes were sad, and he frowned beneath his dark mustache, but his face was still hard. She turned back to the coast, and rested her hand on the dark hilt of the gorum-steel blade he once had made for her. Like him, she hardened herself to her task. "We knew the Groll had been on the waters," she spoke, forcing strength into her voice. "And from the bodies, we know the Marish were with them. But it seems they have all been slain. We will take the girl to Miranae's temple in Tierasol, but we must sail again. We must search the coasts. If the Groll are boarding Marish ships, we must find out where."

"Don't become attached to her, Rue," said Zarue. "It'll be a long time before we can return. She must fight her own battles now."

"Yes," she said. "I just wish it was different. She was in such pain. I just wanted…" She breathed heavy, but did not finish. "It was our failure. Somehow the Groll got by us."

Zarue gave a sigh, and looked towards the darkening coast as well. "What in Gorumgahl is in bloody Norvaine anyway? Just a frozen land with no settlements to speak of. It's good she was near the coast. She'd be dead if they bloodied the snow somewhere else."

"Yes," said Ruegette. "It was good."

The wind whipped over her, setting her own red strands to buffet. She pulled her arms in closer, covering the gold links of her mail with her cloak. Snow began to fall, and light to fade. Whatever was in Norvaine, it was over with now.

THREE MONTHS UPON the sea and nothing. Scouring the Marish coast and moving north into the Frozen Sea, and there were no signs of Groll camps, or Groll ship building. No signs that anything at all was amiss with their sister ally to the North. Still, the Groll had gotten to Norvaine. They had the help of the Marish, and they had hurt that girl. Ruegette still did not like it.

She walked along the streets of Tierasol, moving away from the docks with Zarue at her side. They were always a pair, the Prime and her Second. They both served the Warder of the Eastern Citadel, Jarl Mavrou–her father. Ruegette had done so for most of her life. Since the day she took up the sword, and left behind her role as Princessa. Zarue was her teacher and guardian, chosen for her by her father. When she took the Wardai mark, it had come with a cost, that of home and love and family. Ruegette did not always like its burden, but she was a Tagore, duty before all else was her way.

The Temple of Miranae loomed tall on the hill before them. Visible through the streets over the rooftops of village homes and merchant dwellings, its pearlescent dome, a symbol of tranquility under the silver sky. One of three temples in the sea city, Miranae held particular distaste for those of the sword. Many of her profession believed it invited ill fortune to visit its halls or seek its services, and while she did not nurture such concerns, the same could not be said for her protector.

"I know where you're going," he said, looking up to see the white dome of the Goddess's house. "I'm not going in."

"You won't have to," she said. "I will go."

"You can't help her," said Zarue, shaking his head, and scowling. "Whatever her fate, she's not something we can care for."

Ruegette gave him a scornful look. "You don't think we can give her even a little compassion? Could we not show some caring?"

"It's not that," he said. "It's that what we do does not leave room for it. The fate of a Norvish girl is not the job of the Wardai. She's with the temple now. They will care for her."

"Well, I will care for her too," said Ruegette. "Even if just for a day. And besides, don't you want to know what happened? How she survived it? She killed all of those on the snow that day. There is no other way to explain it."

"We searched," said Zarue. "We searched and searched. There were no Groll on the seas. Whatever the Groll and the Marish were doing in Norvaine, they must have turned on each other, and it ended. She could not have done that on her own."

"That's not what I saw," said Ruegette. "Twenty dead on the snow, and she was the only survivor. They did not fight each other. You saw the blood. The black blood was not on the Marish, only on her. She fought them all. She killed them. We must know."

Zarue rolled his eyes and shook his head some more. "I will go with you to the temple, but I won't go in. I will be waiting outside."

Ruegette did not push him further. Zarue was his own man and he could make his own way. She had thought of the girl many times in her journey away, but he had seldom mentioned her. It was she who wanted to know…wanted to know that she had truly rescued her.

At the steps before the great door, Zarue halted and touched a small iron ingot to his head, a sign to the war god, Kullis, to ward away the ill fortune of injury. Zarue was not often godly, but he did follow a warrior's traditions. Ruegette looked up at him and smiled. "I won't be long," she said. She left him at the stairs, and went to the doors of the temple.

Inside, she looked for the Matron, the one who was there when they first brought in the injured girl. Younger acolytes scurried about, and she walked past them. The woman she sought was older, and wore a blue sash as a symbol of her station within the faith. Ruegette spied her further along the corridor, and waved. The Matron turned her head to see, and walked towards her. She was more aged than Ruegette remembered, with greying hair and a lined face, and her expression as she approached was one of stoic perseverance.

As she came closer, the Matron dipped into a curtsey and smiled widely. "Princessa," she said. "You have returned. Have you come to see the child?"

Ruegette knew her as Lizelle, and nodded before girding herself up. She did not know what to expect or if she were truly up to seeing the young girl again, but she knew she must. "Yes," she said. "I would see her if I may."

The Matron motioned to her, and led the way through the halls at a slow gait. "We did not think she would live, of course," she spoke. "The burns she received should have killed her." But before the entrance to a large room she stopped, and pulled on Ruegette's arm, turning her. "But she didn't die."

"Well... That is good, isn't it?" asked Ruegette.

"Her struggle is not over," said Lizelle. "You must know; it is worse than we first knew. She is with child."

"With child?"

"I know what is written on her," said the Matron. "That child could be twice cursed. If it is of the Groll..."

"Does she know?"

"Yes," said the Matron. "I offered to remove it, but she refused. She does not speak as we do, so it has been difficult. And the sword..."

"The sword?"

"She will not release it. At first we tried to remove it, but she resisted. In time, I came to realize that somehow it comforted her. That as long as she held it, she was calm. I chose to let her keep it."

"And she is inside?" Ruegette looked past her into the room beyond.

"Come I will show you."

The Matron led Ruegette into a large room of grey colored stone.

Many large columns held the roof, and at the top of one wall, a series of large openings let in light from the outside. The room was divided into many small dens for resting, each with a straw mat. There were more than a few who made use of the temple's services, and throughout she could hear the moans of those who fought off sickness or injury. Others moved about, acolytes who tended to the un-well, bringing in water or ointments as needed to the sick and weary. The one Ruegette sought was near the back.

The girl looked much different than when she first came across her. She was covered in a white gown and lay upon a straw mat. Her face was no longer swollen, and the bruises and cuts that once marked her pale skin were gone. Her wrists bore only faint scars, and her feet had been almost completely healed, but she still suffered from the burns to her back and winced as she shifted. Her sword lay at her side, her hand clutching at its hilt. Her flaxen hair had been cut short, but Ruegette took little notice; she was a pretty child, and Ruegette pitied her for what had happened.

The Matron left. Ruegette sat on a stool and looked down. "Do you remember me?" she said. "I found you in the snow."

"Yes," said the girl, her voice still bearing the high tone of a child. She tried to say more, but she could not make the words. Instead she spoke a word in Norvish that Ruegette did not understand, and stopped.

"I am Ruegette of the Eastern Citadel," she said. "Most who know me call me, 'Rue'."

"Ruegette," the girl spoke, her eyes coming back up. She made an effort to say the word with the same inflection that Ruegette had used, but still her voice carried its Norvish sound.

"I wanted to see you," said Ruegette. "To see if you were doing well. I think you are looking much better. And you are very pretty. A little more time, and I think more than a few of our young warriors will want to win your fancy."

"No," she said. "*Shal Mot.*"

Ruegette understood immediately what the girl meant; and became unexpectedly aware that this girl was no longer the child that she appeared. Innocence had been robbed from her, and those Durish words alone would keep suitors away. "I see," she said.

"Perhaps we could give them something else to call you. What is your name?"

"Samiare," said the girl. "Am Samiare."

"Say-mi-ar-ee," said Ruegette, trying to get the inflection right. "That's a lovely name. I like you, Samiare. I admire the strength you must have to survive all this. I am told you are with child."

"Yes," said Samiare, letting her free hand slide onto her abdomen. "With child."

Ruegette felt her heart sink. The sight of the young girl, barely more than a child herself, touching a new life within was somehow both wondrous and tragic. Her breath halted for an instant, and her eyes grew wet.

"I know you are a fighter," she said. "You know this child may be of the Groll."

"Of Samiare," said the girl. The child drew back with a look of caution, and determination was written on her face. At her side, the sword she held firmly in an unending grip shifted upon the floor.

"I will not try to change your mind," said Ruegette. "If you want to be a mother after all that has happened, I will be with you. It will be hard on you, but you must know that already. I must ask you about that day, and what happened. Did you really slay twenty men with that sword?"

The young Samiare gazed at the sword in her hand. Such a strange weapon for her to have, an engraved golden hilt and a broad blade of polished silvery steel. She struggled to speak in her new language. "I...no...think men," she said. "I...fight...was pain."

"Please," offered Ruegette. "Do not trouble yourself. I have only one more question. What does, 'Nechare,' mean?"

The young girl winced back as if that word alone were something she could not bear. "Nechare," she said with a voice much like a whimper. "Nechare."

"Yes," said Ruegette. "What does it mean?"

"Nechare...Like...Like..." Her hand trembled as she struggled for words, and a different kind of emotion played on her face, one that revealed the torment inside of her.
"Nechare...girl...like...blood...like Samiare."

"Like blood," said Ruegette, and then alarmed. "Nechare is a sister?" She vividly remembered that day on the field of snow, and she knew that could not be. "I searched them all," she said. "There was no other but you on that field. There was no other girl at all."

"No," said Samiare. "Nechare...go...men..."

Ruegette stood from her stool. "Oh, my!" she said. "We just assumed that when we found you we had found them all, but there were more." Ruegette's thoughts raced. She knew the Groll were there, but thought them a small band. If they were a large band, they were not just marauders. They must have had a purpose. One she still did not know. "I must go back."

She thought to leave but could not. She looked once more on the small girl. Samiare lifted her hand to her, and Ruegette returned to her side. Kneeling, she took Samiare's hand in hers. "I am sorry," she said. "I must go, but I promise, I will not let anyone hurt you again."

Samiare smiled at her. "With child?"

It was a question that Ruegette could not understand, but it was not hers to ask. "Do not fear," she said. "I will not let them take your child." Ruegette released the girl's hand and left the healing dens. Emotions welled within her, more than she would have expected. Admiration and sorrow and even shame. She had found much more than she expected, the child had far more strength than any should, and through all of her pain, she was preparing for an even greater burden—mother to a fatherless child. It was overwhelming. It drained her.

Zarue was still waiting on the steps when she appeared. As he approached, his face bore a grimace that shown both his distaste for the Temple, and his relief that they would be leaving. "Was she well?" he asked without sounding concerned.

"I have work to do," she said. "I will need to get a ship and go back to Norvaine."

"Back to Norvaine?" he questioned. "Rue, anything that might have been there is too old to find now. There have been three snows since then, you won't even find the same spot."

"I'll find it," she said. "Whatever it is."

"Do you want me to get a party together?"

"No," she said. "I want you to stay here and see to it that nothing happens to our girl."

"*Our girl?*" He blurted out. "When did she become '*our girl*'?"
Ruegette shot him a stern look.
"Oh, Rue," he moaned. "You know I hate temples!"

THE SHIP SKIRTED along the coast of Norvaine for several days before Ruegette called it to anchor. The endless expanse of shimmering snow and the unyielding line of grey mountains made discovering the place most difficult. In the end, it was only by her own belief that they must be near that she moved the search onto land.

She wore her gold mail under a cloak of thick fur, and her dark-hilted sword hung at her side. She carried a pack laden with food and other items, and a bow with arrows was slung over her shoulder. Three men went with her. They were warriors with less experience, but she was unconcerned; she truly did not expect to find anything after so much time had passed.

For two days she explored the coast, hoping to find the place where they had discovered the girl, but she could not. On the third day, she came to the edge of a wide valley overlooking a small settlement; a trapper's outpost with only a few buildings huddled together near a wide stream. She considered that soldiers from Tierinor may not be welcomed by those below, but discounted it. She needed a guide, and trapper's outposts were for trading.

There was no hiding on the snow-covered slope. The gleaming white could not disguise four dark and lumbering figures moving upon it, and so she did not even try. The settlement was home to only a few inhabitants, but seemingly all of them had come forth to stare as warriors, clad in the red and gold of Tierinor, came into their midst. Ruegette looked past them and sought out the one structure that seemed most welcoming, one that was constructed larger than the others and billowed smoke from a stone chimney attached to the end.

A large man dressed in furs and with a face enshrouded by a full beard stood at the entry. He watched as they approached, and nodded as Ruegette met his gaze. She thought it unlikely he would speak Tieran so she addressed him in the language of Morheim, one known inelegantly as 'Trade'.

"We are searching for something in this land," she said. "We could use information."

The man smiled and gave a chuckle. "There's not much to find in Norvaine," he said, his dialect in the Trade tongue was very different from Ruegette's, but it was sufficient. "I think you've come a long way for nothing, but I won't stop you from going in."

Ruegette led her company into the wooden structure. The inside was a fashion typical of many of the gathering dens she had seen in her travels; a large open room with a stone firepit against one wall, a single long table with wooden benches set in the middle, and small barrels full of food stuffs placed on the floor. A simmering kettle hung over the fire, and fur pelts were piled up in a corner. The room was empty but for a single man, he sat at the table and ate from a steaming bowl of stew.

She approached. The man looked up from his meal and eyed her with suspicion, his expression questioning her warrior colors and armed companions. The large man who met them outside walked in from behind and shook off the cold. "That's Stroja there," he said. "He's one of the trappers."

"Does he speak Trade?" she asked.

"We all speak Trade," laughed the man. "Ask him yourself. My name's Bajora. You can have stew if you like, but we're all out of ale. The winter's been quite hard. You have anything to barter?"

"We have silver tierits from Tierinor," offered Ruegette. "They should be worth several Morsh ingots on any of the trade routes."

"I don't have much use for coins," said Bajora.

Ruegette smiled at the simplicity of Norvaine's wild lands. "We have a ship waiting for us off the coast two days north of here. It is to wait for seven days before heading south to Morheim. If you help me, I will see to it that it brings ale when it returns."

Bajora brightened at the promise of ale. He raised his hand and pointed at her as he addressed the trapper who was still watching from the table. "Stroja, speak to the woman."

Ruegette sat upon the bench directly across from the man as those who came with her made their way to the kettle and took up bowls.

Stroja had a thin face weathered with creases. Light colored hair hung in strings about him and a thin beard darkened his chin. He wore the leather and furs of a trapper over a lean body, and his grey eyes betrayed his hardness as he looked across at her.

"I don't like women," he said. His dialect in Trade was struggled, apparently something he did not speak often. "And I don't like women pretending to be warriors." He pulled a mug of strong smelling spice closer to him, cupping it with his mitted hand.

"I see," she said. "Well, I don't like drunkards, and those that hide what they drink."

The man smiled and his head cocked to one side. "You're the one bringing the ale," he scoffed. "What do you want with me?"

"I need to find men who travel with Groll," she said. "Before the winter they would have come south and raided some homes on the plain. I know they came upon the home of two girls."

"I know a home like that," said Stroja. "Out in the Sharin territory. Seen the father, Samael, couple times a year. Seems like a good man. Sami and Necha are the girls. Why would anyone want to raid them?"

"We found the girl, Samiare, out on the plain some months ago. She was only half-alive. We did not find her sister, but I know the father was slain. I am interested in finding the Groll that came upon them."

"Sami half-alive?" said Stroja. He shook his head with a pained look. "She was such a pretty child. So was her sister. And brave... You come from Tierinor where the Groll are common. Out here we call them something different. '*Fal*', means 'foul ones'."

"We know they were on the plain. We think they may still be here. Can you show us to the place where the two girls lived?"

"I'll take you," said Stroja. "I owe the father. He spared me some traps some winters back. If this is true, and they hurt them two girls, I would do 'bout anything to get those who did it."

"We can use you," said Ruegette. "We'll leave when you're ready."

"I'll also take some of the ale when it arrives," said Stroja, drinking deep from his spice-smelling cup.

HATE AND ANGER raged within. Another night she lay in the dark, writhing at the pain of her burns, and seething inside. There was no way to escape. She could not rest. In a release of rage, Samiare sat up from her mat, and pulled the sword up to her breast as tears wet her eyes. At the late hour, none would see or know. She hated it all.

To come in the night, to break through their door, to do what they did. Her Father, her sister—all of it. She held the sword, a music played within her, soothing and full of hope. If she let it, it would take the pain away, but she did not want that. She wanted to scream and lash out at it all. To force violence on all those who came to hurt her. Those monstrous creatures…how could there be such wickedness as what they brought? And those that were with them? She would never forgive.

It was so unfair!

To sit in the dark as pain wracked through her…to be forever damaged by what they did. And to have no way to put back what they have broken, or regain what she had lost—maddening. She held the sword—a true fighting weapon, a broad silver blade almost as tall as she, and a heavy gold hilt that could be used with one or both hands. Somehow, it worked through her. It struck down her foes. It showed her how—it burned with fire. And the music…what even was it? Not music but a feeling that seemed to always hum, and to always know. And at a whim, she could understand, and yet….she could not know any of it. There were no answers, just a tone that felt like words. And all of it, not an answer to her will, but a desire only that she accept and trust.

Trust what?

Why had it even happened?

She held the sword, but where was her foe? What could she do with it? Marindor…Groll… What even were they?

Her back twinged and her face grimaced. She had not stood in so long. She pulled in her legs and winced through the pain. She felt so weak. She pressed her sword the floor and let her head fall against the pommel. She went to stand, but the flesh on her back pulled and tore. Pain shot through her. For an instant she could not breathe, and she trembled, and then she gasped out a sob. Would it be like this always? Would there always be pain? She breathed hard, and tried again. The music soothed into her, it told her to lie still. She did not listen. Her arms trembled, her legs barely moved, her back blazed anew. They took her sister–They took her sister! She fought and awkwardly got a knee under herself, but the pain was too much and she fell again to her side. Gasping out, she rolled onto her back, and fell still as tears flowed.

How could she make it right? How could she have justice–revenge? She knew of only one hope. The one her father taught her of–the one who watched over. The one to whom she prayed when the sword was first delivered to her hand. It offered hope, and wanted trust, but what hope was there? What could she trust?

As she lay, she felt a new movement. Something inside her pressed at her belly. Sharp at first, but then a dull pushing out. Her hand went down instinctively, and she felt it. A new life. A new hope.

She closed her eyes, and listened to the sounds as they soothed, and took away her pain. "Nechare," she said aloud. "I will find you. One day...I promise."

She lay in the darkness and let the song play in her heart. Her loneliness quelled for a time, and her pain slowly drifting into something bearable. She tried to push it all from her mind, but she feared she never would.

ONLY THREE FOLLOWED Stroja into the snow-covered valley. Ruegette had sent one of the soldiers back to release the boat, asking for it to return in three weeks to retrieve them, and leaving orders that it should have ale for the outpost. The two who remained were young men with plenty of youthful strength and hardiness, but they were clumsy and inexperienced in the wilderness, and Ruegette had little use for them other than the gathering of food and wood.

The house of Samael sat on the plain, nearly covered in snow. It was a small structure of meager construction, and not at all what Ruegette was expecting for a girl with a gold-hilted sword. Lost in a wide valley speckled with sparse purple pines, and nestled in the shadow of two large mountains, an iced over stream went past the home, ending at a small lake a short distance away. Outside was a large pile of wood covered with snow. The door to the house was missing, and the stone opening of a low chimney lay cold and unused.

"Not much you gonna find here," said Stroja. "Fal will have taken all they had."

"How could someone have lived out here?" questioned Ruegette.

"Winters are bad up here," said Stroja. "But you can grow crops in the spring, and the elk hunting is good. Just got to store 'em is all. Cold helps with that."

Ruegette ordered her two companions to wait on the plain and watch for Groll before heading with Stroja down the thick snowy field to the lonely house below. Approaching the front and moving for the open hole where the door had once been, Ruegette slid down a short mound of snow and stumbled into the front of the small house.

The house was of log construction with mud filling in the gaps. It had but a single room where the body of a man lay on his side. His torso had been pierced several times by stabbing weapons, and his blood was frozen into a dark stain on the dirt floor. His body showed few signs of decay, preserved as it had fallen by the cold. The room was littered with the debris. Those who came before had spared no effort in destroying all of the items in the room; a wide shelf was pulled from the wall and its contents scattered, the tops of chests and a lone table lay splintered, the stuffing of two wool mattresses were torn and strewn. No items of any value were left behind that Ruegette could see.

"Cursed Fal dogs," said Stroja. "There was no need for this."

Ruegette squatted down next to the corpse, and looked at his face, searching for some resemblance between him and the girl. The man's eyes were open, but death had turned them grey and dark.

"We should burn the body," she said. "We should use some of the wood to build a pyre." The man wore a small wooden token on a leather string about his neck. She pulled at it and examined it in the light. The token was a crude carving of a southern flower in bloom, the type of which Ruegette did not know, but it was broken on its edge, and it bore the stain of blood upon it. She took it.

"Yes," said Stroja. "We should not leave him like this."

Ruegette stood and surveyed. "I see nothing here that can help me," she said. "There is nothing to indicate why the Groll came here,

or where they came from. Are there no passes through the
mountains hereabouts?"

"Most things that happen in Norvaine don't have no reason," said
Stroja. "There are plenty of ways through the mountains but not in
winter."

"The Groll did not cross the frozen sea for no reason," said
Ruegette. "I must keep looking. We will stay here for the night. You
should start a fire if you can."

Ruegette went back onto the plain, returning to the place where
her two companions kept watch. "There is nothing in the house,"
she said. "There was no sign of the Groll or what brought them. We
will have to keep looking."

"No, we won't," spoke the taller of the two, and he pointed back
to the house. "That's what brought them. They just followed the
smoke."

Ruegette looked back. Stroja had started the fire and a plume of
dark smoke was rising into the sky. Ruegette watched it grow taller
and considered its meaning. "The smoke is what brought them," she
said. "The Groll could see it from millas off. If they had a lookout on
a high perch that overlooked this plain, they could be a long way off
and still know where to come." The smoke continued to rise even
higher into the sky and Ruegette began to have no doubt. "We found
the girl on a plain near the coast, but her sister was not there. They
were separated. Those that did not stay on the plain must have gone
back into the mountains. There must be a way through, maybe a day
or two north of here. It's possible they can see the smoke from our
fire even now."

"Then we should put it out," said the second warrior.

"No," said Ruegette. "The fire will bring them, and then I can
follow. We will stay the night. Tomorrow I will go alone and seek
them. Stroja will take you back to the outpost. You may wait there
until our ship returns."

"YOU SHOULD NOT be about," spoke a younger acolyte, but the
wandering Samiare paid her no heed. A pain stabbed in her
abdomen, and she winced as she walked. One hand pressed against
her side as she nearly doubled over; the other dragged the naked

blade of her sword along the stones of the corridor. It was a momentary pain, one that took her quite by surprise, and it passed quickly.

"Are you okay?" asked the acolyte coming closer.

Samiare lingered for a moment and breathed heavy, a tear welling in her eye, but she found the strength to right herself. The acolyte came and put her hand against Samiare's shoulder. "It is really too early for you to leave the dens," she continued to speak, but Samiare held up a hand to quiet her.

"No…want… lie…" she tried to protest.

"Come," said the acolyte. "I will take you back."

Samiare lay upon the same straw mat that was hers since she had arrived. The injuries that put her there were only a small discomfort. Mostly it was the burns on her back that would not completely heal, but they did not occupy her thoughts. She rested the gold hilt of her sword upon her chest and gripped it tightly, letting its soothing tones work against the storm of her torments.

All this time, and still it was a wonder to her—a miracle that she should have it at all, and even as she pressed it against her body she could not be sure it would remain. It was simply too much for her to comprehend: a prayer she had spoken in desperation; a being of light descending as if from the clouds; a sword in its fist given as a gift to her dying hand, and a command that she should use it—and in her delirium, how could she know if any of it was real? But still she held it. She had used it. She had seen it come alive with light and fire, and it had slain them with ease. And it was doing more. It comforted her. It took away her pain, and it was leaving music upon her soul.

The sword was healing her, she knew that, but she could not understand… The words it spoke. It did not demand. It only asked. It wanted her trust, and left her with the choice. She was afraid to have it, and yet she was even more afraid not to. The sword could sustain her, and for the one thing that hurt her the most, the loss of her family, it comforted and soothed her. Her father, her sister, her family… How could she ever have them back?

She let her empty hand slide onto her belly. She could feel the life there. It was innocent, and a part of her—she wanted it. Wanted to know that something she cared for, she could defend. It was her choice, and she did not want it taken away. She thought of Ruegette and her promise. She did not trust the temple Matron or the acolytes that worked under her; they were kind, but they had made their thoughts clear, they would kill the child just because it was not perfect in their eyes. It was perfect in her eyes, but only the one who rescued her had seen that–Ruegette would defend her decision.

Samiare held the sword; the song continued, and she listened. She did not want any more pain. She had lost so much, and it was unbearable already. She was afraid. The pain she had felt while walking worried her. If anything was wrong with her baby the acolytes would not understand. She worried over the sword as well, if the song was to ever stop, she would be truly alone and that would be like death.

It wanted her trust, and she had nothing else. She listened.

RUEGETTE WAITED UNTIL the three had vanished over the horizon before taking her torch to the pyre. She wanted to be sure if any were watching they would be certain to see the smoke from her fire, so she had the pyre built inside the house. Offering a silent prayer to the Seven Gods for the father of the two girls, she lit the wood and left the structure to burn. She followed the same trail away from the house that her companions took as they left. It would not be possible to hide her tracks in the snow, so she decided not to leave them where they could be found. After some distance, she turned to the north and began to skirt the mountains.

The line of spires overlooking the plain went in a northeasterly direction and she followed them until it was dark. It was her guess that no one would be coming for at least a day, so she took few precautions. At night, she found a small cave for shelter. It was near freezing, but she did not light a fire, instead she struggled against the cold and lost sleep.

In the morning, she woke un-rested. She shook snow from her pack and drew back the string of her bow to remove the ice that clung to it. Her food supply was ample, but it was frozen and not at all appetizing. She took a mouthful of flat bread, and then started again to move along the mountains.

Ruegette surveyed as she went, searching for a mountain perch high enough above the plain to see for many millas around, and yet low enough that she could easily climb to it. Her search did not take long. The rocky trunks of the many spires gave her many to choose from, and the one she selected was both high and well-hidden.

She waited in her hidden perch for most of the day, until two dark shapes emerged from the white haze and headed south. She considered letting them pass. The trail they left through the flat white blanket would be easy enough to follow, but she knew she could not let them return, if they followed the trail back to the outpost there could be more violence. She came down from her perch and set out after the two. When the moment was right, she would kill them both.

"HOW ARE WE feeling?"

It was the Matron's voice, Lizelle, and it crept upon Samiare like an icy chill. In her meditation she had not noticed the older woman's approach. She understood her words, another gift of the sword she held, but at the very thought of responding, the language was lost from her mind.

"I am told you are feeling well enough to walk," said the old woman with the blue sash. "I would have you come with me."

Samiare did not enjoy the old woman's company, but still she struggled to her feet and rose, pressing her sword against the stones of the floor for support. And then she lifted it, cradling it against her chest. Lizelle looked on with her nose crinkled in disgust, but it passed from her expression. "Come," she said, and then she led Samiare from the healing dens.

They went down a long hall lit by high openings at either end which let in light from the outside. Lizelle walked at an easy pace, and Samiare followed after, the sword she carried pressed against her as she went.

"This is a good sign," spoke Lizelle in a gentle tone. "To see you walking is quite a blessing, much better than seeing you spend whole days lying in that dreary room."

Samiare listened as the older woman spoke, but remained silent. She did not trust her.

Lizelle waited as if expecting an answer, and when it did not come, she stopped and looked back. "You are healing fast now, child," she said. "Have you given any thought as to what comes after?" Again Samiare was silent, and the Matron must have suspected that would be her response, for she wasted no time in starting in with the obvious. "Come, child," she spoke. "A girl who can barely speak, and one with an unwanted child in her lap at that, is not going to fetch more than a beggar's pittance on the streets of Tierasol. Did you plan to live by that sword, or had you not thought so far ahead?"

Samiare did not know what to answer, she had not thought beyond the present for many months. She gripped her sword tightly and tried to reflect on the question before her, but the Matron did not give her the chance. "A warrior's life is not something that respectable ladies aspire to, and when your child comes…Who will look after it?"

The words of the older woman bit into her, and troubled her greatly. This was not the life she was supposed to have. A child was not supposed to be a burden, and to be a warrior—she had not considered that at all. She would be a good mother, she had practically raised Nechare, with her mother gone, and her father…Her father was gone. The thought of that crushed her, and Nechare…was she gone as well? Again the pain of their memory struck her. Again she tried to shut them out. She tightened her grip upon the sword, letting its song flow, and hoping to soothe the pain of her loss, but it was futile.

"There is another way," continued the Matron. "You could sell the sword; a gold hilt can get you quite a few gillets among the wealthier Ridari, and with them, you could purchase a good life for the child. You could stay here with us, to serve the Goddess is an honorable calling, and in time, perhaps, your baby can look after you. That is, provided there is nothing foul about it."

Samiare was horrified, she could not bear the Matron's words any longer. Everything the old woman spoke was like a poison to her, but she could not escape them. She turned and staggered away from the woman fighting against tears welling in her eyes, but the Matron would not relent; she came forward and touched Samiare's back with her hand, the warmth of it coursing through her burns and she winced.

"You mustn't be so upset, dear. I only wish to prepare you for what is coming. You cling to that sword as if it can save you, but you must think about saving yourself if you are going to survive."

Samiare pulled the sword against her and fell with it to her knees. With her heart, she reached out to it, or the powers beyond it—she did not know, wanting its song to soothe the storm of her torment. For an instant, she felt invulnerable again, but then her abdomen shot anew with pain, and she cried out flinching. Instinctively, her hand moved to touch the cause, but then she stopped herself; the Matron would see and she did not want the reaction that might follow—she did not want anyone threatening her baby.

"Child," spoke Lizelle. "Is something wrong?"

Samiare hid her pain well. "Samiare...work...Miranae," she gritted out. "Samiare...keep sword."

"Well," said Lizelle, seemingly satisfied. "There is no need to rush into a decision. If it helps you to feel safe, I will let you keep the sword a while longer, but it is hardly the tool of a healer. You are free to walk the outer halls, but you cannot carry a weapon exposed like that. I will have one of the girls see about getting you a proper means of carrying it about."

Another acolyte entered the hall, and Lizelle called her over. "I must go into the temple," said the Matron. "Adelle will stay with you a while. You mustn't fear, child. You have friends, and we of the temple will take good care of you. "

Samiare practically draped herself over her sword as she pushed herself up, but still she managed. The pain in her abdomen eased, and for that she felt her strength return. She took up her sword and cradled it against her. In spite of the old woman's words, she was afraid; something was wrong, her pregnancy was not going as it should, and it filled her with dread. In her heart, she prayed to the one thing that had shown her any mercy at all, and its song continued.

THE ENTRANCE TO the pass was obscured by a mound of snow with two guards posted in an outcropping high above. Ruegette had no desire to kill the two, she only wished to escape their notice, and sneaking past guards was a skill at which she was very adept. At night, she easily made her way around the two and by morning had left all thoughts of them behind.

It was in the approaching darkness of the third day when she came upon the site of an ancient ruin, four stone buildings that lay crumbling upon the rock bed where three mountains converged. Caves and trees lined the sides of the three mountains as rock, covered with snow, painted a dull and colorless backdrop. Men moved about the ruin. Ruegette counted about twenty of them, and from their livery of deep blue, she knew that they were of Marindor. But it was not them who drew her attention; within the ruin were also the dark and hunched forms of Groll. Shaped like men with knotted muscles and wide backs, their skin colored in dark hues of rust and green and the look of feral beasts cast in their wide maws and wild eyes, they numbered slightly more than the men, and brought the full count of those within the camp to over forty; more than Ruegette could ever hope to slay on her own.

The perch where she hid was high up on the mountain. It was a small outcropping obscured by a mound of snow and the branches of an evergreen that grew from the rock. From where she lay, she could see two fires lit within the camp; one at the center, where the men gathered, segregating themselves from the Groll, and the other near a well-trodden path to the north. It was at the latter that the Groll huddled together like a pack of wild animals. A third fire was lit inside of one of the stone structures, small and sputtering; it came from a torch in the hands of a Marish soldier who stood near the entry. The structure he guarded had seen the wear of age. The stone crumbled and the roof had long since fallen in. Ruegette could see all inside it.

Three men and three Groll stood to either side of a large stone block. One man seemed to be doing all the talking. He was a tall warrior with dark hair and features clad in chain links and carrying a broad sword at his hip; Ruegette picked him out as the leader of the Marish troop. She could tell from the reaction of the Groll that there must be a disagreement. He was animated and gesturing openly as he spoke, but the Groll seemed just as animated, sneering and smashing their fists down on the stone block.

She watched the men in the structure for some time to see if this was a difference they could resolve, but as she waited, something else began to play out in the crumbling lanes below; Groll warriors slowly began to filter away from their fire and spread themselves throughout the ruin. Their actions seemed innocent enough. They kindled no adverse reaction from the men, but looking down from above, Ruegette could see the signs of treachery at hand; too many wandered close to the center, and too many tested the pull of weapons. The argument in the structure continued and became more animated until, in one telling moment, a large Groll took hold of an axe and raised it against the man. The reaction was quick and lethal; a broad blade left the scabbard of the tall man and cut the Groll open at its chest, sending it spewing black blood and falling upon the stone block before rolling to the snow.

A shriek rose, sparking an instant reaction. As one, the Groll, with axes and swords ready, sprang upon the men at the fire. The men were caught off guard and many fell before they could even stand to face the attack. A melee ensued; the men fought back bravely, but they were surprised and out-numbered; their chances were hopeless. Amid the chaos, a tall Groll with green skin and thick leather plates over dark, gorum-steel, chain rose to orchestrate the butchery. He growled his orders and pushed his warriors to violence. And he allowed no quarter.

Ruegette could do nothing to help the men, and was not sure why she should even care to; she contented herself to watch until the full measure of Groll treachery ran its course.

Inside the structure, the tall Marish warrior who first struck down the Groll brandishing the axe made an accounting of himself; he cut down the two remaining and then burst from the entryway to attack those at the fire. The two men who stood with him also performed well, cutting down more than their number before the end, but slowly, like those at the center fire, they too faded into blood spattered snow. The tall warrior was left alone, and against so many, he could do nothing. The Groll surrounded him, and he dropped to his knees, letting his sword fall onto the snow; the butt of an axe to his head ended his fight.

Many of the Groll had been killed in the battle, but more than a dozen still walked in the ruin, and for them, having slain all but the one warrior, it was time to savor their victory. The Groll desecrated the dead. Removing Marish heads from Marish bodies, they set their severed prizes on wooden stakes as grim reminders to all that they were to be feared, and for the one warrior, they bound him alive to a large piece of inclined stone, letting him look on as they dismembered his men. The green Groll took particular delight in tormenting his captive; standing at the feet of the bound man, he gloated, all the while barking orders and laughing until the rest of his band had finished with their bloody chore. Then he gave the order to gather their supplies and leave.

Ruegette watched as the Groll went about the ruin taking all that they needed and did nothing to intervene. The green Groll did not gather, he continued to wait at the feet of the Marish soldier, goading him into misery until the rummaging was finished, and then, having taken his fill of pleasure from his captive, he rallied those with him and set his course out upon the northern pass. He took his band from the ruin, leaving the Marish soldier to die by any fashion that took him.

Ruegette waited until she was sure the Groll were gone before emerging and making her way down the mountain to the rock bed of the ruin. Cautiously, and with an arrow drawn, she pressed through the crumbling buildings and fallen stone to stand, just as the green Groll had, at the feet of the bound Marish soldier.

The man watched her with a look of complete disbelief on his face. He was a lean cut man with rounded features and dark eyes above a thick goatee on his less than shaven face. He was an attractive man, but Ruegette thought him loathsome; he deserved his fate.

"Are you real?" he said. He spoke in Trade, and his voice was deep and fearless.

"It would seem things did not go your way," she said. She remained at his bound feet, looking up at him from a safe distance. The man struggled to lift his head and look at her.

"It did seem that way," he said, "but now you are here to set me free."

"Who said I would set you free?" she said, changing her language to speak in the tongue of Marindor.

The man looked at her with even more puzzlement, and then realization. "Ah," he moaned, "from Tierinor." He dropped his head onto the cold stone and called out in Ruegette's own language of Tieran. "Well, Tierinor, you have come a long way to find a cold place, and too late to gain what was here."

Ruegette circled him, keeping her bow lowered but her arrow ready. "I am Ruegette," she said. "I would know what a soldier from Marindor is doing here."

"Ruegette!" said the man. "Ruegette de Tagore? ...of Tierinor? ...Ruegette, the daughter of Jarl Mavrou of the Eastern Citadel? ...Ruegette, the woman whose skill with a bow is renown in the four lands, and whose ability with a sword has destroyed both man and Groll alike? You are *the* Ruegette, the one I have heard so much about?"

"It would seem I have a greater reputation than you," she said. "Who are you? And what are you doing here?"

"If you are half the legend I have heard, then you must know that already."

"And if you believe the tales, then you must know I will carve you up and feed you to wolves if you don't answer my questions. What was here? And what does Marindor want with it?"

"This is tiresome," said the man. "I am Darimus of Marindor. Whether by freezing as the Groll would have me, or by your hand, it seems I am meant to die. I see no reason to help you."

Ruegette pulled back her arrow and pointed it at the man's eye as he looked on her. "What is this place?" she demanded coldly.

The man's head tilted slightly, and his eyes grew wide as he stared down at her. He trembled as he took in a breath, but he smiled wide and kept his composure. "Don't you know?" he said. He turned his head away and his chest sank, as if resigned. "Look around, Tierinor. I am sure it will come to you."

Ruegette lowered her bow and walked away from him. Going to the fire at the center of the ruin, she took up a brand and began to investigate the crumbling structures. She went first to the one that held the stone block where the men and the Groll had argued. Looking at the stone in better light, she could see that it was carved with the script of an ancient language, that of the Allarie in its oldest form. She studied the symbols of the language carefully, translating what she could, but Allarish was not a language she could read fluently, and she struggled. Her eyes scanned the surface, skimming over the words, searching for any that leapt out above the others and could reveal the stone's purpose until one word did just that. It was written upon the bottom and carried a graceful elegance above all the others—'*Ilnydrifel*'.

It was more than a word, it was a name, one Ruegette barely knew, and one that only came out of legend—*Ilnydrifel*.

"You see it, don't you," Darimus called out. "It is the marker for his tomb. He came here just as the legend spoke. The Shadow was thrown down and its body divided, but it could not die. To keep it from ever again becoming whole, the pieces of its flesh were divided among the three lands and sealed beyond reaching. But one seal was left imperfect; the key to it was broken, and a shard of it was possessed by the mage, Ilnydrifel. It was also his curse, for he was forced to flee the four lands, and to seek shelter from those who would slay him, but at the moment of his escape, an arrow, fired from the bow of the priestess, Glysandra, struck him and left him stricken by withering magic. It crept upon him, bringing him to a slow doom. It was he who took the shard of the broken key, and it followed him into his burial chamber where we found it still clutched in his hand."

Ruegette emerged from the ancient structure and stood in the arch of the once proud entry. Darimus rolled his head to look at her. "The legend is true," he said. "The Eye of Ebon will soon be found. The Shadow is after it."

Ruegette was without words. The legend of the Dark Beguiler was but a faded memory. The seals that held his prison she thought only myth, and the role of Ilnydrifel was as a traitor to his people. It was a legend that Ruegette did not know well, but somehow a part of it must be true, and the Groll had gained the first hidden piece of its puzzle.

"So Tierinor," said Darimus. "Are you just going to stand there looking beautiful, or are you going to cut me free?"

Ruegette darted a venomous look at the bound warrior from

Marindor. "You are with them," she said. "You are aiding the Groll in finding this key."

"No," said Darimus. "It was they who came to us with its location. We only pretended to help. I was here to gain the Shard and secure it from them."

Ruegette did not know what to believe, but she knew evil. "Two girls were taken on the plain south of here. One we found near death at the hands of your band, but her sister was brought here. What became of her?"

Darimus dropped his head back onto the stone. "What girl?" he said. "There was never any girl brought here. I would not allow it."

"Why should I believe you?"

"Because," said Darimus. "I am a Captain in the army of Marindor. I believe in the judgment of the Seven Gods. I hate the Groll, and if I had planned better, it would be a Groll tied to this stone and not me. We did send a party south, but they never returned. They brought no girl here. I swear it on my honor."

Ruegette threw down her crude torch and readied to leave. She placed her bow across her back and adjusted her quiver.

"We don't have much time," said Darimus. "The Groll are taking it back to Gorginor. If they get on a ship before we can stop them, it will be weeks before we can regain their trail. They already have a lead on us. Our duty is clear, neither Marindor nor Tierinor can allow that."

Ruegette pulled her dark-hilted sword and approached the stone. She stood beside it and studied the man one last time, contemplating her course before taking action, and then she slashed forward with her slender blade. The steel rang out with a loud clang and the man practically fell off the stone as his bonds were cut. Darimus slid onto his knees and rubbed at his wrists.

"There are two of your men guarding this pass," she said.

"We must leave them," said Darimus. "They can find their own way."

SAMIARE HAD FOUGHT against the signs, but this time the pain was too great. It stabbed into her, causing her to fall and crumple; she cried out. There was blood; it stained her dress and ran down the length of her legs. She could not hide it. An urn she held dropped onto the stones of the floor, shattering like a clattering alarm. Her sword rested in a scabbard at her side, and she grasped its hilt in desperation, but the pain would not subside. She looked up to see the many startled faces that looked on. An acolyte gasped, and she was helpless to prevent what came next.

Temple girls rushed to her aid; she was carried to one of the healing tables. The pain in her belly tore and she writhed against it. Her sword belt was removed and taken from her. She reached to retrieve it, but the girls held her down; they said words to soothe her, but she could not understand them. She pleaded, screaming out in both Tieran and Norvish, but they were not responding.

They lifted her dress. It was red with blood. Samiare felt her soul tearing as the temple acolytes did their work. It was not time for this, her baby was not ready. She fought to keep it inside of her, but her body would not obey. She grew frantic and wrestled to escape but still she was held. An odor reached her, a sweet smelling herb that was burned in a bowl at her head; its purpose was to intoxicate her into manageability. She hated it, but its effects were strong.

The Matron was there; she spoke in strange words and moved in such a languid fashion that Samiare could not be sure if she were real or imagined. Hands pushed on her belly and she could not resist them. She screamed and pleaded; she could not bear to lose this last chance at her dreams of family, but still it was being taken. In her anxiety, she called out for the one Tieran warrior who might stop them, but Ruegette was not there to help her.

Soon it came. Temple girls looked at it in horror, and Samiare heard plain the Tieran word—dead.

She cried, and demanded to have it, but the Matron held it in a cloth and went with it from the table.

"No," she screamed. "Don't take my baby from me!" But none could understand her. Her language was not their own. In the distance, she thought she heard an infant's cry, and that alone drove her to frenzy. She thrashed against arms that held her and kicked, but strength was not with her; the drug had seen to that. Acolytes held her fast, and soon lethargy ruled all she could do. At the final moment of her surrender, Samiare had never know such emptiness, a hollowness reached deep into her heart and tore at it with callous viciousness.

She lay upon the straw mat of her healing den without moving. The gold hilt of her sword beckoned from the ground next to her, but she did not wish to hold it. She had never felt so empty, so cold, or so alone; she felt as if she were dead and wished that she was. She did not know how long the acolytes worked on her, or how long it had been since they were at her side, but she knew what they would not say. She would never again have children. More than one offered words of regret, but she could not accept them, she wanted to hate them, but she could not even feel that dark emotion; there was nothing left within her but a cold, fuming anger, and it could not be sated.

She wanted an answer, she wanted to know why. How could this happen? What had she done to deserve such pain? And what was the sense of letting her baby be taken from her? Why was she given deliverance on that snowy plain if misery was to be her fate? She was angry, angry enough to demand an answer. Her hand took hold of the sword at her side, and again she heard the song it played, but her heart was closed and her will set; she did not want consoling. She wanted to be heard.

The moment passed and she was left shaken, some things were not meant to be asked, and some answers came too harshly. Tears streamed down her temples, and she gasped in silent sorrow. If there was a bottom to the dark places she had gone, she learned that she had yet to find it. It was not for her to ask or to understand, it was for her to choose—walk in the light or be forever in darkness. Samiare did not know where her heart was. Dead as it was, she felt only coldness and anger, but she knew what she must do, what she wanted—she wanted to fight. She pulled the sword up onto her chest and held it in a steady grip. It wanted her trust and she wanted rage. To walk in the light, or be forever in darkness…She would choose the light. She would bring it to the Groll.

THE GROLL COULD run for days without rest. They were larger and stronger than men. They needed little in the way of food or water, had survived in the impossible cold of Gorginor, and in the unyielding heat of the Shadow's mountain. When the Groll were fashioned, the Dur had bred war into them. They were a strong and hardy stock, but they enjoyed battle, and too easily turned to the fight.

Groll bodies littered the snow, the bloody result of having to choose a new leader for their band. By Ruegette's count they had whittled themselves down to only eight. They were still formidable but far less of a risk than before. She had more than enough arrows to handle what remained.

"Shargat will have the Shard," said Darimus. "I knew he would gain control when I killed his Dahmor-ra at the ruin. A supply ship comes every four weeks. They will reach the coast before it arrives. We'll have to hurry if we're to do the same. It'll be a Marish ship. It will not take them on board if they are alone. They'll have to kill the crew if they can or find another way."

"Then let us not waste any more time looking at the dead," said Ruegette. "We run until we can no longer. Then we rest and run some more."

Darimus shot her a questioning look. "You wish to run the entire way?"

"If that's what we must do."

"How does a woman become a soldier like you?"

"Perhaps," said Ruegette. "If Tierinor was not alone in fighting against Gorginor, and our allies had remained true, I would be more like the docile women of Marindor."

"All right, Tierinor," said Darimus. "We run."

The two ran along the Groll's trail late into the night, and then again the next morning. The days passed coldly and the nights colder. To keep warm, they rested together under the thick fur of Ruegette's cloak. Both slept in their armor, and Ruegette kept a knife in her hand, lest there be any treachery in the heart of the Marish Captain.

It was near dark when the two arrived at the end of the trial. It had not gone to where the supply ship was to arrive, but instead to a rocky cove against the water far south of the supply point. There was no sign of Shargat or his band, only the makings of a camp and the clear pattern of a small boat upon the ice.

"They're gone!" Ruegette shouted to the winds, and she cursed under her breath.

"We are too late," said Darimus stoically. "They must have had another ship waiting for them, probably stolen from a Marish dock. The Groll have been more prepared than I had thought."

"We must follow them," said Ruegette. "Where is your supply ship going to land?"

"North," said Darimus. "It will take us maybe another day to reach the supply point, then another two before the ship arrives. The Groll may be ahead of us, but they are far from completing Ilnydrifel's quest. The Shard is but a fragment, and the gate it opens is still lost. We do have time."

"I don't know what you dug up at that ruin," seethed Ruegette in a tone that held no equivocation. "But know this: we are going to get it back, and when we do, I will take it back to Tierinor."

"That is a discussion we can have at another time," said Darimus. "For now, we must get to the supply point and wait for our ship. There is nothing we can do until it arrives." For a moment, his expression bore his concern, and then his manner shifted, and a wide smile spread across his face. "Plenty of time for a Captain from Marindor and a beautiful woman from Tierinor to become—"

"Plenty of time for you to tell me what Marindor is really doing here with the Groll," snapped Ruegette. She glared at him. It was not a time for his boyish charm, and Marindor had much to answer for—*He* had much to answer for.

"You wound me, Tierinor," said Darimus. "Do you ever think of anything but duty?"

Ruegette did not answer. She looked straight into him, and smoldered, but his smile only grew wider. A smile, she knew, that had worked on many, but it would not work on her...not this time. She turned away, and fumed.

"I see," said Darimus. "Look but don't touch."

RUEGETTE STOOD AT the bow of the ship. They had been sailing for seven days upon the Norvish Sea, and the sight of land had only just begun to peak on the horizon. Cold winds gusted across the sides and blew against her, whipping her red hair about her face. Ruegette knew they were looking at the coast of Tierinor. They were still north of Tierasol, but the Groll they pursued would have gone east further still.

She was aware her position on the ship was not very secure. The ship was from Marindor; all held fealty to Marindor's Queen and showed proper respect to her captains. There were more than twenty aboard, and she was only their guest until they reached ground. Any disagreement she may have would not go in her favor, but that alone would not keep her from performing her duty.

Darimus approached from the aft deck and came forward to join her. "It is the coast of Tierinor," he said indicating the land on the horizon. "We could part company if you wish. We can deliver you safely to your shores."

Ruegette knew a moment like this would come. It was incumbent on him that he offer, but she was not prepared to give up the chase. "No," she said. "I am not going to Tierinor. I am going after the Groll who took the Shard."

"It would be safer for you if you did," said Darimus. "I would prefer it. A beautiful woman should not be about chasing Groll and fighting with swords. That is for men to do."

Darimus's words ignited a fire in her. She was a true hero of Tierinor, and concern for her safety was not something she appreciated. "I am a proud daughter of Tierinor," she asserted sternly. "I have been doing the work of a soldier all of my life. It's all I know, and you would do well not to test that."

Darimus leaned on the rail next to her, and looked up with baleful eyes. "Is that what you are?" he said. "Ruegette of Tierinor, the soldier. Is there no woman in you?"

"Woman in me?" she said. "You allied with the Groll, and you allowed them to gain something they should never have. All that we know can end, and yet you are concerned about how womanly I am?"

"Now, Tierinor," said Darimus. "We have been through this. It was not my choice to ally with Groll, and it was not my wish to see Shargat gain the Shard. If I could undo the events of that day, I would, but I do not have that power. All I can do is go after them and take back what they have stolen. It's a task I pledge my life to, and one you can trust I will not fail at."

"I appreciate that," said Ruegette. "If only your pledge could take away Shargat's long lead or restore the Shard to where it was before you and the Groll dug it up, then I could return to the safety of Tierinor and rest knowing Marindor is keeping watch. I am sorry, but I think we're in for a long journey."

"I was hoping you and I could get along better," he said, "but I see the woman is still hidden behind duty. It is a shame. I find I like you."

"Now, Captain," she said. "How could your liking me make any difference in what we must do?"

"Because," he said. "Then I could do this." With an abrupt motion, Darimus took hold of Ruegette, pulled her to him and kissed her.

Ruegette's recoil was more instinctual than willed. She raised her arms to push the Marish Captain away, her mind already preparing the long stream of slurs that would follow, but as Darimus was shoved away, he grabbed the hilt of her sword and pulled it from its scabbard, leaving her disarmed and helpless.

"You saved my life at the tomb," he said. "I owe you for that, but I also have a duty, and it does not include a soldier from Tierinor."

Ruegette was instantly angry. "You deceitful cur. Give it back at once."

Darimus shook his head and held up her sword to look on it. "Gorum steel," he said. "Metal of the Groll."

Ruegette knew she had lost. Darimus had gotten the better of her, but she would have her say. "How dare you?" she seethed. "Know this, I will foll–" The words were left unfinished, the hilt of her own sword struck her temple and she lost all consciousness. She fell to the deck and into darkness.

Ruegette woke to find herself on the coast of Tierinor. All her belongings had been returned, and her sword was back in its scabbard. There was no sign of the ship from Marindor or of Captain Darimus. They had long since sailed. Her head throbbed where it had been struck and feeling it with her hand did not help to relieve the pain. Ruegette picked herself up and gathered her things. Inwardly she seethed. The Marish Captain was bolder than she had thought, and had played her well. She was going to make sure that never happened again, and there would be an again.

Tierasol was a day further along the coast and there was no use sitting on the beach; the sooner she got to the city, the sooner she could plan her next move.

RUEGETTE ENTERED THE city by the north gate, and found Zarue already waiting. The gate was next to the guard barracks and several of the more frequented taverns, so it was no great surprise he would see her, but the hour was early, and that alone made his appearance unusual. Ruegette had spent the night on the road and entered the city only a few hours after dawn. Her head still smarted, and her feet were sore, but worse than both, she carried the wound of the Captain's deceit to her pride, and it hurt.

Zarue lumbered towards her from the direction of the barracks. He wore a well-oiled suit of chain armor, but his head remained unclad. His dark hair was unkempt, and his thick mustache was untrimmed. "You all right?" he asked at the sight of her. "You look terrible."

"I've felt better. I will be okay after some rest."

"Something hit you in the head?"

"It was nothing," she said. Instinctively, she touched her hand to the sore spot at her temple and then regretted it. A flare of anger welled up inside her, but she managed it. "I am okay," she said. "What of our girl?"

"Girl?" he said with a blank expression.

"Yes," she said. "The one I told you to stay here and watch."

"Oh," he said. "She's fine."

"When was the last time you saw her?"

"Not long ago. On the day you left, I went into the temple and told the old woman if anything happened to her, I would cut off her hands."

"You did what?" said Ruegette, horrified.

"Rue, you know I hate temples. That very day I got into a brawl with one of the local guardsmen. I busted my finger on his knob and had to go back to that accursed temple before the night was through. And don't think that old rusty axe was gentle with me either. Now, because I broke his jaw, I got pressed into training some boys. I am stationed here for a season."

Ruegette gave him a stern look. "Come on," she ordered. "We are going to the temple to look in on her."

"Oh, come on, Rue," he protested. "I've asked about her, and I looked in on her. They said she was healing up just fine...Isn't it enough that I got stationed?"

Ruegette waited with Zarue just inside the foyer of the Temple for one of the acolytes to come and escort them. Zarue protested loudly, but she would not hear it. Before them, the door to main hall opened and a now familiar old woman appeared dressed in the same white vestures and blue sash that she wore the day Ruegette left for Norvaine.

"Ah!" exclaimed the old woman upon seeing Zarue. "Our brash young brawler has returned, how nice. How is your finger?"

"Don't think I don't know how you enjoyed it, you old witch!" he shouted. "My hand is fine, no thanks to you, and you'll not be seeing me in here for the rest of my days, if the Seven Gods are kind."

Ruegette slapped Zarue across his arm with the back of her hand. The big soldier looked at her with surprise. "What?" he said.

Ruegette stepped forward and addressed the Matron. "We are here to see the girl."

"Yes, of course," said the old woman. "I can take you to her. She has been on her feet for weeks. She works at the temple now. She helps us treat the sick."

"What of the baby?" asked Ruegette. "How is her condition?"

"I'm sorry," said the old woman. "The baby was stillborn shortly after you left."

"Oh," said Ruegette. "I am sorry to hear that."

"It was of the Groll," said the woman. "It is better this way. If it had lived, it would have killed her in the childbirth. Come I will take you to her."

"You go ahead, Rue," said Zarue, "I will just wait here."

Ruegette half-turned in the doorway and shot back with an angry look that made him start.

"Oh, all right," he relented. "I'll go inside."

The child, Samiare, was within. She wore a white gown in the same fashion as the acolytes and she carried water in a long-handled urn. She looked much better than when Ruegette had last seen her and seemed to bare no signs of her injuries. She would have been almost indistinguishable from the other acolytes of the temple if not for the thick sword belt she wore at her waist, and the gold hilt that jutted out from it. She brightened as she saw Ruegette appear in the room and dropped all she was doing to greet her.

"Ruegette," she said, still getting the inflection wrong. "Good ...see Ruegette."

"I am sorry I was not here," said Ruegette. "I am sorry about your baby."

The small girl turned away and her mouth twitched as a forlorn look touched her features. She put her hand on her gold hilt, and then, gaining strength, looked back. "Is...okay," she said. "Is....no for Samiare."

"I see that you still wear your sword," said Ruegette. "Do you still feel unsafe?"

"No," said Samiare. "Want...be like Ruegette. Want...be..."

"You want to be a warrior?" asked Ruegette with astonishment.

"Yes," said Samiare. "Want be warrior like Ruegette."

Ruegette was stunned; the girl before her was too young for any such role, and it was not the type of thing young women should aspire to, but then she remembered how they found her, and the pile of bodies that surrounded her in the snow. Could she have slain them all? And what did it mean if she did?

Ruegette considered her; she was still so small and she did not bear a warrior's body. But the sword was already a part of her. Ruegette already knew the fight in her, she had seen it as the girl struggled to survive against her wounds, and in the courage she displayed as she wished to mother an unwanted child. "It is not easy to live by the sword," she said, "but it seems you already do."

"This is ridiculous," burst Zarue. "She wants to be Wardai? She can't be like you, Rue. She's not ready to be a Wardai. She would not make it as a regular, and the cavalry won't want her either. Don't fill her head with foolishness."

"Twenty dead in the snow thought the same as you," said Ruegette. "Do you want to test her?"

"Maybe I do," declared Zarue. He reached for his sword, but never got it from his belt. Samiare stepped back and pulled her sword faster than he could tug the blade free. Zarue's hand was knocked away from his blade, and then the silver edge of the young girl's blade dug into the soft flesh under his chin. The girl shouted something in her own language and backed him up, pushing him with her sword. Zarue retreated until he was backed into a pillar. Samiare glared at him with anger in her eyes. Zarue struggled but could not get free of the blade. He rolled his eyes until he looked at Ruegette's surprised face. "Oh, yeah," he said. "I think she's ready."

"Samiare!" snapped Ruegette. She grabbed the child's arm and pulled it down to release her Second.

The girl was trembling. She turned away from Zarue and walked several steps away. She put her sword back into its scabbard and fell to a knee with her head down. Zarue rubbed at his chin, his face was flushed white and his eyes still wide. "I have never seen such speed with a sword," he said bewildered.

Ruegette looked at Samiare's small form kneeling upon the floor. She too was amazed at her quickness, but part of her wondered what the girl would have done if she had not interceded. "You will train her," she said, steadily. "I want you to start with her today."

"What will you do?" he said.

"I must visit the Esilecolm Library at the Citadel. Something is happening in Marindor, and I must know what it is about."

"Fine," he said. "I will get her cleaning mail by days end. She can start by learning how to care for her gear." Zarue turned to leave but was stopped by the old acolyte in the blue sash.

"You are bleeding," Lizelle accused.

"What?" said Zarue. He looked at himself and noticed the blood dripping out from beneath his gauntlet. "She cut me!" he shouted. He examined his arm and saw the clean line cut into his mail. "She cut through my mail!" he said even more alarmed.

"Come on," said Lizelle. "Let's have a look at that hand."

Ruegette looked at Zarue with concern. "Zarue, I'm sure she did not mean to…"

"I don't blame the girl, Rue," screamed the big warrior. "I blame you! It was your idea to come to the temple." The old woman pulled at his gauntlet, and Zarue pulled away. "Leave me alone, you old crone."

"Stop being a baby," said Lizelle and she slapped him across his shoulder.

Ruegette looked back to Samiare kneeling upon the floor. Her hand had returned to her sword and she was rocking slightly. How could she have slain twenty men with only that sword? And how could she strike so suddenly against a warrior as experienced as Zarue? There was a mystery to the child, one Ruegette hoped could be controlled.

SOMETHING WAS WRONG; the priestess knew it in her heart. She stood in her white evening robe beneath the main arch of the infirmary. The healing dens always looked bleak, and the moans of the ailing were commonplace in Miranae's Temple, but seldom was it a place for the dying. The Allarie did not die; that was why the arrival of the wanderer from across the mountains was so strange. Something afflicted him. His arm was swollen, and his flesh was streaked with lines of purple and black; they went up his arm and across most of his chest. The man was thin, even for an Allarie, and nothing of the priestess' healing powers could cure him.

She remembered the night he entered; amid a freezing rain he stumbled through the doors of the temple and pleaded for healing. She helped him then, even though it was beneath her station, but she could have done no differently; his pleas were to her directly and his affliction was beyond the skills of any other. Many were the acolytes that said prayers and tried to comfort him but it was Glysandra herself, Glysandra the Keeper of Souls, who brought him the most comfort. He could not state how the affliction had come upon him, but his death was near, and Glysandra could not ignore him.

For three nights she prayed over him, calling forth the miracles of Miranae to end the strange disease, but to no avail. To her, it seemed as if there was a malevolent force preventing her cure. Desperate and willing to make the sacrifice for his aid, she entered into a deep prayer over his dying body. Calling on all the light of her own Allarish spirit, Glysandra cast herself into a prayer of offering, asking for that which only the Seven Gods could wield, the power to restore life to the dead. The cost of her prayer had been high, it left her spent and weary, unable think or to fathom the many things she saw as her spirit touched the light; and the results were only faintly shown. The affliction that had crept across his body had only receded. Still it was enough; the healing of Miranae could not be undone and soon, she knew, the afflicting process that had spread in the wanderer would reverse. It was only with this knowledge she allowed herself rest, but her rest was not peaceful.

For two days Glysandra took repose, and with each hour she turned and grew cold. In the sanctuary of her dreams, she learned the truth of the Wanderer; his soul was in conflict with an evil in his heart, an evil he fought against but could not defeat. Somehow, it was the will of the Shadow that worked within him. When at last she woke, she came to know a new fear, one that sent her flying from her bed, through the halls of the ancient temple, and finally to the very place she had left him; but something was wrong.

"Where is he?" she demanded of the acolytes who meandered between the healing dens. "Where is the afflicted man?"

"Keeper," spoke one. "He wished to walk the halls. We let him. He is with one of the healers."

Glysandra feared the worst. She knew what he sought. In her rest, she could not perform her role, and without the Keeper of Souls the dead must not be approached. She burst through the halls to the dark places of the temple, through corridors and rooms long since forbidden to all but the highest of station, and to the one place that belonged to the Keeper of Souls alone, a bronze door that opened the way to the dead. It was there that she found the body; a young healer lay strangled at the precipice of the door that should not be opened, yet was.

Screams rang out from those who followed her, but Glysandra did not heed them. She did not need to enter to know he had already been below, and there was only one way to put a stop to the evil of the Wanderer. A guard of the temple rushed towards the sound of the screams and from him Glysandra snatched away his bow and drew an arrow from his quiver.

"He is fleeing the city," she pronounced. "Send word to the streets. He is not to leave Tierasol."

THE COURT WAS full of young men and boys all dressed in chain armor. Zarue stood near a rack containing wooden swords, his arm wrapped in a sling, and Samiare stood next to him. Like the others, she wore a chain shirt, but it was too large on her small frame; the links bunched over the belt she used to cinch them in, and sleeves billowed loosely about her thin arms. She had spent the entire day before with a steel brush and oil in an effort to remove the rust from her links, but still they did not pass Zarue's inspection. Beneath the loose chain, and jutting out from her side, was her sword, her hand resting on its golden pommel; she was the only one in the court to wear a weapon.

"Come get your wood!" ordered Zarue to the boys.

Samiare watched as all the young men filtered past a weapons rack and took up a wooden sword. She looked at Zarue for direction and was met by a solid glare from the tall warrior.

"You too!" he commanded, gesturing to the rack.

Startled by his forcefulness, she took up a wooden practice sword just like the others. She was uncertain as to what was expected of her, but she did not want to disappoint. She noticed the boys had moved onto the grass and stood beside each other in a large ring; making the assumption that she was to be included, she went to join them.

"We don't carry swords into training," growled Zarue. "Only wood. And trust me; that will hurt enough."

She did not like that condition at all, her sword sustained her, and she needed the gifts it bestowed; without it, she would lose the song, and without the song, she would not understand their language. She started to speak in protest but did not know the words. "I...keep," was all she could get out.

"No exceptions," said Zarue sternly, then he pointed back to the weapons rack. "It will be safe there."

Not knowing how to rectify her position, but wishing to embrace the life she had chosen, Samiare decided to follow the order. She went to the rack, took off her sword belt, and left the gold-hilted weapon on the grass. When she rejoined the ring, her link to the one thing that gave her understanding of the Tieran tongue was gone from her side and without it she could not understand Zarue's language any better than she could speak it.

She felt their eyes upon her. She had been feeling them since she arrived, and she heard the comments about the '*girl warrior*'; they were ridiculing and mocking her. She listened as one copied her speech, saying '*I keep*' as if it were something funny, and then suffered through the faint laughter of several nearby. Zarue began to address the boys and she heard her name. In unison the boys all looked at her. Zarue went on saying even more words, few of which she understood. He pointed to one at the circle, a tall boy with dark hair and a slender build, and the boy moved into the center of the ring.

Samiare watched the boy intently as he took up a position near the middle, and then turned to face her. It was plain he was expecting something from her, but she did not know what. Zarue called her name again, and from his tone, she knew she had missed something important. She cast her eyes to the big warrior and saw he was pointing into the center of the ring. Hesitantly she stepped forward, and as she did the boy lifted his wooden sword as if to engage her. She understood she was to fight him.

The boy began to circle her as the others cheered him on. Samiare turned as he went, trying to keep him to the front, but the boy was only baiting her. Seizing upon her predictability, he feinted with a move to flank her and then lunged in with his wooden sword, driving it at her face. Samiare gave into his trickery and was caught off guard, awkwardly she swatted at his wooden sword with her own, catching it in mid-thrust but leaving herself exposed and off-balance. The boy tested his strength against hers as their swords pushed against each other, and she could not hold him. Breaking her guard with his strength, the boy swept her weapon aside and spun forward, thrusting into her with his back and shoulder. Samiare tried to lift her wooden blade out of the tangle of wood and limbs, but she made the wrong choice. The boy extended his arms to gain power and then he jammed the butt of his wooden blade into her abdomen just below her ribs.

The wooden end bit into her organs, and she was reduced to her knees. She fell into a crumpled heap on the ground and gasped for breath as the boy lifted his arms to the cheering of the others. Savoring his easy victory, he turned to her and spat out venomous words, "*Shal mot.*"

The boy went to rejoin the ring but was laid flat by a blow from Zarue. Words were screamed out. Terse and cutting, berating the boys, but she barely heard them. She vomited on the ground.

Samiare sat upon the grass near the weapons rack. She held her sword in her lap. Zarue spent the morning training the boys on the sword, but at midday he grew tired of sparring, and sent them to practice at archery instead. When the last of them cleared the court, he gave her a long look, and then came over to where she sat.

"What's going on?" he said. "When you disarmed me in the temple, I believed you did kill those men upon the snow, but after what I saw today…"

Samiare did not know how to respond, so she said nothing.

"Is that an Allarish blade?" he asked. "Is it the sword that does the fighting?"

She pulled her sword closer and lowered her head. "Is no Allarish," she spoke.

"But there is an enchantment to it."

"With magic…yes," she spoke. "It speaks…I listen. With sword…I hear."

"I speak four languages," said Zarue. "Ruegette speaks five. You are going to have to learn to speak them as well."

Samiare kept her head down as she spoke. "I learn," she said.

"I don't know what that sword can do," said Zarue, "but I am going to teach you how to fight so you don't need it…if that is what you want?"

"I want," said Samiare.

"Tonight we start with languages. You can keep the sword if you need it to understand, but you must learn to speak Tieran, and you must learn Trade."

Samiare lowered her head, and looked on her sword. She wanted to be like Ruegette. She wanted to fight the Groll. She would do whatever it took.

"There is one other thing," said Zarue, "If any of those boys calls you 'Shal Mot' again you send them to me. I will remind them of the proper fashion to address a Wardai of Tierinor."

GINOUX, THE STEWARD of the library of the Eastern Citadel, was a thin man long past his youth. He was pale from the lack of Mirneth's light and his eyes were as yellow as the musty parchments he watched over. He walked with an amazing quickness for his age and seemed to know every dusty scroll and frail document that was hidden among the many crates and shelves of the library complex.

Esilecolm was hidden deep in the rock under the Eastern Citadel. Far from the light of Mirneth's orb, the corridors and rooms remained unaffected by the passage of ages, and the coolness of the underground chambers kept the ancient parchments from fading into ruin.

"You know the tales," said the Steward, his voice as cracked and withered as an old scroll. "The Shadow took to flesh and rose as the dragon against Allarie, but he was defeated. The warriors of the light, led by a prince of their race, and wielding a sword of fire in his hands, cut him down and tore his body asunder. But the victory could not hold. The Shadow was not of flesh, and cannot die. The Allarie knew if it ever found again the strength to make itself whole, its reign would return, and the victory would be undone. And so they took what pieces remained and scattered them across the four lands. Sealing each to never be found."

"I know the legend," said Ruegette. "But there must be more. The Groll seem to have found a source of knowledge, they are seeking the Ebon Eye. I must learn as much as I can."

"I can show you all that is written," said the Steward. "All that we keep safe in these stone walls."

"Yes," insisted Ruegette. "I need it all, and I don't have much time."

"Of course, Milady, I will bring what we have."

Ruegette sat in a small alcove with scrolls piled around her. The library was a dark and musty place filled with the wafting fumes of oil lamps and the gritty dust of ancient stone. She had asked the

Steward for anything on the Shadow and the legends of the keys that
held his prison, and the Steward provided dutifully. He brought
tomes and scrolls and bits of parchment, adding them to the pile.

Ruegette struggled to read all she could, skimming each scroll and
book, looking for something–anything–that could shed light on the
myth that was becoming real before her. She was determined, she did
not like that she knew less about the ancient lore than the Captain
from Marindor, and she would not be so unprepared again, nor
would she be so taken by him a second time. Thinking on it still
made her angry. *How could she have been played for such a fool? How could
she have let him steal a kiss?*

Ruegette did not know what she hoped to find, but she knew the
legends of the Shadow would be the best place to start. The writings
provided were all written in an ancient form of Tieran and all bore
the same familiar stories of the past. Three seals hidden among the
three kingdoms, and within each, a piece of the dragon's flesh, that if
recovered, could release the Shadow from his long prison. The keys
were protected by unknown magic and a mystery that could not be
solved in one land alone. The Eye of Ebon was one of these, cut
from the head of the dragon, this item alone could bring a threat
upon four lands as yet unseen since the war against the Shadow.

Ruegette had heard these tales before, but as she read, she
became increasingly aware the accounts were lacking any information
about the seals or the keys that undid them, and nowhere was there
any mention of the locations, or what they might do if released. She
read further; letting hours pass into days, she read about the ages
before the Allarie, of the old ones and of the silver people of the
Sharal, and of their fall. Of Tokoron, a hero of that silver race, who
succumbed to dark beguilings, and brought the first age of darkness.
And of the Shadow, who rose from the ashes of Tokoron's defeat, to
bring a new age of darkness to the Allarie who followed him. Of
Shateel, the dragon, who in ages past, fought a battle against the
light, and had his blood spilled upon the land, and of Shalee, his
serpent mate, who plots in secret and whispers in the night. And of
Ereth, the great darkness beyond, who once took form and battled
with the Gods, and was thrown down before the face of Meridel in
the night, but cannot die. All of them agents of the dark, testing and

tempting and deceiving, always looking to bring down the Light, and the Gods, and pull them into the darkness of their abyss. She read of the wars between Allarie and Dur, and then of the rise of Groll from foul magic deep within the cold mountains of Dark Gorginor, and then the rise her own race, the Morkind, when the Allarie faded into the east. But it was not enough.

On the third day, she summoned the Steward. "There must be more," she insisted. "I am missing the tale of Ilnydrifel. I am in need of that."

"Ilnydrifel?" balked the Steward. "The Allarish mage, who for his own aims tried to steal the Eye of Ebon and was wounded by an arrow as he boarded a ship to flee from Tierinor, fired from the bow of no other than a Priestess of Miranae."

"A Priestess of Miranae," said Ruegette. "Glysandra was a Priestess of Miranae?"

"If I remember the tale correctly."

"Could it be he was at the temple of Miranae when she discovered him? And if he was, what did he do to provoke Glysandra to fire her arrow?"

"I do not believe that is revealed in the story," said the Steward, "but I will fetch the tale and perhaps you may learn."

"Wait," said Ruegette. "All of the texts I have seen are written in Tieran. Why are none of them in Allarish?"

"They have been translated. The Allarish texts have been forbidden. None may look at them without the permission of the Koning."

"Why?"

"I don't know."

"Then get them."

"I will need the permission of the Koning."

"But, you know who I am?"

"You are a daughter of the Jarl, a Princessa of the Citadel."

"I am not just a Princessa," asserted Ruegette. "Look at my hand." Ruegette held up her palm before him, revealing the deep mark of a dragon over Mirneth's rising orb burned into her flesh. A mark born only by the Wardai. "I am a Wardai of Tierinor," she said. "And like all Wardai, I made an oath to defend this land and its

people, even at the cost of my own life if I must, and by the
Koning's direct order, the Wardai act in his name in all matters. It is
a sacred honor; one never betrayed by any who bore a Wardai title,
and one I hold above even my own father's throne. I speak with the
permission of the Koning, and I must see the Allarish texts."

"I am sorry, Princessa," said the Steward. "I did not know you
were a Wardai."

"How can you not know of me?" she said, incredulous at his
answer. "I thought the name of *Ruegette de Tagore* was quite notorious
within the Citadel."

"The Jarl has more than one daughter."

"Yes, but there is only one whose name is renown in the Four
Lands."

"Princessa," started the Steward. "The translated texts are every
bit as detailed as the Allarish scripts, perhaps…"

Ruegette shot the man a glaring look that turned his yellow
features pale.

"I will get them," he said.

"There is one other thing," she said. "I need a messenger sent to
Tierasol. He is to deliver a message bearing my seal to a man named
Zarue at the north barracks. If what I suspect is true, then we must
have guards posted at the temple of Miranae."

SAMIARE STOOD BEFORE a door made of bronze and fought
against sleep. For four nights, the boys had given her this duty,
hoping that she would wear out or lose interest. She barely knew
them. They were all just faces without names, the same form of one
large, mocking antagonizer after the next. She would not give in. She
would be like Ruegette. She would fight the Groll.

Zarue walked in the hall, muttering as he approached from places
closer to the entrance of the Temple. She had seen him argue with
the Matron, and knew he did not like being in the halls, but he was a
good teacher, and dedicated. Something had happened, something
that made him decide to place them all as guards. She did not know
what, but she would not disappoint.

The halls were dark, but for a few scattered torches that lit the
halls. She held her sword, and listened to its song. She was tired, but

in its soothing, she did not feel the need to sleep. She had been
about the temple many times, but the area of the bronze door was
strange to her. Each night, shadows moved in the periphery of her
awareness that left her with feelings of uneasiness and made her
wary. Earlier in the night, a torch had gone out in the connecting hall
only a short distance away. She had felt the shadows then, but they
faded. She saw shadows everywhere, even in people. They troubled
her.

Zarue drew closer and then stood before her, his eyes inspecting.
"We don't touch our swords unless we plan to use them," he said.
She dropped her hold and stood straighter. He reached forward and
pulled at the loose mail of her armor, turning it in the light. "Still
some rust." He touched her chin and looked into her eyes. "The
boys are still treating you unkindly?"

"Am okay," she said. "Boys no hurt."

"Your speech is better," he said. "What is your duty? Speak it in
Tieran."

Samiare struggled with the words. They formed in her head only
with difficulty, and she spoke them slow. "To guard this…door," she
stammered. "To keep…safe from…enemies of Tierinor."

"Describe the events of the last hour."

"All halls…dark," she spoke again, the inflections of her Norvish
home still carrying through. "Two guards pass by, twice.
Healer…Lizelle…pass by, looking for you. Torch…burn out in hall
to left. All quiet."

Zarue smiled down at her. "I think, maybe tomorrow, I will let
you decide where we place the guards."

Samiare smiled as well, and shared a laugh.

"One of the torches has gone out, you say?"

"Yes," she said. "Fli…Fl…um…" The word would not come.
She gestured with her hand, opening and closing it in rapid
succession.

"Flicker," said Zarue.

"Flicker, then out. Not long."

"Okay, young Wardai," he said. "I will take a look at it. Keep up
the good work."

Zarue walked towards the hall where the torch had gone out and looked down its passage. "No one has been through here?" he asked, turning back to her. "Both torches are out." He gestured to one of the sconces nearest. "Bring me that one."

Samiare went to it, and reaching up, pulled it from the sconce. She brought it to his hand and looked down the hall as well. It was dark, and trailed off beyond her sight.

"Wait here," he said. He went forward and held the torch up to the one that was out, and then stopped. "You sure no one has been here? It's not spent, did someone put it out?" He lit it and moved further down towards the other, but then he stopped again, holding his torch out in front of him. "Is someone there?" he called out.

Samiare watched from a distance away. Ahead, she could feel only darkness. In spite of the torch light that flickered in the hall, she felt something like a presence, but it was distant and oddly cold.

Zarue walked past the second sconce and went even further down the hall. Before him, a door waited at the edge of the light. It was slightly ajar. He took a step towards it, and then stopped. Around its frame, an eerie orange glow began to filter through and seep into the hall before him. He drew back several steps, and reached for his sword. "What sorcery?" he spoke.

Samiare watched, but did not understand. She took hold of her sword as well, and went to call out, but then there was motion. The door itself was thrown open by an unseen force, and from it, a dark creature emerged. Not like the thick and misshapen form of a Groll, but a tall and regal creature in dark robes, with flesh like a shadow, dark and grey. Its face bore long angular features, and orange light hung about it like a shroud; seeping away from its body in a haze. It glowed in its eyes and hair, and flowed as if blown by a foul wind. And though it was still many strides away, it reached for Zarue with long needle like fingers. It spoke, a strange language that clouded in Samiare's head as she heard it, "*The words, they are here.*"

Zarue pulled his sword and cried out in alarm; his torch falling to the floor. From ahead, the creature lowered its hand and clouds of orange vapor formed before it. The vapors swirled violently and then collapsed into glowing disks of haze before bursting with a new light that brought forth the hulking forms of three Groll warriors. The closest, one with skin of deep green, gave him no time to consider. It leapt forward with a dark axe raised and brought the weapon crashing down at his head.

Samiare gasped as she saw, and her own sword came into the light. Zarue brought his blade up against the axe and a loud clang rang out. The two of them scuffled as the others moved to flank. Samiare screamed out as well and rushed forward. Zarue canted his head to look back on her, his eyes revealing dread, and then he turned on the Groll with a new ferocity.

One with red skin and a spiked club met him first. It hurried to his flank and swung in with a broad stroke. Zarue caught its arm with his hand and cleaved down into its neck, dropping it to the floor. He hastened to pull his blade free as the first swung its axe again. Zarue cut against the weapon, deflecting the blade down, but it went askew, and sliced into his leg. Zarue cried out, and nearly fell. The green Groll hissed in glee as it yanked the axe out, pulling Zarue's stance off center, but Zarue pitched himself forward, driving his broad blade forward, and stabbing the green monster through the torso. Black blood spilled next to his own, and wet the floor as the creature fell. Zarue braced his hand against the wall to keep from falling with it.

The last Groll, a black monster, bulled its way past his dying companion as Zarue shifted to square-off against it, but as the big man turned, his leg folded, and he fell, his own red blood pooling in the hall.

Samiare ran forward with all her might, crying out in her exertion. Her feet fell heavy, her armor shifting with the motion of her legs, her own blade pulled back to thrust. Before her, the black Groll stood over Zarue with its sword raised, but then it lingered; for only a heartbeat, it paused to savor its kill, and for him it was a heartbeat too long. Samiare lanced in from the side, driving her sword forward, and piercing him through both armor and ribs. The Groll monster looked on her, disbelieving, but with fading sight, he slumped and fell.

She pulled her sword free, light emanating from the blade as black blood dripped down its length. At the end of the hall, the dark creature looked on as well with glowing eyes. Its arms dropped to its sides, its body giving no movements. Samiare opened her arms to it, letting her sword cast to the side. She could see the darkness of it, see it deep into its being. She knew it must be one of the completely lost.

Zarue reached up to her, and touched her leg. "Child," he said.

Samiare took a step closer to it, and glared. "Fight me," she said in her native Norvish.

A motion more, the hand lifted. The hall filled again with orange clouds, only this time, it was five and not three, and from each another foul Groll came to be. She pulled her sword back with both hands on its hilt. From behind, she heard Zarue call out again. "Run," he screamed. She did not run. She looked on them, and hated. And behind them all, the creature of shadow faded, and she felt its presence sweep away from where she stood, leaving her with only the Groll before her.

And then they clashed.

The first moved, and then the others with them. Samiare gained her stance. Her sword held close to her body, she heard its song, and felt again the impulse of its call. She saw the movements of her foes, almost as if they were slow and languid, like heavy sand moving through water. She cut through the first before his blow could land, sending him in pieces to the floor, spattering his blood against the walls. The second, she evaded, and stepped past his blow to cleave down another who was behind him. Her sword grew in brightness, lighting the hall, causing the Groll before her to turn their heads away. She met the blade of another, casting it aside in a close circle, and bringing her sword around to cut its wielder through its side and torso. More music played. She could see it all—all of their motions and thrusts and wards, and she knew their actions even before they made them. She wheeled around, and brought her sword slicing through the one she had stepped past as flame of purest white rose from her blade. The last stepped to back away, and held a heavy mace up to ward, but she would not let it escape. All she saw was the face of a fiend that killed her father, and took her sister, and burned her with fire. She hated it, and in her rage, she stuck him down as well. Letting his pieces fall and his blood wet the floor. She kicked the corpse in anger and cursed at its dead form until her rage passed.

Becoming calmer, she turned with tears welling in her eyes, and saw Zarue struggling where he fell. Her sense returning, her sword growing dim, she rushed to his side, and put her hand on him.

"I am hurt," he said, looking up at her. "He cut past the bone. It's bad."

"Samiare...get healer," she said. "Samiare get Lizelle."

"Yes," he said. "Go."

She stood and ran down the hall with her sword held low and pointing behind. At the corner stood one of the boys, an older lad of the patrol; his expression one of bewilderment and shock. She ran by him and left him where he stood.

"THEY TOOK MY leg, Rue," moaned Zarue. "What can I do without my leg?"

Ruegette sat next to the big warrior with her hand on his. "I'm sorry," she said. "I am sorry I was not here."

"My whole life spent chasing Groll," Zarue continued. "My whole life out in the passes, and forests, and canyons; my whole life spent with you in the service of Tierinor, and now what? I can't even stand."

"You must not say that, Zarue," pleaded Ruegette. "You mustn't quit. We will find a new place for you."

"As what?" Zarue burst out. "A beggar?"

"You will never beg," she said. "As a daughter to the Jarl of the Eastern Citadel, I promise you shall not want."

"I know you will look after me, Rue," he said softly.

"You are one of the best. There is still much you can do. Teach your skills to a new line of Wardai. Stay in the service of Tierinor."

"You should have seen her. I cannot teach what she did. She killed those twenty out on the plain. I have no doubt."

"You are speaking of the incident in the hall?" asked Ruegette.

"It was a Maygar," he said. "It stood before us in the hall, with all its dark sorcery. I thought it would kill us all...but the girl... She was not afraid, and somehow, it was. It withdrew before her, leaving only a rabble of filthy Groll that she slew with ease. I have never witnessed such a display."

"There is something here in the temple," said Ruegette. "What do you think it was after?"

"I don't know," said Zarue. "I think it said something. It might have been '*words*', but its language was strange, not Durish, and not Allarish."

"I learned things, Zarue. I know where the Eye of Ebon is. I have a map. I copied it from a book I found in Esilecolm."

"The Eye of Ebon?"

"Yes," she said, "but others have been on its trail long before me. A Maygar would not risk coming here, or use its dark sorcery to travel so far, if the need were not dire, and for one to do so without a summoning stone to guide it… It would not have left here without the secret it came to retrieve. I must learn what it learned. The Eye of Ebon must never be unsealed."

"It withdrew from the girl," said Zarue. "She was holding the bronze door in the south corridor. You should start looking in there."

"I will look," she said. "And then I'll return. I will stay with you tonight."

"Don't worry about me, Rue," said Zarue. "You do what you must to keep them from the Eye."

Ruegette stood and started to leave the big warrior's side, but he stopped her with his voice.

"One other thing," he said. "Take that girl with you. She's ready."

GLYSANDRA KNEW THE streets would not be the path the Wanderer took from the city, there was only one place he could go to escape, and none would be able to bar his way. She ran through the streets of Tierasol ahead of the alarm, and ahead of those who rose in the night to answer it. In her evening robes and with her red-gold hair billowing behind, she looked as a flaming ghost descending upon the one site Ilnydrifel was sure to be.

A fire burned at the docks, once proud ships with wide reinforced hulls bound with bronze filigree burned with all the rage that a dark mage could set them to. Of the many trading vessels and war barges, only a single craft was not in flames, a low merchant ship that loomed like a dark shadow upon the water and drifting slowly away. Bodies lay upon the dock, those of workers and watchmen who could not know the danger the afflicted man posed and were brought down with fire to lie in smoking heaps on its boards. Flames danced about, threatening to engulf the entire platform into a raging inferno, but Glysandra did not pause; charging through, she raced to the edge of the pier, cursing that she had ever helped the Wanderer. Upon the water, a single large sail billowed to life, and beneath it, a lone dark figure stood with his decrepit arm raised to the dark powers that filled him.

Glysandra had only one hope to stop him. Drawing back her one arrow, she said a final prayer, "Goddess of the healing gift, I rescind all my petitions to make him whole. Withdraw your arts and make my arrow true." Glysandra let the arrow fly.

In the darkness, it struck. The man cried out and staggered upon the deck as his affliction raged upon him once more. He clutched at the rail and writhed in his pain, and in his misery, lost his hold on an object that he held in his one good hand, letting it fall into the darkness of the Sea of Floes where it could not be saved.

Glysandra stood and watched as the ship drifted slowly into the night. Behind her raged the flames, her escape was cut off. In her last act as the Keeper of Souls, she leapt from the flaming dock into the freezing waters below, where only darkness and ice awaited.

"THIS HAS NOT been opened since the Allarie faded into the east and the Morkind took on their burden," said an ancient and frail voice. It belonged to an old man in white robes who was bent with age and walked forward only with the aid of the Matron, Lizelle. In his right hand, he held a slender white staff that tapped upon the flagstones of the hall. Ruegette knew him as Saurul, the Keeper of Souls.

"It will not open for any," Saurul's withered voice continued. "Only for the Keeper of Souls alone. None have been beyond this door. None should ever disturb the souls below."

Ruegette stood with Samiare at her side. The young girl shifted and fidgeted constantly, her hand still upon her sword and her oversized mail still hanging loosely about her small frame. She did not appear to Ruegette as 'being ready', but she had heard and seen too much to doubt her. Ruegette held a torch and stepped aside to let the Keeper of Souls approach the door.

"I apologize to you," said Ruegette. "I know the hour is late and this is a most unusual request, but I fear something has been beyond this door, even if it has not been opened."

The old priest barely waved his hand and grunted to dismiss her apology. "I pray you are wrong," he said in a voice barely audible. "If it is for the Koning then I will do it for you."

Lizelle helped the old priest to stand before it and then stepped away as he laid the tip of his staff against the bronze surface and began to chant with words that were barely audible. Ruegette waited patiently, watching the priest, but Samiare was too anxious; she took hold of Ruegette's arm and spoke, "What is behind?"

Ruegette opened her mouth to answer, but it was the voice of Lizelle that spoke first. "It is the door to a burial chamber," she said. "This temple, like many things in Tierinor, was made by the Allarie long ago. They were destined to live forever, but sadly some of them did not. Below the temple is a chamber that holds many of their remains."

"It is a sacred place," said Ruegette.

A sharp metallic ring signaled the unlatching of the great door, and then slowly it began to open into the hall. Ruegette moved closer to it with her torch held high, but Samiare stood back and gripped her sword, ready to pull it free. Gusts of air, filled with the smell of old dust, rose from the passage buffeting the flames of Ruegette's torch, and from deep within, the mournful sound of a howling wind wailed in lonely resonance. The bronze door swung freely until it stopped with a loud and lurching clang, leaving the four before an opening that went forward into darkness and revealing the top of a long descending stairs.

"They have rested for thousands of years," said Saurul. "Be mindful of their peace." He slowly shuffled away from the door, and Lizelle came forward to take hold of his arm.

Ruegette cast a glance back at Samiare. The girl's eyes were wide and uncertain. "I hear you have earned a new name for yourself," she said. "I hear some are calling you '*Shal Comaire*,' the 'Groll Slayer'."

Samiare seemed startled by Ruegette's attention and cast her eyes up to look at her unknowingly.

"I do not know what lies beyond," said Ruegette, "but we will face it together." Samiare nodded her head, and Ruegette started onto the stairs.

The stairs descended far below the temple, dropping into darkness for what seemed like thousands of steps. After the first hundred, one of the side walls fell away leaving an open side that would plummet any to their deaths if there was a misstep. It was cold in the underground chamber and only grew colder as they descended. At the very bottom was a large stone arch; it stretched high overhead and was carved with Allarish symbols.

Ruegette looked on them, but they were too ancient for her to decipher them all. "It's Allarish," she said. "But it's old. It seems to speak of souls that cannot die, and sleep that must not be disturbed."

Samiare looked up at the script and gave a shudder. She gazed out into darkness as the wind gusted along the curve of the stair and howled.

"It is a warning," said Ruegette. "We will heed it. We will disturb nothing." She put her torch before her and moved down the last dozen steps with caution. Samiare stayed close and made no sound at all.

The two came to stand in a large cavern with walls well beyond the reach of their torchlight. The floor was rock and covered with a loose layer of grit, but where they stood, a path of carved stones was laid before them. Ruegette set upon it, going forward without fear, but Samiare was not the same; she turned at every shadow, and every low howl of the wind.

Ruegette lit the way forward, following the path until the walls of the cavern became visible and the carved stones led them to a naturally formed opening in the rock. Within the opening, a pedestal made of a silvery metal glinted, and upon it was a thick book opened to a page near the middle. She put her fingers against the book; it was not brittle and there was writing upon it, clean and unfaded. She studied it further, turning some of the pages, she found only Allarish symbols.

"It is a book about the dead," she said, "but it cannot have been here all this time. It shows no signs of age." She stopped on one of the pages and struggled with the words as she read them. "Here it speaks of an Allarish warrior who fell to Groll in the Silver Woods and was brought home." She turned to another. "And here it tells of an Allarish woman felled by a Groll arrow. It says she was a beloved child to a mage." Ruegette flipped through more pages. "They are all the same, epithets to the dead of long ago, remembrances of who they were, and how they fell."

No sooner had she finished speaking than a strong wind gusted up from the emptiness before her. It blew hard against her, buffeting the torch she held to near extinguishment. Ruegette backed away from the pedestal, but Samiare stepped forward and looked long into the darkness, surveying in all directions. The wind died down as the young girl stood vigil, and when it was gone, she turned to look at Ruegette. "Something disturbed here," she spoke. "Before we come…Samiare feel it."

Ruegette returned to the book and flipped through more pages finding more names and more descriptions. She flipped back, looking at each new page with uncertainty, and wondering if the Maygar had come here and made use of it. Her fingers felt along the edges of the thin paper and caught on an uneven spacing near the middle.

She flipped it open to that spot, and there before her was the torn edge of a page that had been removed, a page in the tale of an Allarish woman named Ellyndil.

"We seek the resting place of Ellyndil," she called out, but her words were overshadowed by a low moan that rose from out of the darkness. In an instant, Samiare turned on it and pulled her sword to hold the naked blade, glowing faintly, before her. The low moan gave way to a loud shriek that ripped through the darkness, and then more rose to join it, bursting out from all directions.

Samiare turned at each new emanation, waving her sword about to ward away the noise, but the shrieking only rose in volume until Ruegette could not even shout above it. In the darkness, white shapes of glowing vapor raced through the gloom, too thin to be material but with too much shape to be mist. They weaved through the chamber like it was a sea, not held by any restriction as to direction or elevation. And they came by the hundreds, seeping in from every dark space, rising up from the floor, and descending from high above where the cavern's heights could not be seen, swarming ever closer until they became a great vortex around both Ruegette and Samiare with her glowing sword before her.

And it was Samiare they moved against. They lashed in, and she struck out wildly. When they touched her, she would recoil, and when she cut at them, they flew back. Her sword began to glow even brighter, forming a radiance around which the misty forms swarmed. Faces appeared in them, full of rage and dark despair, and at each move the girl took, each swipe of her sword, the howling grew louder. They hissed at her and the blade she held before her.

Ruegette knew it was the sword that enraged them. The glowing blade threatened them, and they reacted. She shouted at Samiare to release it, but it was to no avail; the girl could not hear. Ghostly shapes swooped in from the edge, touching her as they passed near, and where they touched, Ruegette felt her skin freeze and her stamina drained. Desperately, she called out again, but the noise was too much. Not knowing how else to reach her, Ruegette rushed forward and leapt upon the young girl, knocking her to the ground and falling upon her. Samiare struggled to break free, but Ruegette wrestled to contain her—to take control of her sword arm. Samiare cried out, and Ruegette screamed at her, her face so close that gold hair touched her mouth. "Let it go!" she yelled. "Let go of the sword."

Samiare continued to resist, but Ruegette held her too tightly; she could not escape the older woman's grasp or get her arm free. She struggled and writhed until she could no longer and then, defeated, she released her hold, letting the sword clatter to the stone floor. Ruegette stayed upon her, cradling her from the danger that swirled above. The phantoms continued to move at them, sweeping in and out and touching Ruegette's back with wispy hands that caused her to writhe, but still the she remained, and all the while calling out in the Allarish tongue, "Peace, we wish peace."

The torrent continued, not subsiding for many long moments, but slowly the fury passed and the shrieking died down to a low moan. When they settled, both she and Samiare were left panting upon the floor. Ruegette was first to move; slowly she stood. Her torch lay upon the floor barely lighting the pedestal it had fallen near, but she did not need it to see, all about the chamber were glowing shapes flowing like sheets in a storm, passing through air and stone as if they were the same. Samiare stood next to her and looked at them too. Her sword lay within reach, but she dared not pick it up.

"We seek the resting place of Ellyndil," Ruegette called out in Allarish.

There was a long silence and then a clamor of moaning and wailing. The shapes moved, flowing in mass out into the darkness, seemingly to lead a way. Ruegette went back to the pedestal and picked up her torch. She turned to follow after the spirits, but her eyes caught on a sight that filled her with dread. Samiare, with no semblance of concern, reached down and took hold of her sword yet again. Ruegette's heart sank at seeing it, and she prepared for the worst, but the girl slid the blade back into its scabbard, and the spirits gave it no reaction at all. With a sigh of relief, Ruegette put aside her fear and set out to follow where the spirits led.

The cavern gave way to a narrow corridor of carved rock dotted with dark openings along its length. The openings were the entries to many small chambers that served as resting dens for the dead, and within them Ruegette expected to find only sealed burial vaults or ornate sarcophagi, but that was not what she saw; instead many of the chambers had been violated. Lids had been ripped open and seals had been broken, and the bodies of fallen Allarie had been moved; many spilled onto the floor and still others were left to hang from the sides of the containers that held them. The bodies themselves were also not what Ruegette expected; they were not rotted or skeletal like those she had seen in her many journeys, most appeared as if they had only just passed, with only the smallest cast of death's pallor upon them; a visage that caused even her to feel uneasy, let alone the girl who followed her.

Giving a shudder, she turned her eyes away from the macabre displays, and steeling herself further, set again on the trail of the spirits. The way passed through a labyrinth of interlocking corridors and musty chambers, all desecrated and left in a fashion similar to those she first saw. Ruegette became more comfortable with the grim visages of death as she passed, but they were still unsettling, and by the end of her journey, she came to feel only anger, and even upset at the vandalisms she witnessed. The path she followed led her to a small chamber containing only a single stone sarcophagus. The lid on this too had been opened and the body of a young Allarish woman had been partially pulled from it; her remains slumped over the side until her head and a single arm dangled loosely over the floor. Near the coffin was a torn page, the one missing from the book.

Ruegette handed the torch to Samiare and took the page. She studied it; like the tome it was torn from, it was written in the old Allarish tongue, but it was not a tale of the Allarish woman's death, or even a recounting of her life; the words were strange and unknown to her. She struggled to say them aloud but doing so seemed to have no effect.

"These are not words I know," said Ruegette. She tried again to say them, but could not be sure, and then spoke them again working on her inflection, and this time there was a change. No sooner had she uttered the last syllable than a voice began to trail out from the Allarish woman's corpse, even as it lay lifeless upon the edge of her stone sarcophagus.

"*My word is Yamoth.*"

The corpse repeated the words again and again, her voice as faded and drifting as the life that left her. Ruegette stood right beside her and listened. "My...word...*Yamoth*," she repeated.

"Oh, my," she said. "Zarue told me the Maygar had spoken to him in the halls. He said it might have been 'words' that it spoke. The Maygar was looking for this secret."

Ruegette thought on what it would mean if the Maygar had learned this word and knew that it could not be good. She looked sadly upon Ellyndil's corpse and wondered how she had come to hold such a secret, but then decided she must restore the Allarish woman to her rest. She took hold of the corpse and eased it back into the comfort of its final resting place. The corpse continued to speak with the voice of the dead woman even after Ruegette laid her back down, but in time, her words trailed off into silence. Ruegette had Samiare help her put the stone lid back over the body and then took notice of the name carved into it.

"Look," she said pointing at the Allarish script. "This says 'Tolilzin'. This is not the sarcophagus of Ellyndil."

Samiare looked at the Allarish word blankly. "We find Tolilzin?" she said almost uncertain.

"Yes," said Ruegette. "I think we'd better."

They found the sarcophagus of Tolilzin in similar fashion to that of Ellyndil, and like the first, it too bore the name of another upon its surface, that of a fallen hero, Rafangil, and then his bore the name of Ellyndil. At each burial room there was a torn page upon the floor and as each was read another word was revealed. "Yamoth," "Eomil," "Enshu." Each word a secret for more than a thousand years, and, as Ruegette feared, each word bringing the Eye of Ebon closer to Groll hands.

PART 2
WHITE WITCH

TAKEN FROM THE icy waters, the body of the once Keeper of Souls was as beautiful in death as it was in life. How could any know the Wanderer would bring such ruin when he first appeared at the doors of the temple? Once the priestess who guarded the bronze door to the dead, now to be taken down the long stair a last time, not under her own power or as guardian of the dead, but on the mournful arms of acolytes to be an occupant.

That it was the Shadow once again acting his evil upon the land there was no question, and the tomb beneath Miranae's Temple was full of those who had also lost in the struggle to rid their lands of his influence. With great accolades and many tears, Glysandra's name was added to the Book of Lives Lost and slowly her body was carried to a place of honor where it would rest until the seven Gods came to claim her.

The fate of the afflicted man was unknown to those in the temple. It was several days before any could follow after him and nowhere was his vessel reported to have docked. Many thought he had returned to Gorginor with his prize, but a few saw Glysandra loose her arrow and strike him at the helm. Speculation rose that he must have died from her shot.

It was not known what he stole from the temple, or even if he had taken anything at all, but what he left behind brought a cold fear into the hearts of the Temple priests. Fished from the water was more than just an object, it was a leather-bound book with bronze clasps and thick vellum, and in it was something frightful, for it was not a book of wisdom or a tome of history, but a book that tried to unlock the intricate puzzle that was the Eye of Ebon.

The ink on its vellum pages was smeared and ruined from the water but where it could be read, it told the tale of the Eye, and in it was the one page that had no damage at all, the page that bore a map of the region between the lands of Tieran and Alasdain. A map that had strange markings and showed a path through the Forest of Silver to a region clearly marked, and the village it was near–Sahlohir.

The secrets held in the book were not meant to be discovered, and it was decided it should never be opened again, but it was not destroyed. The great task of hiding the book was entrusted to the one Allarish lord whom even the Dursharal had come to fear, Rivin de Tagorlyarde, Warder of the Eastern Citadel. And so its secrets were locked away deep within rock passages far beneath the gleaming spire that watched the east.

THE TIERAN SCOUT ship skirted the shoreline of the wide river. It was a long and narrow vessel with a single row of ten oars on either side, and a mast, there to carry the vessels only quilted sail, lay lengthwise across the deck, removed as a precaution when the company left the Sea of Floes and entered the Aillsdale River. The bow of the ship hung low over the water, and beneath it, the bronze protrusion of a ram peeked above the surface. The rear beam rose high and curved in over the deck like the tail of a scorpion, where a large tarp was hung, making a small quarters for its captain and passengers. The vessel had but a single deck and a shallow cargo space beneath. Forty soldiers of Tierinor worked her oars, their shields hanging about the sides and adding to its protection.

Any voyage from Tierinor to the Aillsdale River went through the Sea of Floes and past the coast of Gorginor. The Aills was a series of interconnecting lochs and channels that cut a deep path between the Drisari Mountains to the west and the Silver Mountains to the east. The land between the two ranges, once called the Southern Passes, because it was only through them that the forces of Gorginor could gain entry into the lands beyond, was now called the Wastes. With the retreat of Alasdain centuries ago and the inability of Tierinor to control the land, the Southern Passes had fallen mostly into Groll hands, and had become only a place of ambush and battle. Ruegette led the men deep into danger. It was unlikely they could travel the river unseen, and to gain the best chance of surprise they moved the ship at night, hiding it as best they could during the day.

The banks of the river had seen much war and death. A pine forest, once called the Silver Forest by the Allarie of old, spread across the hard ground on both banks, tall and thick spires with needles of white silver, pine green, and faded purple crowded the shores and spread through the hills and crags beyond. The entire region from the lower tip of Gorginor to the farthest extension of the Southern Passes were Groll lands. It was a land of trees and rock and war, and it bore the scars of many battles. Many were the towers and posts set throughout and along the shore to guard against invasion, and many were those who had been lost and broken and burned in long ago battles.

It was cold on the river. Winter always lasted long in the four lands and even in the breezes of the early spring, it would be sometime before the snow completely melted, a condition which would last only a few months and then snows would return just as thick as before. Ruegette was used to cold, and so it seemed was the girl from Norvaine.

Samiare stood upon the deck with her. She wore a finer suit of chain than Zarue had first given her, and a small helm adorned her head. Her gold-hilted sword hung from a belt at her waist, and still she grasped it like it was a touchstone to calm her heart. When Ruegette first found her, lying near dead on a snowy plain, she spoke not a word of Tieran, but after many months she was speaking it well enough.

"I have prayed," said Samiare. "I feel great evil upon...land."

"It is said," Ruegette spoke, "that the Shadow is never far from what is his. We are nearing the Eye of Ebon. It may be his presence you feel, but he has no power while his prison holds. There is nothing to fear." Ruegette was still uncertain about the girl, and the Wastes were a place full of danger; in the past she would only enter them with Zarue at her side, but with his injury, he could not any longer, and it was he who picked the girl to replace him.

"I...no with fear," said Samiare.

"Ship ahead," announced one of the soldiers.

A silence fell upon the deck as Captain Ambrue strode forward to survey, an action followed by many of the crew. The ship hung like a dark shape lumbering in the water. It was not whole. Many of its side planks were missing, opening it to the sky like a cracked bowl. The smell of burnt wood was the first indication as to its fate, and as they drew closer, a faint wafting of smoke could still be seen to rise from it.

"It was of Marindor," spoke the Captain in a hushed voice. "Not one of ours."

The low sleek shape of the Tieran scout ship drifted towards the broken vessel, every man on board standing to look upon it. As they passed, a score of jutting arrows could be seen marking the wood that remained.

"A war ship by the shape of it," Captain Ambrue declared. "Smoke still rises from her; this fate could not have befallen too long ago."

Ruegette looked upon the lost vessel with particular interest. This close to where she knew the Eye of Ebon would be, a Marish ship must have carried those who were tasked with quest of it. *Could Captain Darimus have been aboard?* It was a disappointing thought, and in spite of the fact that he had taken advantage of her, it saddened her. She believed he would keep his word and take back the Shard he lost from Groll hands. She did not want him to die in the effort.

She turned away from the rail, no longer wishing to look upon the drifting hulk. "Captain Ambrue," she called. "We have come far enough. I need to get to the shore."

The Captain gave her a long and pensive stare, and then he called the men to orders. "Put her to shore," he commanded. "The Wardai has spoken. Look lively."

Samiare came and stood next to her. "We go together?" she asked in a quiet voice.

"No," said Ruegette. "I need to go alone. There are Groll about, many of them. I must use stealth in the woods, and I fear you would only slow me down. Some distance south of here is the village of Yeshale, it is little more than a ruin now, but once the village was devoted to the worship of Emshallet, the God of light and water. A shrine still stands there; it marks the ground where the village once stood. The shrine holds a pool that opens onto the river. Take the ship into the pool and hide it. The Groll openly avoid the holy places of the Allarie, so they will be afraid to enter the ruin. When I have done all that I can, I will go to Yeshale and seek you there."

"I understand," said Samiare, her head lowered and her disappointment clearly visible upon her face. "I wait for Ruegette to return."

"Be wary," said Ruegette. "The Groll fear the shrine, but that will not stop them from entering. The Wastes are always full of danger, and these trees hide wickedness in every shadow. You must always be ready. If things go poorly, other ways across the river lie too far to the south to be of use. Your only choice will be to press east for Alasdain. I am going to find a way to the Eye. It was hidden in the mountains near the village of Sahlohir. The Groll must have learned this as well, and the Shadow will spend many of their lives to retrieve it. The Groll must not be allowed to capture it no matter what the risk or sacrifice. Keep that in mind always."

"I will pray for you," said Samiare, lifting her eyes to look straight into Ruegette's. Ruegette smiled and then turned to gather her things.

RUEGETTE DID NOT like to disappoint the young girl, but her duty left no room for errors. The Wastes were not a kind teacher, and the Groll would be only too willing to repeat their wicked tortures upon her again if she should fall into their hands. A similar fate awaited herself as well if she were not careful, but she had skills to keep herself safe in the wilderness, the girl could only fight to the death; she did not doubt the wisdom of her decision.

She moved away from the Aillsdale with an arrow ready in her bow. If the Groll were near, they would be watching the river, and

she knew her safety depended on putting a good distance between
herself and the water. She moved cautiously, and though it was
thought the blood of the Allarie ran in her family, she had no gift of
dark-sight as that ancient race was reputed to possess. To snap a
fallen limb, or to wander too long away from tree cover could bring
an army of Groll upon her–she would be too careful for that.

Sahlohir was rumored to be lost within the Silver Mountains to
the east, but she had a good idea of where it lay. The map she copied
from the tome in Esilecolm was not an exact representation of the
land, but it gave her enough to get started. Ruegette did not know
much about Sahlohir, only the rumors and legends. Once a city of
splendor and a source of fine metals, it fell to Groll even before the
Allarie had vanished into the east. Its location was lost to time by
centuries full of warfare and strife. Ruegette held what may be a copy
of the only map in existence that revealed its location, but the
discovery of a ship from Marindor, and its ambush by Groll so far
south along the Aills, was enough for her to know the city was no
longer lost to one or both of these armies, and if armies guarded the
entrance, then perhaps she could follow their movements right to its
gates. All she had to do was find one.

There was a road along the eastern side of the Aills. It was
ancient and un-kept by the Groll, decaying until it was nothing more
than a rutted and broken stone path, but it ran from the Sea of Floes
to places far south of the Wastes. It was even rumored to cross the
hills of sand and lead to wild lands far beyond the shipping lanes.
Though worn, the road still serviced the armies of Morkind and
Groll, and Ruegette knew she could not long follow it without
finding those set to watch it. The road however was not always
recognizable, and she understood that in its current state, she could
very easily pass over it and take no notice. She was determined to be
careful she did not pass it by.

She traveled straight east for more than an hour before a line of
jutting stones, half-buried in the dirt and cutting a straight path
through trees, left no doubt where she was. In the distance was the
sound of armored figures moving in the dark. They approached from
the north and by the noise of them, they were a large band. Ruegette
always assumed an unknown force in the Wastes to be Groll, and she

had no desire to be seen by them. Moving well off to the side, she hid herself behind a large tree and crouched low as she readied an arrow in her bow. Shortly, the noise of grunting and barked out commands in their foul Durish language let her know who they were.

The Groll came at a fast pace but remained distant. The sound of them was full of clanking metal and rhythmic grunts, but it did not hold the snapping of branches or the rustle of low brambles as it would if they moved in the woods. To her, it meant they would be on the road and easy to follow. She waited for them to pass and listened as they headed off to the south.

Ruegette had spent too many days in the Wastes chasing Groll to miss the significance of their movements after dark. Groll could go for days without sleep, but they did not do so by choice. If they were moving at night, then there was something pushing them. She waited until the sound of them began to trail off in the distance before following, and even then, she moved as quietly as she could. She did not want any risk of being discovered. She knew better than to move openly onto the road, she stayed inside the tree line and headed south after the Groll.

The Groll greatly outpaced her, but the sound of them running upon the road lingered long after they had departed. Some distance further new sounds added to their clatter, they had moved off the road and by doing so, the noise of snapping branches along with the occasional ring of metal cutting into wood added to their racket. Still their echoes grew faint as she made her way along their trail, growing so distant that she thought they would fade entirely until another, more telling, sound rose in the darkness—metal ringing out in reverberation as steel impacted steel.

Somewhere ahead there was a battle. She knew it could not be a battle joined against her own soldiers left upon the river; they could not have moved so quickly as to be this deep in the woods. It might be Groll upon Groll, and given their nature it was always a possibility, but it might also be that some of Marindor had survived beyond the encounter that lost them their ship. A new thought sprang up, one that was both welcome and concerning. *Might it be that Captain Darimus was in the battle ahead?* She knew only one way to find out. She picked up her pace and set her course on the sounds of the battle.

The battle raged like a grim beacon in the night. As she drew closer, she could hear the crash of metal, the pounding of wood, and the screams of those dying, but it was too distant for her to play a role in its outcome. In its fury, it seemed to move about the woods, first seemingly a distance in front, but then it broke off and moved some distance to the east, and then another clamor rose from the west. The combatants were moving and taking their battle to new locations, all of them further still from where the battle had started, its indication being only that the Groll she followed were pushing back against whoever they battled.

Small fires lit the woods ahead, and she decided to approach one. Wary of being discovered, she went stealthily towards the nearest until she had eased close enough to make out figures moving about it. They were Groll warriors, and they were scattered in a hasty camp. Banners stained with blood and painted with grim imagery marked their ground and were placed at the edge of the well fueled fire. The noise of Groll moving in the woods beyond the camp crashed out in the darkness, and within the radiance, shadowy shapes scurried about. Occasionally, their voices rose above the clamor, and sporadically, Ruegette could make out their words. For a time she listened, but nothing useful was in their conversation, only the cackling of Durish speaking mongrels basking in their enjoyment of cruelty. Tired of it, she prepared to leave, but was stopped by the rise of a new voice speaking in the language of Marindor.

"Who leads you?" growled the voice. It was thick and gruff with the accent of Groll upon it. "What is your purpose here?"

There was no reply. In the light of the fire there were three that had been brought forth. Two were stood upon by Groll guards; the third was on his knees before the speaker.

"Umgot would have you speak. Put out his eye."

The order was quickly obeyed, and it came with the wild screams of their victim over the wicked taunting of the Groll. The questioning continued, as did the resistance, and so did the Groll teach cruelty to their captive. It could not last.

"Darimus," screamed the man held at their hands. "Darimus is our Captain. He leads a contingent past your lines. He goes after Shargat, and a secret hidden in the mountains."

His answers did not come easily and Ruegette pitied him, but there was nothing she could do. If she tried, the Groll would simply capture her as well. The mention of Darimus did cause a stir in her, it brought both a relief and an anger to her heart; relief he had not perished, and then anger she was going to have to find him to keep the Eye of Ebon from his hands as well. She had not forgotten his actions on the boat, there would be a score to settle on that.

"Kill him," barked the Groll in his own language. "Kill them all. Shargat wastes us here. Umgot goes east to find this Dar'mis. I will have his head."

There was nothing Ruegette could do to help any of those held by Umgot, and she did not even try. She hid herself in the darkness and heard as each prisoner was put to death. In time, Umgot gathered his band and moved east. Ruegette let them get a lead, and then she started to follow.

"GENTLY STROKE," ORDERED the Captain.

The sleek shape of the scout ship moved slowly upon the water, her pace of the last hour no more than one walking, and the sound of her as she moved over the glassy surface was little more than a rustle.

The Captain led his ship further south into the uncontrolled waters of the Aillsdale. None put voice to it, but the deck was thick with fear. They were far from the gates to the Eastern Citadel, and few from Tierinor ever came this far south in the Wastes, fewer still had come this far and returned. The east bank was darkened by the forms of tall trees, and the fires of Groll camps glinted out from many places within the woods, their number growing as they passed slowly by.

Samiare sat in the darkness under the tarp that covered the aft of the ship, her sword, still in its scabbard, pulled onto her lap where she grasped it with both hands. She would help the men at the rowing if they would have her, but she was considered too weak to pull the oars, and her small size and slight reach would only hinder others if she tried. Captain Ambrue seemed nervous. He paced the

deck with his hands clasped behind him, his head cast down in a
determined fashion. He barely spoke the words, but at a steady pace,
his order repeated, "Stroke," he said. "Stroke." His Lieutenant,
Izarou, worked the tiller, and another, thought to have good eyes,
looked over the bow.

"Ship ahead," spoke the hushed voice of the forward lookout.

"Ship?" uttered Captain Ambrue.

"Two ships," whispered the lookout. "Near the shore."

Captain Ambrue held his hand high to steady the oars. "Two
ships?" he breathed. "Not a stroke."

The men went quiet. Many cast their heads to listen. The sounds
of movement along the bank were unmistakable. Samiare could hear
them as well. Rustlings that rose from places nearby, enough that it
could not be merely the wind through the trees. She turned her head
to face them, but the Captain spoke again and drew her attention
back. "Ahead," he commanded. "Full stroke!" It was too late. A
reverberating twang broke through the darkness like the sound of
plucked strings ringing out from too many locations. "Ambush!"
cried the Captain as hidden darts whistled towards them in the night
air.

Samiare gave a gasp and stood as arrows landed, but she could
only watch. The darts came unseen, pounding into the ship and its
crew like the tapping of a new rain upon a dry roof, and amid the
noise was the sharp ring of metal, and the cries of men struck.
Several fell beneath the hail, and many took arrows; among them,
Captain Ambrue. His leg shot through, he fell and rolled on the deck
before her. He did not cry out, instead he kept his bearing and gave
his orders. "Turn the ship, you mongrels," he screamed. "Put us to
shore. Let us take the fight to them."

Slowly the ship turned as another volley landed. More men fell
beneath the shower, but the Captain kept at them. "Stroke, curse
you! Stroke for all you're worth!"

The ship picked up pace and began to drift swiftly towards the
east bank, where the sound of archers grew in volume. In the dark of
the forest, small fires sputtered to life, and arrows set with flame
were cast into bows. More movements resounded, the Groll were
making ready for the melee, but the Captain had set their course.

There was no backing away from the danger now.

Bow strings let loose again, this time bringing fire and striking both man and vessel with a fierce assault. Under the volley, the Captain was delivered a fatal blow, his body slumped upon the deck next to others who shared his fate. Flames darted up from many shafts stuck deep into the wood.

Samiare stood motionless at the aft, her small form lost among the tall and burly shapes of men dressed for war. She saw the chaos that broke upon the deck. No longer held by the command of their captain, the men gave into fear. Many fell against the rails to hide, or took up their shields from the sides, as others shouted to keep order, but none would follow. Another volley landed, this time falling upon the aft, one arrow punching through the chain of her skirt to slice across the inside of her thigh. She fell to a knee.

The ship drifted loose upon the water at a rapid pace. More arrows slammed into her sides and deck, flames licked upward and began to catch the wood. The ship started a slow drift to the side, and then it struck ground with a lurch. Her prow rising up as she slid onto the bank, and with planks creaking under the stress, she ground to a stop. For a moment there was safety, the cast of the ship, with its bow high and deck at a steep angle, shielded those within from more arrows, but it could not last.

Samiare snapped the shaft caught in her skirt and let its pieces fall onto the deck. Her leg burned where it had made its gash but she managed the pain of it. She looked up to see the men frantic before her, fear gripping them like a snare. She felt it too. Arrows punched into the ship's bow, the sound of it maddening, rapid and sharp, like the beat of a carpenter's hammer pounding into planks and sealing their fate with fire. Below, the sound of the Groll beating on shields and jeering was deafening. Samiare pulled her sword free and dropped its point into the deck before her. It glowed faintly in the dark. She prayed over it for valor, then stood and moved forward. A round white shield lay upon the path and she took it up as she went.

She passed by cowering men as she made her way to the fore. Some were too wounded to move but most were simply too afraid to try. At the rail, she turned to look at them, all of them warriors with more years and brawn than she, and each of them staring back with

eyes wide in the grip of fear, even the Lieutenant in his red plumed
helm was frozen with fright. Samiare glared at them for the span of a
few heartbeats, then slid over the rail and dropped to the ground.

She hit hard but had no time to consider her pain. Arrows leapt
through the darkness, two of them impacting her shield as she stood
and a third coming over its edge to bite into her shoulder. One arrow
bore fire and flames danced over the white face of her shield, but she
gave them no heed. With her face twisted into rage, she charged
forward, her shield held before her, and her dimly glowing sword
held back to strike. Arrows came again, some pounding into her
shield, and others flying past into what she did not know. At the tree
line, dark shapes made ready. Behind, she heard the war cries of
Tieran soldiers rising up; some had followed her lead to come and
fight for all they were worth. And from ahead, the sound of insidious
delight.

At the edge of the forest, Groll warriors with heavy blades moved
to meet her, and Samiare did not disappoint. She cut through the
first as he raised an axe to strike, gashing him open across the mid-
section and leaving him near in half on the ground. A second she cut
the legs from as he swiped at her with a glinting curved sword, and
then a third she skewered through the neck after bashing down his
short spear with her shield. As the third Groll fell, Samiare screamed
at him with all of her fury. Filled with hatred and rage, she threw
herself deeper into the woods, the sword in her hand cutting a
merciless path of limbs and split torsos as it went, and glowing
brighter with each Groll it slew.

"THE WAY WAS blocked," sneered the figure. He bore the lithe
and regal continence of an Allarie. His clothes were mage robes of
deep blue, but they dripped with water and were stained with grime.
"I took it as far as I could. I found a new way, but still I could not
approach it. The spirits were upon me. I could not go forward." In
his hands, he held a slender fragment of stone, one partially etched
with runes, but the rest was gone completely.

He stood in a cluttered room of hewn stone. About him were
podiums and tables piled with scrolls and dusty tomes. Bottles,
empty and discarded, lay strewn throughout, while glass vials and

strange containers were packed onto shelves and mixed in the clutter. These, he seemed to care nothing for. Given to rage, he swept his arm over one of the podiums, throwing its contents onto the ground, and then he threw himself upon it and wept. From his agony, his hand that held the fragment rose from his folded arms as his head twisted to look at it. With one eye upon it, he trembled.

"Why!" he screamed. "Why should I continue? Have I not served you better than any other?"

His face drew into a sneer, and he slammed the fragment down upon the podium, leaving it there. In a rage, he stormed about the dank room flailing his arms violently and crushing all that was loose. He overturned tables and cleared shelves until there was nothing left but a pile of clutter and the one podium left alone. He would not look at it; he swore it to himself.

"I am sorry," he wheezed out, and he turned to face it. "You are right and I was wrong." He walked towards it quickly and took up the fragment again in his hand to hold it before him. "How could I not see?"

He bowed his head in shame and shook. "I can get past them," he spoke as in a whisper. "What must I do?"

"No!" he screamed out. "If they see they will know what I have done. They will know!" The figure fell upon his knees and pleaded. "Let me do it. I will go as Ilnydrifel. They will allow me."

Pain wracked him, and he slumped to the floor, and then he laughed. "Yes, of course," he grinned. "Ilnydrifel is dead. I will hide myself in shadow." His face twisted with alarm and concern played in his wide eyes. "But how shall I take you?"

The shard began to glow red with fire and burned into his hand. The figure screamed and writhed but he could not let it go. It sank into his flesh and burrowed into his arm. When it was concealed, the flesh became restored. The figure openly cried and for many long moments fought against the pain, but then he stood.

"I am ready," he spoke with vigor. "I will leave at once." He strode from the room towards a long stairway that would take him out into the light.

RUEGETTE FOLLOWED AS Umgot led his Groll quickly

through the trees. His pace was almost that of a full run, and the noise of his band carried through the night like a storm. For Ruegette, staying close was not necessary, but as Umgot moved his band first through one Groll camp, and then another, she found it impossible to follow. She left his trail to move east on her own. All through the night, she could hear skirmishes to the south. It seemed that there were more of Marindor in the Wastes than she first assumed.

She made her way as stealthily as she could. The Groll were spread throughout the woods in great numbers, more than she thought them capable of, and it would take all her skills to avoid them. She did not know how many days travel it was from the river to the ruin of Sahlohir, but she knew the mountains were still several days off, and that was too far for her to go without sleep.

Near the first light of dawn, she began to look for a suitable shelter to hide in. She spied the remains of a ruined tower sitting upon the top of a high hill. The tower was wide at its base and grew thinner as it rose. From its partial battlement and flat top, Ruegette thought it to be an ancient watchtower, one that would have been used to watch the north long before the Groll had advanced into the south. It was nearly complete, only broken to the sky near the top where it appeared as if a diagonal slice had been cut from it. The tower was blackened by fire and several of its stones lay on the ground around it, but it was not abandoned.

From where she watched, she could see dark shapes moving inside of narrow windows that were spread around the circumference. There were three windows in all and each set at a different elevation upon the shaft. The Groll would have no reason to hide, so Ruegette thought it likely the shapes belonged to men, and if the men were soldiers from Marindor, then perhaps they could be of use to her.

Trying to stay hidden, she moved for the tower, but as she approached a party of Groll came into the valley. She hid herself and watched them. They went towards the tower seemingly unaware that others were within; they did not offer any signal before approaching, and none came out to greet them. She counted fifteen, likely a scouting party. She considered her chances against them; with surprise she could kill quite a few with her bow, and if she were correct, that it was Morkind and not Groll that hid within, fifteen seemed like a manageable number; but she was well out of arrow range, and she was going to have to act quickly if she wanted to help, the Groll were already closing in on the ruin.

She made ready an arrow and started for the tower at a fast pace. The Groll continued their approach as well, coming very close to the broken wall before those within ignited into action. Two arrows sailed out from the highest window and struck the front of the Groll rabble, an instant later a third lanced out from the lowest window as well.

Two Groll fell, and a third was struck and cried out. The Groll reacted quickly. Warriors with axes and spears and heavy maces rushed for the tower as four lingered back to raise bows and loose arrows as well. Closing on the base, spears were thrust into windows as others took to the wooden door with axes pounding.

Ruegette was practically running to get within range. She did not know how many were inside, but her concern grew. If Captain Darimus was one of those inside, she did not want to see him fall. Groll arrows flew up at the windows, some striking the tower, others lancing in. The door shook under the jarring blows and wood splintered. Spears were thrust through the wood, both from those inside, and from the Groll jamming their own dark tips in. More fell, but the door could not hold.

Coming close enough, Ruegette slid to her knees and pulled back her first arrow to loose. The Groll archers were scattered in an uneven line. She knew she could kill the closest unseen, and maybe others as well, but she must be quick, already the door cracked and wood fell from the frame. She took hasty aim at the one closest and let her arrow fly. As it sailed, she pulled three others, holding them between her fingers to set them quickly. Ahead, the first Groll was shot through the neck and fell silently on the hill. The next was also behind the others and could fall unseen. She drew back with one arrow strung and let fly. She stood and ran closer as her arrow struck, and the second fell.

Her range became shorter, and she slid forward again, pulling back her string and releasing in haste. A third arrow struck the next

from behind, driving in near his spine. The Groll pitched forward
and fell, but not before giving a cry of pain. His companion took
notice. He turned and in an instant, locked his eyes on her. Ruegette,
strung her last arrow and released, her hand open as she waited. The
arrow flew without drop, and struck him through the face as he
flinched. He fell next to his companions.

At the tower, the door splintered, and Groll warriors pushed in.
Fighting could be heard, and men screamed out. Desperate, Ruegette
rushed forward. Her hand grabbing the hilt of her sword. She saw
more than one Groll fall near the entrance, and heard more screams
from inside, but the men gave ground and the Groll piled in. She
cried out in her exertion. The battle had moved inside, she wanted to
be quicker.

Groll fought past the entry, and steel rang out as more ground
was given. Running with all her might, Ruegette gained the tower
and pushed through the door. Both Groll and Morkind lay dead at
her feet, and at the base of a wide stair, more had fallen. The stair
was made of stone and spiraled up around the tower. Two men
fought with four remaining Groll. The men had been pushed back
until they came precariously close to a gap where the stone had
broken away, and to retreat further would see them plummet to the
hard floor below.

Ruegette whipped up her bow and snatched out more arrows.
The twist and breadth of the stair prevented her from sighting all
who were upon it, but she only needed a small opportunity to lessen
the threat. A Groll close to the edge presented his head and at such
close range she could not miss. The arrow left her bow and cut
through his skull. The Groll stiffened and pitched sideways from the
stairs.

She strung another, but she could not be fast enough; in an
exchange of blows one of the men was cut through and fell from the
stairs as well. An instant later, his killer was cut down beneath the
sword of the last to fight against them, and also rolled limply down.
Behind it, another tried to rush over and fill the rank, but she was
ready as he leapt. Her arrow slid beneath his ribs and brought him
shrieking from above.

The last man stood against the last Groll. Ruegette readied

another arrow but she could not get a clean shot. On the stairs, a Groll axe crashed against a Marish sword. Ruegette circled, looking for an opportunity. The shoulder of the man came into view as his sword whipped back and then forward, followed by the dull clang of metal. The Groll gave off a grunt and thrashed at the man. The man retreated up another step, his foot resting on the very last step before there was only a drop. The Groll lunged forward and for an instant exposed its shoulder and ribs. She fired. Her arrow slid beneath the Groll's arm and skewered its shoulder. The Groll gave a yelp and recoiled. The man's sword flashed back and then finished the contest with a cleaving blow to its ribs.

Ruegette drew another arrow and waited. The man stood at the edge of the stairs and looked down, his face so familiar that it gave her a start just to see it.

"Tierinor?" he questioned, bewildered.

Ruegette could barely speak. "Darimus," was all she said.

THE NORTHERN CHILL of the night air blew against Samiare, seeping into her like the wash of a cold rain. It had been blowing for some time, but she had only just become aware of it. Another sensation swept over her, quite the opposite of the cool air; it was a burning deep in her shoulder. She reached up to feel and then remembered the arrow. She did not know when, but at some point during the battle the shaft of it had been broken, leaving only the smallest bit of wood above her skin. She had lost her shield as well, splintered to an unknown blow. She did not remember much of the battle, or even how many she slew; she was left with only the feeling it was not enough.

She felt the arrow. The head protruded slightly from behind her collar, and a long steel edge could be felt along the surface of her skin. One of the barbs rose above the flesh, but the other was sunk into her shoulder. The wound hurt immensely, but there was nothing to help that. Her sword lay at her side, no longer glowing as it had during the battle, but still she held it tightly as if it alone could give her comfort. Gathering her strength, she put her fingers around the bit of shaft and twisted the arrow free. It was painful work. It took all she had not to cry out, and when she was done tears openly fell down along her temples. She trembled and bled, but it would pass. She would not get up from where she lay. Instead she pulled her sword up onto her chest and rested.

She heard the voices of Tieran soldiers who had survived the battle. They were organizing, gathering the dead and wounded. She listened as they took an accounting of who could continue, and who could not. Names were spoken and fear at what would become of them if left to Groll hands, and then a decision was reached. She listened as those who would continue offered accolades and assurances to those who could not. At the end, there was the promise that they would be remembered as heroes in the great halls of Tierinor. She heard their prayers, and then their final sacrifice. It was a hard decision and men openly wept as they carried out the grim task.

Samiare wanted to cry for them as well, but she could not. Too many were the strange emotions that twisted inside of her. She understood the loss but could not express it, and that made her angry. For her, there was no feeling of loss, or even elation for surviving the battle. Instead she felt cold and detached. She hated the Groll.

She did not move, even when she heard someone calling her name. She spent her last resting moments trying to calm the torrent inside of her. She heard as men drew closer in the dark, and the pop and crackle of their ship as it burned. She heard her own breath and the beat of her own heart, and then she heard a faint ringing in the night. It stirred her, and she tried to hear it again. It was there, the clatter of metal and the echoes of sharp cries. Samiare stood and looked for it through the darkness. Ruegette…

"There you are!" called one of those near. "Are you wounded?"

"There is a battle," she said. She waited, still looking into the darkness, and then, hearing it again, she pointed with her sword. "There…We go." She half started to leave but was stopped by the voice of the man nearest her.

"We go?" he said questioning.

Samiare turned to see the ashen face of the armored man who stood before her. He was tall and held his helm in his hands, his unshaven face lit orange in the light cast from the fires of the ship.

Others came to join him, all with weariness and despair set in their faces. She dropped her sword to her side and stood glaring at them, just as she had before leaping from the ship. Somehow they all disappointed.

"A battle?" questioned another. "We have just had a battle. We don't need another one."

Samiare slid her sword back into its scabbard. She examined each of them and took in their measure. None of their faces gave any indication of support for her action, and that only served to irritate her further. "A battle," she repeated. "Groll against who? We find out. We go."

"It is probably just Groll against Groll," said a third. A dark-haired man with a round head, his manner was dismissive. "We should stay away."

Samiare turned from the men and faced the direction of the battle. Her hand slid back onto her sword, and she breathed deeply. She wanted to kill more. She wanted to kill them all. "You stay," she said. "I go," and then she started out into the dark.

RUEGETTE STOOD UNMOVING as she looked upon the man's face above her. In an instant, her heart raced at seeing him alive, and then in another she turned cold and seethed with anger as she brought to mind her last encounter with the Marish Captain. She remembered too well what he had done to take advantage as they stood together on the bow of his ship. Darimus of Marindor had much to answer for.

"You are starting to make a habit of coming to my rescue," he said with a wide smile on his face. "It is a feat I am becoming rather fond of." He paused to wipe his sword clean on the garments of the Groll he last slew, and then strode down the stairs.

Ruegette lowered her bow and prepared, she knew that the needs of Tierinor came before her own, but she would not be made a fool a second time. She steadied herself and grew calm as she waited for him to descend, but her eyes followed him with a volcanic fire burning within. Darimus came to stand before her, and then, reaching forward, he brushed red locks from her face. "I should thank you," he said.

Ruegette did not reciprocate. Instead she cast her head away and let her hand slide on to the dark haft of her slender blade. "I would thank you for returning my sword," she said with a measured tone.

"Ah, yes," said Darimus. He turned to survey the tower and took in a breath, a pained expression came over his features, but he kept his bearing. He looked over the bodies and came to rest over one near the entry, a young soldier slain by a spear. A frown touched his face, and he looked away, then he spoke as if deciding to push aside who they were. "I suppose I do owe you an apology," he said, "but we have no time for that now." He moved to a pile of leather packs once belonging to his now dead companions and began to rummage through them, secreting small items in his bag as he went. At one, he paid special attention, pulling from it a small bottle. "Dragon cedar," he said before hiding it away, then he recovered a bone scroll tube from it as well. "We need to leave this tower before these Groll are missed."

Ruegette watched him gather the items as he prepared for their journey and fumed at his assumption. It was not her duty to help him gain the Eye, quite the contrary, she meant to keep him from it. She moved to stand before the battered door; her hand resting on the dark hilt of her sword and her demeanor cold. "I wish to know your intentions," she said. "Are you here to stop the Groll, or are you here to claim the Eye of Ebon?"

Darimus paid her little attention at first, but his manner changed when he looked up to see her blocking the way out. He stood and considered her, and then calmly spoke. "Ruegette of Tierinor, do you mean to kill me?"

"I don't want to kill you," she said, "but I will not allow you to have the Eye. I need to know you can be trusted, or I cannot allow you to continue. It is best we settle this."

Darimus looked into her eyes for several long moments before speaking again, and when he did his voice was both boyish and playful. "Is this because of our encounter on the ship?" he mused. "I do apologize that our parting was so abrupt, but I did offer to take you ashore. It was your own fault that you refused."

"It's more than that," said Ruegette. "We are soldiers. You thought of Marindor above Tierinor, and I would expect no different, but this is the Shadow's eye. If it is recovered, the four lands will be broken by an evil whose name we dare not speak. That which keeps the Eye from the hands of the Groll cannot be compromised."

"The Eye is already compromised," said Darimus. "It was the Groll who came to Marindor looking for aid, and it was only because of this that Queen Karkella made the decision to help them. We had no other choice; we needed to learn what they knew before we could act to stop them. It was my mission to keep the Groll from gaining it, and that is what I am still trying to do. It's only if the Eye cannot be kept safe that I am to take it, and then only to bring it before my Queen so that a new fate can be decided for it." Darimus held up the bone tube before her as an offering. "But none of that will matter if the Groll claim it first. I will share with you all I have. Can we at least agree that it'll be easier to keep the Eye from the Groll if we work together?"

Ruegette stepped forward to examine the tube. "What is this?"

"It's a map," said Darimus. "It is ancient enough to have been written by the hand of Ilnydrifel himself, and it shows a land beyond a land, or at least it was thought by the one who carried it until a moment ago. It is marked in old Allarish and bears a location Ilnydrifel must have used when he tried to put together the puzzle. This, he would have used before he was struck by Glysandra's withering arrow. Shargat looks for the Eye in mountains, and his Groll guard the way east. If we try to find a way into the mountains, we will face much peril. I think there is another way, one that was used by Ilnydrifel, but he could not undo the magic that held it. He needed to gather the pieces left behind. If we follow in his footsteps, we may be able to avoid the Groll altogether."

"That is not likely," said Ruegette. "I overheard a Dahmor-ra named Umgot order his band to look for you. He called you by name."

Darimus cast his eyes down and took in a breath. "That complicates things," he said, then his expression changed, and his eyes flashed up to Ruegette's own. "It is good then that I have Tierinor's finest Wardai to help me."

"Why should I?" she said. "I don't trust you."

"Nor should you, but if you wanted a reason let it be because I have met a woman that makes me think in foolish ways, and maybe she feels the same."

Ruegette gave a dry and dismissive laugh, and then she slid the tube into her belt. "You presume too much. You owe me another apology."

"I do?"

"You kissed me."

"Oh," said Darimus. "I'm not sorry for that."

Ruegette took in a deep breath and let it out. She wanted to be bigger than the Marish Captain and let go of the kiss for the good of her nation, but she could not. "If you try it again, I will run you through with my sword." Even as she said it, she thought it to be weak and unnecessary, but still she had to say something.

"Tierinor," Darimus chided. "I was only trying to bring out the woman in you, even if it was for only a moment. Besides you cannot say you didn't like it. Perhaps you are hoping I will do it again?"

"You cannot possibly think…" Ruegette burst out, but the look on Darimus' face told her otherwise. "Oh, by the Seven Gods…"

"We are wasting time," he said. "The Groll will be after us, and we have a long distance to travel. We had best be leaving."

"Why do you think I will go with you?" Ruegette snapped out.

"How else can you assure that I will not claim the Eye before you? Like it or not, we are a pair."

"I could kill you," she offered dryly.

"Come now, Tierinor. We both know you will not do that."

Ruegette considered the smug young Captain and cursed to herself. In spite of her desire that it was otherwise, he was right. She was not going to cut him down for only a stolen kiss, and she was not in a position to refuse his offer to travel together. Once again, it seemed he knew more than she about the quest for the Eye, and she could not afford to dismiss him while that was still true. Quietly, she resigned herself to the necessities of her mission. "Okay," she relented. "I will lead you, if only to keep Marindor from claiming the Eye as her own. Where do we find this other way into the mountains?"

"You have misunderstood," said Darimus. "It's not a way into the mountains we are looking for. We must head north and find a place called the 'Whispering Glade'. It is there that Ilnydrifel began his quest, and there that we can begin anew to piece together the puzzle he tried to solve."

"That cannot be the way," said Ruegette. "North of here is the Unfrozen Marsh. It may be a good place to avoid the Groll, but we will find nothing there."

"I don't know what is there," he said. "I know only that Ilnydrifel would not have left a map if he did not think it a place to find what he was looking for. He came very close to retrieving it, and we would be very blessed if we come half as close as he did."

"Or cursed," said Ruegette under her breath. She looked about the bodies of the Groll and the Marish soldiers as she weighed the choices before her. She did not enjoy being in this position, where Darimus knew more than she, and there was only one way to see to it that his knowledge would benefit them both; whatever they did, it would have to be together. Darimus threw some rations to her feet, and she took them, then she started to gather arrows to refill her quiver. "I will take us to the edge of a stream that flows from the marsh," she said. "From there, we will turn north. I will lead you, but you must mind what I say and keep quiet while we are in the Wastes."

Darimus smiled widely. "Ruegette of Tierinor, I would mind you anywhere."

Ruegette let a thin smirk play on her lips. "I'm going to hold you to that," she said, and then she left the tower.

SAMIARE STOOD AT the top of a wide hill and looked down. A fire burned in the flat below. A camp for the Groll.

Light fluttered against dull colored standards that draped down from long poles. Painted with the wicked symbols of Groll bands, they formed a crescent behind the fire, the thickness of them making for a crude barrier. An ancient war-wagon, with wheels askew, lay rotting near the edge of the light, the beast that carried it, only a pile of bones. Groll gathered in the camp. More than twenty, their forms like hunched shadows against the light. Some lingered near the edges of the radiance, but most were at the center where they held a captive to the ground and pulled his bound arms up from behind as he screamed.

A large Groll with red skin, and rust colored plates over his shoulders and torso stood over them all. He watched with his arms folded; a curved, cleaver-like sword hung from his belt. She heard them speak, they called him Tuz.

There were other captives. Four Morkind males in tattered clothes and thick ropes lay bound near the wagon. They writhed at the feet of two with clubs, and suffered blows whenever it pleased their twisted manner.

Samiare glared. The torture served no purpose. There were no questions, no reason other than its terror; more cruelty only because it brought mirth and fed their monstrous lust. Iron shafts waited in the fire. She knew what they would do. She had felt shafts like those before. The wounds of them still burned upon her, still caused her back to twinge in restful moments. She hated the monsters that they were. She would kill them all.

There was noise behind her. The low rustling of movement through the trees and the clamor of armed men approaching over the ground. The men of the ship came to be with her. They crawled along the slope, coming to where she stood. In the distance, battles still raged to the south and east. There were more in the woods than they had first known, but Ruegette was still to the north. She prayed she would be safe.

"We have come to be with you, Wardai," spoke one from the ground. The lieutenant, Izarou, who had worked the tiller. He lived and spoke for the group. "It is our duty to protect you. We go wherever you go."

"Tuz," she said. "Groll is named Tuz, he speaks it."

"I don't know of Tuz," said Izarou. "The Groll have many tribes. This area of the Wastes should belong to a Feng named Rumsha. He has been strong here for many years. Maybe Tuz is one of his Dahmor-ra, the standards would indicate that."

"And the men?"

"They are of Marindor. It would be useful if we could free them, but it will be difficult. If Tuz is a Dahmor-ra then those with him will be his chosen. There is much risk if we attack. We should avoid these. We cannot help them."

Samiare did not care if the men were rescued or not. They were of Marindor. She knew their sin. "We will kill them all," she said.

Izarou gave an incredulous laugh. "I would kill them all too. How would we do that?"

She did not answer; instead she slid her scabbard forward until the hilt of her sword was within easy reach of her right hand.

"You mean you want to just charge down there with your sword held ready and butcher them." It was a jest that he spoke, but Samiare's silence left little doubt as to her intention. "Please," he pleaded. "If they hear our approach, they will slay their captives, and we will have gained nothing. While I do not doubt your courage, this is something my men are better suited for. If this is something we must do, if this is your will, let *us* do it."

Samiare looked at Izarou as he lay on the ground, and then back to the camp where the Groll went about their mirth seemingly unaware of the wrath she meant to deliver to them. "You lead," she said. "I follow."

The men of Izarou's troop slid through the woods like an uncoiling snake. Izarou gave a clear set of orders; move with stealth, strike with speed, gain control over the prisoners, and prevent retreat. Four of his bravest shed their loose items, took up Groll spears, and moved to gain a position on the wagon as nine others moved onto a hilltop behind the standards. The remaining two encircled the camp and hid in the dark on the far side. It was a simple plan, and it was well-orchestrated. The Groll seemed unaware of the trap being laid for them.

Samiare waited as Izarou stood near and kept his hand over her arm, keeping her from pulling her sword. "It will start shortly," he said. "You and I will make for the center. Do not pull your sword until we are right on them. We can't afford for its light to give us away." He watched, and when he was sure, he mimicked a night bird's call to give the signal. "Slowly," he said. "Let the Groll react before we strike." His hold on her arm released and he began to creep slowly forward.

Samiare walked after him, her hand ready on her sword, but she did not pull it. As she followed, Izarou's plan began to unfold. Those on the hill let out with cries of battle and began a full charge at the camp. Below, the warriors of Tuz scrambled to make sense of it all, many looking up at the approaching assailants with eyes wide, others lifting a sword or an axe and rising to meet the new challenge, but Tuz himself did not appear confused in the least. In an instant, he pulled his thick curved blade and rallied his warriors; issuing commands in his native Durish, he sent his killers out to meet the rush.

In the woods, Groll and Morkind clashed. Tuz, flanked by two of his guard, shouted more commands. Behind him, those that stood over the captives moved in answer. They drew blades and raised them up to slay, but their blades never fell.

The four tasked with securing the prisoners rushed from the darkness and swept over those at the wagon with grim precision. In only a few quick motions, the two guarding the captives fell beneath a thrust of spears to die gasping and writhing from many wounds.

Tuz grew in rage. He screamed out as his two guards turned on the new threat from the rear. Defiant of the four warriors, he thrust his own thick blade down into the one Marish captive at his feet and twisted the blade in spite. The four Tieran soldiers rounded the rotting war-wagon; leaving their spears in the bodies of the slain, they came with swords drawn and ready to engage the red-skinned Dahmor-ra with his two warriors.

Samiare strode behind as Izarou took to a run. She quickened her pace to run as well, but he was too fast and out distanced her. She heard his foot falls land heavy on the wet ground, and saw his blade glint in the light as it waved in his stride. In the woods outside the camp, the clamor of battle continued, and in the camp, the four who swept in to rescue the captives engaged the two who defended their Dahmor-ra.

For an instant, it looked as if there would be a complete victory; one of the Groll fell beneath the swords of Izarou's four, and the other was driven away from Tuz's flank—but the instant passed. The Groll leader met the blade of one who tested him, casting the straight Tieran sword awkwardly low, and then finishing the warrior by driving the point of his curved blade into his gut. A second pressed in with a downward blow, but was easily evaded and then struck into his ribs. A third was engaged by Tuz's last guard and forced to halt, and the last, Tuz finished in a growl, cleaving him across his shoulder and neck.

Samiare rushed to clear the distance, but Izarou was too far ahead. He arrived first and threw himself into the light of the camp with his sword held in both hands. She saw him go straight for the red savage. He drove his sword forward like a spear, but it was cast wide by a sweep of the red Groll's cleaver. He slashed in again with a blow meant for its head, but Tuz met the blade with his own dark saber, and twisted it down, causing the Lieutenant to stumble. Izarou tried to recover; he drove the point of his sword at Tuz's exposed chest, but was struck instead by a well-timed counter. Twisting away from Izarou's lunge, Tuz drove his own curved blade into Izarou's exposed leg, cutting into his thigh and grating against the bone. Izarou gave a cry, and fell as Tuz jerked out his blade.

Samiare screamed and stormed into the radius of the fire. She would not let the red savage finish his work. She drove in with her sword, cutting at him in a wide swath that forced him to take steps back. In her hands, her sword burst with light, a brilliance that swept over the camp and saw the Groll Leader turn his head away; he staggered backwards and held up his hand to shield. Samiare went before him with her sword low and arms wide, her white blade glowing bright as her gaze fixed upon him. "*Whar-Shumura,*" he spat out in Durish trying to focus his eyes. She heard his words, he had called her 'White Witch'. She struck. Cutting him across the throat in one lightning blow, Tuz's head flew from his body, and fell without ceremony onto the damp ground.

Samiare paused to take measure. Izarou rolled in the dirt, pressing his hands against his wound. The last of his four was struck and lay dying from a wound to her left, and the shouts and clang of battle raged from the woods around her, but from behind, the heavy feet of Tuz's last guard scurried near. In her mind she gained his distance and timed his strike. At the instant of his blow, she wheeled on him with her sword sweeping wide. His axe lashed in, grazing her hair, but her own blade cut across, taking his arm from his body, sending it sailing through the air. The Groll staggered forward, and fell to his knees two paces further.

And then she was on him. Pressing her boot into his back, she pushed him until he lay sprawled upon the blood-soaked ground and drove the point of her sword at his side-turned face, forcing its edge into his black skin and pinning him beneath it. She saw a course, a way she might bring the Groll to her. With a cold wrath in her voice, she spoke in her own native Norvish. "You live because I choose to let you," she said. "You will deliver a message for me. You will take the head of this 'Tuz' to your Feng, and then tell your 'Rumsha' that the White Witch is coming for him."

The Groll did not fight or struggle beneath Samiare's glowing blade. Instead he lay motionless and winced as light washed over his black and bestial face. "Rumsha will kill me if do," the Groll snarled back in his own Durish.

"And I will kill you if you don't," she answered still in her own Norvish. "You will be put to death no matter where you are found, now go before I take more of your limbs."

She released her captive and stood back from him. The black Groll drew in breath as if a weight had been removed. Gazing about with eyes wide, he sprang into motion, scampering over the ground to where 'Tuz's head lay, he snatched it up and rushed off into the darkness.

"What are you doing?" screamed Izarou, still near. "Kill him before he gives us away!"

Samiare looked into the fiery eyes of the injured Lieutenant but she did not answer him. A battle was still being fought in the woods about the camp, and she was still un-sated. With her sword still lighting her path to battle, she left Izarou to join his men in the woods.

"MASTER, DID YOU hear?"

The voice rose from behind. The inlaid door of the marble chamber had just closed, and at it stood a young Allarie in a well-fashioned tunic of soft leather, a dagger rested at his belt, and a large ring glinted from his right hand. His hair was deep brown, and his angular eyes were as green as leaves in summer. Within the room, a lone figure crouched over a silver-lined chest upon a low table.

The figure was of another Allarie, much older and dressed in deep blue. His features were not like that of the younger, his face was gaunt and his color near pallid. His hair was thin and streaked with age but still he had a regality to him that could not exist in youth.

"Someone has tried the stone gate," said the younger. "The one they guard that leads into the mountains."

"Yes," said the figure, "but entry was not granted."

"How so?" asked the younger. "The stones were broken and knocked askew from their hinges as if a great force was hurled upon it."

"And the guards who held it were slain with fire," said the figure, "but that is not the true gate. A much greater seal than guarded stone must be broken to find what lies in the mountains."

"Then you've heard?" said the younger. "But you've been locked in here all the night. You forbade me to allow visitors into your sanctum."

"This sanctum no longer suits me," said the figure. "The way is poisoned, and so I must find another. It is unfortunate, and I am left with regret."

The youth came closer to look at the objects strewn on the low table. "You are packing to leave?" he said.

"I must leave Sahlohir," said the figure. "And you must also keep my secret." An orange fire welled in his hand and grew hot as furnaced steel. He turned on the younger, and with his flaming hand, he reached towards him.

IN THE DARKNESS before dawn, Samiare came back to the camp. She could see bodies laying about, both Groll and Morkind, and others moaned out in the night, but she did not care for any of those. The four Marish warriors had been rescued, and for them she held anger. She knew both their wickedness and their dark pursuits. They would be made to answer.

She strode in a frightful sight, still covered in Groll spatter and the red streaks of her own blood down her sleeve. She held her sword before her and pointed it with menace at the four. In her own tongue, she spoke words full of threat and anger. "Hold fast and pray, men of Marindor, for mine is a sword of justice and I know well your sins."

Unarmed and left with only tattered under-tunics, the four from Marindor could not defend themselves before her. Helpless, they looked at her without comprehension and shrank back. Samiare stepped forward as one of the four fell to the ground and gasped out a breathless plea in his own tongue, "What is this? What have I done?"

About the camp, men looked on, their faces questioning and not understanding. She raised her sword high and Izarou screamed at her. "What are you doing?" Fighting the pain of his wounded leg, he lurched forward and threw himself upon her arm, pulling down her sword and knocking her away. "Stop this," he shouted.

Samiare turned on Izarou with a flash of rage. She shoved him aside with her blood-covered hand, and pulled her sword free. Izarou stumbled under the pain of his wound, and fell. He clawed at her legs with his hands, but she held her sword high above his reach, and stepped away. His hold faltered and he fell fully upon the wet ground. He pleaded with her to stop.

Samiare stood back and cast her eyes on him with scorn. She looked about to see only faces flush with bewilderment. She hesitated but did not relent. "These men..." she stammered in accented Tieran as she pointed to the Marish four with her sword. "In Norvaine...with the 'Fal'." She withdrew a few more steps and took in breath to calm herself before speaking again. She struggled with the words. "With the Groll," she said deliberately. "They did seek the Ebon Eye. They did wicked things."

"That cannot be," shouted Izarou. He fought to regain his feet but faltered. One of his men came to his aid, but he refused it. Trying again, he rose with gritted teeth, and spat out, challenging, "These men have never been to Norvaine. What could they have done?"

Within the camp, men grew in apprehension. The four from Marindor protested their innocence, and though their languages were not the same, some of Izarou's troop spoke in agreement. One, an older soldier with thick muscles and a weathered face, spoke above the lot of them. "Wardai," he said. "These men have suffered at the hands of our enemies. We cannot judge them so harshly."

Samiare recognized him as Mirathue, one she barely knew, but as she looked on him, in his rent chain and bloodied tabard, she saw in him the wisdom of her father, and she softened. Lowering her sword, she turned to face Izarou. She was no longer filled with rage, but instead a deliberate coldness carried in her voice. "No," she said. "Not them in Norvaine, but Marindor. Wicked is their Queen."

"You speak of Queen Karkella?" Izarou said, incredulous. "What if she is 'wicked'? What is that to us? We are in a land full of Groll. Our ship is gone, most of our provisions have been lost, and we have already seen too much battle. That any of us might survive in this wretched land is more than we dare hope. I gave my blood to free these men. I will not let you put them to the sword."

Samiare glared at him. She heard as the pleas of the four grew in volume and looked on as some of Izarou's troop acted to calm them. A circle had formed around the four and voices rang out chaotically. Some of Izarou's troop spoke at them in Marish, but the four did not react favorably to it. She had brought this, the men did not understand, and the Groll would soon be coming again. This was not a time for confusion, and she knew only one action that could end it. Putting aside her rage, she yielded before the determined Izarou. Deliberately, she turned back her sword and slid it into its scabbard. "I no wish...kill men," she said. "Marindor is with Groll. Must answer—"

"Marindor is fighting the Groll," Izarou cut her off. "And we are in need of good warriors." Izarou turned from her and limped his way over to stand before the four as his men parted to make way for him. He held his hand high as a gesture of peace and spoke to them in their own tongue. "I am Izarou of Tierinor," he said. "We fight against the Groll. You men are free to take up weapons with us or make your own way in these woods."

The four sons of Marindor were a disheveled lot. All of them wore dark tunics that hung in tatters about their stocky frames. Their features were dark and rounded like all of Marindor, but their faces were marred by Groll brutality. One of the four spoke before the others. "What of the girl?" he demanded. "She agrees to this?"

Samiare watched as Izarou turned his head to study her. She did not want to be a part of it. She turned from them and walked out into the woods away from the fire. Pulling her sword, she knelt down in prayer. "Yes," she heard Izarou speak behind her. "All of my troop will welcome your swords."

One of the Marish stood, and took heavy steps towards her. When he spoke, it was as a jeer, and loud enough to be sure she heard. "I have no fear of a woman's sword," he called. "This land is no place for her. She will need saving before this is done, and perhaps then she will come to appreciate the courage of Marindor. I am Krellus. We serve in the army of Carand Kellenus of Marindor. We will go with you until such time as we can rejoin our ranks."

Samiare felt the weight of all their eyes looking on her, but she made no motion. She held her sword with its point to the ground and leaned her head against it. Behind, there was only silence until Izarou gave the command. The men would be joining their troop.

Long moments passed as she prayed and listened. She wanted to find Ruegette, to be with her, to kill more Groll, and to know what she must do, but she found no answers. Instead, the music soothed and worked its way to heal her. She wished to know what was wanted, but as always, it was only to trust. Whatever had brought it to her hand, whatever it was that she prayed to, it wanted something from her—and she did not understand. But she would trust. It was the only thing she could do. She heard the approach of Izarou. He limped towards her and groaned in his exertion.

"I would speak with you, Wardai," he said quietly. "Our time is short, and the men are questioning our purpose here."

She said silent words and let her head sway as she prayed. She did not know what was wanted, but she knew what she must do. To her, the answer was plain. "The Ebon Eye our duty is," she spoke aloud.

Izarou hobbled a few more steps and then half fell onto the ground beside her. "I believe all that I have heard," he said, his eyes looking on her with earnestness. "You are 'Shal Comair', but the rest of us are just men. We cannot survive another battle. Allarish blades are very rare, but even that will not see you through every battle."

"No," she said. "Is not Allarish. Allarie are fallen. They cannot wield sword I have."

"Listen to me," said Izarou. "I need to trust you. I need to know you will not lead my men into battles they cannot win, and I need to understand why we fought a battle to free men you would put to death. What is it that Marindor has done that we should be so wary of them? And why didn't you kill that Groll dog as he fled from the camp? You are risking us, and I see no purpose in it."

Samiare looked fully at Izarou. She could not comprehend his lack of understanding. "The Ebon Eye," she said, becoming indignant. "Ruegette seeks it...far from here." She stood and pointed to the north with her sword, the same direction taken by the one fleeing Groll. "We bring Groll here. We fight...They no find Ruegette."

"We cannot help Ruegette if we die," said Izarou. "We cannot fight the Groll. We need an army. We need the Marish. We need those—."

"Marindor in Norvaine with Groll," she cut him off. Her agitation grew. She pointed to the four as her sword drifted back. "They do evil deeds. Kill my..." She tried to finish the words but choked on them. Fighting for composure she started again. "Take us...in...snow they did..." She could not finish. Tears welling in her eyes and anger rising, she pointed her sword at the four and ranted. "They stood with 'Fal' and aided."

Izarou's face displayed his sympathy, but it was too much to ask. "Please," he pleaded. "You know these men have done nothing. I do not know what befell in Norvaine, but you must come to your senses. If Marindor is guilty of some sin let these men atone with their deeds and not with their lives. We need to look away from the things of the past and confront the evil before us. We need Marindor to succeed against the Groll. If you truly want to draw the Groll away from Ruegette, you will need their army to do it. I cannot leave my command to you if you cannot see what we must do."

Samiare stopped and fell still. "What mean you?" she said, her voice quiet and concerned. She looked down at his wounded leg and remembered the prayers at the boat over those who could not continue. She was filled with dread at what he might say.

"It is our way," said Izarou. "It is the final duty we give to Tierinor. Four of us have been gravely injured. If we tried to continue, our injuries would slow the troop and our blood would leave a trail that could be followed. You are Wardai, and I must give up my command. I must obey the code we all follow."

She would not listen further. She took up her sword and strode into the light of the fire. Holding her blade high, she stood before the men. "I am Wardai," she asserted. "You listen. We no kill men with wounds. No code do we follow here."

Izarou stood behind her and struggled to join her in the light. "Mirathue," he called. "You know the code. I place you in command. You know what you must do."

Mirathue stood near the edge of the light, hidden among a group of Tieran warriors with his grizzled face cast in befuddlement. Izarou stumbled forward and addressed him again. "Mirathue," he called. "The code is clear. I demand you see to it."

Mirathue looked into the fiery eyes of Samiare with her sword held high, and then the hobbling form of Izarou. "Lieutenant," he spoke gingerly. "I dare not disobey a Wardai."

Samiare lowered her sword and Izarou stopped in his efforts to advance. In the camp the men of the troop fell in behind Mirathue, and then the decision was sealed by one who bore the scars and wear of many battles on a toothless face. "We fight as brothers, we die as brothers." Samiare knew him as Janthro, and he too fell in behind Mirathue.

Mirathue looked both left and right, and then to Izarou. "It seems the men do not wish a change in command," he said. "Where do we march, Lieutenant?"

Izarou rose up straight and turned to face Samiare. "Wardai?" he said passing the decision on to her, and her station.

Samiare cast her eyes at him and accepted. "South," she said. "We must leave this place."

SAMIARE WALKED AT a brisk pace, but with her mail, and small stature, she could not keep the pace. She drifted back towards the rear of the line, and breathed heavily. Izarou struggled near her, his injured leg slowed him greatly, and she worried that he might fall out or give into his injury. The way was over low hills and steep rises. There was no easy path through, and already the pounding of war drums thrummed in the distance. Another battle loomed. It would be coming sooner than she wanted.

The labor of Izarou was palpable. His desperation carried in his heavy breaths and pain bearing grunts. She heard him with every step he took. In the distance, the drums grew louder, and she heard him cry out. "They're coming! Mirathue, do you hear? ...They are coming!" There was no response from ahead, and the distance to those in front was widening. She did not like it, but she held her sword. She kept her faith.

"Mirathue," she heard Izarou call again.

She drew in closer to him. "Calm yourself," she said. "They are near. Listen...be ready." Izarou paused and looked about, but she did not do the same, she kept her gaze on the path and went ahead. The noises grew louder. The sound of drums was not the only rhythm to be heard; the heavy tromp of boots came from places nearby.

"We are doomed," said Izarou.

Samiare halted and for an instant she looked down at her feet. "Stay with me," she said softly, and then she resumed walking.

Ahead, one of the men stopped; Janthro of the ship's crew. Holding an axe in one hand and a sword in the other, he held out his arms and drew in breath. "I grow tired of this," he said, calling out so all could hear him. "Why do we not turn and fight them? Why do we give them our backs? I wish to die in battle as a warrior of Tierinor, not as prey struck down in flight." He stood with his arms outstretched until both she and Izarou moved past.

"What of you?" Janthro called to her. "The one we call 'Shal Comair'. Is there enough enchantment in your Allarish blade to see us through one more battle?"

Samiare did not answer him, but Izarou stopped and stood straighter. "Mirathue," he called to the front of the troop. "Look for high ground. Find us a place to fight."

"Yes," agreed Janthro. "Let us look for high ground, and let us there settle our differences."

Samiare waited as men took up positions along the line. It was a small hill that Mirathue had chosen. Steep rises along two sides, and a shallower swath where Groll could more easily ascend to the east.

She knelt behind them; she prayed. Water gently flowed in a creek below.

Across the way, the Groll came. Cresting the top of a wide hill, they formed into a long line and looked down. Their number was great, and growing still. War drums beat in a rhythmic rumble and grew louder, thrumming out until the drummers themselves became visible, and stood behind the line.

Izarou took to the steep rise of the wide berm with a spear in his hands. He would mark the center and guard against the Groll assault. Mirathue would lead men to hold the steeper flank to the west, and Janthro would defend the shallower slope of the east. Samiare did not need to be told. She knew where she would be.

Drums beat and Groll pounded on their shields. Before them, a green monster with a thick jaw and gold rings glinting from his ears, stood before his horde. He held an axe of gorum-steel high and thrust it forth. He shouted out to give the command, and before him, his band began their march, menacing down the hill.

Arrows were let loose. Izarou screamed the orders, and a small few with bows lashed out to thin their number. Some struck, others deflected, but few fell. The Groll broke into a run. Men at the berm made ready. Samiare stood and moved behind both Janthro and Krellus of the Marish. She held her sword up and pressed her head against it. One final prayer. The Groll numbers were great, greater than she had seen before—maybe too great.

Heavy feet splashed in the shallow water, and cries of fury and rage rose up. Men lunged down with spears and poleaxes as Groll warriors crashed upon the rise. Screams followed and then the clash of battle. Groll warriors spread along the flanks.

Janthro ran along the crest; his axe crushing in, his sword defending. Krellus of Marindor followed, trying to guard his flank with a heavy Groll cleaver, but the number of the enemy grew too quickly, and Groll ascended rapidly up the slope. Samiare moved with them as well, she saw the gap grow wide. Krellus clashed with one, and another slipped behind him. It raised its axe to strike, and she stepped in. Her sword drawn back, its music guiding, its blade gleaming white; she brought it tearing across, slashing through the axe wielder's body, and leaving him in pieces in the mud.

Another rushed up the slope. Krellus stumbled back in his haste to ward and slipped onto his back on the wet ground; she moved past him, and cleaved in. Her sword cut through, its blade becoming bright, the Groll fell. She went forward still. She cut through another, and as he faded, white flames openly licked from the blade. More Groll came. She could see them all. Their movements and their guards. They were many, but they were crude in their motions, and trusted in their ferocity and their strength. With speed and faith, she could best them. She cut past another, lashing in beneath his descending blow, splitting him to his spine. And then another as he lunged in from below and she cleaved into him with a wide crushing arc. A Tieran warrior fell near her, and the hole became wider; another came. She tore through him as well. She saw Janthro move along the crest with Groll on all sides. She would not let him fall. Krellus stood next to her again, and she moved along the line with him guarding her flank. She cut down more as they ascended, and pushed into those who had already swarmed the top. Janthro was ahead, and Krellus behind, and Groll were all around. The White Sword gushed with fire, and she wielded it to exhaustion, slicing through bodies and limbs, driving into her foes until they littered the ground like dark shapes spilled onto each other, and the three of them held the top. But still they fought on.

The cries of war raged around her, men died and Groll fell, the drums of war becoming only a distant thrum, Izarou's voice only a distant call, Janthro screaming near...She could not listen. She held the sword, burning white and filling her with its song, she drove at the lumbering shapes before her. But in the distance a new sound rang out—the low and throaty groan of a war horn, its closeness wringing confusion in the swarming Groll. Even from those before her, she could see it. They looked east, and showed fear. She did not care. Her sword flashed with an unquenchable fire, consuming all who drew close, and she wanted to kill them all. To show them forever that she could.

Mirathue's voice called out above the din. "It's Marindor," he hailed. "It's Marindor come to fight."

She barely listened; she went in further. Her sword burning hot with fire, Groll warriors drew back. She cut through another, slicing through his axe held up to ward and cutting him deep into his body. She pressed down towards the creek bed, and Groll warriors, once full of hate and rage, bore only fear at her approach. The horn sounded again, closer still, and their trepidation grew. They backed away, some turning to run.

Across the way, Marish warriors appeared on the wide hill; running hard and with weapons drawn, their numbers were enough to overwhelm, and at the sight of them, the Groll openly broke into flight. Only a few who had engaged too deeply fought on, and their lives were quickly cut from them. Finally, even the green Groll who led them turned to flee.

Samiare cut through a last and stood defiant; screaming at them in challenge, but more would not come; her sword dropping low, her chest rising from her exertion, they openly ran before her. Holding the sword out to her side, she held her arms wide, and watched them flee until, exhausted, she fell back onto the cold ground and yielded. Her body trembled, and her arms shook, but inside…inside she felt something new, she felt sated. Something she did not think she could.

The soldiers from Marindor swarmed through the trees and rushed over their small hill. They were many, numbering more than thirty, and all bore the wild look of men who had spent too much time in the Wastes. Some paused to deliver blows upon the bodies of fallen Groll, assuring they would never rise again, as others moved past and reformed a line along the crest of the western slope. A small number took up a position below where Samiare lay, poking at the dead, and coming to stop near her. One pointed, and called her out to his commander.

Samiare took in more breaths and then rose. Looking on the hill, she could see those that still remained. Of the forty that came with her on the boat, only nine still lived, and of the Marish they had rescued, another had fallen in the battle. She saw the Marish commander look on her. He was a lean man with gaunt features and a beard of thick dark hair jutting from beneath his helm. Izarou too had survived. He limped to greet them with his hand held high and a wide smile on his face, behind him, those that remained shouted in jubilance.

The Marish commander came to stand before them all and considered. When he spoke it was to Izarou, and in his own Marish tongue. "I am Sararth, a Placent in the service of Carand, Kellenus, who leads the effort of Marindor in these lands. I am pleased to see Tierinor has taken an interest in our struggle."

Samiare watched and listened. She did not speak his language, but as she held her sword and heard its soothing tones, she could understand his speech.

"Likewise are we," replied Izarou in the same tongue. "The woods are full of Groll, and we have had our share of battle. I am Izarou, a Lieutenant in the army of Tierinor. I lead these men through the Wastes."

The Marish Placent looked on the troop and gestured with his hand to indicate where she and others stood. "I see three in your group are of Marish blood, and that you have given a sword to a girl child. How did that come to be?"

Izarou looked towards her, and then at the three. "These belong to you," he said, gesturing that they should cross back into the Marish ranks. "We rescued them from the Groll but a few hours ago. They offered to aid us until we could deliver them back to Marish hands. The girl is more than she seems. She is a Wardai. It was she who led us to free your men."

"A Wardai?" spoke Sararth, his eyes looking on her with disbelief. "She is not even Tieran?"

Izarou nodded his head. "She is the second to Ruegette of the Eastern Citadel, and she has been called 'Shal Comair' from all that have seen her in battle. A title that I think is well-deserved."

Sararth's shook his head, an incredulous look still on his face. "How can this be true?" he said.

"It is true," said one from behind, Krellus of the rescued. He came forward and pointed to the eastern ridge where the bodies of Groll lay in heaped clusters upon it. "That is where she stood. She alone slew them all. The same she did to the Groll who held us captive, and it was she who slew Tuz the Red-Hand, cutting his head from his body in one pass. She possesses an Allarish blade and wields it with a terrible swiftness. When first she approached us, I thought she meant to kill us all, but here she fought bravely, and defended my life."

Sararth followed the line of Groll with his eyes, and then cast his look back at Samiare. "You are the Second to Ruegette de Tagore?"

"I am," said Samiare, stepping forward, her words in Tieran.

"Then I would be honored to meet this renowned Lady and Wardai of Tierinor." He did not share her language, but still she understood. "I would propose an arrangement where both our forces can work together against this common foe."

"I fear that is not possible," said Izarou, again in Marish. "We separated with the Lady in the north, and our way through the forest has not been gentle. There are no more Tieran forces loose in the Wastes."

Sararth moaned his disappointment and lowered his head. "I see," he spoke. "The Wastes are about the death of armies, and so it is with both our forces. When we came south, I stood with three thousand brave souls, but two weeks of battles have played on our number. Defeat has seen our force scattered and our supplies dwindle. We have been separated from the Carand, and I have been about the woods for several days looking for disparate units to regroup. Our lack of supplies has us pushing for the river where seven Marish ships should lie along the banks to the south. You are welcome to join our ranks if you like. We will pursue the Groll who fled this battle and kill them by nightfall, then we will head for the river, and seek a place to cross. Hopefully there will be safety on the Tieran side of the Aills."

Samiare heard, but could not believe his words; to leave the Wastes while Ruegette still fought, and the fate of the Eye was still uncertain... "No," she said, still in Tieran. She came fully to the front to stand next to Izarou, but she did not look on him, instead her eyes were fixed on the hardened face of the Marish Placent. "We take men of his and fight Groll near mountains."

Izarou looked at her without comprehending, and at this, she grew annoyed. "Tell him!" she snapped out.

Izarou seemed shaken by the forcefulness of her command and flustered. His eyes looked disapprovingly at her, but, as was his duty, he turned to the Placent and spoke on her behalf. "The Wardai humbly asks that we take your army east."

"East?" moaned Sararth. "We cannot go back east. There are not enough of us to pass again through these woods. We must go west."

"No," said Samiare again, insisting. "The Ebon Eye his duty is. Ebon Eye is not where river is…Groll no matter to river. We take army to mountains…east. We find Carand of his. We seek the Eye."

"Wardai," spoke Izarou, cautioning. "It is not for us to issue orders to an army of Marindor."

Samiare cast a glaring look at Izarou that spoke without words what she thought of his concern over protocol. "I am Wardai," she asserted. "Tell him."

Izarou's face bore his distaste for speaking the words, but he addressed the Placent. "The Wardai insists we must head east and seek the Carand," he said. "She reminds the Placent that his duty is to the Eye of Ebon, and we must not give up the struggle. I remind the Placent that the request of a Wardai bears the weight of Koning Huedrus of Tierinor. It is a proper request that may sew favor between our two lands."

"I know well the position of your Wardai," spat Sararth. He drew his hand to his beard and turned his back to Izarou. He took a breath, and then, abruptly, he looked to Krellus. "You," he barked out. "You, who have suffered at Groll hands and then spoke for this girl. Would you follow her into the heart of Groll lands?"

Krellus looked at Samiare and placed his hands upon his hips, then he spoke in a morose tone. "Death will follow her," he said. "I fear to be with her." Then he turned his head away and looked directly at the Placent. "But I cannot question her valorous heart. If I had to fight with Groll again, I would want her sword cutting us a path to victory. Aye, Placent, I would follow her."

Sararth cursed aloud and looked away. He cast a glance at his men, and then up to the silver firmament above. "So be it," he relented. "Tell the Wardai we must gain supplies before we can return east. We must still press for the river."

"Wardai," said Izarou. "The Placent says…"

"I hear him," Samiare cut off. "Only few go to river. South along river is Yeshale village. You take others with wounds and find supplies. I go with Marindor…east!"

"You want me to lead the wounded to Yeshale?" asked Izarou.

"But my mission…" Izarou stopped. He looked on her, wincing as he shifted his wounded leg, and then nodded his understanding. He lowered his head and spoke. "I will lead the way to Yeshale," he said. "Is there anything else you wish?"

"Yes. Tell Placent we go east."

RUEGETTE KEPT HER bow ready as she led a trail towards the mountains. Darimus followed closely behind, and to Ruegette's surprise, he made very little noise in the woods. He was packed heavy; laden with too much armor, supplies and rations, but other than that, Ruegette could only assume he had spent time in the Wastes before. They had moved well beyond sight of the ruined tower and came to a low valley where a small stream cut through the freshly thawed land. It was only here, where the noise of running water would mask his voice, that Darimus spoke.

"There was more in the caves at Norvaine than just the Shard," he said. He did not look at Ruegette, but rather stared into the distance and spoke as if he were reciting a verse he had given voice to many times. "Ilnydrifel left behind much that he knew about the Eye; much that if it were known to Shargat, our quest would have already been futile. The caves were marked in many places, but the markings were in the language of the old race and Shargat could not read them. Of the Groll that went with us into Norvaine, only his Dahmor-ra, Guryot, could read Allarish, but I slew him with my first stroke when the Groll turned on us. I knew that our cooperation would not last, and so I did not write what I had learned for fear it would be taken from me, but that did not keep written documents from Groll hands. As we searched the caves, one of those who served in my command found a chamber full of parchments and vellum scrolls, and in revealing his find, he brought me that map."

Ruegette loosened her arrow in its string and lowered her bow. She listened to Darimus intently. She no longer felt weary or fatigued. He knew more than she did and this was a tale she knew she must hear. "But how?" she questioned. "I saw them capture you and rummage the camp. You didn't have it when I found you, and you didn't leave my sight after I rescued you."

Darimus smiled wide and chuckled. "If Shargat had cared to

remove my tunic, he would certainly have found the map, as would have you, but as I recall you turned down my advances. I rolled the vellum in linen and lashed it across my back, where it stayed until we boarded my ship and left for your home of Tierinor."

Ruegette darted a chilling glance at Darimus. "Yes," she said. "And it was very kind of you to give me safe passage to my home, even if that was not my choice."

"Of course," said Darimus. "Such was not your choice. Really it wasn't what I preferred either, but I couldn't simply bring an agent of Tierinor before my Queen, especially one with your...ah...reputation, but I was honorable, I left you unharmed and with all your belongings in the safety of your home."

Ruegette caught the way he drew out his words and felt them creep into her. "What do you mean, my '*reputation*'?" she shot.

"Well," said Darimus. "Only that you are well-known for your devotion to Tierinor. More than that, I dare not venture in your presence. I've heard the rumors of your swordplay."

Ruegette glared at him and hardened her expression. "You think you are sly," she said, "but I have known men like you before."

"Ruegette," said Darimus. "I have never had anything but honorable intentions towards you." He held his hands away from his sides until she cast her angry expression aside, and then he could not resist prodding her once more. "And, no, you have never met a man like me before."

Ruegette turned on him with her anger rising. "You presume too much," she lashed out. "And we have no time for this childishness. Finish your tale or I will leave you here."

"The map," said Darimus seemingly unmoved by Ruegette's posturing. "It is not like any I have seen."

"What do you mean?" She put down her bow and pulled the scroll tube from her belt, unrolling it in the open air.

"As you can see," said Darimus. "It's not a map with traditional landmarks. The region it shows is clearly where we stand. You can see where he has included the Aillsdale and the Silver Mountains along the east, but the rest?"

Ruegette studied the map. Like the one she had copied in Esilecolm, it was cleanly drawn and the inks seemed as fresh as the day they were scribed, but the vellum was thin, almost transparent. A long uneven line drawn in blue ink was used to mark the river, but the rest was in black. Near the edges were the jagged shapes of mountains, clearly making this a map of the region where they stood, but it was the land that was oddly indicated. It seemed as if Ilnydrifel was trying to account for every river and stream that flowed from the mountains; marking their paths as they curved and winded, thickened and thinned, crossed and overlapped. To have accounted for this number of them he must have spent years charting their courses, but they were not all correct, they were far too numerous, and Ruegette could attest that many of them did not flow in the Wastes; further, the lines were in black, and not the blue he had used for the water of the Aillsdale.

There was more. In many places, the map was marked with the spidery script of Ilnydrifel's own hand; scrawlings of old Allarish that Ruegette could only read with difficulty; and the one of most interest was in a region between the river and the mountains bearing the Allarish words, '*Chol Junat*.' Words Ruegette roughly translated as '*Our Sanctuary*'.

"Our Sanctuary," she repeated.

"Our Sanctum," corrected Darimus. "An odd thing to write to be sure, but the difference is important. Ilnydrifel marked that place above all others and called it his 'Sanctum.' The map is not drawn with any clear landmarks other than the river, and the river is not accurate. With no scale, we misjudged the location and landed too far to the south. It wasn't I who found the error, but I'm all who lives that can make use of it. This 'Sanctum' is to the north. We must find it."

"But it says, 'Our'," Ruegette pointed out. "Who are the others?"

"I don't know," said Darimus. "When I learned of a room that held Ilnydrifel's writings, I swore its finder to secrecy, and ordered that he should return in stealth to destroy the entire body of Ilnydrifel's writings. This he did, or at least I was told as much by Guryot. It was that which led to his turning against us, and to Shargat betraying my men while we argued. The Groll were cleverer than I thought, and we were not ready. But it was not all bad; I was rescued by a very pretty woman, and she turned out to be Tierinor's finest Wardai."

Ruegette raised an eyebrow and shot Darimus a fiery glance tempered beneath her own cool demeanor. "Don't you ever stop?"

"No," said Darimus.

"Perhaps you should," said Ruegette in a measured tone. She took down the map and began to roll it back up. "The land has changed," she said. "It may be that the river used to flow this way, or that the unfrozen marsh did not exist when Ilnydrifel made this map. This place you are looking for may not be there to find anymore."

"I think that's unlikely," said Darimus. "Look at the ink. This map was made to last forever. I do not think Ilnydrifel would have taken less care with other things that pertained to the Eye of Ebon. There is something in the marsh waiting for us; all we have to do is find it."

"What else?" said Ruegette. "What else was written in the caves? How can you know that while we seek this, 'Sanctum,' Shargat will not simply find the Eye of Ebon and return with it to Gorginor? We can ill afford a misadventure in this. How can you be sure this is our way?"

"I cannot be certain," said Darimus. "But I can assure, we will not overcome his forces if we continue to push straight at him, and I think we can safely assume the way to the Eye, even with a map, will be fraught with peril. Shargat is not prepared for that. He will go recklessly forward and ignore the dangers ahead, but still, he may succeed, and we cannot count on the Groll to fail. The only way we can assure the Eye of Ebon is not returned to Gorginor is to claim it first, and we will fare better following Ilnydrifel than Shargat."

"Okay," said Ruegette, disliking her choice but finally committing herself. "I will go with you and find this 'Sanctum'."

"I knew you could not resist me," said Darimus. "You look tired. I think you should find a place to rest while I keep watch. We have time, just not a lot of it."

"I don't think so," said Ruegette dryly. "I don't trust you. I fear I shall wake and not like the liberties you have taken. Then I would have to cut out your heart."

"You wound me, Tierinor," chided Darimus. "I would never take advantage."

Darimus started north along the water, but Ruegette did not

move to follow. Instead, she looked to the east and hoped her decision would not be the wrong one. She let out a sigh, and then slid an arrow back into the string of her bow. As an afterthought, she looked to the south and wondered about the girl she had rescued in Norvaine, and in that, at least, she took comfort. Come what may in the Wastes, Samiare would be safe in Yeshale.

MISTS ROSE IN the valleys between the hills. In the darkness of the early morning, the flicking light of twenty small fires marked the camps of a Groll army. Their enemy scattered and their camps far from any battle, they sought mirth in the ways that suited their violent manner. The cries of Morkind echoed in the dark, those of the few who had fallen captive, and with their screams, the wicked laughter of their tormentors hovered in the cold morning air. Another sound thundered in the darkness as well, it was the beat of drums that marked the approach of a new band. Umgot the Foul-Tongue entered from the west, and he spared no time as he pushed his way to the center, looking for the One Hill, the one that held the throne.

The 'One Hill' rose upon a wide expanse long devoid of trees. Banners in crude colors and standards on torn leather streaked with blood were adorned with the severed heads of men, and beneath them, on a throne made of Morkind hide, sat the Feng. Rumsha the Bone Reader was not like other Groll. His stature was well below that of his warriors and silver hair matted against the low pate of his oblong skull, framed only by long pointed ears that jutted from behind his temples. His squat form and mottled green color made him almost toad like, but the angle of his features showed the Allarish lineage one such as he must have oozed from. He was aged and respected, a station few Groll ever achieved, and he carried a cunning savagery behind his deep black eyes. He wore a tattered robe and skulls hung from a cord that sealed a pouch at his belt, not the skulls of Morkind, but those of other Groll who did not win his favor. He did not carry a weapon of any sort, only a large staff adorned with a Morkind skull to lean on. Near him always were his chosen, Groll who had proven themselves and won his favor. If a challenge was in order, he had the muscle to sort the weak from the strong. The old Feng lifted his thin, wide lips into a snarl as Umgot approached, revealing his blackened and pointed teeth.

Umgot made his way into an audience with the Feng as his band filled the ranks behind him. Umgot was a tall and proud warrior of his race. He wore hard leather plates over iron links with thick muscles swelling beneath them. His helm was of a grey metal, and he wore a wide leather patch over one eye, the only seeming flaw on his well-formed and black-skinned body. In his hand was a heavy, single-bladed axe, the edge of it gleaming white against the dark gorum-steel of its head.

"Why come you here, Foul-Tongue?" sneered Rumsha through a voice that no longer bore vocal inflection, only a guttural grunt that rose from deep in his throat. His language was Durish. "I have called no Dahmor-ra to answer."

Umgot removed his helm revealing thick tufts of black hair that jutted out from a scalp marred with scars. He strode forward and fell to one knee before the Feng. "Forgive me, Great One," he spoke, "but I must speak about our enemy."

"Speak then, fool," ordered the Feng. "My patience is thin." The old Groll shifted forward in his chair and leaned against his staff, holding it against him with both hands.

"I fear, Great One, that our enemy to the south is no longer of concern. I have extracted information from prisoners. A small band has moved past us to the north. They seek to avoid us in their quest to lay claim to what is hidden."

Rumsha's eyes narrowed, and his wide lips drooped into frown. "Why have you brought this to me," he demanded. "Do you not think the rattling bones would tell me if we were in jeopardy? You should have dealt with this, now I fear I have two problems, eh?"

"Half my band pursues them," snarled Umgot. "And I come to you with this news. I learned his name. He is called Dar-mis, and he is the one they have placed their hope in. He will head towards the mountains, and there he will meet those loyal to this, Shargat. I fear we are wasted here, Great One."

"Ah yes," hissed Rumsha sinking back into his throne of flesh. "Shargat!" He spat the name as if it were bile in his gut. "Yet another from Gorginor who thinks he can rule in the Wastes, but the Wastes are what I have made them."

"He is a fool, my Feng," spoke Umgot. "He thinks he can call forth the Shadow. He wastes us, and is honored by those weakling, Allarie-fallen Magi who dare not venture from the Shadow's land. We should not serve him."

"You think as I do," smiled the Feng. "I will consult the bones." Rumsha sprang into motion; reaching into the pouch at his side, he pulled forth a fist full of darkened bones, and in a motion that was more an extension of his will than an effort, he cast them onto the ground. As they landed, he flew from his throne and fell upon them. On his hands and knees, he studied them, examining their every turn and tangle with one eye wide and the other unmoving. "The bones do not lie," he cooed as he cast his eye first to one and then to another. "The Shadow," he spoke. "The Shadow has been hidden." He darted about on the ground looking deeper. "I see a champion of light and darkness, and a wicked hand holding a key." The Feng ran his hand over some of the scattered pieces. "Here," he said. "There is a danger, but it is not east, it is north in the unfrozen marsh." Rumsha stood and thrust his hand at Umgot pushing him back with an unseen touch and sending him stumbling to the ground. "I feel the Shadow," he spoke. "This land is fresh with his presence. Shargat is close, but I see him as blind."

Umgot rose to his feet with a growl, which drew a malicious and darting glance from the Feng. "You have done well to bring this to my attention," spoke the Feng. "Shargat is a fool who will soon pay the price. The Shadow is near, and his enemy is to the north. We must come to his aid."

Rumsha stood taller and swept up his staff for support. Umgot bowed low as his axe dangled in his hand. "I will do as you command, my Feng," he spoke. "I, too, serve the Shadow." Rumsha stepped forward and put his hand on Umgot's uncovered head, bestowing his blessing, but something else drew his attention away, a new disturbance within the camp.

In the throngs of the Groll horde, a stirring in the ranks rose above the clamor, and a wave of motion moved rapidly towards the hill of the throne, drawing in an ever-increasing crowd of onlookers and participants. The cause of this commotion was unclear, but as it moved closer Rumsha turned to face it with his staff held wide to his side. With his hand, he bid Umgot to stand and serve as one of his chosen while events unfolded.

Screams reached them and then a hunched figure, beaten and tormented by those around him, came into view. He seemed like a miserable wretch, and he was being pushed through the lines at the point of a broad spear held by a large, black Groll. The black Groll gave him no rest. He kicked at the wretch when he fell and jabbed him with his spear when he strayed from moving forward. It lasted in this manner for several moments, but soon the captive was thrust before Rumsha to cringe at his feet. The maligned creature wept openly and squirmed with pain, but it was not one of the Morkind that had been delivered, it was another Groll who lay beneath Rumsha's gaze, and with him, the severed head of yet another Groll was tossed onto the ground.

The captive Groll had only one arm, and it was lashed to his side. As the wretch lay upon the cold dirt the black Groll who brought him called out through a face twisted with disgust. "We found this one near the road to the south," he jeered. "He was fleeing through the woods, and carried with him that, the head of Tuz the Red-Hand."

Rumsha's eyes burned. With his staff, he smashed the side of the fallen one and barked out. "What is the meaning of this, eh?"

The Groll squirmed to his knees. "Forgive me, my Feng," spoke the captive. "I had no choice. She told me to deliver Tuz's head to you."

Rumsha snarled with rage and cracked his staff against the hide of the Groll beneath him. "Why did you listen to any but your Feng?" he demanded. "Who told you to bring this to me?"

"The 'Whar-Shumura'," the Groll sniveled. "The 'Whar-Shumura' told me to do it. She said I should deliver a message."

At the mention of that name there was a noticeable gasp from all present. Rumsha himself recoiled and turned pale, his eyes grew wide with concern. The silence was telling, but Rumsha could not be fazed long. "Dare you speak that name to me?" he hissed.

"I sought to flee," wept the Groll upon the ground. "So you would never hear it, but they discovered me. I know what was revealed."

Rumsha regained his composure and fell into a chilling calmness. "What was revealed?" he demanded. "Do you think I wait here to die?" He waited, but the Groll beneath him gave no answer. "Fool," he spat. "I have lived in these Wastes for three hundred years, for that was the revelation: that I would not die until it was at the hands of the Whar-Shumura. Do you think you have seen this, '*Whar-Shumura*'?"

"My Feng," spoke the Groll. "I saw her cut the head from Tuz the Red-Hand in one stroke. Then I saw her slay our best warriors with a white flame dancing from her hand. I moved against her, and she struck off my arm as if it were nothing. If she is not the 'Whar-Shumura' than I do not know what else could have been revealed. You must fear, my Feng. She said she would come for you."

A murmur spread through the ranks of Groll, but Rumsha did not indulge it. His anger was swift and severe. He pulled up his staff and clutched it with one whitening hand. "I will not fear!" he shouted. "I will not fear! I am Rumsha the Bone Reader."

Rumsha turned to those who stood around him. "Take this fool from my sight. I wish to hear his screams. Cut from him his other arm and throw him into the meat worm pit where his screams may please me for days without end. I will not fear! If there is a girl in my Wastes who dares call herself by that name, then she will pay the price for drawing my wrath. Bring in my Dahmor-ra. We will gather into one and crush her."

Rumsha shambled back to sit upon his throne as Umgot came before him, falling upon his knee. "My Feng," spoke the one-eyed Groll. "We will go with you to crush this 'Whar-Shumura'."

"No," said Rumsha with a sinister coldness. "We must not forget the Shadow. Go to any camp you wish and take command of those within it. If anyone questions you, cut off his head and bring it to me so that his skull may dangle upon my cord. You seek out this danger to the North, and I will destroy the Whar-Shumura."

PART 3
RULER OF THE
WASTES

IN THE DIMNESS of the torch lit chamber a Prince of the Allarie stood as a witness before the closing of the final gate. The room held a great seal, one that was carved into a circular disk set beneath a stone arch that marked the boundaries of a prison deep in the rock. A wide platform protruded beneath the arch, and the curved spiral of two separate stairways, one to each side, connected the platform to the floor below. Allarish symbols marked the stones of the arch and were carved into the seal itself. The seal was open and only a dark void waited beyond.

The Prince stood in silver scales with an ornate breast plate. Black hair framed his angular face and thin braids dangled before his slender ears. With piercing green eyes, he watched all that happened, missing no detail. At his hip he wore a broad-bladed sword with a gold hilt, the haft wrapped in white leather. He was Raefendal, and it was his sword that took the Eye.

The Prince did not stand alone. With him were champions of his race, warriors who gave of all they had to bring about this day and had fought by him to the fall of the Dark Beguiler. Not all wore a sword; here also were the priests and priestesses of the Seven Gods, and mages who could bend the elements or channel the silver energies at their whim. All had played a role in this; all were worthy.

Raefendal stood at the base of the two spiraling stairs while others took to their tasks. Prayers were offered at his side, and on the platform above, mages prepared a great spell. Before the seal was a crystal box inlaid with silver and writ with symbols, and inside a dark and shadowy object floated. Not unlike an orb, the object turned of itself, ebbing and scintillating in shades of black and dull grey. It seemed at times to stop and grow dark before turning again.

Upon the great seal was a triangular depression, a receptacle for the one key that could close it and leave anything placed inside trapped forever; or to be used once again to open the seal if the Seven Gods had turned their back upon the toils of good peoples. It was the mage, Tiragel, who held the key; a single piece of metallic stone, shaped as a triangle and inlaid with silver, itself carved in Allarish runes. Tiragel was the greatest enemy of Shadow. His war with the Dark Beguiler began long before the armies of Gorginor were met in battle, and long before Raefendal appeared with the one sword, for this began as a war of mages; a battle between those who had turned from the path of light and those who held true to the powers that formed them.

"It has been a long struggle," said Raefendal addressing all in the chamber. "There is much we have sacrificed. We have all given, and we have all lost something dear. For many, the sacrifices continue still, but this evil was our burden to bear. It was the sin of our people who brought this to be, and it was our obligation to set it right. Our sins fractured the heavens and cost us our immortality, and we must pay the price.

"The Shadow must never again be free. Let us cast away this fell creature and seal it forever in the void from whence it came."

At the Prince's word, Tiragel gave the signal. Two who had served with him for many years began an incantation that would weave a great spell, one that when focused into the prepared object could move the seal and leave it forever closed. Two others came forward to lift the crystal box, taking it up and holding it before the open void with unflinching resolve. Tiragel lifted the triangular key high and using his own arcane powers, brought it to life in a brilliance of scintillating colors. He thrust the key forward, making it the object the others focused their spell upon, and letting them add their power to his. One thing remained, the seal must be closed.

The dark shape within the crystal box began to shake and pull at the arms of the two who carried it. They struggled to hold it, but their will was strong, and their course could not be averted. Slowly the sealed box was delivered into the void, and the path made clear for Tiragel with the key.

The great seal moved of its own power, closing in on the darkness behind it, its edges recessing into the void as Tiragel pressed the key into the depression and worked his magic. An instant remained, an instant that would seal away the Dark Beguiler until the great dragon fell from the sky and Mirneth's orb no longer burned, but an instant was an instant too long.

Fighting against the powers that sought to imprison it, the Shadow finally shattered its crystal cage. In the one instant that remained an inky finger reached past the seal and turned to touch the key. Dark was the explosion that followed.

"WARDAI," SPOKE A voice.

Samiare barely heard him. She had gone outside of the camp to pray, but too strongly did weariness play against her. She leaned against a small tree with her sword pulled up to her chest. She had only just begun to nod off and fought to open her eyes when she recognized it.

"Mirathue," she answered groggily, her accent still present in her inflection.

The light of Meridel shown pale in the dark sky, and the chill of a night in the Wastes was only just beginning. Samiare had passed the day traveling in the company of Marish soldiers, and of those who served Tierinor, only two remained to accompany her; she opened her eyes to see both before her. Mirathue, the oldest of his troop, appeared strong and steady, his only wound a cut at his side; and Janthro, the toothless brawler, his armor a patchwork of chain and iron plates, his body marked with lacerations, a condition his scarred flesh must have experienced many times.

"You should not wander too far from the group," said Mirathue.

Samiare barely made any movement to acknowledge him. "I came to pray," she said. "Not gone long."

"I'd not lose sleep over that," scoffed Janthro. "Sec is the only one who listens, and that's just cause Gorumgahl never runs out of room."

She opened her eyes to look at Janthro but said nothing. Mirathue knelt beside her and began to work at the chain of her punctured sleeve. "You were wounded," he said. "I should look at it." Even more fitted to her small size, the links were still loose, and the older warrior had little difficulty in turning back the small rings to reveal the wound she had taken at the river's edge. Mirathue pulled at the cloth of her red stained sleeve, tearing the entry hole bigger.

"Is not injured," she said coming more awake and showing annoyance at his ministrations. "Wound no hurt."

Mirathue probed at her, even as she writhed away from his touch, and upon seeing the marks of her injury, he lifted his brows in astonishment. "Wound no hurt?" he said. "It's almost healed. How can that be?"

"It's that Allarish blade," said Janthro. "It has some enchantment."

"No," she said. "Is no enchanted. Is no Allarish, is blessed."

"Blessed," exclaimed Janthro. "You really do think the Gods are listening. I'm going back to camp." Janthro did not wait for any reply, and did just as he said; leaving the two alone, he strode away.

"Pay no attention to Janthro," said Mirathue. "If it eases your heart to pray, then who are we to steer you otherwise? Still the blade is remarkable."

Samiare gathered her strength and stood. "I can no change men's heart," she spoke. "Warriors fear Gods. Gods give reason to die for."

Mirathue let out a chuckle. "I had not thought of it that way. I suppose some Gods anyway."

"All Gods," she said, not sharing in his mirth. "All Gods bring fear."

"You are a strange girl," said Mirathue. "Sararth says we will be staying here through the night. You should return to the camp if you are going to sleep."

"I am no ready for sleep," she said. "I will pray."

"Maybe I will pray with you," said Mirathue. "To which God do we pray?"

"Which God favor you?"

"Any of the seven Gods will do," said Mirathue. He cast a glance towards her, but she gave no reaction. "I suppose I favor Kullis," he continued. "He is a God of warriors and courage."

"Is god for trial and growth," she said. "A hard way is his. This god looks over Tierinor. This god will favor you."

"Is that to whom you pray?"

Samiare held up her sword in both hands and looked past Mirathue into the darkening forest. "No," she said. "I belong to another. One you no know."

"Maybe I do," offered Mirathue. "Is it a Norvish god? What is his name?"

Samiare cast her eyes back and looked into Mirathue's. "I pray to one who watches over," she said. "I can no speak his name. A name can no describe him. He watches us...Watches you. He knows this trial, knows our heart. He brings me. I can no know why. I must do."

"Wardai," spoke Mirathue. "You speak as if this God talks to you directly. That cannot be."

"All Gods speak," she answered. "Can Mirathue listen?"

"Well," said Mirathue uncomfortably. "Do not talk of this before Sararth. It is already a miracle that you moved him to take us east. If he hears of this, he will leave us alone in these woods."

"Sararth is of Marindor," she said. "His heart is in shadow. His trial will be great. I will not help him. He chooses this struggle, or we will leave him."

"Leaving him will mean our deaths," said Mirathue.

She turned from him and what little expression she held in her face left her. "Trials await also you," she said. "Kullis will give you courage."

"Maybe I should pray," said Mirathue.

Samiare did not answer, instead she knelt and brought her sword close to lean her head against its hilt. Trials awaited her as well. To choose the light, or be lost to the dark. Even after all she had done, she did not know which was before her. More Groll slain, and still she felt empty. But her anger had changed, to kill Groll was not enough. She must become something greater. She prayed she would choose right.

Mirathue stayed with her for a time, but soon grew tired and left.

FOR THREE DAYS, Ruegette led the way north. Ahead of the Marish Captain, she moved along the edge of a wide stream, following it against its flow as it cut a deep gulley through the Wastes. With the noise of water to mask her sound, she took a quicker pace than she had through the woods. In the softer soil near the stream, the ground too easily left signs of their passage. Wherever she could, she avoided stepping upon patches of bare ground, and she did not dare to move on the mud along the banks of the water itself.

The way was quiet; she did not converse with Darimus during their movements. In a land controlled by Groll, even if there was little risk of being overheard, speaking aloud was not wise; and but for brief conversations during times of rest, the days were passed in silence. As they moved further into the north, the stream widened and its flow grew faster. Ahead, the far away sound of crashing water rising above the rush signaled the location of a distant waterfall, and as with any area of high ground, she knew there could be danger. She slowed her pace and moved towards it with more caution.

Even before she came to stand beneath the fall, she could see the jagged face of its high rock cliff jutting up above the trees. It loomed over the forest floor by the length of two bow shots and traversed across the land far beyond seeing. Water gushed from the top with great force, crashing into a deafening roar at the bottom, where centuries of downpour had cut a deep well into the rock floor. Ruegette had scouted it well. She was quite sure there were no Groll at the top, but that was not the whole of the danger; to follow the stream further, both she and Darimus were going to have to get to the top.

"What do you want to do?" Darimus called above the din.

Ruegette looked at it closely; the face had many fissures and jagged outcroppings suitable to climbing but the stones were wet and covered with a mossy film, a condition that could only add to its treachery. She gave a sigh and leaned with her back against a large stone near the base. "We could skirt it to the west," she said in a raised voice, and then she pointed along the length of the cliff with her hand. "If we follow the face, it will sink when we move closer to the river...but that may take a day or more."

Darimus followed the edge of the rock face with his eyes. It stretched off to the west until it could no longer be seen through the trees. Shaking his head, he looked back to Ruegette. "I don't think so," he shouted.

Ruegette smiled and looked up the face. "Then we climb," she said. "I think you should lead."

"I have no rope," said Darimus. "And I could do little to help you with the climb. It would seem to make little difference who goes first."

"It has nothing to do with rope," said Ruegette. "I'll not have you looking up at my rear as we go."

Darimus let his face twist into a wide smile. "Now Tierinor, what do you think I've been doing for the last two days?"

"Keeping your thoughts on the Eye of Ebon, I would hope," she snapped, not sharing in his mirth.

"It's a steep climb," said Darimus ignoring her tone. "Do you think you can make it?"

Ruegette stood and tugged at the straps of her breastplate. "I'll make it," she gritted out. She pulled the large plate from her chest and tossed it into the foaming well beneath the waterfall, leaving only her gold-colored chain above her red undertunic. She made a sling of her sword belt and placed the slender blade over her shoulder, then, unstringing her bow, she tied it across her back and secured her arrows. Last, she adjusted the small pack about her waist and turned to Darimus. "You should do the same," she said. "You have been heavy with armor since we left the tower."

Darimus stood admiring her with a wide smile. "You fascinate me," he said. "How does a Princessa of Tierinor become a creature like you?"

Ruegette shot Darimus an icy stare and only half smiled. "By standing up to the Groll when our sister nations did not."

"Come, now," said Darimus, pleading. "There must be a story."

"Not one I would care to share."

"Why would that be so bad?" he probed. "You treat me like I was less than the Groll, and I did share my map with you. You could try to be a little more pleasant."

"Pleasant?" Ruegette burst out, her anger finally pushing through her militant demeanor. "You think I should be pleasant?"

"I think if you tried you would find I am not all that bad."

"You stole a kiss from me!"

"Is that what this is about? The kiss!"

"Apologize."

Darimus stood motionless with his brow bent in puzzlement, and only after a long pause did he answer. "No."

"Why?"

"I wanted to."

"You hit me with a sword."

"I had to do that. You are Ruegette de Tagore. How else could I have gotten you to go ashore?"

"It hurt."

"I do apologize for that."

"I don't accept your apology." She turned from Darimus in a huff and stormed over to the base of the cliff where she stood with her arms folded for several long moments. She considered just leaving him where he stood; she had his map and knew the land. She would get much further than he, but she could not help feeling it was she who was the one being childish about the whole thing, and for an instant, it softened her. "Perhaps," she said without looking at him. "Perhaps...I will tell you when we reach the top...But you will go up first."

"Fair enough," said Darimus. He went to the edge of the water and stripped down to his chain shirt, discarding all his metal plates into the foaming water of the fall, and then he too secured his sword and belongings over his back. When he was ready, he walked over to Ruegette as she stood studying the way up, and quite deliberately, reached forward with his hand to place it against her rear and give it a gentle squeeze. Ruegette jumped with a start, and Darimus only winked at her. "I'll be waiting for you at the top," he said, leaving her to grumble foul words beneath her breath.

SAMAIRE WALKED AT a slow pace. The river far behind, and the mountains still days away, she followed at the rear of the Marish troop and let them take the lead. Mirathue and Janthro walked with her. She knew they would not leave her side.

It was no secret that the Marish Placent did not enjoy retracing their steps through the woods. He was wary of Groll ambushes and too quickly called a halt whenever they might be exposed. She did not enjoy his caution or delays. She would push them harder if she could, but Mirathue had warned against it. She knew they were not favored. There were grumblings about the 'girl Wardai' and her insistence at going back. Many thought it foolish that they should have listened to her at all. At times, Sararth would turn and look at her, as if still trying to decide if his course was wise, but he seldom came to speak. He seemed afraid to come near.

For two days, they had travelled with no sign of the Groll. The mountains drew closer, but the Marish leader only grew more troubled. He commented frequently about not knowing what was ahead, and of the possibility of an attack. Questions arose from his men as well. Could the Groll have truly vanished? Samaire held a different concern. Could something else have pulled them away? Could they have moved north instead? Could they have found the Ebon Eye, or worse, could they have found Ruegette? She did not like to think on any of it.

Near the top of a rise, the troop was called to a halt, and for this, again, she did not understand. Why must they always stop when no Groll were ahead? About her, men gathered into small groups to rest, and runners moved up and down the lanes. Frustrated, she set herself against a stump and shifted her sword onto her lap as both Mirathue and Janthro came to sit next to her. One of the Marish soldiers emerged to check on them, and she bid Mirathue to ask him why they had stopped, a question that brought only a dismissive stare from the man. "We are scouting," he said. Then he left them, and Samiare took hold of her sword to pray.

Again, there was talk about the lack of food, and their mistake at not heading for the river, and again they questioned why they were listening to a girl from a far away land. Samiare grew flustered. She looked towards the front and saw Sararth standing between the trees. He met her gaze, and his face hardened. He approached.

"There are six thousand Groll loose in these woods," he said. "More than can be made to disappear, and yet we have seen no sign of them since we turned towards the mountains. I do not like it."

Mirathue rose as Sararth came before them, and Janthro followed his lead, but Samiare remained where she was, turning her sword in her hand. When she spoke it was to Mirathue, her tone sullen. "Ask Placent why we have stopped," she said in accented Tieran.

"Wardai," Mirathue admonished. "The Placent has sent out scouts to look for Groll. This you know already."

She gave a sigh; even Mirathue did not understand her. "Where Groll no matter," she said. "Take army to mountains."

Mirathue grimaced and shook his head. He turned his attention back to the Placent, and spoke in his own form of imperfect Marish. "The Wardai wants to know why we have stopped."

"We cannot move an army through these woods with no supplies," said Sararth. "If we cannot find another camp to loot, we could make it to the mountains, but we won't have enough food to return. Tell the Wardai my scouts are looking..."

Samiare became agitated. She stood and threw back her hand, thrusting it to the northeast. "The Groll gather," she said. "The Eye of Ebon is near to them. We find Carand of yours...No delay with scouts."

Sararth's face twisted into a scowl. "Tell her to be calm."

"Wardai!" said Mirathue sternly and then his tone changed, "Samiare..."

Samiare flinched at the mention of her name and cast a questioning glare back to the older warrior.

"We cannot talk to the Placent in such a tone," he continued. "We are guests in his company."

Samiare kept her gaze on Mirathue, and then spoke with an icy determination in her tone. "Am calm," she said. "Groll no wait for us... Must no delay." She turned her back on the older warrior and stepped away from the group. Coming to rest near the stump, she pulled out her sword and knelt.

"I like her," said Janthro.

Mirathue gave a huff.

Samiare could feel their eyes upon her, but she would not turn to look back. She said a prayer for them, a prayer that they might live up to their call. She heard Mirathue speak again, pleading with the Placent, but in a gentler tone.

"I apologize," he said. "The Wardai is anxious to rejoin this force with that of your Carand. Her mind is on the Eye of Ebon. She fears the Groll are close to reaching it and are gathering to assure their control. If she is right, your scouts will find nothing that can help us. We must not delay. We must put together an army and attack them before all is lost. We must head east and reach the mountains even if it means that we will not be able to sustain a return to the river. You command this host; it is you who must decide if we take this risk."

There was a long pause, and finally, Sararth gave his answer. "I will wait for my scouts to return," he said. "If they find nothing, we will put our faith in the Wardai and press on to the mountains without delay, but if something is discovered, we will act on our own."

Samiare waited as the day passed. In small groups, the scouts returned, and their tales were all the same, the Groll were not ahead. For Samiare, it was a small victory. If the Groll found the Eye, or if Ruegette was made to battle alone, it would mean nothing. She would not rest, not until the woman she so looked up to was safe, and the Eye was far from Groll hands.

RUEGETTE MOVED BEHIND Darimus.

The climb was slow and taxing. The rock face was not difficult to navigate, but it was steep, and it played wickedly against tired muscles not used to such activity. Darimus reached the top first. He pulled himself up by his forearms, and then, swinging one of his legs onto the precipice, he rolled onto the plateau above. Ruegette was only just behind but as she neared the top, she found his hand reaching down to help her, and his warm face smiling wide. She darted her eyes towards him, and considered her action, but then she accepted and let him pull her up over the edge.

For many long moments, she did not move or speak, instead she lay next to him resting on the ground. It was late in the day; Mirneth's orb was only just a short distance above the western tree line, and it was sinking fast. From the top of the cliff, the land below them was visible for many millas before fading into the silver light of the world mist. To the south, winter pines, lit purple and green in the fading light, lay unevenly on rolling hills like the waves of a sea; and beyond them, glistening ice sparkled in a myriad of scintillating colors that beaded out from far off places. Below, the spray of crashing water was lit into two wide and prominent rainbow rings, and far to the east, the outline of mountains, grey and violet in the approaching twilight, loomed like ancient pillars holding up the sky, the tops of them hidden in grey clouds and silver mist.

Darimus was first to recover. He sat up and watched over Ruegette as she rested, but when she rolled forward to prop herself up, he stood and looked out over the tree covered plain. It was quieter at the top, and there was no need for him to shout to be heard above the noise. "It is beautiful," he said. "To think this should be in a land torn by so much war and strife."

Ruegette rose to her feet and came to stand next to him. "I have spent most of my life here," she said. "I know this land as well as any. It is a land full of strange wonders and much peril. There is only death here for those who are not careful. We should not linger."

Darimus turned his head to look at her, and his hand lifted to stroke her hair and then touch her shoulder. "Ah, Tierinor," he said. "How like this land you are; strong, vibrant, and very beautiful, but sadly I know you are just as dangerous."

Ruegette turned in his grasp and touched his hand with hers. She smiled widely but hid a fire behind her eyes. "Is that what you were trying to do?" she asked in a playful tone. "Make me less dangerous?"

"Of course, I would never wish to...," cooed Darimus drawing in closer to her.

"Good," she said, brushing his hand away and thrusting him back. "Then we have an understanding." She turned from him and walked away. Finding a large rock, she sat against it and undid her pack, fishing in it until she found something to eat.

Darimus watched her as she went through her machinations and smiled to himself. With the sting of rejection still plastered on his face, he broached a different subject. "You owe me a story."

"Well don't hold your breath," she said between bites of foul-tasting flat bread.

"Oh, come on," he groaned. "It's not like we have much else to do."

"Yes," she agreed. "But I know you are only asking because you cannot find a way to tame me. You don't truly care."

Darimus held his arms wide and looked at her with baleful eyes. "You misjudge me," he protested. "I really would like to know."

Ruegette studied him for several moments and considered his plea. From somewhere inside rose the thought that perhaps, for the first time, he was actually being genuine with her, which was all she really wanted. "Alright," she said. "If you really want to know." She pulled her legs in and made herself more comfortable. She thought on it for a moment and then began.

"When I was a girl, I used to watch my father go off to war. I was young and could not understand what it meant for him, but my father was Warder of the Citadel and so that was his duty, and as a consequence, I barely knew him. I did have many siblings, some I knew well, but of all them, I was closest to my oldest brother, Rendid. It was he who was to be the Warder after my father, but sadly that will never be.

"Like all first sons of the Citadel, Rendid reached an age where he was expected to take up the service of my father and lead our armies into battle. His first challenge came on a spring day much like this one; news that an army of Groll had crossed the river came to our walls, and my brother took the lead in organizing a force to engage them. It was a large company he gathered and before it was to set out, he asked that a small band of women come with the men and tend to them. It was mostly the servants of Miranae that went, but there were a few who were there for other reasons. I remember being very excited about the invitation, and I asked my brother if he would let me go with him, but he refused, saying that it was not proper for a Princessa to mingle in the campsites of men preparing for war. Disobeying him, I disguised myself in the robes of a Red Sister and hid among the other women where I went undetected until well after our army passed through the gates.

"Rendid was not happy when I was discovered, but at the time there was little he could do. He reluctantly decided that there was little risk for letting me stay; our army was large, and the enemy was far off; it was never thought that the women would be caught up in the fighting, we were to be kept safe in a hidden camp and protected by the swords of brave men stationed there to guard us. But the army ran into difficulties, the Groll were hidden, and we could not find them. We looked for them everywhere, but without finding we were unable to settle into a normal camp or make regular defenses, and on a night when we were still unsure of their location, they attacked us with surprise.

"I was too naive to know the danger; I ran onto the battlefield to tend the wounded as was my role. It was dark and the smoke of fires rose from the ground like a blackened fog. It was everywhere, blocking my vision and filling my lungs until I choked. I thought the enemy had been put into retreat but I was wrong; they feigned a collapse of their line and pulled our forces into a snare. In quick measure, they skirted our lines and were at our flanks. In the chaos, the fighting drew near. I remember watching as men scrambled in seemingly random directions to face this horrid enemy, but the Groll could not be repulsed.

"Our numbers were all that saved us. The battle did not go well; many of our soldiers were slain, and of the women, only myself and one other was spared. The men were in confusion and my brother...his voice was no longer on the field to issue orders. I remember asking of those who still lingered where I could find him, but no one would answer. I feared he might have been hurt and so I ran about the field calling for him.

"And I found him. His outline was like a phantom coming at me in the smoke. He was not hurt, he was worse. His body was held above the ground on the pinions of a long spear, and his blood colored the shaft down to the dirt that held it. Looking on him was like seeing a shadowy ghost frozen above the plain; an image that will be burned into my memory forever.

"I barely remember the rest of that wicked day, but before it was done, I had taken up my brother's sword and called together the remnants of his army into a cohesive whole. Some of the Groll had

fled the battle and made for the river, but I swore they would pay
with their lives for what they had done. I led our soldiers against
them and destroyed them all on a field near the water. I became a
hero on that day, and I have been in the service of Tierinor ever
since. I am a Wardai. I hardly play the role of Princessa anymore."

Darimus looked at her speechless for more than a moment. "I am
sorry for your brother's death," he said. "I am sure it was not easy for
you at the time."

Darimus's caring words surprised her, she did not really think
him capable of showing concern, and she did not wish to squander
it. "That was a lifetime ago," she said. "I barely remember who he
was anymore."

"Still," said Darimus, "I am sorry."

She swallowed hard and cast her eyes away from the Marish
Captain. "Yes." she said quietly.

Darimus stood and looked out at the path the stream took as it
cut through forest below, and then he pointed. "Groll," he said.

"Groll," said Ruegette with alarm, her thoughts no longer on the
past. "Where?" She stood and looked to the land below.

"There," said Darimus pointing along the river. "Near the water.
They have stopped to drink."

He was right. Along the river there was movement. She cursed
and then pulled Darimus away from the edge of the cliff.

"I saw about ten," he said. "It could be just a wandering band
loose in the Wastes."

"No," said Ruegette. "With both Tieran and Marish forces
fighting in the south, they would have joined the rest in their lust for
war. They are a scouting party. They're here looking for us. That
accursed Umgot must have gotten our trail."

"Then we must face them," said Darimus. "We could hold them
here at the cliff face."

"They will not come here," she said. "At their distance, they won't
be able to scale the falls before it is dark, and they will not camp if
they are here to find us; they will skirt this cliff. That will put them
further behind us, but the marsh is still more than five days from
here, and that is too long. We will have to deal with these another
way. We should get as much distance on them as we can and look

for a place that will give us enough advantage to risk fighting them."

"Well," said Darimus. "You are the Princessa. We will do as you say."

"Good," she said. "Then don't call me Princessa."

BLACK BLOOD STREAKED along the floors of Sahlohir's largest palace; marble flag stones that once gleamed white with splendid majesty lay stained and covered with grime, and corridors of grey stone that were once the avenues of nobles and servants alike had fallen into disuse and disrepair. The palace was not alone in its ruin. The whole of the city shared in its fate; spires that once shimmered in the light of Mirneth's orb lay fallen upon the wide streets, shrines that were once a testament to the best of Allarish stone-craft bore the weathered cracks of time, and great halls that once held all the splendor of Allarish art and lore had become the gathering dens of a wicked host. Banners once marked the city, streaming ribbons of purple and blue that had waved proudly in the high mountain winds but waved no longer; faded into the dust of ages, they had long since disappeared, only to be replaced by the grim standards of the Groll. There was little left in Sahlohir that time did not touch, or the Groll destroy; only a dingy throne room deep within the largest palace still served its original purpose.

The blood that fell freely through the halls trailed from a gaping wound in the side of a moaning Groll. His hands bound tightly and his arms lifted behind him by two of his kind, he was dragged through the halls. The captive was not unlike those who bore him; he wore the chain and thick hide plates of a warrior, his skin was black, like many of his race, and an empty socket where an eye once rested bore testament to his courage in battle, but nothing of his past could save him from the treachery ahead.

A spear in the hand of one of the bearers dripped with his blood, held by a green-skinned savage, it was this weapon that ruined the captive's gut; and the other, a slavering, black-faced rodent offered no greater kindness; he held a heavy iron mace in his fist and bore no hesitation at using it. The two took glee in the pain they inflicted and gave the captive no mercy; they pulled him along without ceremony or dignity, punching him as he struggled, and cracking him with the butt of their weapons when he fell. His blood flowed in a rapid stream and soon it filled the entire length of the hall.

At the entry to the throne room, the two threw the captive to the floor. Kicking and smashing him with weapons, they drove him forward, pushing him further into the room and towards the throne. At this, the captive struggled all the more, but it only brought him more bitterness and violence.

The throne room was not as it once was, the marble floor was stained with blood and scarred by large patches of crumbling rock, the walls were beset with stains, and banners, bearing the primitive symbols of Groll tribes, hung from skull adorned poles. Where sconces had once been set into the walls, only marred holes remained, and high above, a rotted roof lay broken to the sky. A dais, covered with mold and stained by filth, jutted from the far wall, and upon it, a seat of marble, covered in Morkind hide and adorned with skulls.

A large Groll with green skin sat stoically on the defaced throne; dressed in chain and metal plates, he rested a large single-bladed axe across his lap. The Groll was thick with muscle and his features were squarely cut into his wide face; yellow eyes narrowed with hatred; a wide mouth twisted into a snarl; and teeth like sharp needles bared behind thick lips. The Groll was comfortable on his throne, if such could ever be felt by one of his station, for here in Sahlohir, he was a chief among the Groll, and its reason was clear; a thin stone hanging from a thick leather cord about his neck–the Shard he had taken from a tomb in Norvaine; and Shargat the Shard Bearer kept it by might and cunning.

Shargat was not the only to inhabit the room, other Groll were present as well; the Dahmor-ra of several bands; those who followed the Shard Bearer since they came south from Gorginor, and whose station they owed solely to him. Shargat chose only the strongest and most ruthless of his race to serve as his chiefs of war, but he knew enough to keep them in line; better to keep them gnashing at each other's throats than let them come at his.

Shargat considered the captive as he lay like a discarded sack upon the floor, and listened to the jeers of his Dahmor-ra as they mocked him and called him traitor. Some even took the liberty to cast stones upon him, which brought sharp cries of pain from the victim's lips, but Shargat could not be moved by his suffering; it was his blood that he wanted.

"We found this one, Shard Bearer," spoke the green-skinned Groll with the long spear in guttural Durish. "He resisted being taken, but he soon gave into his betters when my spear split his guts." The Groll shook his spear so that all could savor the weapon.

"What...What is this?" sputtered the injured Groll. "I have done nothing..."

"Quiet, dog!" growled the green Groll, and the butt of his long spear cracked against the back of his captive's head.

"Is this the one?" said Shargat as if in a breath. "Is this traitorous pile of dung the one who slew our Shuma-ra before he could begin the summoning?"

"He had this," spoke the green Groll. He pulled from his belt a stone and held it up for all to see. The stone was no bigger than his hand, and it bore a single mark, a rune that had been carved into its face and filled with gold. "We found it on him," he snarled and then he walked before Shargat and placed it into the Shard-Bearer's ready hand.

"A lie," shrieked the captive, but he recoiled back into whimpering when a stone, cast from the crowd, struck his head.

"The summoning stone," snarled Shargat standing from his chair. "Proof of his guilt!"

The captive gave one last effort to be heard. "I took no stone," he screamed. "Rumsha..."

"Finish him!" demanded Shargat with a scowl of disgust.

The impact of a heavy mace broke open the back of the captive's head, shattering his skull and leaving him in a crumpled heap on the ground.

Shargat put the head of his axe to the stained marble of the dais and held the engraved stone before the crowd. "You have seen it," he oozed in princely confidence. "This agent of Rumsha has slain our Shuma-ra. On the very day we discovered the trail hidden in the caves, he took from us the one who could make use of the summoning stone and bring the Maygar here. This agent of Rumsha was sent to keep us from the Eye while his master plots a way to steal what we have earned before the Shadow."

Cries of outrage sprang from the host of Shargat's Dahmor-ra, followed by the call for blood, vengeance for the Feng's vile treachery. Shargat stood and listened to it, basked in the sound of it, and let it feed his ambition. Soon a chant arose, one that all Groll spoke in the face of treachery—the chant of war. Spurred by it, Shargat thrust forth his axe. "We know what this means!" he screamed out. "The treachery of Rumsha cannot go unanswered. If it is to be war between our tribes, then it is war!"

Holding up their weapons before their leader, the gathered Dahmor-ra continued their chant, their voices rising in volume and their arms beating on their chests. Like the pounding of the war-drum their voices spoke as one, and above it all, Shargat stood with the broken Shard tied about his neck, and his axe high. "Our duty is clear," he snarled, "Death to Rumsha! Death to any who oppose the will of the Shadow!"

The host erupted into a wild frenzy of murderous lust, and Shargat pushed them further. "I call you forth my Dahmor-ra. Let us purge our ranks of Rumsha's influence. Let no Groll who follows his putrid hide survive this night in Sahlohir. Let us open the gates and loose our wrath upon him in the forests. Let there be war upon him until his entire host lies dead under our heel, and his blood has been drained from his lifeless body." Shargat lowered his axe and pointed it at the main entrance the throne room. "Now go!" he shrieked. "He that takes Rumsha's head will be second before me!"

Groll warriors burst from the chamber into the halls of the palace, and as they went, the cries for blood followed them. Soon the ring of clanging metal and the screams of dying Groll echoed from the dark places beyond, but Shargat gave it little attention; he sat on his throne toying with the summoning stone in his hand, and at his side stood two others; two who did not leave when his commanders spilled from the room, two who had been with him since his rise in Norvaine and were now complicit in his crime.

"Keep a close eye on the Dahmor-ra," he spoke without taking his gaze from the rune-carved stone. "If any starts asking questions, cut his throat in the night and feed his heart to dogs. Keep them at each other and none will come to remember this stone."

One of the two, a red-colored brute with hair that fell in long greasy strands down his back, hefted a heavy spiked mor-macil and spoke without apprehension. "I will keep the Dahmor-ra in line," he said. "I savor crushing their skulls."

The other, a black mottled Groll who bore the caste of impassionate evil on a skull-like face, seemed to absorb the command with a malicious glee. He did not wear the thick plates of a warrior, but instead a mesh of ring-sewn cloth above two slender blades that hung from his belt. "What of the two who planted the summoning stone on that wretch?" he asked with a sinister hint of mirth behind his foul expression.

"You know what you must do," said Shargat. "See to it."

At Shargat's command the two left his side and oozed from the throne room with malevolence seeping through the grim smiles upon their thin lips. Shargat watched them as they departed; contemplating them from the precipice of his stained marble throne until at last he made another grim determination—they too must die, and the sooner he saw to it, the better, for he alone would have the Eye of Ebon.

THE SILVER MOUNTAINS loomed over the purple pines and winter trees like towering gods, stern in their grey continence, unassailable in their indomitable majesty. High above, where even the clouds did not reach, the white snow-covered peaks glistened in the light of Mirneth's orb, and below them, the jagged stone of the mountain itself was a pallet of purples and grays that fell like the folds of crumpled robes from old kings. Below, the ground was broken. Rocks, both large and small, were spilled throughout the damp soil, leaving the path gritty and uneven. Snow still clung in places, more numerous here than in the lit areas closer to the river, and the cold clime assured that the white patches would not soon vanish from the Wastes.

More days passed as Samiare moved east with the Company. They took a quicker pace than before, but the lack of food still had many questioning their purpose. She did not care. Everyday they were closer to joining the larger force, and everyday they were closer to confronting the Groll. She knew she was not liked, she could hear it in the many hushed conversations that rose up in the ranks. But another rumor also spread—one that brought hope. She wielded an Allarish blade. Some had seen her use it. It glowed with light and fire, and it slew many. The weapon alone gave many comfort, comfort they might yet overcome in this dangerous land, and survive against the Groll. And she was prayerful. Some believed the Gods may even bless them for keeping her.

But the way was still hard, with each lessoning of the rations, and each new day's march, the voices questioning grew louder, and the stares contesting grew more challenging. In the morning of the third day, she found absolution. Two Marish scouts of the Carand chanced upon them, and carried the promise that they would all soon be delivered to his camp.

They also brought news of the war, and it was not good. The army had suffered many losses; of its original force, less than half remained. And there were many wounded. To escape the Groll, the army had retreated far to the south. It was said to have enough supplies to last for several weeks, but with no expectation of reinforcements, it was likely they would soon disband and abandon the Wastes. Worse, it was said the Carand himself had taken injury and a deathwatch lingered over his fading body, waiting for his final moment. It was this news most of all that hastened the troop further, and carried them quickly to the Marish camp.

The place where the Marish had hidden was defensible; spread in the cradle of two rocky spars, and set at the base of a large mountain, the natural barriers formed a large ring with only a small gap as an opening. The crest of each spur was raised above the forest floor, and at the top of each, a Marish bowmen stood ready. On the mountain itself, a narrow incline rose to a high shelf that gave a good vantage of the land about, and further to the south, the rush of flowing water could be heard. The entire army was not held within the ring; many were camped in the surrounding woods, but all were well within reach of its protection. It was a good position, one that would give any army an advantage against a determined foe, but if the enemy were large enough, it would only make for a good last stand.

The arrival of Sararth's troop and the appearance of three who were not of Marindor caused a stir within the camps. Rumblings that

Tierinor had come at last to join the fight rose from the lips of many, and with it, the spirits of a defeated army seemed to come alive with a new hope. Samiare heard the rumors spread, but she had brought no army, instead she brought only a task. She held the hilt of her sword and moved passed them. She could not stop the rumblings if she wanted to.

At the gap between spars, a small contingent of soldiers waited to greet them. Three men in the blue of Marindor, one bearing a plumed helm in his arms to show his rank. Samiare took him for the Carand, but the reaction of Sararth spoke otherwise. He seemed wary, and addressed him with a cautions tone. "Eklar de Mouge," he said. "You hold the helm of the Carand. Has there been a change in leadership?"

"Sararth of the Rock Village," spoke the man who was Eklar, smiling wide and raising his hand. "Surely you must feel at home against the mountain."

Sararth looked up at the peaks above and then back to him. "We have traveled the Wastes for many days," he said. "And heard only recently that the Carand had taken injury. Does he yet live?"

Eklar's chest sank a little at the mention of the Carand and his face hardened. When he spoke, it was in a somber tone. "The Carand was cut through his armor in a skirmish, and has been pierced through his side. The wound has grown to infection. He is feverish. It is not likely he will live, but we watch over him in the hope he may revive. Until then I am the Carand-in-Lieu. I lead the army."

"Very well," said Sararth. "I serve Marindor and pledge loyalty to your position as Carand-in-Lieu until I am instructed otherwise. I wish to know how I may serve the cause of our Queen and ask that I may see Carand Kellenus to speak with him."

"The Carand rests now," said Eklar, "but you will see him soon enough. I would ask that you speak of these Tierans who have come with you."

Sararth looked back at Samiare, but it was Mirathue who went forward to stand before them. "These," said Sararth. "We found these holding the top of a hill in a battle of few against many. The noise of war drums brought us, and our numbers frightened away a host of Groll meant to destroy them. They had in their ranks three of our own that they had rescued from the feet of Tuz the Red Hand, a Dahmor-ra of the Groll."

Eklar looked upon them, and quickly his face opened into bewilderment. "What is this girl?" he said. "She is not a Tieran. She is from Morheim or someplace further."

"The girl is a Wardai," said Sararth. "I am told she is the second of Ruegette de Tagore. I have no reason to doubt it."

"A Wardai?" questioned Eklar. "But she is far too young to be one of their kind." He walked closer, studying Samiare's small form. "Yet I see she wears the blood of Groll upon her. Can this be true?"

"I meant to lead my men to the river," said Sararth, "but it was this girl who insisted we come back to the mountains and find the Carand. She was adamant he was needed to keep the Groll from the Eye of Ebon. It was my decision to bring her here."

Eklar considered Samiare for only a moment longer and then turned away from her in dismissal of the hope she represented. "I fear this '*Tieran*' Wardai may have come too late," said Eklar. "It is the wish of Carand Kellenus that we push north again into the Groll and try to break through their lines, but I do not agree with this. The Groll are too numerous, and our army has taken too many losses. If the Carand should die, and I take charge of the army, it is my intention to press for the river and escape this horrid land. This I will reconsider if the Tieran army wishes to negotiate an alliance."

"I regret that Tierinor has not sent an army," said Sararth. "Only a small handful of those that came with this Wardai still live, and they are already seeking to flee the Wastes."

"Then I see no other recourse but to do the same," said Eklar.

Samiare listened as the two men spoke, and again she was aghast at their decision. "No!" she said, using the Marish word, and stepping forward. She tugged at Mirathue's arm; beckoning him to be her voice. "Tell new Carand he must not flee," she demanded in Tieran. "Is no time for cowardice...Army must fight."

Mirathue looked uneasy about her request and opened his mouth to speak with trepidation, but his hesitation was unnecessary; Carand-in-Lieu Eklar seemed to understand Samiare's outburst quite well, and his expression changed the instant she hinted at his cowardice. "My lady," he spoke with an indignant tone, but plainly in the language of Tierinor. "I will not be called a coward for making the wise decision to leave. Too many Groll guard the way north. We cannot prevail…"

"You are a coward," insisted Samiare. She pushed her way past Mirathue and stood rigidly before Eklar, pointing at him to make clear her distaste. "You have many soldiers and look to flee. The Ebon Eye must not be found. This army must fight." She held up her head defiantly before the stunned visages of Marish and Tieran faces alike; Sararth looked on with disbelief, Mirathue cast up his hands and took a step back, while Janthro exclaimed beneath his breath and shook his head. Fire grew in Eklar's eyes and his scorn could not be contained.

"When last I looked it was Eklar who commanded this army," he crowed. "Not some foreign girl who pretends to be Wardai. I will not have my command questioned."

"You are no fit to command," she charged, pointing at him with renewed anger. "Sararth shall lead!"

Eklar drew back as if struck by blow, and in cold restraint of his temper, he spoke in a stern tone. "I have heard enough of this," he said. "We are grateful Tierinor has cared enough to send a Wardai to do her speaking, but sadly we must decline your offer to engage the Groll."

Samiare started to speak again but Mirathue intervened. He took hold of her arm and turned her away, then speaking over her, he drowned out her words. "Steady child," he said. "It would be best if you did not open your mouth again before the Carand-in-Lieu."

"Placent Sararth," bellowed Eklar in his native Marish. "Take this 'Wardai' from my sight. See to it she and her fellows are well cared for, but do not bring her before me again." Sararth lowered his head in acknowledgement, and the Carand-in-Lieu turned his back on the three, leaving them where they stood as he disappeared within the cradle of the mountain spars.

Samiare glared at him as he left, and thought to pursue him further, but many were the men who pulled at her to prevent it. Samiare pushed at those who put hands upon her, growing angrier at their efforts, but finally it was Mirathue who convinced her to yield. "We will rest," he said in a calm tone. "After a night's sleep, I will see if I can win us another audience with the new Carand. Maybe in the morning he will be more amenable to hearing you."

"He is no fit to lead," she protested.

"I cannot help that," said Mirathue, "but you must still come away from here."

IT WAS KRELLUS who led Samiare and her two Tieran guardians to a place near the water, and it was there she finally came to rest. Sararth had given orders the three should be supplied with rations and treated with the courtesy worthy of commanders from a foreign army, but it was clear they were less than welcome inside the Marish camp. Samiare did not stay long with Mirathue and Janthro; she went with them to the water's edge where she washed away the filth of Groll gore from her skin and clothes, but she did not follow them back to their crude camp. On the rocks near the water, she held her sword in both hands, cradling the naked blade that had carried her through so much already against her. Her mind dwelled on the events of only an hour ago, and emotions swirled within, consuming her thoughts. Inside, she felt as if her heart were a sunken pit that pulled in all around it. She knew she had failed before the Carand-in-lieu, and knew there was little she could do to remedy it. It tore at her. Fighting off tears she began to pray; her only refuge in the dark.

For a long while, she was lost. Left alone until Mirneth's orb began to fade behind the mountains, and the light of Meridel rose dimly in the haze, she spent the entire afternoon in prayer. She asked for an answer. How could she make right what seemed so impossible? How could she defeat the Groll with so little, or protect Ruegette when so many with her wished to flee? How was she to do what was needed, and how was she to do what she wanted most to do? But the answer was, as always, to have faith and to trust—to believe.

She did believe. She was devoted. Through all of her pain and loss, there was only one light that comforted her. Only one that could heal her. She did have faith, and she did trust. She wanted so much that was lost, but always it was too much and too far out of reach. Would she ever find Nechare again? Could she protect what she loved? The answers were not given. Still the song played and soothed, but it angered her. She believed, but was that enough? Was it just that she was to be alone? What were her gifts even for if she could not use them for others? And then, in her prayer, she understood.

She rose from the rocks, a new purpose filling her. She heard the voices of Mirathue and Janthro speaking, but another voice was there as well. Sararth was with them, and he spoke about the new plans of Carand-in-lieu Eklar. She approached them in the dark, drawing near as the Placent continued. His tone carried the ease of confidence that had been missing from him for many days, and his posture bore all the regality of command, but he went silent, and his expression changed noticeably when he looked out and saw her coming near.

"I could not understand what passed between you and Eklar," he said as she entered the circle, "but he is not pleased. I saw Carand Kellenus. He is badly wounded and is weak with fever. A Groll sword pierced him below his ribs, and it cannot be healed in the Wastes. It is a wonder he has lived this long. I do not think he will survive much longer."

"Eklar must not control army," declared Samiare. "Carand must not die." Turning to Mirathue, she bade the older warrior to translate for her. "Tell Placent...take me to Carand, I wish to see him."

Mirathue did as he was bid, and Sararth shook his head at her demand. "Impossible," he said. "Eklar has made it clear he no longer wishes to see the Wardai. He has given orders to keep her from the camp."

"I no seek Eklar," said Samiare. "You are leader. You get me to Carand who is dying." Again she indicated to Mirathue to speak for her, and again he complied.

"What good would it do to see Kellenus?" said Sararth. "He will be dead shortly, and Eklar will take his place."

"I have prayed," she said. "I had not understood before, but now I do. I can help him."

Marish soldiers guarded the entry to the gap between spars, but Sararth had no difficulty in using his rank to escort the three from Tierinor past them. Carand Kellenus was kept at the far side of the

ring in a crude shelter made of draped cloth, and it was there that
Sararth led the three with some haste. The hour was late, and none
but the sentries at the gap were about to challenge his purpose. Once
beyond them, he was able to move all of them quickly to where he
lay.

Samiare was first to push open the cloth and enter the tent. A
soldier sat within and rose as she entered, issuing a challenge, but
Samiare paid him no heed. Mirathue entered next with Sararth and
Janthro looking in from the outside. The guard moved to intervene,
but Janthro gave a grunt that warded him back.

The Carand lay upon the ground with a bloody cloth tied over his
wound. He was pale and breathed in shallow breaths, his eyes
opened only for an instant as Samiare stood over him, but then
closed; his mouth moved, but he lacked the strength to speak.
Samiare knelt beside him and then began to feel for his injury. He
was cold to the touch and winced uncomfortably as she examined
him, but the wounded Carand had not the strength to prevent her.

"You must not do that," ordered the guard. "None must disturb
his rest."

"Be calm," said Samiare. "I must see."

Mirathue moved to allay the guard and spoke in a soothing tone.
"The Wardai wishes to comfort the Carand. There is no reason to
dismay."

"I know of you," spoke the guard. "Eklar gave orders you were
not to come here."

"The Carand is dying," said Sararth, letting the conviction of
command carry in his voice. "The girl can do no harm. She will
continue."

Samiare drew her sword and laid it over top of the dying
Kellenus. He coughed, and lifted his hand to remove it, but she
prevented him; she took his hand in hers and then began to pray.
For a time, nothing happened, but soon the blade began to glow, and
with it Samiare's hands began to ebb with a faint light as well. She
spoke aloud, saying her prayers in Norvish, asking that the gift that
had so healed her since that day in the snow, be given from her to
the dying Carand as well.

"What is she doing?" demanded the guard. "Is she a healer?"

"I don't know," said Mirathue. "I have never seen this."

"I will get Carand Eklar," burst the guard and he went to push his way out of the tent, but Janthro moved to stand before him with his arms folded, and his demeanor threatening.

"Let him go," said Sararth.

Janthro could not have understood Sararth's words, but he turned at the sound of them as if he did. Sararth came forward to put his hand on the lean brawlers shoulder, easing him aside, and then he turned his attention to the guard. "Go on your way," he said. "You have your duty, we have ours." At this the guard shot from the tent and disappeared into the darkness to alert the Carand-in-Lieu.

Samiare's prayer continued but not with the same fervor as when she started; her voice had died down to only a low chant and the light that ebbed from her hand had grown to a radiance of pure and brilliant white. She lifted the bloody rag that covered the deep wound in Kellenus' side, and in the light that ebbed from her, she could see it plainly; his flesh was dark and sundered, and his wound oozed with an infection that colored his side both green and purple. Mirathue winced at the sight of it, but Samiare did not hesitate, she placed both her hands upon it.

Light pulsed from beneath her palms as she pushed her hands against Kellenus' side, and beneath her, the dying Carand rose up on an arched back and cried out. Darkness seemed to envelope him, it hung about his features like a cloud, but the light from Samiare's touch seeped forward and penetrated his flesh as deep as the sword that cut him; soon he fell silent, and soon it all faded.

Samiare was spent; the light inside her was gone entirely, and the words that flowed from her mouth as a mantra were spoken no longer. She panted, but it was more from bewilderment than exhaustion; she lingered unmoving for a time, but then took up her sword and stood. "I can do no more," she said. She went to withdraw, but no sooner did she turn from Kellenus's side than the curtain wall of the tent was ripped down, and the dark form of Eklar burst upon them.

"What is the meaning of this?" bellowed Eklar in a rage. Guards stood behind him, their torches casting flickering shadows across his face.

Samiare turned with a start but was not intimidated; she glared at Eklar from behind cold grey eyes and smiled with a hint of wickedness. "Your Carand must not die," she said. "I prayed for him."

Eklar thrust forward his finger and shouted to all who could hear. "I gave orders she was not to enter here." He turned on her and screamed in his own accented Tieran. "You are no longer welcome here. You will leave us!"

Samiare did not care about his ranting, her task was done. Slowly, she bowed her head in acquiescence of Eklar's order and drifted away from the side of Kellenus. Eklar watched her with an expression of utter contempt; his eyes smoldering; daring her to disobey again, but he did not understand what she had done: beneath the posturing and screaming of the Carand-in-lieu, the Carand, Kellenus, suddenly took in a deep breath and began to writhe. Eklar turned with surprise, and his eyes went wide with concern; without any hesitation he fell to his knees beside his commander. "My Lord Kellenus," he exclaimed.

"I was falling into a dark place," said Kellenus in a weak voice, "but I felt such warmth; it was as if a hand took hold of me and pulled me back from oblivion."

"My lord," said Eklar. "You must not speak; your wound is still grave."

Kellenus reached up to grab hold of Eklar's collar and then he pulled the Carand-in-Lieu to him. "How?" he asked, it was a question that turned Eklar's features white, and caused him to draw back in realization of the answer.

"It was the Wardai," spoke Sararth. "Somehow...she healed you."

"A Wardai," said Kellenus. "A Wardai from Tierinor ...here?"

Samiare stood behind the wide shapes of both Mirathue and Janthro, expressionless and calm, her hand again on her sword. Sararth gestured to her as Kellenus lifted his head to look. "I thank you," he said.

Samiare nodded and then turned to leave, as she did both Mirathue and Janthro fell in behind. The three of them crossed quietly to the opening between spars, and there Mirathue broke the silence. "How did you heal the Carand?"

Samiare stopped and looked at him. "I prayed," she said.

"Yes," said Mirathue, "but..."

"I was led," she continued, "but I could no heal wound, only stop...only reverse. I was no strong enough. Is all I could do."

"The Carand will live?" asked Mirathue.

"Yes," said Samiare. "Will live, but must more heal."

"So what do we do now?" grumbled Janthro. "Injured or not, the Groll will find us here, and we are still too few."

"Is true," said Samiare. "Army is too small. We seek more Army. We must go for Alasdain."

"Alasdain!" growled Janthro. "Why not ask the rocks to help us? Alasdain will never come into the Wastes."

"Faith," said Samiare. "We must have faith."

TWO DAYS INTO her northward journey, Ruegette started to lay the seeds of an ambush. Choosing to move near the water and leave visible signs of her passing, it was her hope the pursuing Groll would find her trail and soon follow. The ground where she chose to make her stand was a good one; at the top of a steep slope cut into the rock by the flow of rough water. The slope gave way to a treacherous expanse of slime covered stones and slippery shelf like expanses that rose one above the other like the steps of an uneven stair. The rise of each step varied in height, some manageable by only a hasty stride, others rising high enough that the Groll would have to slow to surmount them; enough to break any charge. Both she and Darimus hid themselves; she at the top of the rise, and Darimus in an outcropping on the shelf below. She knew the danger in letting even one Groll escape with its life, if any survived, it would be able to tell others and greater trouble would be ahead. To assure that her ambush would get them all, she knew she must wait until the Groll were well upon the rise before springing her attack.

It was late into the day when the Groll finally appeared at the base of the slope, and even then they lingered. Peeking down, Ruegette could see that one, a black-skinned giant with a rust-colored helm and a chain shirt, seemed to command the others; he barked out orders in sharp grunts and beat his will into his band with a short club. "Drink," he grunted in guttural Durish. "By dawn, we will have them; there will be no more water until then."

Another, a red-skinned brute with a heavy mace, came to the bottom of the rise and began to sniff the air. His face twisted into a menacing smile. "So close I can smell 'em," he basked. "I want these scrawny mice. I want to taste their flesh while it is still dripping with blood."

Ruegette ducked her head down lower. She feared his expression, if he had even the slightest suspicion of an ambush, her trap would spring badly, and the peril would be greater. From where she lay, she could see Darimus pressed against the rocks, his breath growing heavy and his dark eyes wide with concern, the sight of him gave her a bad feeling. She tried to allay her fear, she knew the moist current of the air rose from the bottom up and not the reverse; indeed, she could smell the stink of Groll that it brought. It could not be that he could scent them.

"What is it?" barked another Groll voice. "Do you suspect something?"

"I smell their women," said the brutish Groll.

The other began to sniff about, and then grew annoyed. "I smell nothing," he growled. "You are sick with bloodlust. You smell only your own meat-wormy self."

The first sniffed again. "She was here," he said. "Not far. We'll catch her soon. Then she'll hurt."

"Drink," came the voice of their commander.

Ruegette heard the two moving off, and raised her head to look down. They were gathered near the water, all dressed in thick leather and patches of chain. She counted twelve. Some wore the pieces of gorum-steel plate; grieves, or a breastplate, or a rusted helm, but none had a full suit. There were many spears, and some large axes; each had a weapon for close fighting, and four had bows. It was these that she knew she must slay at the onset, if the Groll could manage a return volley of arrows, they could cover their charge and she would lose her advantage. Three had shields, but not one had it in hand.

Their leader watched over them defiantly. He held a club, and his offhand rested on the hilt of a curved sword at his belt. He waited for only a moment and then grunted out a new order. "No more water. Every one of you filth laden dogs up the hill."

Ruegette's heart grew tight as she heard him, and she prepared; making her bow ready, she tested an arrow in its string. They had moved onto the slope; she could hear them drawing closer from the sounds of their grunts and the clamor of their metal plates grating against the rock. She was eager to start the fight, but knew she must wait; she had to let them come close enough that retreat could not be possible. She feared their numbers, she must kill the four archers before they could recover from their shock, and the ascent of the Groll would be quick. Even with obstacles, they may still gain the top. She looked at Darimus, hidden in the rocks with his sword ready, he still seemed anxious. She steeled herself. When she heard the Groll begin to move past the first rise that could pose an obstacle to their approach, she moved. Leaping to her feet at the top of the slope, she sighted the black Groll who led them and let her arrow fly.

The black Groll was struck through the throat, and fell back down the rocks. On the slope behind him, those that remained shouted out and scrambled to pull their weapons. Shields were brought forth and some leapt for cover behind large rocks, but not before Ruegette unloaded into them with terrible speed. One arrow pierced a Groll archer near the rear, and then a second feathered a spear holder as he charged for cover; a third struck down another bowman as he drew back an arrow of his own. But the Groll were too numerous and in spite of her efforts, arrows raced up, and she dropped low to avoid them.

She could not see them, but knew they were coming. She made ready another arrow and then held it until her instincts told her to move. When they beckoned, she rolled from the rock that hid her and stood. Two archers shifted their bows to loose as a third surmounted the largest rise and closed. Ruegette tried to sight the fast-approaching monster, but she could not get a clean shot before the two below released their arrows. Forced to fall again, the Groll would be upon her. She reached for her sword, but it was not needed; as the Groll took to the last rise, Darimus sprang from his outcropping, and charged. With a crash of metal, he plunged his sword deep into the attacker's side, crumpling him to the ground. Exposed, he turned from the dying body and leapt down two more steps to where another with a curved sword rose to meet him.

Ruegette was filled with dread. Two archers remained and in only a few heartbeats their arrows would cut Darimus down if she did not act. She rose to her feet and pulled two arrows as both archers below took aim.

"Darimus!" she screamed, but he was committed to his attack. He could not disengage. Hastily she sent her arrow at one, a shot which pierced his chest and threw him wheezing to the ground, but as she strung her second shaft, a Groll arrow found its mark, not into the side of the fighting Captain, but into her instead. The broad head punctured the chain of her collar and shot clean through her body. Ruegette let out squeak as she was pierced and was knocked to the ground by its force; her bow left her hand, and arrows flew from her quiver to scatter about the stones. Stunned, she lay where she fell as pain welled over her.

For an instant, she tried to manage it, but quickly she felt faint, and struggled to stay aware. Below her, she could hear the clamor of battle; steel fell against steel, and grunts, both savage and menacing, bore all the passion of life trying to avoid death. Her concern grew, the task before Darimus was impossible. He could not slay all that remained with only his sword; and her concern overwhelmed her pain. She searched for her bow. It had fallen upon the rocks near her feet; she snatched it back up. Two arrows lay near it, and she took them as well. Grunting through her pain, she stood and strung an arrow, and with a shaky hand, took aim.

Down on the slope, Darimus had clashed with several of the Groll. Two lay dead upon the rocks, and a third rolled limply towards the bottom. A fourth stood before him with an axe held high and another with a spear lowered to kill rushed at him from the side; she let the one with the spear be her next target. Struggling to make a good shot, but with fading strength, she sent her dart. The arrow lanced forward and struck the spear's carrier through its arm; it cried out and dropped down its point, but it was not a fatal wound. Frantically she strung her last arrow, but she was too slow to repeat her effort, far below the shelf where Darimus battled against the one who held an axe, the last of the Groll archers fired at her again. She had no choice but to evade.

Ruegette fell instinctively, but in doing so, she pulled at the arrow piecing her collar; the pain was immense and nearly pushed her to unconsciousness. Below she heard the clash of axe against sword, and the dull impact a blade makes as it cuts into mail. Pushing back tears, she made ready her last arrow and stood. Darimus still held the shelf, the axe wielding Groll lay dead at his feet, but he was not free from danger, already the spear of the Groll she could not slay lashed in at him, and already he was leaping back to avoid it. Below, she saw the Groll archer line up on her again and she grew determined her last arrow would finish him. Hastily, she pulled back her bowstring and steadied herself to take aim. The two released together. Ruegette's arrow flew with a precision that few others could match and struck her Groll counterpart full in the chest, while his arrow sailed high and flew beyond the rocks. Thrown back by the force of her arrow, and screaming out its life, the Groll archer tumbled over the rocks and slid limply to the floor below.

Ruegette watched as Darimus warded against the jabbing spear of the last Groll standing. The warrior kept its distance and favored its arm, but the thrust of its spear was still wickedly lethal; and the length of its weapon offered it the advantage. Darimus leapt back from one thrust, and then another until he found himself full in the water that flowed rapidly down the slope. In fear of the outcome, Ruegette let go of her bow and pulled her slender blade. She leapt down onto the slope, and raced forward, hoping to be of aid.

Darimus retreated back through the rushing water and stumbled in the stream as the Groll moved to take advantage. Lunging into the torrent with its broad spear forward, the Groll thrust the point of its weapon at him, but the Marish Captain had only been toying with him. Quickly gaining his feet and casting his sword in a low arc, he beat aside the Groll's thrust, and with the sweep of his hand, he took hold of the weapon's shaft.

The Groll shrieked as Darimus latched onto its spear, and then, giving the weapon up for lost, it released its hold and pulled at a short blade upon its belt. Darimus raised his sword to strike and leapt upon him. The Groll held up its dagger as Darimus fell, but it did not save it. Darimus plunged his sword into the Groll, pulled it free, and then drove it in again. Black blood flowed with the water down the slope and Darimus stood victorious; his armor was rent at his side, but no blood flowed between the links.

Ruegette stopped for a moment and watched him; then in weakness, she dropped her sword and fell to her knees. She saw Darimus look up at her and then leap into action at the realization. Below him, a single Groll, one that she had seen rolling down the slope under Darimus's assault, rose and fled into the woods. She could not follow it. She felt faint and slumped upon the rocks. In an instant Darimus was holding her. "Ruegette," he said with anguish. "You've been struck."

She looked up at him with a weak smile upon her lips. "I'm okay," she said.

"Don't jest with me," said Darimus, compassion showing on his face. "It'll be okay. I'll take care of you."

"Just let me rest," she said. "It hurts, but I can bear it. Just let me rest." She closed her eyes, and darkness fell upon her.

"WHAT IS THIS, Rumsha," spoke a tall Groll with red skin and black hair that fell in braids about his wide face. "I have waited three days to know why you have summoned us."

"Some say the Whar-Shumura has appeared, and that it is she that brings about this fear in you," spoke another, a green-skinned monster with strange yellow eyes sunken into deep pits. "We had the Marish pigs scattered and broken; slaves and playthings for the taking."

"Keep your tongue, toad," spoke another, also with skin of green but bearing gold rings upon long ears, and a granite slab of a jaw beneath a wide, flat face. "I saw the one you speak of; days back we fought against a small band of Tieran dogs, and the female led them. She must be Allar born for she moved with the swiftness of an Allar, and a white flame danced in her hands like a scourge. Against sixty of my warriors, she littered a creek bed with our bodies. She forced us to flee."

"You fled because you are weak and jump from shadows," shouted the yellow-eyed monster. "If she was Allar, then I would have cut off her tits and burned them in front of her."

"I heard she killed Tuz the Red Hand," spoke yet another, a fiend with black skin and large tusk-like fangs that jutted above thick lips. "I saw his head as it was thrown into the meat-worm pit along with the sniveling dung that brought it."

"Is that what this is about?" spoke the red Groll with braided hair again, but this time his tone held defiance. "The Whar-Shumura! Is this what you have brought us for, Rumsha?"

Rumsha stood near the center of the gathered Groll and leaned upon his knotted skull-adorned staff with both hands. His face was twisted into a scowl as he listened to the bickering. These were his Dahmor-ra, and it was his army that lined the woods beyond, an army almost six thousand strong, and he disliked his commander's tone. The old bone-reader remained calm amid the storm of rumor and posturing, and he lingered long and steady before answering the accusations of his defiant Dahmor-ra. "Who is it that reads the bones?" he hissed. His question was meant for all, but his gaze was fixed on just the one with red skin and long braids. "Be it you, Murg the Mor-Slayer, or is it I who has the gift?" Rumsha rattled the bones in his pouch.

"I don't fear you, Rumsha," spat Murg. "The only one threatened by the revelation was you. I'll not give up slaying Marish pigs for what you fear."

"Murg speaks right," said a black-skinned Groll, a warrior whose face was scarred with a spattering of pink colored burns. "The Whar-Shumura is not our problem, Rumsha, she's yours. You should not have wasted us with this fairy tale."

"Dare you question me?" snapped Rumsha turning on all around him with his staff held wide. "Do you forget that I am the Feng? That I rule in the Wastes? If you think otherwise, come show me the error I have made."

Murg the Mor-Slayer gave a huff and pulled a curved sword from his belt. "I will show you more than that—"

The boasting of Murg went unfinished, even as he strode forward to battle the Feng, he was ensnared at the neck by a shadowy tendril that snaked out from the staff of Rumsha. With callous indifference, Rumsha constricted the inky ribbon to block his air and lifted Murg to twice his height above the ground. The red Groll sputtered and fought, but he could not gain release. With delight, Rumsha manipulated the tendril, making it even tighter so not even a cry could escape from his suspended victim, and then, with Murg the Mor-Slayer dying for all to see, Rumsha looked at those he had gathered. "I rule in the Wastes," he hissed. "I will have the disloyal die, or I will kill you all!"

The yellow-eyed Groll pulled a long straight blade into the light and roared as he turned on those beside him, and more followed in kind. The sweep of a broad axe cutting into the flesh of a black Groll deemed disloyal ignited the hill into bedlam. In the span of an axe-blow, Groll turned on Groll; all fighting for the favor, or the removal, of the Feng. Rumsha stood in the middle of it, not fighting or even commanding; the old bone reader merely watched as his warriors cut into each other, and took pleasure at the sight of it. The battle spread into the camps and soon the entire host of Groll moved at each other in a storm of bloodletting and murder.

Long into the night the butchery continued; and by dawn the dead littered the field like dark lumps discarded and spilled upon the muck. More than two thousand lay dead, and many more were injured. In the night the battle had descended from a test of loyalty to an ignoble purging of the weak, and in all of it the Feng reveled. Untouched by axe or sword, the old Groll walked about the camps and surveyed. Most of his Dahmor-ra had fallen in the night but he remained unconcerned; by midday, he would replace them all. As he went, the survivors began to chant his name, and Rumsha knew just how to restore the order.

At the top of a large hill and set upon the wide stump of a tree cut long ago, was his throne; an ancient chair taken from the halls of an Allarish lord and tainted with blood and sacrifice; it was there that Rumsha stood before his entire host, and there he held up his skull staff to the low throng of those who chanted his name. Beneath him, the few that remained of his Dahmor-ra assembled; covered in gore and dripping with blood, they held their weapons haft first towards the Feng; a show of their tribute and subjugation. Slowly banners were erected in the camps, one from each band; the mark of their loyalty.

Rumsha held his staff above his head and set it aflame with an un-consuming fire. "Who rules in the Wastes?" he shouted, and as

one the host answered with the chant of his name. "There is a
usurper about us," he hissed. "One calling herself the Whar-
Shumura. And she is a threat." Rumsha let down his staff and
pointed it at his warriors. "I have seen the fear she has brought to us
all. She comes at a time when the Shadow stirs under our feet and
seeks to undo his will. It has even been said that she wishes to kill
your Feng... She must die!"

This pronouncement of Rumsha brought a chant for death from
his assembled host, and it grew in fervor until even Rumsha himself
could barely be heard above it. "She does not go to where the fool,
Shargat, wastes his time. She did not head into the north or lead an
army to the walls of Gorginor. We know where she is. She is here! In
our woods! On *our* hills, and in *our* valleys! We will not waste our time
chasing the remnants of a defeated army such as the Marish. I
command her to be found, and I will take the head of any who seeks
to do otherwise." At this, the Feng ripped off the cord of Groll
skulls that hung at his belt and threw it to the feet of his Dahmor-ra.
"Go!" he shouted. "Find her, kill her, and bring me her head!"

SAMIARE WAITED AS Mirathue packed his bag with food and
Janthro filled his skins with water.

"There's no point going to the wall," the toothless brawler said,
growling to himself and any who would listen. "Those bastards
haven't come out of their hole for so long, I doubt any of them even
knows how to hold a sword. They won't come back into the
Wastes."

Samiare turned her head away to let him grumble. "Faith," was all
she said.

Sararth stood near with a small band of six warriors. The Carand
was too weak to take full command of his army, and so it was Eklar
who had selected him for the mission. He would accompany her as
they approached the Alasdani. He brought a shield and offered it to
her. She lifted it and thought it too heavy. She put it down.

"Seems like a complete waste of time," Janthro grumbled some
more.

Mirathue stood tall and slung on his pack. He looked to his
friend. "You ready?" he asked.

Janthro smiled. He hefted his axe, and touched iron to his head. "Been ready," he said.

Samiare stood as well, and pulled her pack up to her shoulder. She looked to Sararth, and saw only his questioning expression. "We go," she said in badly accented Marish.

"Yes," said Sararth. "We go."

For two days, she followed as Sararth took the lead. He went north along the mountains, seeking what he called, 'the Passage of the Immortals', a pathway through the rock that was to lead to the very gates of Alasdain herself. Again the pace was slow, and again, Samiare would have preferred a faster one, but the Placent was cautious. Against the mountains, the ground was harder, and the days colder. The jagged peaks were high, and choked the light of Mirneth's orb from the land, keeping its warmth from lingering too long on the frozen ground. But in the shadows they were also more hidden, and the hard ground prevented signs of their movements.

The 'Passage of the Immortals' was not easy to find; made of many smaller and intersecting paths, it could lie on any trail that went between the mountains. Sararth could never be sure which would lead to the wall and which would end impassable. It was only at the discovery of a ruined gatehouse lining the entrance to a snow-covered pass that he ended his search. There were many passes, and many ruined structures against the mountain, but at this one, he seemed certain. The gatehouse could serve no other purpose, and he led them beyond it.

As they moved between the walls of rock, and onto the gritty, snow-covered path, Samiare could not help but feel uneasy. If the Groll were ahead, or if they came from behind, there would be no place for them to go. Even with her sword burning brightly, she still had to wonder at how many would be too many, and how many she could protect others against. For her, to hate and fight and fall could not solely be her way. And for the men with her, they were not many, and she had already seen too many fall. She said a silent prayer, but kept to the path. If she was to help Ruegette, or bring defeat to the Groll, Sararth would have to be right.

None of them had ever before seen the wall, but Mirathue spoke of its legend. Thickly built and towering above the reach of bowmen, it had never been breached, and not so much as a single stone had ever been broken. He spoke of the land and people as well, reciting their legends with reverence. A people who believed in old ways, and old traditions, and Kings with long lives that could trace their lineage back to the Allarie themselves. "Long life was their gift," he recited. "Not to be spent in endless wars with Dark Gorginor and her Groll."

"It's good they have walls," Janthro retorted. "Something to comfort them while the rest of us burn."

Samiare did not know what to expect, or why they had abandoned the Wastes, but she knew they were needed. She did not know how, but she was going to bring them back into the war.

The path they travelled was worn with disuse; erosion had washed away much of the trail as it rose against the mountainside, and fallen stone covered it in patches. For much of the day, the trail twisted into the depth of the range, but before Mirneth's orb fell, it cut across the breadth of a larger trail, and then soon that cut into another. To Sararth, it seemed as if the trails were like the tributaries of a river leading back into the main flow. From what he knew of the path, and its crisscrossing nature, he was sure they were heading in the right direction.

Leading them further, Sararth stayed to the passages where the path was widest, and pushed east until, cresting the rise of a small hill, it was there. Towering before them like the sheer edge of a cliff, the Great Wall of Alasdain loomed high above. Made of cut stones and stretched between the foundations of two mountains, it rose higher than the tallest trees of the Wastes, and buttressed against the rocks as if it were part of the mountains themselves. The large gates were tiny next to the massive construction, looking only as the slatted panels that might mark the entrance to a mine, but still they were formidable; made of thick wood, banded with metal straps, each was higher than Samiare by more than four times her height, and sealed tight. Above the doors were two small towers, and from them, large lavender pennants, bearing the silver winter-tree crest of Alasdain, wisped in the wind. A platform of laid stone jutted out from beneath the towers; sitting only the height of a man beneath the top, it was accessible by a short stairs from above, and it was from it that men could be seen to move.

Samiare could not know what other defenses the wall held, but she could see plainly the impossibility of breaching it. The men of Sararth's troop came to a stop, and looked at it with a daunting hesitation. She too was unsure of how to approach it and remained still. Sararth took a step to the front. "I will go," he said.

He went ahead of them all, and walked down the center of the path. As he approached, the dull reverberation of a struck metal gong filled the air, and even before the brash tone faded, armed men began to fill in the battlements above.

Dressed in bone-colored scales, and draped in the lavender livery of Alasdain, men with bows took positions between the ramparts and readied their arrows. Their numbers grew and grew, and for a short time it seemed as if the entire Alasdani army must be above, but soon a smaller contingent moved onto the lower platform, and one came before the others. Dressed in the same lavender and scales as his soldiers, the leader bore a plumed helm and gold crest, marking him as their commander, and when he spoke, his voice was loud and sharp.

"Warriors of the Wastes," he said. "I am Leondis, Damar of Alasdain, and defender of this road. Who are you, and what is your business here?"

His language was strange. Samiare could only know it through the gift of her sword, but none of those with her seemed to know it at all; they all looked blankly at each other. Finally, Sararth, standing before their company, turned his head to look back, his expression questioning.

Samiare held the hilt of her sword in her hand, and took in a breath. She looked over and saw Mirathue watching her. "Come with me," she said, and she started forward.

She closed the distance and came to stand next to Sararth on the open road. She waited as Mirathue went before them all, and spoke out in the Marish tongue to make clear their intention. "We are of Tierinor and Marindor," he said. "We wish to enter Alasdain."

A discussion ensued from those atop the wall, and soon the man spoke at them again, only this time his language was in perfect Marish. "You are warriors," he called. "We are not interested in what you bring. Go now, before more follow you."

Samiare spoke for Mirathue to answer. "Tell Alasdain, we wish to speak to King. Only then we leave."

Mirathue did as he was bid. "We are here to speak with your King. We require an audience before him to petition his aid against the Groll. We cannot leave until we have seen him."

"You will not speak to the King," shouted the Damar. "We care not about your wars with Gorginor, and you shall not be allowed to pass. Go back to whence you came, before I decide not to release you." At this he raised his hand and signaled to one of his archers. An arrow flew down from the top of the wall and planted into the ground at Mirathue's feet.

Mirathue stood back as the arrow bit, but Samiare took exception. She went forward and kicked the arrow away with her foot, and then took hold of the hilt of her sword with her hand. As she did, and almost as one, the entire body of archers upon the wall drew back their bowstrings and took aim. She stopped and glared up at them, but the Damar only looked impassively down.

Mirathue came forward and took hold of her arm. "Come," he said. "We are not welcome here."

Samiare said nothing. She resisted being pulled by Mirathue, but slowly she was turned away from the wall and led back into rocky avenues of the Passage of the Immortals.

RUEGETTE OPENED HER eyes to the sight of unfamiliar surroundings. She went to move her head but winced from the pain at her collar and lowered it back to the ground. As she lay, she took in what was around her; she was in the ruin of a small stone structure, probably an outpost of long ago; the roof was missing, as well as many of the stones that would once have added definition to the walls, and the ground was littered with the rubble of them; one of the walls was nearly gone entirely, and along another, a doorway was still outlined but no door remained within it.

She examined herself; her chain armor was missing, and she wore only a blood stained under-tunic. A crude bandage had been tied about her torso and shoulder, the material of which was less than clean, and a terrible pain throbbed and burned from her shoulder. She remembered the arrow that struck her and the sickening feeling she had as it drained the strength from her body. Her hand instinctively reached for the arrow, but it was gone. She felt along the bone of her collar, it burned greatly and the pain of it told her it may be broken. She feared to think what else may be wrong with her, or the manner used to save her from death, but she knew that she lived only because of the ministrations of one man.

From outside, she could hear the faint sound of singing, and at once the voice was both familiar and soothing. Filled with exuberance, and a hint of caution, she called out to him. "Darimus?"

The Marish Captain appeared at the door almost instantly. "You're awake," he said. "Good."

"How long?"

"It's been days," said Darimus. "That arrow should have killed you, but I had a little healing to bear—the dragon-cedar, it burns with fire, and hurts like mad, but it makes bleeding stop. I emptied its contents into the wound. It'll leave a scar, and you won't like its effect on you, but it did what was needed. I also had to set the bone. That will hurt too for a time."

"It'll do," said Ruegette. "I thank you, but we cannot rest. One of the Groll escaped and will soon bring others. The best thing we can do is keep moving."

"You are right, of course," he said. "We cannot stay here."

"Where are we?" she asked. "And dare I ask what you have done with my armor?"

"We are not far from where you fell," said Darimus. "I carried you for a time but moved away from the water to hide us better. I saw this structure peeking out through the trees and thought it'd be as good a place as any to hole up. I had to remove your armor. It is with your things in the corner there." He indicated a small pile of her belongings that lay along one of the less crumbling walls. "I had to use something from the Groll to cover your wound. I washed it first, but it was all I had." Darimus gave a sly smile. "I promise I didn't see anything."

Ruegette blushed as she considered the circumstance and would not look at him. "I don't want to know," she said. She tried to rise, and with effort, got to her feet. Her collar burned and throbbed and she doubted she could lift her arm over her head. "You have done such a good job with my bandage," she said. "Do you think you can help me with my mail and belongings?"

"Of course," said Darimus. "I would never want to miss an opportunity to help you with your clothes."

"Yes," she said, "and my fear is you have already had too much opportunity."

"Tierinor," burst Darimus. "You wound me. And after all I've done for you."

She was not missing any of her items, but her wound was debilitating. It burned at her badly, and rubbed no matter how she wore the mail. She tested her bow and found the pain was just too much to draw back an arrow. She walked, and bore her load, but she was slowed. Her items felt as if they grew heavier with each step she took, but she could not let them slow her down. Gritting through the worst, she indicated to Darimus they should set out. Though it was still her knowledge that guided them, it was she who trailed behind, and the tall Marish Captain who lead the way upstream.

More days passed as she nursed her arm. The pain had subsided some, but it still was enough to make her wince if she pulled at it wrong. Though she was becoming more capable, she continued to let Darimus take the lead; and somehow, through the toil of her wound and his caring over her, she could no longer look on him with the disdain she'd once had—and to her surprise, she even thought of him as 'honorable'. The land had slowly begun to change in their passing; the ground seemed to level off, and the stream, which often rushed past in a white foaming torrent, had widened and become calm. Trees grew thicker and the vegetation was changing; no longer did they move on hardened ground patched with snow, or the rutted roots of great trees; instead they pressed through a land with soft soil and fields of smaller broad-leafed plants that sprouted in an ever increasing abundance. Evergreens and purple pines still dotted the land, but an occasional willow grew among them, and soon, they too grew more numerous. The air was warm and the ground moist, and in the scattering of a few secluded pools, steam could be seen to rise into the air. In time, the moist ground gave way to wet, and then to an area of thick, muddy mounds rising above a layer of surface water that stretched as far as the world mist would let them see.

"Well," said Ruegette. "We are here. The Unfrozen Marsh. It is bigger than I remember."

"I have never seen such a thing," said Darimus. "How can it be so different than the land about it?"

"I don't know," she said, "I don't think anyone knows. And if what we are looking for is in here, I am not sure how we will find it. It would take us five days at least to walk around, and even then, we may still find nothing."

"It is in here," said Darimus. "In the middle, else it would've been found already." Darimus broke off two long branches from a nearby willow and pulled the leaves from them. "I will lead," he said. "It may get deep so probe ahead with this." He handed one of the two branches to her.

"This is just lovely," said Ruegette, accepting the long branch. She went to the water's edge and pushed it in. The branch sank to the length of her knees and then pushed into the mud on the bottom.

"Ready?" asked Darimus coming up behind her.

"At least, in the water we won't have to fear leaving tracks." She tested the water with her hand. "It's warm."

"Good," said Darimus. "Then let's get started."

SHE FUMED.

Away from the gate, Samiare walked in silence as Mirathue tried to say words to calm her. She held her sword and reached out for answers, but there were none. Again, she was to trust.

Moving back along the same path that brought them, she heard the grumbling of the Marish soldiers. She knew they did not believe. Some said openly that she should have listened, and they should not have bothered with the Alasdani. Sararth ordered them to silence.

During the night, the temperature dropped and by morning a light snow had begun to fall. It was cold, but there was no fire lit. The troop was slow to rise, and Sararth had to assert himself get his men in order, but by dawn, they were all back on the trail.

For much of the morning the men trudged upon the snow-covered paths, and Sararth spoke more than once of his concern for the lack of Groll, it was just unimaginable that they would leave the

road unguarded. He led them at a quicker pace than before, but at
the crest of a stony rise, his concern became real, and a small band of
Groll came into view. For the troop, there was no hiding from them,
both groups looked on each other in the same instant, and each
knew what it meant. From the Groll, one reached for a horn as
others drew weapons and started forward.

Sararth cursed aloud as he pulled his sword. He gave a rallying cry
to those around him, pulling the men together into a line as ahead
the sharp sound of the horn blared out.

"They blew a horn," shouted Janthro, hefting his axe and sword.
"More will be coming."

Mirathue joined him, standing at his shoulder. Samiare stood
behind and pulled her sword slowly, holding it in both hands, and
looking upon the rise.

The Groll came as one, and as they closed, Sararth gave the order
to meet them. The men charged forward, and Samiare ran with them,
but quickly she lagged behind, unable to match their stride. At the
impact, two of Sararth's men fell, and Groll broke apart their line.
Janthro evened the toll with his savagery; he split the skull of one
with his axe, and then cut down a second with a thrust of his sword.
Mirathue became engaged, and Sararth struggled with several that
moved against him. The Groll had greater numbers, the men grew
desperate. In single combat, they were pushed back, and Groll
moved to gain their flanks. Another fell, and Groll began to swarm.

Samiare closed the gap, and when she entered the fray not a
single Groll moved to engage her. In an instant, she cut through the
defenses of a sword wielding monster, letting it die in pieces, and
then she cut down a second with similar ease. A third, she skewered
in a great display of swiftness, and a fourth practically fell over
backwards as it tried to escape her. It was not her, but rather the
sword that caused such fear; burning with a light that shed forth in
an ever-increasing brilliance, it seemed to grow brighter with each kill
she made, and before it, the entire host of Groll took notice.

"It's her!" screamed the retreating Groll as he scrambled to back
away from the glowing blade. "It's the Whar-Shumura–"

Samiare did not care what he feared. He was Groll, and she
would not let any escape. She cut through his defenses, and split his

torso open under the fire of the white flaming blade. For an instant, she felt the twinge of darkness, but quickly it passed. Another lingered close and she lashed in, striking him down as well.

The Groll tried to draw back, but for them, the realization had come too late; they could not break away, and escape was not possible. Against the might of very skilled Marish and Tieran soldiers, and the wrath of the foreign Wardai, they were quickly dispatched. Only one had survived; standing on the rise with his hand still upon his horn, the last Groll had witnessed it all, and he turned to run.

Samiare pointed to the fleeing Groll with her sword, and frantically called out to Mirathue to stop it, but she was too late; the Groll had already disappeared from the hill. Janthro took off after it and ran all the way to the top of the rise, but it was in vain. Cursing, he gave up the chase and returned. "He was too far gone," Janthro said as he panted and rejoined the group. "I would never catch him."

"He'll be back," said Mirathue. "He blew that horn as a signal. This was a scouting party."

Sararth gathered the bodies of the three who had fallen and laid them in rest. Another of his men bore a large gash to his arm, but he would live. Sararth considered the dead, and spoke over them. "I would honor you brothers if there were time." Then he shook his head and turned back to those who had lived. "We cannot stay here. We must leave without delay. A larger force will be coming, and if they heard that horn we won't have much time."

"I agree," said Mirathue, "but we cannot go forward. They will control any split in the path ahead, and if they know we are here, they will gather more and move to control others."

"Then we go back to the wall," said Sararth. "And pray they do not send us away a second time."

Samiare did not stand with them. She remained on the road and looked towards the rise with her sword still in her hand. She did not like that even one had escaped. In the distance the horn blew again, its sound reverberating through the mountains for all to hear. When she turned, she could see the dread that had come over the faces of those behind. Only six remained.

"We must make haste!" said Sararth, and he turned from her to begin the retreat back to the Great Wall of Alasdain.

RUEGETTE TRUDGED THROUGH the waters of the unfrozen marsh, following Darimus as he moved through a mire of long-standing pools. He plodded a course that led straight into the heart of the strange land. Though warm, the marsh seemed devoid of other living creatures, not even insects could be seen upon its surface, but large leafy trees grew from the water as far as she could see, standing like giant pillars of deep greens and faded purples above a reflective glass. Both of them had learned early that the trees grew mostly from the shallows, and stayed near them as much as possible. Travel through the marsh was slower than either of them had wanted, but the mud proved most difficult to navigate, and in many places, to step upon it was to sink into a thick sludge that possessed a suction all its own. More than once she had to rely on Darimus's aid to escape these deadly traps, and each time, she could not help but admire the strength and concern he showed when he pulled her free.

The water was unusual as well, it grew warmer the further in they went, and steam continued to rise from many areas; at times bubbling over with the boil of foul smelling gas. In spite of the water's warmth, the air was still cool, and that, combined with the wetness that clung to them, made standing outside of it difficult to bear.

Neither of them knew what they were looking for, but it was Darimus's hope that whatever it was, it would just be something they could not mistake. The words, 'Our Sanctum,' did not leave much in way of a description, and Ruegette knew, whatever this 'Sanctum' was, it could be completely submerged.

Ruegette did not like being in this part of the Wastes, along with the discomfort of her wet clothes and the filth of slimy mud, there was also an uneasiness that she felt; a feeling that there was something sentient in the land about her, and it assailed her with a coldness beyond just the wind. She did not want to mention it to Darimus, she could not dismiss that it might not be just an irrational fear, but somehow, the feeling grew stronger the deeper in they went, and before long, she could predict the direction they should

travel solely by the uneasiness she felt. Dusk was fast settling on the
land, and she was extremely wary of spending a night out on the
water. She pressed on Darimus to make haste in his plodding ahead
and was determined to use the last moments before nightfall
searching for a place they might use to hole up. Her instincts told her
to move in the direction of her discomfort, and she was less than
surprised when Darimus shoved aside a large cluster of leaves to
reveal the object she knew they sought.

Resting upon a high mound, and so overgrown it was almost
impossible to see, the ruin of a small stone structure sat exposed to
the ages. Older than even the marsh itself, the ruin must have
survived in this harsh environment for hundreds of years, and
impossibly showed little wear for all it had endured. The island about
it was also odd in that it was devoid of trees, even though such grew
in abundance around it, and steam actively rose from its muddy
surface in a wispy haze.

Darimus was first to approach. Wading out into the depths of
chest deep water, he slowly crossed the distance to the small island
before climbing out on the other side and shaking the wetness from
his clothes.

Ruegette was only a moment behind and came to stand next to
him, but she did not wring away the water as Darimus had done,
instead she folded her arms over her chest, and stood nervously; the
uneasiness she had felt throughout the day was now strong, and she
could not ignore it any longer. "I do not like this place," she said. "It
is unsettling."

"What do you mean?" said Darimus. "It's just a ruin, like so many
others; hardly a danger to you or me. The ground is harder. We can
stand here."

"I feel a presence," she said. "Something callous and cold."

Darimus looked about the mound, and then stilled himself to
experience whatever it was that was unsettling her, but he could not.
"I feel nothing. Are you sure?"

"No," she said. "I'm not as sure as I would like to be, but I have
been feeling it most of the day. There is something here, something
that creeps on me. Like there is a watcher in the shadows, but it
remains hidden. I don't know what it is, but it feels wrong." She

looked on him with her arms pulled in close, and her eyes darting, she took in a nervous breath.

"What do you want to do?" he said, watching her.

She considered the question, and even though she thought it would be best if they left the stone structure just as it was found, in her devotion to duty, she knew she could not. "We must continue," she said. "It's too late to do anything else."

"Okay," he nodded. "I will look around."

He went to the structure and examined it.

Ruegette stood warily behind, looking on it as well. Made of stone and covered with both mud and withered vines, its shape was that of a near perfect cube, but it was half sunken into the wet ground. The top of it was low, rising only about as high as her head, and a section along the western face was cut away, revealing a short stairs that descended into a water-filled well before a partially submerged stone door.

"There's something on top," said Darimus. He climbed up onto it, and started to kick away some of the mud. "There's a symbol and some writing, but it's old. I don't think I can read it." He kicked at it some more, trying to clear all of the mud away. He moved towards the center.

Ruegette watched him from the ground and saw as he kicked at the mud, but no sooner did his foot brush the surface near the center than a voice shrieked in her head. Screaming as a raspy, breathless whisper, it shouted as if coming suddenly alive, and it said only a single word, but Ruegette could not comprehend it. Startled, she gasped in spite of herself.

Darimus turned the instant he heard her. "What is it?" he asked, his voice full of concern.

"I heard something," she said. "I heard a voice…it whispered at me."

Darimus grabbed hold of his sword and went to jump down from the roof, but Ruegette held up her hand to stop him. "No," she said. "It's gone now. What did you find?"

Concern shown in Darimus's features as he regained his stance atop the structure, but he did not let it slow his response; "I don't know," he said. "There is Allarish writing upon the symbol, but it's hard to read in this light. I think it's a magic symbol, but for what purpose I cannot know."

Ruegette listened, her hand moving onto her sword, her eyes surveying the marsh through the encroaching darkness.

"Are you okay?" he said.

"I don't understand," she said. "I am sure I heard a voice. Did you not hear it as well?"

"I heard nothing," said Darimus, "but if this is what I think it is, then this place was once called the 'Whispering Glade'. Maybe what you heard was a trick of the wind or a gust through the trees."

Ruegette considered the possibility and shook her head. "I don't think it was the wind," she said. "It was more substantial than that. It said something, but I did not understand it."

"Well," said Darimus. "Whatever it was, if it's here, then it must be inside. I'm going to try the door."

"Yes," said Ruegette as she drew forth her sword. "And I will be right behind you."

Darimus went down the steps and stood in the small pool at the bottom. The water had filled the stairwell three steps high and lapped against the stone door but did not seem to go through. The door was large enough for one as tall as him to enter by, but there was no ring or obvious mechanism to open it.

He pushed on the door, moving it almost not at all, but from within there was the faint crack of breaking wood. He tried again, only this time he threw all his weight against it, and the door could not hold. Bursting open into a dark hall and letting the water of the stairwell empty onto the stone floor, the door flung wide and clattered against the inside wall. From within a blast of heated air came forth, and an ancient beam, once used to bar the door, fell like dust from brass clamps set into the frame. Darimus pulled his sword and peered into the darkness, waiting for anything that might scurry at him from beyond, but nothing came except the sound of dripping water. Turning to Ruegette, he flashed a faint smile. "It certainly seems to have been abandoned long ago," he said. "We'll need something to light."

Ruegette gave a laugh. "Everything is wet."

Darimus stepped into the hall and lifted the remains of the

wooden beam. "This has been spared. Can you light it?"

Ruegette took the beam and held it in the light; it was rotted and crumbling, and she tore at it easily with her hands; pulling it apart in wide strips. Much of it was made wet by the water that had flooded in from the stairwell, but a portion of it was dry enough that she thought it could light. She had a flint with which to make a fire, but with no paper or kindling it could not help. Seeing no other way, she brought forward her bow and looped the string around a piece of her branch probe. Though it may ruin her string, she went to work pushing and pulling on her bow, causing the piece of branch to twirl against the dry strip, until smoke and then fire appeared.

Gathering up the remaining strips, she went into the structure. Inside, she found that Darimus had moved down a narrow hall and stood at the top of another stairs leading down into even more darkness. The hall was for the most part dry, but the sound of water dripping echoed from places below. As she approached, Darimus turned to look at her and a pleased expression lit up his now unshaven face.

"Good," he said. "You got it to light."

"I've only enough for five," she said. "The wood is wet, but it will burn quickly."

"It's dry in here," said Darimus. "And nothing has been through that door in centuries. We are safe. I'll go and cut more branches that we can leave here to dry. Then I'll pry a brick from the wall and use it to bar the door. We'll rest here tonight, and tomorrow make a full investigation."

Ruegette looked into the darkness below, and it did nothing to allay the anxious or uneasy feelings she had. "I will go with you," she said. "I do not want to be left alone in here."

"Good," said Darimus. "Then maybe you can tell me about this Zarue I heard you mention when you were sleeping away your injury?"

"Zarue," she said, not understanding.

"Yes," said Darimus, "Zarue."

RUMSHA SAT UPON his Mor-hide throne and waited. He wanted the 'Whar-Shumura'–with all his being he wanted her, but he had read the bones; they spoke nothing of her. Not even did he get the revelation of his death, as he had in every past reading; it was as if she had been hidden in some way, and it consumed him. He held the bones in one hand and toyed with them, letting them pass through his fingers and dropping them like grains of sand into his other. His readings had not been without fruit; he knew all he needed about the treachery of Shargat and his horde. Even as he sat, he could hear battles raging in the hills about him, but they were battles he had no interest in; whether the victory be his or Shargat's, the life of Rumsha was not in question–his revelation had seen to that.

"Who rules in the Wastes?" thought Rumsha to himself. "Is it I, or this Whar-Shumura?"

The battle could have easily been won by Rumsha if he had cared; he had four thousand warriors to command, and Shargat only two; but he would not give up his pursuit of the Whar-Shumura. He kept only five hundred with him for this battle; the rest he made to search in the south. He cursed Shargat that he even had to partake of this distraction. There would be a heavy price to exact for this, he would see to it.

The battle was drawing closer. Rumsha's forces were in retreat and that displeased him greatly. From his throne, he could see the woods come alive with fires and fast-moving shapes. The pitched tones of ringing metal pounded out from nearby hills, and the sound of war drums came like a distant thunder drawing nearer; not his, but those of Shargat, the traitor. A Groll warrior came to stand next to him; one of his trusted Dahmor-ra.

"They are close, my Feng," spoke the Dahmor-ra. He was a large Groll clad in darkened leather and adorned with a smattering of chain mail for armor; in his hand, he held a notched pole axe. "If we lose the blackened hill, we should flee. We can gather our forces in the south, and then return to crush this Shargat and his band under our heel."

Rumsha sat lost in his thoughts, giving no reaction to the words just spoken, and misreading the mood of his master, the Dahmor-ra intruded upon him again. "My Feng…"

"Silence, fool!" spat Rumsha. "I tire of your cowardice." On the hills beneath his gaze, he could see a mass of movement shifting through the trees; that of his warriors pulling back and fleeing before Shargat's host. It was not entirely against his wishes; he had not sent them to engage Shargat's horde, but rather to dwindle away their numbers; to fight them at the passes and water crossings, to lay a siege against their ranks and then retreat only to draw them into another snare; but it was his hope that it would not come to this, a battle on the hill of his throne. "Cursed upstart," growled Rumsha. "May he rot in a meat-worm pit for all eternity!"

The retreat brought a host of Rumsha's warriors running onto his hill, and more would soon follow. Among them came Morgal, the Skull Wearer; it was he that Rumsha commanded to go and engage the forces of Shargat, and he that drew the most contempt from the festering Feng. Morgal was powerfully built, chain links stretched to their limit over his muscular frame, and black skin rippled with grim definition on his massive arms. Blood trickled from a wound to his shoulder, but it seemed not to faze him. He wore a dark helm shaped like a skull with thick horns curling down about his wide face, and he held a thick, curved cleaver that dripped with the blood of his enemies. He came before the Feng and fell to one knee in front of him.

"We have fought them as you wished, my Feng. We cut six hundred of their number and took few losses. We will fight with you till the end."

"Six hundred, eh?" sneered Rumsha "It seems it was not enough. Why do I have to suffer enemies on my hill?"

"My Feng," growled Morgal. "Shargat has sent his entire band, and they show no fear of our arrows, but they are weak. They do not fight like Morgal Who-Wears-the-Skull. Here they will die." The large Groll held forth his dripping cleaver and set it into the ground before the Mor-hide throne.

Rumsha smiled through his thin lips, and his thoughts turned towards reprieve for this Dahmor-ra. "So be it," he spoke. "Call your warriors back and set a line here. We shall see the truth of what you say."

Morgal stood waving his cleaver and rallied his forces. Beneath the throne, he set a new line, one with poleaxes and arrows that could test the mettle of any host, and as he did, the warriors of

Shargat crested the blackened hill. They numbered over a thousand, more than twice that of Morgal, and they carried the heavier mail and weapons of Gorginor. Quickly, they formed a crude line that covered the entire summit.

On both sides, drums beat and warriors chanted songs of death and victory, Dahmor-ra stood before their warriors and gave forth calls to rally them, and archers made ready their bows as fires were lit to add flame to their arrows. Morgal stood before his entire company with his cleaver raised. "Make them run," he shouted. "Let our arrows cut them down until they reach the bottom; then the axe; then the sword. We take them on the low ground. They must not pierce our line. They must not reach the Feng."

Rumsha sat and watched as his ranks were formed and rubbed the bones in his hands. On the blackened hill, Shargat's forces began to descend, and Morgal responded. Arrows were fired across the gulf and withered his enemies, but they did not break them. Soon the warriors of Shargat moved into the valley and it was then that Morgal gave the order to charge. The two armies clashed. At the break Morgal's warriors engaged with such ferocity it seemed they may overcome the numbers arrayed against them, but it quickly subsided.

Rumsha spat upon the ground as he saw his warriors starting to be pushed back and in his anger he cast the bones; they fell in a telling pattern. At the bottom of his hill, the forces of Shargat started to break apart his line, and to his dismay, he watched as the center dissipated letting a thrust of Shargat's warriors burst through to charge the throne. Rumsha rose in a fury.

"Dare you come to lay hands on Rumsha, the Feng?" he ranted. "Know this, and know it always: only Rumsha rules in the Wastes!" With a swipe of his skull staff, he sent a crescent wave of flames cutting into those who charged forth, and in an instant their burning bodies lit the hill like blackened smoldering lumps. The Feng scowled at the rest of Shargat's host before descending the hill towards them. His anger driving him and his wicked powers far from spent, he would not be a captive to any. He had read the bones, and the bones never lied—they told him he would travel to Sahlohir, but the manner of how remained unclear.

PART 4
SWORD OF
RAEFENDAL

THE PRINCE ROSE slowly as blood trickled from his mouth. About him lay many dead. He had not seen what became of the mage, Tiragel, but the two who stood with him lay near, crumpled upon the floor. Others stirred: a Priestess of Miranae, two servants of Tiragel, and the warrior, Rafangil, his friend for two millennia. Raefendal could barely recall the explosion, but what little he could conjure put the cold grip of death upon his heart. With terrible dread, he looked to the seal, afraid that he would find it still opened, but it was closed. And the key that sealed it…The key still lay dormant within the cut stone, only it was not the same; somehow it had been broken.

"Will it not end?" Raefendal shouted through his bloodied lips. "Will we not be atoned?"

"We cannot know," said a woman's voice. It was the Priestess of Miranae, the fair and beautiful Ellyndil; one he loved dearly and whose wisdom he trusted. "We cannot trust what we have seen. We must seal this chamber, and all that lies beyond. None must ever come to test this seal."

"And the way must be guarded," spoke the one that Raefendal knew best; Rafangil, his lifelong friend. "A duty beyond flesh and blood is required. Only then can we be certain."

"Of what do you speak?" said the Prince, fear rising in his voice.

"I will make the sacrifice to guard the Shadow," said a third. Tolilzin, the mage, a friend and companion to Tiragel, and he spoke without any hint of trepidation.

"No!" said the Prince. "I cannot allow it." But conviction was not in his words. He knew the truth they all spoke, and he yielded. "Let it be me who makes this sacrifice."

"You cannot, my Prince," spoke Ellyndil. "The duty you bear defends us all. None must know the sacrifice we make, and none must again come upon this chamber. For our secret to be held, only we three must know the seals we lay. Only you can see to it that we are forgotten."

"I cannot forget you," said Raefendal near tears.

"You must," spoke Rafangil. "Take the key and hide it. Then hide all that you know. Keep our names from the annuals of history, remove us from all legend and lore, and then take your secret and flee this land so that what we give up will hold for eternity."

Raefendal fell to his knee and bowed his head. "It will be done, I swear it."

Atop the stair, the last who survived the dark explosion took hold of the key and delivered it to his hand of the Prince. "Come, my Prince," he said. "Like you, I too must leave, but for now, let us go together."

Raefendal knew the mage well. Second only to Tiragel in his hatred of the Shadow, Mylindrifel was always a friend in Raefendal's darkest moments. "You comfort me as always," said the Prince. "Speak to me of your son so I may dwell on life, and give up this evil on my heart."

"Ilnydrifel," spoke the old Allarish mage, helping the Prince to his feet and leading him towards the yawning opening of the wide corridor. "He will be a great Mage someday, a legend in the four lands."

SHARGAT STOOD BEFORE a bronze door. Set upon a stone rise
within a deep underground cavern, the door was both tall and thick,
and the bronze of it was beaten into a mural that displayed an
Allarish figure standing within a field of flowers beneath the rays of
Mirneth's orb. The rock that framed the door was ornately carved;
above were passages written in an Allarish script, and on each side
was a stone figure; one, an Allarish woman in a flowing robe with
her hands folded in prayer; and the other, a tall Allarish warrior
dressed in scale armor, plumed helm, and a long flowing cape. The
warrior held before him a sword carved to show radiating light from
its blade.

Below the rise was a wide shelf that overhung a deep and
seemingly bottomless canyon. The shelf was covered in a grey gritty
dust that bore the imprint of those who tread the surface, and many
were the dark tunnels that emptied onto its expanse. The cavern was
not still, somewhere within, it rumbled, and it was hot; warm air blew
up from the canyon below and heated the chamber with a current all
its own. Shargat did not dare venture alone into this unknown; with
him were fifty warriors, those he claimed worthy of witnessing his
rise, but more likely his fodder for the unexpected.

The door was sealed, but Shargat could not be kept from his
prize. "Open it," he barked, and letting his yellowed gaze fall upon
one near the front.

Warily, a tall and thickly muscled Groll dressed in leather and
bearing the heavy hammer and spikes of a builder approached the
bronze door. He studied it; there were no hinges or rings, no handles
or devices to manipulate; only the smooth surface of hard bronze
sealed flush against the frame. Gingerly the builder tapped the face
with his hammer but it brought about only the deep resonance of
thick metal. "It is sealed," he said. "Allar magic has been at work in
this."

Shargat's eyes narrowed with a seething anger. "Allar magic
cannot keep us from the Shadow's Eye," he hissed. "You are the
siege builder, break it down!"

"It is too thick, Shard Bearer," complained the Groll. "Only a
Maygar can undo…"

In a rage, Shargat swept forward with his axe, planting its thick head into the builder's side and crumpling him to the floor; then he kicked the gurgling body off the rise to the stone shelf below. "There will be no Maygar!" he shouted to the rest. "Our Shuma-Ra is dead and his summoning stone lost, but Allar wards or not, the Shadow demands we enter; so break it in you filthy swine before I split every one of your skulls to the teeth!"

Shargat was unrelenting in his will and with threats and punishments he drove them. Two at a time could bash at the door, and for hours he made them work at it. With each pounding of the mace, or the hammer, or the axe, the door gave a little, until, crumpled and folded at the corners, it finally broke away from the rock to swing open into a chamber beyond.

Pushing his way to the front, Shargat gazed into the room behind as slowly the light from his torch cast away the darkness. "A tomb," he spat. "A tomb of dead Allar." At the very mention of his find, lust appeared in the eyes of his warriors, and whispers full of malice followed by rough laughter rose from their ranks. "Touch nothing," sneered Shargat. "We do not defile tombs today."

Shargat stepped past the mangled door and entered the tomb. It was a large chamber with row upon row of sarcophagi, each ornately carved with fine filigree, and large columns that rose to a vaulted ceiling high above. Braziers, cold for a millennium, lined the aisles, and large openings cut into the walls led into darkened corridors beyond. Statues and monuments were scattered throughout, and in the center was a single stone pedestal bearing a thick leather-bound tome.

The Groll poured into the room, savoring and lusting to destroy what took centuries to create. One Groll moved for the tome. "Look," he grinned. "A pretty Allar book!" But he was crushed from behind by the angry axe of Shargat.

"Find me the Eye of Ebon!" Shargat screamed as the dying offender writhed upon the ground, and black blood dripped from his axe.

The Groll spread throughout the tomb while Shargat took to the center and stood before the thick tome. In disgust, he swept the ancient book to the floor, letting it land with an echoing clap, but no sooner did the sound of it filter through the corridors and chambers beyond then a wind began to swirl, and with it came the swooning of a howling current. Torches began to buffet and cast their flames sideways under the power of strong gusts, and eerie glowing shapes could be seen to rise in the darkness.

The warriors of Shargat grew nervous and their smug expressions changed from visages of lust to abhorrent fear, and some began to speak openly of their terror. "This is a cursed tomb," spoke one. "We wake the dead!"

"What do you fear?" shouted Shargat to his warriors. "The dead of Allar? They lie here because of our might."

The light of a flickering fire sprang up from a side chamber, and then again in another, and then another, and another, lighting each with an eerie glow of red until not a single corridor remained dark. These same fires burst from the braziers spread throughout the main chamber; filling each in turn and burning with a strange redness that cast ghastly shadows upon the walls and high vaulted ceiling. In the one chamber that lay ahead, the ghostly shape of an Allarish woman formed in the darkness. Sitting in a large side-turned throne, her head looked over her shoulder and gazed upon the podium, and at the one standing before it. The woman's arm was extended and her palm upturned, beckoning those before her to stop.

Ignoring the fears of his warriors, Shargat curled his lip into a sneer and strode forward. As he approached, the glowing of the ghostly shape receded, fading into a large statue carved in white stone. He considered the stone figure for an instant, and then lifted his axe. "I come seeking the Eye of Ebon," he called. "I bear the Shard that will free it. I will have it, you stinking Allar whore."

From someplace within the statue, the voice of a woman wafted into the chamber. It was a gentle tone, soothing and melodic, but it was spoken in Allarish and he could not comprehend.

Shargat stood bewildered, and astonishment played on his face. "What?" he said. In an instant, he knew there was a demand before him, and he could not satisfy. His eyes grew wide with fear, and the realization of his error came rushing upon him. He turned to run.

Around the fleeing Shargat, the chamber came alive with the souls of the dead. They rose from the very sarcophagi that held them, passing through the stone lids as if they offered no barrier at all. More came through the walls and still more from the floor, and all about him, Shargat heard the screams of his warriors ringing out with curdling terror. He saw as many swung their blades in futility, and witnessed as one after another fell beneath withering caresses that drained them of color and strength and life.

He ran for the entrance where the battered bronze door offered the only hope of escape. Icy hands brushed against his skin and seeped into his body. He screamed and summoned all his strength for the flight. Another Groll fell in his path, its body swarmed over by the ghastly entities and its screams wailing out until its empty lungs could no longer make a sound, but he could not be made to slow. He ran under a swarm of ghostly spirits of his own and felt the strain of ever increasing weakness pressing upon him, but somehow the swarming apparitions seemed not to be able to bind him. The entrance gaped before him like a portal to salvation and he burst forward, daring not to look back at what pursued.

He made one last leap for his freedom, but something snared him. He was pulled to the ground by his throat and fell to his horror still within the chamber. Frantically, he turned and saw it was not a spirit, but the Shard itself that held him; bursting with darkness like light from a fire, the thing floated from the string at his neck, and pulled him not away, but towards the statue he had just stood before. It denied him escape and left him powerless to stand. About him, a thousand ghostly shapes swarmed in a great fury, and many rushed forward to assault, but somehow, the darkness of the Shard repelled them.

Shargat grinned in near madness at his fortune, but then fell back into terror at the sight he next beheld; in the chamber beyond the pedestal, the clear shape of the woman stood from her chair. Her white robe billowing in unknown winds and anger burning in her angled eyes, she spoke menacing words in incomprehensible Allarish and strode forward. Her hand pointing at him as she approached, Shargat knew she would not be thwarted by the power of the Shard alone; indeed, he knew she meant death.

He wrestled with the Shard to free it from his neck, but it could not be removed. Within his thoughts a voice arose; hissing at him

like a whisper of evil, it spoke a single command, "Kill her!" Its
language was strange, but he knew it plainly, and he screamed with
an all-consuming terror. In his hands, the Shard freed itself from the
string about his neck, and unable to control his own thoughts,
Shargat hurled it at the apparition, casting it in an arc of shimmering
darkness that seemed to suck in all of the light.

"YOU MUST LET us pass!"
Samiare watched as Sararth pleaded their plight again before the
wall.
"We are pursued," he shouted. "A large number of Groll nip at
our heels!"
She breathed hard, and felt the same anxiety they all did. They
had been at a fast pace for most of a day, but still the Groll were
within hearing—their drums and war-horns resounded through the
valleys and chasms of the Passage of the Immortals to echo even
against the stones of the great wall before them.
"Can you not hear their drums?"
Again, the wall was lined with Alasdani archers, and again the
plume-helmed Damar stood on the platform above and called down.
"You should not have come here," he shouted at them in Marish.
"What passes between you and the Groll is of no concern to us. You
must leave."
Samiare expected their indifference, but she prayed it would be
different.
"Where would we go?" screamed Sararth.
The drums beat louder, rising in volume with each passing
heartbeat. They would not be allowed entry. Samiare turned to face
back towards the rise, her hand holding her sword. She watched. The
arrival of the Groll was imminent.
"I care not," spoke the Damar. "If you do not leave, anything that
comes, we will hold against Marindor for bringing it here."
Mirathue watched with her. He spoke words Samiare already
knew. "They are upon us."
Groll warriors crested the rise, fifty or more, spreading
themselves into a long line that completely filled the road. Their
faces cast in savage anticipation, the Groll looked down on their prey

and paused. Two with drums beat their instruments in a thunderous, doom-filled rhythm, while two others with stained leather banners came to stand ahead of the line. One, a red-colored Groll with a cleaver-like axe, moved to the front and held his axe high as a beacon to rally his band. They were terrible to behold, more than Samiare knew they could fight.

Around her, the men all turned to face them, standing with their shields and weapons ready. Samiare could see the look of hopelessness on their faces. She turned towards the wall, and the Alasdani upon it. The archers shifted their bows, aiming them at the line of Groll instead, but the Damar stood with his scowl unyielding; not one arrow would be loosed on their behalf. On the crest, the sight of the archers gave pause to the Groll, but the command of the Damar saw it would not last; he spoke his final words in his own tongue; he would not intercede.

Samiare seethed with scorn, but it would not change what must follow. Glaring up at the Damar, she resigned herself to her fate. She took up her gold-hilted sword and held it against her forehead as she said a silent prayer. The Groll began to chant and beat on their chests. She could feel the fear of those who stood with her; there was nowhere to hide, and nothing they could do.

Her prayer was short. She lowered her blade and took several steps backwards before turning to face the Groll. She did not stop when she turned; she continued walking, she was the reason they were here, she was the reason they may all die, she would face them. She threw open her arms holding them in a wide gesture, inviting any to come test her. Behind, she heard Janthro start to come forward, and Mirathue call to her, but she dismissed them with a wave of her hand. The Groll line broke into coarse laughter at the sight of her and five warriors came forth with dull-colored weapons hefted in their hands.

As they drew close, one charged before the others. With a heavy spiked mace held high, he swung for her head, but she was too fast for him; in an instant she cut past his swing and ripped her sword through his vitals, cleaving him to his spine. The Groll shrieked as he was struck and fell in a crumpled heap. A second sought to catch her as she was occupied, and he thrust forward with a hooked sword, but she effortlessly beat down his blow and struck; cutting him at the shoulder, and slicing through his arm and ribs. The Groll fell onto his knees and gasped for air with deep wheezing breaths.

She pushed him into the dirt with her foot and turned her icy gaze upon the remaining three, and they hesitated. The sword in her hand gave off a dim glow in the well-lit field, and it only seemed to grow brighter with each blow she landed. She heard one speak. "Whar-Shumura," it said. Sensing their apprehension, she stood erect and again let her sword cant to the side, only this time she let a malicious smile slide across her lips.

Overcoming their trepidation, the three charged as one. A spear was thrust forward to skewer, and another cleaved at her with an axe, but she bounded away from both. She cast the spear aside with a swipe of her sword, and ran up a low rock to leap past the one with the axe. Landing in a crouch, she cast a wicked blow back, cutting the axe wielder across the back of both his legs and dropping him limbless to the ground. The spear carrier twisted to follow her, and she wheeled on him, pulling up her sword and cutting him under both arms. He gave a huff and fell to the ground.

The last stepped in and flailed at her with a heavy sword. Two blows, he sent at her small form, one to slash open her vitals, and the other to take her head. She rolled from the first, and warded back from the second. A third blow was sent, and she countered it with her own; cutting into his swing to catch his weapon, she glanced her blade from his to cleave into his torso. The Groll fell without a sound and she wrenched free her sword; the blood of five dripping from its edge, and light bursting from its length in a dance of white flames.

Drums no longer beat from the Groll line, and laughter no longer rang. The red Groll stood before his band with disbelief upon his face, but he would not yield. Samiare did not relent either. One Groll still lived. Writhing on the ground with his legs missing, he crawled aimlessly in the dirt. She went to him with hate in her heart, and turned her sword down. He craned his head back to look but she did not care. Looking to the red Groll on the rise, she raised up her blade, and without ceremony, drove its point into his spine.

She took satisfaction in it, another Groll slain, but for the first time, she felt a change. Somehow, there was a darkness that ebbed from her to the blade, and from it back to her. It shook her, and she paused.

But it was still one insult too many. Upon the rise, the red Groll leader screamed out his rage. Raising his axe-cleaver high, he gave forth a cry, and behind him, his warriors opened their fanged maws to echo his sentiment. The red Groll thrust forward his axe and strode forward, and as he did his entire band followed him.

Samiare stood confused. Was there something she had not understood? Behind, she heard the words of Janthro as he called out to rally those around him, and then his approach as he came forward to stand with her. Mirathue came next to her as well, and the Marish troop filled out the line. She turned to face the approaching enemy. How could it be dark? Where they not her foe? Were they not wicked? Did she not do what was wanted?

The Groll advanced, slowly at first, but as they drew nearer their leader gave forth a cry, and as one they burst into a run. Though it seemed fatalistic, the men crouched behind their shields and pointed their weapons. Samiare waited with her sword still strange in her hands, she did not know what to think. The gap narrowed, cries of war rang out, and the men braced themselves. She had no time. The light still shown and flames still burned. She would use it again. She must. She took it back up and readied herself in her stance. In the seconds before the clash, Sararth gave a last desperate cry, but then…salvation.

Falling from the sky and striking the Groll ranks like raining spikes, the arrows of the Alasdani broke apart the Groll charge. Many fell beneath the rain of steel and many more would follow. Upon the Great Wall the order had been given. The Damar stood with his hand forward, and his sharp voice rising above the din. The archers had fired in unison, and in wild abandon they pulled back arrows to let fly again.

In the rocky gap, the two lines collided and quickly became a tangle of slashing blades and dark forms locked in mortal combat, and Samiare joined them; forgetting the darkness, and giving into the call of the flaming white blade, she let it rise and fall, slaying her foes with its own deadly precision and bursting out with its light for all to see. In only a moment, the battle that should have belonged to the Groll was stolen from them. Their numbers cut to size by Alasdani arrows, their swords set against warriors with few equals, and their lives consumed by the unquenchable fire of the Whar-Shumura, not one survived; of those that broke and tried to flee, Alasdani arrows struck them down.

The battle over, four warriors of Marindor and two from Tierinor still stood in the gap, and with them, Samiare lowered her sword. At the wall, a low rumble signaled the lifting of the bar, and slowly the thick gates began to open. In the space between the gaping doors, warriors in pale lavender emerged, and before them all was the Damar, Leondis, in his purple plumed helm.

The Damar strode forward with his entourage fanning out behind him. He had a broad-bladed sword at his belt, but there it stayed. He came at a quick pace, and his eyes beamed with astonishment. His hands extended, he stood before Samiare. "Can it be?" he asked in well-spoken Marish. "Can that be the Sword of Raefendal?"

Samiare looked at him and puzzled. With the back of her sleeve, she wiped the Groll blood from her face. She did not know what he meant, *Sword of Raefendal*, but she lifted her blade, which now only bore the faintest trace of glowing light, and held it high. "Is no sword of mortals," she spoke with the Tieran tongue. "Is sword given to me."

The Damar fell to his knees as she lifted the blade and bowed his head. "Forgive me," he pleaded. "I am just a lowly Damar in the service of King Avaugnol. I did not know you possessed it. You must go to Avanrill at once. You must stand before our King."

Samiare looked to Mirathue, and then to the Damar. The tremor of darkness still shook inside of her. She did not know what it meant, but she knew what they must do. "Tell him, take us there," she said.

RUEGETTE PASSED THE night at Darimus's side. Ensconced within the stone walls of the structure Darimus seemed able to sleep well, though uncomfortably, on the stone floor, but not so for her; the feelings of unease would not subside, and as she lay in the darkness, a voice whispered in her head.

The voice was not steady, at times it spoke softly; barely louder than her own heartbeat, and at others, it ranted as if given over to madness, but never did it echo, as it would if it came from deeper within the structure, and even at its loudest, she was not sure if she were truly hearing it. She was not afraid, though it was unsettling, and she tried to listen, but the voice was too inarticulate; many of its syllables were slurred, and even in moments of clarity, its language was simply unknown to her. She thought it was speaking in an old form of Allarish, and the words at times did seem familiar, but always they were out of reach of her mind's ability to interpret. And often there was no voice whispering at all.

Ruegette dozed in the quiet times, and as she did, her mind raced. Half in dream, the images of a dark and wandering figure took precedence in her thoughts. An outcast full of woeful self-hatred, and suffering from the scorn of many, she found him at once to be pitiable. She sought to follow him, and perhaps to pull him back from his isolation, but he was far too removed. She studied him. At first, he was misunderstood, an odd figure who wished to be kind, but ever so slowly he changed; rejection turned to indifference. He wandered far, often where there was no trail, and his way was difficult, but his determination was intense, and on his own, he developed the power to proceed. Where stones blocked his way, he moved them with a sheer force of his will, and where forests grew to hinder, he brought down fire to consume them. His name became known; a whispered label for something malign, and his heart turned again; indifference fell to wickedness.

The figure retreated from those who scorned him. Leaving behind the boundaries of civilization, he sought his own way without the judgment of others, and he learned new skills; fire could be made to melt stone and stone could be made to flow like water, there was no barrier that could hold him. And then there was the voice. It whispered so that only he could hear, and he listened to it, coddled it, kept it precious within his heart; and it drove him to madness.

The voice never relented once it had found its way within him. It pushed him and prodded him, and slowly it took away who he was. The figure resisted, ranting and gnashing against the unseen force that came to rule him, but the voice was too strong, and what it wanted it would not be without. "The Eye," it would say. "Get me the Eye." The figure struggled against it, for deep in his heart, he knew it should not be, but his will was not his own, and in time the voice came to whisper something new.

A single word in its own strange language. "Soon…"

Ruegette woke with a start. In her mind, the voice was trailing away as if it had nothing more to add, but its last word she had heard clear—*Soon*. It had said it, and then she understood.

Ruegette rose from where she lay and went to the entrance of her stone hideaway. She removed the brick that barred her in and pulled open the door. A red sky shimmered behind the mountains, a signal of the approaching dawn. Leaving the safety of the dark hall, she climbed onto the roof and stood upon it, looking out into the murky darkness. Somehow she knew: deep beneath her feet there flowed a river of fire, and the flames of that river had made this land into what it was; the occurrence of this river was not natural, and it was instead Ilnydrifel who had made it; a fire from deep below the surface had been ripped upwards with an unimaginable power, and all at the behest of the Shadow; but why, she could only guess. There was one other thing that was clear as well, something that even she did not want to consider: the Shadow still had a voice, and that voice was counting down the days to its freedom.

Ruegette grew cold at the thought that any part of the Shadow might no longer be imprisoned, and it sickened her to think that just below her feet that same voice drove an Allarish mage to insanity. Once the Shadow had found its host, it would have pursued no other purpose than to destroy its prison, and this 'Sanctum' must have been a part of its design. There was a sigil upon the roof, and it too had a purpose.

Ruegette turned to the strange symbol and studied it. In the growing light of the early dawn, she could just barely see its outline etched into the stone; much of it was still covered. With her feet and hands, she scrapped away the remaining mud to look upon it. There were words.

Ruegette struggled with them, but as best she could tell, the symbol and its letters were an enchantment to protect something within, but what she could not know. Part of the script spoke of seeing all, and from that she became alarmed; if the Shadow could speak in this place, perhaps it could also see.

Ruegette leapt down from the roof and moved hurriedly back into the structure. She had been a fool to think she could follow in the steps of Ilnydrifel and not also find the Shadow. She had already been too careless, and the cost had been high.

"*Soon*," the voice had said. Soon Shargat would have his prize. Soon the Shadow would have the Eye of Ebon. Soon its prison would be broken, and soon it would be free to renew its conquest of the four lands. She did not know what lay hidden in the dark halls of the structure, but it was time she found out.

AVANRILL LAY IN a wide plain along the western edge of the Seryon River. Its high walls, made of white stone, surrounded the city on three sides and buttressed against the flow, completely sealing it against the water. From the walls, streamed banners of lavender and blue that waved in the breezes of the valley like long flowing ribbons, built by Allarish hands when their race was still young, Avanrill was less of a place constructed of necessity as it was a work of art; tall palaces and great houses made of white stone lined the cobblestone streets like points of light gleaming within the plain, white towers with round bases, and cone shaped roofs above flanged apses, rose as giant pedestals reaching to the silver sky, and seven temples set upon seven hills ringed the city; at each, a silver spire shimmered in the light of Mirneth's orb with an almost magical splendor. Below the grand constructs, gardens and fountains spread like patches of green and purple in a sea of white, and streets, alive with the endless flow of people, weaved through the city like a patchwork.

Above the splendor there was one structure that stood out as greater than the rest. Made of white stone and holding five towers of its own, the palace of the King was shaped as a giant cross; four wings, large enough to be great houses of their own, connected by four great halls to a central spire that towered above the rest.

There were only three gates that allowed entry through the city wall, and at the rivers edge a wide series of docks stretched out into the water where ships, both large and small, came to port. Spanning the river was a wide bridge that linked the city to a tranquil village beyond, and fields, dotted with sheep and livestock, speckled the lands of the east and north. Many were the well-worn roads that marked the plain, and many more were the carts and ox-pulled wagons that moved about them.

Avanrill was to be five days walking from the Great Wall, but Leondis had intervened to make it three; he provided horses for the journey and then took it upon himself to lead the way so they could reach the city in all haste. It was he who pressed the locals for fresh horses whenever there was need, and he who petitioned provisions in the villages they passed to ease the strain, and when they arrived at the western gate of the ancient city, it was he again who got them through.

Samiare did not ride on a horse of her own, she had never been trained in equestrian arts and Leondis had thought it improper for a girl to ride, a sensibility held by many within the plains of Alasdain. Instead, she rode with Mirathue, sitting in front of him with her legs cast to the side, and holding onto the horn of his saddle for the entire journey; a condition she continued even after they had passed through the gates.

The streets of Avanrill were full of merchants and craftsmen, and many were the strange faces that milled about in the crowded avenues. Leondis continued in his self-appointed role as guide and he led the small band through the city, but he was not quiet; speaking openly, he boasted of the sword of Raefendal being returned; a tale that made Samiare feel very uncomfortable, and as his words spread through the streets, enthusiastic onlookers began to gather in great numbers. The attention was more than she was used to, and she tried to hide herself by pressing into the armored chest of Mirathue, but there was little she could do.

Leondis seemed to enjoy the crowds and stayed with the small troop all the way to the palace gate where palace guards barred their entry. Again, Leondis pleaded their business, and petitioned the guardsmen for an audience with the King, but in his deliberation, he put his foreign entourage on display, speaking of them all as great champions, and even claiming Samiare had come to speak for Koning Huedrus himself. And then he spoke of the Sword of Raefendal, and that which he had witnessed in the battle before the

Great Wall, a story which drew both suspicion and awe from the guardsmen. But his rank gave him stature, and the Damar of the Great Wall was known to the Palace.

Admittance was only a formality, and soon the seven 'great champions' were delivered into an entry hall and attended to by young palace-girls and servants. Filthy from the road and disheveled from days spent in the Wastes, they would not be allowed admittance to the King until they had been bathed and were given something more suitable to wear; an offer the men eagerly accepted, but Samiare objected; she did not wish to undress in front of others, and she would not relinquish her sword to strangers.

The servants of the palace did their best to accommodate; she was assigned a single girl as an attendant and taken to a private chamber that contained a small pool, heated with coals, for bathing. The attendant tried to help her with her armor and sword, but Samiare grew annoyed and sent her away. Only when she was alone in the chamber did she remove her garments, and then quickly she slipped into the warm water. Leaving her mail and clothing upon the wet stone floor, Samiare took her sword with her to the water's edge and kept it within easy reach; of them all, only she would be allowed to carry her sword before the King, and that only because of the legend.

As she bathed, the servant returned. Carrying a bundle of fine cloth, the palace girl left behind an elegant robe of shimmering blue cloth for her rent armor, soft shoes for her boots, and a fresh white gown in favor of the torn and blood-stained undergarment she had worn all the while before. The servant did not look at her as she made the exchange, nor did she make any attempt to approach the sword, but she did leave behind a silver inlaid scabbard and sword belt befitting a great prince to carry the blade.

When Samiare emerged from the chamber, she did not look as one who had been fighting with Groll or as one who had slept a week on muddy ground. Instead, she was a creature of grace and beauty; her eyes shimmered like blue crystals against the color of her robe, her foreign features carried a hint of exotic innocence, and her pale skin rivaled the hue of a winter goddess, but the heavy sword strapped to her side in a silver inlaid scabbard marked her as not like

any noble woman of the palace, and when the servant girl returned
with combs and ribbons to do her hair, even she bowed low as if
entering the presence of a queen or princess.

A great arched door marked the entrance to the throne room of
Avaugnol and it was before this that Samiare first appeared to those
she had traveled with. At her approach, neither Janthro, nor Sararth,
nor even Mirathue recognized her, but as her transformation became
clear, they looked on her with astonishment and gave whistles of
approval.

"Kullis and Sec!" exclaimed Janthro with a wolfish grin upon his
face, and then walking around her to ogle. "Is this our young
Wardai?"

"Child," said Mirathue, not able to hold his tongue. "You're
beautiful!"

Samiare blushed at their attention and shooed away their
comments with a bashful discomfort, but she did not forget their
reason for coming; at the door stood two men with pikes who were
dressed in the livery and scales of Alasdain, and beyond waited the
King; they would need much from him.

Leondis appeared; emerging from one of the great arched doors,
he informed them the King had taken his throne, and indicated that
when they were ready, he would have them announced. Sararth went
and stood before the doors and Samiare took to his side. Behind
them, the others fell into a line. Samiare had never stood before a
King before, and the thought of it made her nervous. Rumors of her
had abounded throughout the palace, and even in the hall where she
waited, many had gathered to look on her; the sword that brought
them hung prominently from her hip, and she held its pommel for
comfort.

Sararth gave a nod, and Leondis went through the doors to give
the announcement. Soon the great doors swung open and those who
stood guard bid them to enter. Sararth took the lead, walking
forward with his chest high and his eyes forward. Before him was an
immense chamber laid out at the crux of the giant cross. Four grand
corridors met at a large circular dais in the center of the room, and in
each, throngs of people crowded to witness an event that could only
be likened to a coronation. Upon the raised dais sat a high throne of

white marble and silver filigree, and above it, the roof gave way to a great spire that rose beyond seeing. Banners of lavender and blue streamed down from above like billowing sheets, and ringed the central seat like curtain walls, and upon that all important chair sat Avaugnol.

The King was aged; thinning silver hair receded to baldness and a gaunt face that held tired eyes. He was dressed in a princely white tunic with gold trim, and a fur lined cape of deep purple rested on his shoulders. A gemmed broach sat at his shoulder, and jeweled rings were set upon several of his fingers. His crown was little more than a gold circlet, but it held within it a single tear shaped amethyst the size of a man's eye. Behind the King, six warriors stood in a crescent, adorned in scale armor and holding pikes to attention, they held guard over their sovereign.

Sararth strode forward until he was only a few paces from the King, and then he fell onto his knee with his head bowed low. Samiare followed his example, and behind her, all of her companions did the same.

"Great King of Alasdain," Sararth spoke. "I come in a time of great peril and humbly ask that you receive me as you would our Queen."

Avaugnol waved his hand to dismiss the formalities. "Yes, of course," he spoke in a deep throated voice that was both tired and dismissive, but his use of the Marish tongue was without accent. "Your Queen is young and impatient, and her dark schemes will one day be the ruin of her."

Sararth shifted uncomfortably, and his eyes darted up. At his throne, the King stood and took a step forward. "Fear not, warrior," he soothed. "I am quite fond of your Queen, and wish her no ill, but it is not your Queen we are here to discuss. I must know, is that the sword that has filled my halls with so much gossip since you passed through our gates?"

Samiare raised her eyes to the King; he stood like a child looking at her with a tangible curiosity playing on his features. He smiled at her and with a brush of his fingers, beckoned her to come forward. "It is okay, child," he spoke. "Rise and stand before me."

Samiare dared not deny the King. She stood, and apprehensively looked about the great chamber. Instinctively, she put her hand upon the gold hilt of her sword, drawing an instant shift of movement from the guards at the throne. Realizing her folly, she released her grip and held her hands wide as she slowly came forward. When she had moved within two paces of the King, she fell again to one knee and bowed her head.

Avaugnol looked down upon her, accepting of the recognition of her place in his hall. "I have been told you are Samiare, of a place not of the four lands. Is this true?"

"Of Norvaine, am I," she spoke in accented Tieran. "Across Frozen Sea, I came."

"Show it to me," said the King, changing his speech to that of Tierinor. "I would look upon it."

Samiare undid her belt and pulled the sword, scabbard and all, free of her waist. Gently, she held it forth so that the King could look upon it.

Avaugnol reached down to take hold of the weapon, but Samiare reacted poorly, pulling it back from his reach and raising her eyes. The King smiled and lifted his hand. "May I?" he asked as a chuckle murmured from the crowd.

She did not know what to do, it was not her wish to relinquish her sword, but she did not want to refuse a King. She relaxed her grip and held the sword up for the King to take.

Avaugnol took hold of the scabbard and lifted it from her. He did not touch the hilt of it, only turned it under his gaze. "How came you to have this?" he asked.

"I prayed," said Samiare. "It…was given."

"Have you received the gifts?" he continued. "Do you strike down the heart of evil in one stroke? Do you send away the dark with a brilliant light? Do you speak to all as one voice?"

Samiare looked up at him with growing bewilderment. "I do not," she said but then hesitated. "I have… I am just…girl, like any other."

"You seem so uncertain," said Avaugnol. "I see by your poor use of Tieran that you know not how to use it. Perhaps in time…"

"I need army of yours," she interrupted.

"Patience, dear child," he spoke. "First, I must hold it." He placed his hands upon the hilt and drew the blade into the light. For an instant, he looked on it with wonder, but quickly his expression changed, and a look full of fear set into his face. He staggered backwards, falling against his throne where he let out a great cry.

From within the hall, gasps of disbelief rang out, and Samiare grew frightened as well. She took to her feet and moved to aid the King, but pikes were lowered at her, and she was driven back. From the arched doors, more guards appeared and quickly their pikes were set low as well.

At the throne, the King dropped the gold-hilted sword and gasped for air in deep breaths. His face still held despair and tears began to stream down his face. He shook, and then enraged, he stood. Pointing at Samiare and her companions with a trembling hand, he shouted at them with all his vigor. "Seize them," he screamed in his own language, and he practically pushed his guards at them. "Take them from my sight and lock them in our darkest tower. These who are of Marindor and Tierinor we will ransom back to their lands. But the girl...*She has no land*...We will deliver Koning Huedrus a blessing and remove her head from her body. So be it at dawn tomorrow."

Samiare gasped in disbelief, but as pikes were pressed against her, she could doubt no longer. She turned to escape but the pinions of a pike caught her by the ankle, and she was sent stumbling to the floor. Before she could recover, the heavy bodies of armored men fell against her, pinning her underneath.

At the throne, the King took up the sword and thrust it back into its scabbard; whereupon he turned and strode from the hall, never releasing his grip on the blade encased in leather.

"FATHER," CALLED A young Allarie as an old wizard returned from his long journey. "You have come back. Is it truly over? Is the Shadow finally destroyed?"

Mylindrifel's face lit up, and he smiled. "Ilnydrifel, my son," he spoke. "Do help your old father with his things."

Mylindrifel dismounted from his cream-colored horse and embraced his son. "It is good to see you, boy," he beamed. "How have been your studies? I hear you are quite a master of fire."

"And more," said Ilnydrifel with pride. "I can bend the rocks as

well." Ilnydrifel went behind his father and helped to remove his
riding cloak. The material was made of red cloth, and was too heavy
for a summer day, it was something his father no longer required,
but as the boy slung it over his arm, a small piece of rock fell from it
to the ground.

"Let's go and see your mother," spoke the wizard, looking past
his son's ministrations and focusing his attention on the door of his
home. "Long it has been, and I have so waited to see her." The older
Allarie went forward and took to a wide stair that went into the
marble hall of his home. "There will be stories to be told," he
boasted, "and matters I must make right after my long absence."

Ilnydrifel would have thought nothing of the rock, but dark lines
marked its edge and they drew his eye. Looking at it again, he saw
that it had been a piece of something carved, and he snatched it up.
His first inclination was to bring it before his father, but something
else took hold within him, like a shadow clouding his mind. At the
instant of his touching it, he was filled with a desire to keep it, and to
protect it. It was as if a command had been spoken, and he could not
refuse.

Mylindrifel turned at the top of the stairs. "Do hurry, boy," he
spoke. "Do not stand there gawking when the master beckons."

"I am coming, father," spoke the young Ilnydrifel. Then he slid
the fragment into his pocket and went to remove the bags from his
father's horse.

RUEGETTE TORE AT her own bandages as she hastened to wrap
the ends of thickly cut braches. She had resealed the door, and
replaced the brick between the copper brackets, but it was not just
the things outside that concerned her.

Darimus stood over her, a sputtering torch in his hand, and in the
shifting light, she could see well her work, but little else. Before her
the hall proceeded into darkness, but a short distance away it would
open onto the top of a dank stairs; that much she had learned the
night before. She knew Darimus did not understand the sudden
urgency with which she pushed him, and she had offered him only a
brief explanation as to why, but to say she heard voices did not seem
her most persuasive argument. There were only enough materials for

ten torches, and even those were only crude instruments at best, but she had just one course in mind, find whatever was in here, and leave before anything found them.

Darimus was kind. He did not require a long explanation; it was enough for him that she seemed concerned. When she was ready, he took the lead and went before her in the hall, but at the top of the stairs, he paused. Looking down into the darkness there was only the occasional trickle of dripping water; nothing at all stirred below. "We are alone in here," he said.

Ruegette stood close behind him, and fidgeted in a way that seemed unlike her. "I know," she said. "Still, I want us to go quickly."

"You're not going soft on me, are you?"

"What do you mean?"

"I mean, you took a bad wound from a Groll arrow, and now you seem to be jumping at shadows. I want to know you're okay."

"Please," she said. "I am whole, and you would do well not to think otherwise." She looked away, but still felt his eyes upon her. "Can we proceed?" she snapped out.

"Of course," said Darimus with reproach, and then he started down into the unknown. The stairs itself was very long, and continued for more steps than Ruegette cared to count before emptying into a narrow hall, flooded with calf-deep water. The water was warm and murky, and its surface ebbed with a constant ripple, but it seemingly held no danger. The passageway ahead stretched into darkness, and along the walls beside, narrow openings formed dark voids into unknown chambers. Not trusting the floor to be sound, Darimus prodded ahead with his tree-branch staff, and then trudged through the water with caution. Before him, small white fish could be seen scurrying away, and the thick water sloshed against the stone walls, but nowhere did the floor seem less than solid. As he drew nearer to the first of the small openings, the light from his torch touched upon the wide surface of a stone door that lay ahead. Set with brass rings, it was once meant to bar the entrance of anything behind, but the bar was long since missing.

"Here," said Darimus, handing his torch to Ruegette. "Hold this while I take a look."

Ruegette took hold of the torch and peeked her head into each of the dark openings, as Darimus went forward. There were three openings in all, two of which had long ago seen all within them rot away, but the third opened into a cluttered room full of floating debris and half-sunken objects. She started to move into the room, but Darimus called out to her and she stopped. Seeing that he had begun to tug on the brass rings of the sealed door, she left the cluttered room to join him.

Darimus pulled the door open with a huff to reveal a long passage beyond. Made of hewn stone instead of cut bricks, water filled the passage to the calf, and air, hot like a tavern kitchen, gusted forth. The hall was pitched in a slow decent that went only deeper underground, and the level of the water rose in accordance with the grade. The hall was damp and musty, and moisture trickled from the ceiling and walls.

"Looks inviting," he said with the hint of a smile.

"It looks impassable," Ruegette corrected not sharing in his mirth.

"Oh," he mocked. "And just what did you find?"

"Only this," she said, and she led Darimus into the cluttered room.

The room was like the tunnel in that it was fashioned of hewn rock instead of laid bricks, and water trickled from one of the corners with a faint and rhythmic reverberation, but unlike all else within the structure, there was much to sift through; two stone tables, covered with film, and a podium of white marble stood sturdy above the water; glass vials and pieces of pottery, mostly broken, floated in the murk, and along the walls, niches and stone brackets marked the location of shelves that no longer remained. There were two rusted chests made of an unrecognizable metal, and painted into the wall above one of the tables was a map similar to the one she had copied in the library of Esilecolm.

"Look," she said. "I've seen this picture before." She fished around in her pack and produced the copy she had made. "There," she spoke, presenting it. "They are the same."

"What is that?" questioned Darimus with accusation rising in his voice and his finger pointing at the map in her hand.

Ruegette cursed to herself, she realized her mistake in producing her hidden copy, but there was nothing she could do about it. "It's a map," she said sheepishly. "One I copied from the library of Esilecolm. It is from an ancient tome that was written in Ilnydrifel's own hand."

"A map!" Darimus burst out with surprise. "Why did you not mention it before?"

"Because..." she stammered fully regretting her misstep. "Because it holds nothing more than the location of Sahlohir–information you must have already known."

"Yes," said Darimus, "but I trusted you with the things I had learned, and you did not trust me."

"You are right," she said. "And I am sorry. I guess... I guess, I thought less of you then."

"Well," he said indignantly. "How comforting this is. Why, if not for our finding this image upon the wall, you would still be keeping it secret and thinking less of me."

"I have kept no secret," she defended. "I came with you to this place, and in doing so, gave up the pursuit of Sahlohir. I trusted you when I lead you–"

"I would like to see it, if I may," Darimus said coldly.

"Of course," she said, her voice wavering. With a nervous step, she went to the stone table beneath the painted wall, and swept away the filmy dust. As she did, sheets of vellum paper appeared beneath.

She looked on them with astonishment and even Darimus expressed wonder that they could have lain for so long without ruin. They were sketched upon and penned with the same ink that had preserved other items of Ilnydrifel. One was of an arched door, and another was of a woman sitting in a throne with her head turned over her shoulder; a third contained only writing.

Darimus had the greater knowledge of ancient Allarish, and it was he who translated the document. "It says he knows the name of the woman," he spoke, "and that he knows where she will hide. I must presume he means the woman in the chair. Notice the paper seems to pair up with the one beneath so each would be unusable without the other. Perhaps he was making something but it was left unfinished."

"Wait," said Ruegette. She put her map flat upon the stone table, and then pulled out the oddly marked scroll Darimus had given her. When the vellum rested upon Ruegette's own handmade copy they complimented each other perfectly, and the lines, that looked much like rivers cutting across the Wastes, now seemed to point a path between the site Ilnydrifel called 'Our Sanctum' and the hidden location of Sahlohir.

"Oh, Darimus," she said, feeling very small, and suddenly realizing the value of what she had. "I did not know. I am sorry."

"It seems to be marking another way into Sahlohir," he said, dismissing her apology with a cold demeanor. "I bet it starts beyond that door in the hall. It is a map of the underground."

"But it's flooded," Ruegette said with an expression of dread. "We cannot use it. We have wasted our time." She turned to look beyond the room and into the darkened hall, and her sense of urgency was renewed. "We should leave."

"No," said Darimus. "We will look for more."

"It's of no use," she said, feeling the futility of their venture. "There's nothing here."

"Perhaps," he said. "But I think you owe me a little indulgence."

"Okay," said Ruegette cowing to her guilt, "but only because I am so sorry."

Ruegette began to collect the bottles and pottery that floated in the water, and then set them upon the second table. None were labeled and only a few were left with their seals intact. She broke the top off one and tested the liquid within. "Oil," she said. "Enough to make a few good torches." She tested three others; two contained an unknown powder, and the third smelled of vinegar.

Darimus wasted no time in going to the two sealed metal chests. He lifted one onto the center table, but the other broke out its bottom as he lifted, and spilled its destroyed contents into the murky water. At the table, Darimus played with the clasps of the one, but they were too rusted to be moved. Recognizing the futility, he pulled out his sword and beat upon it. The metal was still strong, even after its long stay in the flooded room, but it could not take the pounding he could deliver, the top yielded and a small hole was dented inward.

Within were four glass flasks containing a clear colored ooze. The stuff was viscous and speckled with impurities and was nothing that

Darimus cared to see removed from its bottle, but he did hold one before his eyes and shook it to see what qualities it contained. From inside the flask, a soft light began to glow, and as he shook it harder, it grew brighter still, until it was almost as radiant as Ruegette's crudely made torch. "It glows," he said, "I have never seen anything like it before."

"Me either," said Ruegette, "but there are many things of the Allarie that are a mystery to me. Such a thing would have served Ilnydrifel well if he was searching underground passages, but it won't be of much use to us."

"I'm going to follow the tunnel and see where it leads," said Darimus.

"Darimus," said Ruegette. "I am sorry I didn't share my map with you."

"Forget it," he said. "We are both soldiers from different lands. I understand what that means."

"Yes," she said, but for the first time in years, she regretted she was a soldier from Tierinor.

Darimus led Ruegette beyond the stone door and into the dark flooded passage. As he went, the water became deeper, and soon it rose to above his waist; a distance later, and they came to a place where the roof sank beneath the waterline.

"It's blocked," said Ruegette, "and it's just as well. I don't like this place, and I think it's past time we left."

"Perhaps it continues still," said Darimus, and he began to undo his sword belt.

"What are you doing?" Ruegette let out with rising concern in her voice.

"I will go a little further," he announced. Then he gave a sly smile and started to work on removing his armor.

"You cannot," she said. "It may be flooded from here to Sahlohir; if you were to become trapped or lost…," but before she could finish her words, a loud pounding reverberated throughout the long hall. Ruegette turned with a start and looked back towards the entrance. The pounding came again.

"It's the door," said Darimus. "Someone's breaking in."

"The Groll," said Ruegette with a fierce anger. "It's Umgot and his band. They have followed us."

"There will be too many for us to fight," said Darimus. "Especially in this narrow hall. There's only one course we can follow."

Ruegette cursed out loud, and then she too started to remove her armor.

SAMIARE SAT IN the cold dampness of an underground room. She had been stripped of her robe and shoes and was left with only her white under-gown to cover her. It was dark in her cell and her hands were shackled to the walls by a short length of chain. She did not know where her companions were, and she had no hope of getting free to find them. Much time had passed since she was taken into the halls beneath the palace, and very little time was all she was given. Afraid and unable to make sense of the events that saw her placed in her cold cell, she anguished.

Without her sword at her side, she felt naked in a way she had not since the night her home was invaded on the plains of Norvaine. Her sword was her link to all that made her powerful, and she needed it to bring light into her darkness. Separated from her weapon, she feared that the gifts it provided would be gone from her forever, and worse, she suffered a terrible feeling of woe; it was not something of hers that she lost, it was something divine; its loss was her failure. The pain of that realization hurt her more than all the blows and punishments she had suffered since Norvaine, and she despaired. Was this her punishment for the darkness that flowed from her when she slew the helpless Groll? Was she now to be abandoned? Would the watching God no longer see her? In the cold and dark, she turned to the one thing in which she had placed all of her faith: she prayed…prayed and hoped she was watched over still.

Above the scurry of rats and the infrequent drip of water, she could hear voices speaking. They came from beyond her cell, and wafted in through the thick wood of the locked door that sealed her. They were not voices she recognized, but she knew them to be those of palace guards. They drew closer and she feared it meant the dawn was upon her, but as a door opened from somewhere above, she could hear their words plainly.

"It's cold," spoke one. "Can you not give a condemned girl a warmer cell?"

"It was the King's wish she be kept away from the others," said the second. "I have no place else to keep her that is quiet, but don't you worry; the little strumpet is not going to die from the chill."

Samiare listened with disbelief. Their words were spoken in their own tongue, but she understood them still–even without the hilt of her sword to grasp, she understood, and no longer did she feel abandoned. Whatever it was that had happened, whatever it was that she had done, the watching God was still a part of her, a part she never wished to lose again.

The two figures moved closer to her, and she heard every word of their conversation. A flickering light appeared through the cracks in her door, and then the jingle of keys worked at the lock.

She was near blinded as the door creaked open. Her eyes, accustomed to the total darkness, could not look on the brightness of the torch that one held above his head. The other, who controlled the keys, came forward, and then crouched down in front of her.

"It's your lucky day, pretty," he spoke. "The King wishes to see you."

"Don't waste your breath," said the bearer of the torch. "She can't understand you." The crouching guardsmen grinned widely and then took hold of Samiare's chin. Turning her head in the light, he dug his fingers into her cheeks and pushed her lips forward. "A pity this one has to die," he said. "I would've liked to know her." Releasing her, he fished through his keys and then undid her shackles. "Come!" he ordered, and he pulled her away from the wall by her hands.

Samiare was pushed through the halls of the palace in her gown and bare feet. Through windows, she could see it was dark, and the complete lack of any activity about the palace told her it was late. At the entrance to the throne room, the two guards took her by the arms and pulled her in.

The room was cast in shadows, the only light came from a flickering sconce beside the throne itself. Avaugnol, the King, slumped rather than sat in his throne. He was twisted sideways with one leg over an arm, and one hand draping on the marble floor. His clothes were disheveled and stained with wine, and on his chest, he

held a silver decanter. The sword he had taken from her lay on the
ground before him.

The two guards strode forward, dragging her as they went, but
stopped when the King held up his hand. "Release her," he ordered.
"Then leave us." The two guards obeyed without question; bowing
low, they left Samiare to stand before Avaugnol alone.

For a long moment, the King did not speak, nor did he even lift
his eyes to look on her. Samiare did not know what to do or say, she
stood quietly and rubbed at her wrists.

"Do you know what it is to fear death?" the King spoke as if to
no one, his words wafting up from his languid form to hang like
dissipating smoke, but that is not how he left them; looking finally
upon the frightened Samiare, he spoke in a voice full of passion.
"Can you imagine what it is like to displease the Gods?"

Samiare did not speak, she could not comprehend his meaning.

"Of course, you don't," Avaugnol answered for her, dropping his
attempt to converse in Tieran as an absent-minded gesture. "One
such as you has always pleased."

"I feared I had not pleased when in battle, I felt darkness creep
upon me, and when before the throne, I let you take the sword that
was given to me," she said. She spoke the King's language with a
proficiency that surprised even her, and though it still bore her native
accent, she found that the words came in a miraculous fashion just as
she needed them.

"I see your use of the gifts has improved," he spoke with a laugh.
"Tell me child, what is the secret of the Seven Gods?"

"That there are not Seven Gods," she answered. "There may be
many gods, and in many lands, but there is only one who watches
over, and he is above them. The Seven Gods can only share in his
form. I do not follow them. I follow the one above."

The King shifted in his throne and sat upright with all the regality
he could manage. "How do you know this?" he demanded.

"I see it in the way he reveals himself to me," she said. "I saw it
the instant I first held the sword…as I lay dying on a frozen plain."

"Do you know what I saw when I held it?"

She shook her head to indicate she did not.

"I saw damnation," Avaugnol spoke, and he withered in his

throne. "The watching God is displeased with me. The Seven Gods are silent." The King began to weep, and then grew angry. "How can it be?" he shouted. "Have I not kept the old ways true? Have I not made offerings at the temples? Have I not ruled with wisdom and temperance? How can I have earned such displeasure? How can the Seven Gods remain so silent? How can I be so judged?" The King wept openly and shrank again in his throne. Holding his hand to his eyes in bitter despair, he made one pitiful plea. "How can I be redeemed?"

Samiare was moved, but she knew no way to give him what he wanted. "I cannot redeem you," she said. "I have no such power."

At her words, Avaugnol took away his hands and looked at her with madness in his eyes. "How can it be that you were chosen?" he ranted. "How can it be that the sword that was part of our legacy was delivered to your hands?"

Samiare folded her arms across her bosom to ward away the cold. "I do not know," was all she could answer.

"Do you not fear death?" pleaded Avaugnol. "I must be redeemed, and you must help me. I will take you as a wife and consort. You will council me, and I will know what is wanted from me."

"I cannot," she said. "That is not what is wanted from me."

"Then what?" asked Avaugnol. "What must I do?"

"You must stand up against evil," she said. "You must not stand by while the agents of the Shadow walk freely. You must not abandon the armies of Tierinor and Marindor to fight alone against the Shadow, and you must not deny your responsibility in the struggle for the Eye of Ebon. You must do what the watching God wants of you. You must act, and do so for the rest of your days."

The King shrank beneath her words, and hid himself under his hand as they bit into him. For many long moments, neither of them spoke, until finally, Samiare decided she had too much else to worry over. "Only you can decide to seek redemption," she said, "but I do not have much time. The dawn is approaching."

The King stood on his throne, letting the wine decanter fall away from him to clatter against the marble floor. "The Eye of Ebon has the power to give the Shadow all seeing sight," spoke the King with a new sense of sobriety. "With it, his influence will reach beyond his prison, and soon he will use it.to find and gather to himself all that he has lost. The King of Alasdain will not let this occur. By the dawn, I shall have five hundred cavalry soldiers ready to ride and within two days another two thousand footmen."

Samiare trembled as she heard the King speak the words and fell to her knees. An astonished smile lit up her face as she felt the great burden lifted from her.

"I don't know why you were chosen," spoke Avaugnol, "but you were meant to wield the sword. It is no longer the sword of Raefendal. It is the Sword of Samiare, and I would have no other than the bearer of this sword lead my armies. Take it and wield it well."

The King took up the sword, holding it by its leather scabbard, and held it out for Samiare to take; an invitation she eagerly accepted, pulling it from its scabbard and holding it up high as the King knelt and white flames lit the room.

RUEGETTE WAS RUNNING out of breath. She had long since passed the point where she could return to the air of the stone complex; her only option was to keep going forward. Darimus had shaken one of the illuminating flasks and tied it to his belt; it was the glow of this light that she followed through the murky waters, and it was truly the only thing she could see. She had stripped herself of her armor and left behind her bow; all she carried was what could be strapped to her body or fit into her pack. The walls of the tunnel were anything but smooth, and she used the bumps and edges within to pull herself along much faster than she could swim otherwise, but even that became tiresome.

The tunnel seemed endless, and pain rose in her lungs as she struggled against her body's desire to breathe. She lost track of whether they were heading down or moving up, and soon it became a struggle just to see the light of Darimus ahead of her. She grew weary as she moved forward, and taxed her breathless body until the movement of any muscle was a challenge of will, and at her side, her sword became an unbearable weight. Her chest began to convulse of its own volition, trying to pull something into her lungs, and desperately she resisted. She pushed herself as hard as she could, and just as she came to the end of her will, she surfaced onto a mound of rock.

Darimus was there already; he lay face down upon the mound and sucked in wind with heavy pants. Ruegette could not help but do the same, and practically wept as she filled her lungs. For many moments the two lay together, half in water, half out, and both gasping life. When she was finally able to move, she rolled onto her back and stared up at the rocky ceiling high above, still in the throes of recuperation, her wet hair streamed across her face in red ribbons, and her water soaked under-tunic clung to her like a skin of red vellum.

Darimus moved as well; he pulled the glowing flask from his belt and put it above his head on the rock mound, then he rolled onto his side and looked at her.

Ruegette turned to look on him. She smiled widely. "We're alive!" she said.

"You're beautiful," he said.

"What?"

"I'm going to kiss you."

"Don't," she said, but before she could protest, Darimus pulled her to him, and kissed her full on the mouth. Ruegette put her hands on his shoulders to push him away but then she did not. Instead she let him continue and even kissed him back. He kissed her harder, and her hands tightened on his arm, pulling him closer still. His mouth moved, and hers with it. She felt his hands glide over her, feeling her shape, and coming to rest at her breast. When finally he pulled back his head, he smiled widely at her. "You see," he said. "I'm not all that bad."

Ruegette fell back and lay still, trying to sort through what just happened. Darimus rose and got to his feet. Finally, she burst out, "I told you if you did that again I would kill you."

Yes," he said. "But I think I would rather die than never do that again. And besides, you are starting to like me."

Ruegette could not move. She was simply too stunned. Inside she wanted to get up and make some defense of her position, but there was a part of her that wanted him to come back—indeed she had started to like him. And there was something else… something she thought she had lost, something she thought forgotten. She wanted what she did not have, wanted what, in her duty, she had given up. She wanted to love him.

Darimus picked up the glowing flask and looked about. He stood on a rocky outcropping within a large underground cavern. A lake filled most of the chamber, its edges spanning off into darkness, and water dripped in from the roof to splash against it like a sporadic rain. The tunnel they had used was not visible under the water, but their way out loomed before them like a wide yawning mouth. Glistening with moisture and crystal-like flecks, a wide corridor waited on the edge of their small outcropping.

The corridor was wet with a slimy film and smooth like hardened glass. The rock was unusual in appearance, unlike the grey stone of the mountains it was near black in color and its surface was blistered as if baked. Long glass-like stalactites hung from a ceiling that was more than high enough for any man, or woman, to stand in or walk. The path went up steeply for only a few strides and then seemed to level off before drifting back into darkness. "Are you coming?" said Darimus looking down at her.

Ruegette sat up, but was still not herself. She stared at him for a long, silent moment, and drank in his form; wet clothes clung to him like gossamer, and his muscular build shown through the fabric; thick arms pressed through translucent sleeves and a wide chest bulged beneath the wet cloth. In a new light, she actually found him quite attractive.

"Why did you kiss me?" she snapped out with as much outrage as she could muster.

"You know why," he said.

"Well, I just thought…." In truth, Ruegette did not know what she thought. "Never mind," was all she could say. She rose and pressed the water out of her dripping clothes. "Where do you think we are?"

"We cannot be too far along," he said. "There must still be marsh above us."

"Somehow," she said, her sense slowly drifting back. "Somehow, I think this passage will take us beyond any need to fear the water. It

seems that Ilnydrifel found a way through, and I suspect he used his
wizardry to see that it was passable."

"The map didn't show any alternate passages for some distance,"
he said. "So, we'll just have to follow the trail until there's a reason to
stop."

"It could be many days to Sahlohir," said Ruegette. "And I don't
have much to eat. What I did have is now soaked."

"There were fish in this water," Darimus pointed out. "We only
need catch a few. If we eat sparingly, we should be able to make it; at
worst, we will just have to remember our way back."

Ruegette looked to the water, and then back at Darimus, and the
way they must go. Even in the dark, with only the light he held to
frame him, she wanted nothing more than to go together.

"THE SHADOW HAS many forms," spoke Avaugnol, "and it was
the one sword alone that could bite his flesh no matter how he
appeared."

Samiare stood upon a low balcony at the end of a great corridor
within the palace. Below her, men in the armor and purple livery of
Alasdain formed ranks upon barded warhorses. Pikes were held at
attention, and silver plumed helms glinted in the morning light. The
King had kept true to his word; his knights, near five hundred
strong, were ready to do his bidding, and their orders were Samiare's
own: that they should ride ahead to secure the Passage of the
Immortals, that they should deliver the Placent, Sararth, back to his
Carand, and that they should wait while the armies of Marindor and
Alasdain converged into one force ready to march on Rumsha, the
Feng.

Mirathue and Janthro remained with her, they lingered in the hall
behind the balcony; somehow she knew they would not leave, even if
she asked. The King of Alasdain stood next to her, and as the
captains of his cavalry made ready, he spoke of legends few others
would know.

"It was said once, the Allarie were given endless life. That they
would live through millennia as we spend a day; looking at the events
of an age as if it were only the difference between infancy and
childhood, or adolescence and manhood. It was said at the

foundation there was no Shadow, but it may be that he too has always been."

Samiare listened, and though she need not, she still rested her hand on the pommel of her sword; only this time it was not because she sought comfort in something that had sustained her, but instead because it had been lost, and now it was returned. "But the Allarie fell," she said, half in question. "They were made to leave."

"Yes," spoke the King. "But like so many things that are told, much is forgotten. It matters not how the Shadow came to be, only that he deceived. Many were our Allarish forbearers that turned away from the light and gave up on their gods. Their choice to accept the darkness and to embrace the deceiver is what brought an end to their grace, and for that immortal race, death was their punishment.

"But it did not end at just the fall; many were those who sought to return to the favor of the Gods, and in their quest for redemption they were given a path: they would not be forsaken if they placed in them their faith. It was then that the Allarie began to fight against the Shadow, and then that Raefendal appeared with a weapon that could destroy it–Ifrangul was its name."

Samiare shifted where she stood, and ever so slightly she pulled the hilt of her sword closer to her.

"Yes," said the King, taking notice. "That is the weapon of which the legend speaks, but you should take no comfort in it. The Shadow is more than flesh and blood. He cannot be fought on a battlefield or trapped in a castle. It took all the Allarie had to offer to bring him down, and if he should rise again, then it will fall to the Morkind to repeat their trial. Armies can fight against armies, but what can kill a creature of the dark?"

Samiare stiffened at the thought and then steeled herself to the role. "I do not know," she said, "I will do what the watching God asks of me."

"Ah," said the King, "but isn't that the challenge that stands before us all? Can it be so easy? To do and not question? Those that had turned from the light became the Dur and soon the Groll appeared to spread war through the four lands. Many were the heroes of that time, and many more were those who held faith to their Gods; they should have lived forever but did not because they fell on a field of battle. Did they remain true, or was the promise taken from them?"

"Whether I live or die is not for me to choose," said Samiare. "I cannot change what will befall, I can only choose to follow or not."

"Yes," said Avaugnol. "But you can prepare."

"Then I will prepare."

The King took a step forward and looked out upon his court. There was a somberness in his posture, but his voice carried with it the vigor of portent. "It was as the dragon that the Shadow chose his most physical manifestation, and it was against this form that the Allarish armies sought to slay him, for they thought if just one form could be made to die, then all of his forms would suffer. It was Raefendal, a true warrior of the light, wielding the sword, Ifrangul, who forced the Shadow to assume the wyrm, and he again who brought it low. But an evil like the Shadow cannot be destroyed forever, and there was a cost."

Avaugnol turned from his court and looked straight into Samiare. "The dragon never died," he said. "Oh, his power was taken from him, and his body was gravely weakened, but he lingers still, seething and plotting, waiting for a new age of darkness to see his rise."

"And you think this age is upon us?"

"I don't know," said the King. "The Allarie had many secrets and to keep them, Raefendal led his race away from this land. It is said that he died, and that his sword was lost. Many thought the weapon was hidden in the East, but others thought it was returned to the powers above for an age when it might appear again—and now it has. Should we rejoice, or despair that it has resurfaced? Is this a gift to the Morkind that we may stand against evil, or a warning that evil has been among us and its power is strong?"

"I know not what it means," said Samiare.

"Of course, and how could you?" spoke Avaugnol. "It is a new struggle that awaits us, a time for the Morkind to show their worth. It was written long ago that the Allarie would not truly abandon us; that they left their bloodline in the lineage of Kings, and that in our darkest hour they would return to fight at our side. Perhaps that time is approaching."

The King fell silent and returned to looking out at his assembled army. Samiare stood with him for a long time and pondered the things of which he spoke. In her mind she had no doubt that a new war with the Shadow was brewing, but she thought it would not be soon; the Shadow was still far from escaping his prison, and it was still unclear if he could reclaim his missing eye. Avaugnol seemed a wise man, with a good understanding of what he must do, but she wondered if he were truly ready to take up the fight against the Shadow. If the quest for the Eye of Ebon was only the start of something greater, and if they were seeing just the early stages of a long war, then there would be a high cost to pay before it was done.

The army departed shortly before midday, and it was then that Samiare left the balcony. It was her wish to visit each of the seven temples and pray, for each shared something with the light, but the King wished from her one more indulgence. Taking her into a heavily guarded area of the palace, he led her through a maze of hallways and doors that ended at the bottom of a spiraling stair within a dark cellar. There, a small room, lit by the flames of an oil brazier, was hidden like a vault, and within it, a man of many years busied himself with a small treasure. The treasure had but one purpose, and as Samiare came to look upon it, she was made speechless with surprise. Upon the slender frame of a wooden stand was a small suit of armor shaped for a woman; silver scales like fine leaves covering the shoulders and torso; woven chain at the slender arms, and a skirt of delicate links draped the floor. Upon it was a silver breast plate etched in ornate filigree, slightly purple in hue, cupped at the breasts, flared slightly at the hips, and embedded with a pale amethyst below the neck.

"This fine mail once belonged to Raeshabel," said Avaugnol. "The sister of Raefendal. A great enemy of the Shadow was she. Made of the finest mined metal and strengthened by Allarish craftsmen, it is said that the scales cannot be pierced, and that the cuirass can ward away even dragon fire. It is light and supple, and it is yours if you will have it."

Samiare stood abashed. "I cannot accept this," she said. "It is more than I can repay."

"No," said the King. "It is I who cannot repay; for you have brought me back to life. You have reminded me that Alasdain is a great nation, and that she has good allies. Please put it on and have it. May it protect you all of your days."

Samiare went to the armor and examined it; it was a larger in the chest than she, and shaped for a more full-figured woman, but the size of it was very near her own, and with the help of the one who had prepared it, she was able to wear it comfortably. It was very light, and far less cumbersome than the chain she had worn in the Wastes. In it, she looked like a Princess of Alasdain, but she knew better than to think herself such; she had come to understand that she could not belong to any nation; that she was to be a part of each, and though her heart was with Tierinor, Tierinor alone could not defeat the Shadow.

When she returned to the front corridor, she was rejoined by both Mirathue and Janthro. The two had been gifted with suits of scale armor as well, and both wore them in fine fashion; looking as if they were noble kinsmen of Alasdain. Neither of the two refused the armor, for it was of better condition than their own, but Janthro complained openly; he did not think it proper to wear anything but Tieran mail. Mirathue seemed to hold the issue in indifference, but both wore red livery to display their Tieran loyalty.

Samiare still clung to her desire to visit the seven temples, and to accommodate, the King offered her an escort, but she refused, she was more than comfortable with the protection of Tierinor's two finest warriors. Both Mirathue, and especially Janthro, did not find her desire to be worthwhile, but she made sure to drag both along. It would be two days before they left the city and she had much to be grateful for.

FOR RUEGETTE, FINDING a way in the dark was no easy task. The path was difficult to follow and even with a map, the way forward was often a steep climb or a quick decent, and at times there were passages that were not marked or accounted for at all. There was much to them that confused, and little to indicate their direction. Undaunted, she took to marking the path with small piles of stones. In the early stages of their underground journey, water crossings proved to be their greatest challenge, but at each sunken passage or half-filled tunnel, the way continued to be passable.

She lost track of how many days they had spent in the underground, but she thought it must be many. She did not like to be where she could not see the sky, but she found the blackened tunnels more pleasing than Ilnydrifel's Sanctum. The feelings of uneasiness that had assaulted her in that dark place were not present in the underground, and she found her time was better spent enjoying the company of the Marish Captain.

Darimus stood in the shallow water of an underground pool. He made no motion. Ripples moved along the surface, but the water was clear as glass. White fish moved in the pool beneath him, and he gently stalked them. It was slow work, they were fast and quick to scatter, but he knew how to catch them if he needed.

Ruegette waited at the wide bank where the chamber ended and the tunnel continued. She sat near the water, and touched her hand to her recovering shoulder. It was sore, the bone was still not fully healed, but the burns of the dragon cedar had receded to just a scar. She was wet from having moved through the water with him, and started to lay her wet things out.

Darimus snatched at one of the fish with a splash, and stomped forward, but then he cursed aloud. Ruegette looked up at him and smiled. His motions were loud and echoed in the tunnels. He stood straight, and laughed to himself. In the distance there was a loud squeal, and a small number of squeaks followed. Looking in their direction, he listened some more before proclaiming their source. "Bats," he said. He took his glow flask and shook it, letting it become brighter. "There must be a way to the outside from here. We should mark this. When we have the Eye, we can use this to escape the Groll."

Ruegette stopped what she was doing and looked at him again. *After all they had done, was he still looking to claim it?* She stood and took up her sword in her hand. Darimus turned away from the sounds and trudged through the water towards her, but then he stopped as he saw her.

"You still mean to take it," she said.

"Do you still mean to kill me?" He came forward with his hand before him. "My duty is to my Queen."

"Your Queen is wrong. It must not be claimed. Your duty is to us all."

Darimus came to stand before her, his eyes wide and determined. "You can't fight me," he said. "You are still injured."

"I can if I must," she said. She pulled the scabbard from her dark blade and let it fall.

Darimus's hand reached at the hilt of his own broad blade. "Please," he said.

Ruegette stared at him; she hated this moment. Her heart ached just to think on it. Inside, she knew she did not want to, she had chosen duty over love for so long, she hated that she even had the thought. But she could not let any release the Eye. The threat was too great. His eyes looked back at hers. She could see the anguish in him. And then motion.

His sword came free and glinted in the light. He thrust it forward and stepped in. She backed up a step, and slashed her sword across. Their blades met. He looked to push against her, but she rolled her blade over and then under, caught his thumb and sent his weapon spinning from his grasp. It clattered to the ground as her own came up to his throat. She looked on him again, wanting him to surrender, but instead he lunged forward with his forearm driving at her. Smashing against her collar, he pushed her back to the wall and pressed in.

Ruegette gritted through the pain. Her sword still at his throat, his arm at hers. The pain of her collar was sharp and agonizing. His eyes blazed with anger, and a tear fell from hers. "Don't make me," she said, the edge of her blade poised at his flesh, her hand trembling.

For a moment he held her pinned as emotions played on his face, and then the intensity in his eyes softened and his hold relaxed. "I can't," he said. "I love you."

Ruegette felt her heart stop, and she shook. To hear those words...they stunned her.

"I love you, Ruegette de Tagore," he said again. "I will not hurt you. Whatever we find at the end of this trail. I will let you decide what becomes of it."

Tears flowed down her cheeks, and her sword lowered. "You would do that for me?" she asked.

"Yes," he said. "For you."

She smiled wide, and looked at him so differently. All she had given up for duty and for Tierinor, and now he was giving it up for her. "I love you too," she said.

Darimus reached around her and pulled her to him, and her sword dropped. Her arms came up to embrace as his mouth fell upon hers, and she kissed him hard. So long since she had given all of it up, and now to have it. She would not dare let it go again. It would ruin her.

THE GATES OF Alasdain lay open like a sluice before the mountains. Beneath the stone wall, a wide column of soldiers filed past in high spirits. At the head, a small band of mounted armsmen with pennant flags streaming from the ends of raised lances marked the pace, and before them all, a horse that carried two took the lead.

Samiare sat sideways in the saddle of Mirathue's heavy steed as the latter worked the reins. It was not a comfortable ride, but she understood what was required of her; the peoples of Alasdain were a principled folk, they would not accept a woman to ride as did a soldier. They were also more than a little mistrusting to have her at the head of their army, and that she was foreign, even to Tierinor, did not help. She did not want to invite further wariness from her host.

The mountain road before them was not empty; waiting atop the wide slope, another group of riders set to the reins and approached at a trot. It was a mixed group, most wearing the lavender of Alasdain, but two bore the dark blue of Marindor. Even at a distance, Mirathue could recognize the Marish Placent at the fore, and he turned his mount to meet him.

Sararth looked no better for having returned to the Wastes, and the marred plates of his horse's barding spoke of his circumstances since he departed. The Placent seemed not to dwell on formalities, he raised his hand as a standard cavalryman's greeting, but made no formal gesture. "I see the King has kept his word and more," he spoke as he came within hearing. "Two thousand he promised, but it seems there are more."

"You've a good eye for numbers," said Mirathue stopping his

mount. "We have almost five hundred more than expected. How goes it beyond the Passage?"

"I have been sent to claim you," said Sararth coming to rest, and looking on Samiare still with a strange expression of bewilderment on his face. "Much has changed since our parting, and we must speak as we travel."

"It is well, I hope?" questioned Mirathue.

"Yes," said Sararth. "As we left the Passage near two weeks past, we were met by a small band of Groll sealing the way, but five-hundred men on horses were more than a match for their paltry mob. Two days later we joined the Damar with my Carand, and since that time the Wastes have been different. Scouting parties have been sent out and there have been several skirmishes, but the Groll are disorganized, and their assaults have been ineffective. Carand Kellenus ordered us north to secure the Passage for your arrival, and two days back we fought a battle against a large host, but they were quick to retreat. The Carand believes that the Groll are testing our strength, and are amassing elsewhere for a large assault, but he also believes them to be weak, and that they are unaware of this force. It is his wish to press on to the Hill of the Feng and take control of the south while they are still at their disadvantage. His fear in waiting is that more Groll may arrive from Gorginor, and this opportunity will be lost."

"The Shadow does not send his Groll," said Samiare, engaging the Placent in his own tongue. "He is still trapped and is not ready to begin his conquest. It was his fear that if he left Gorginor with a large force the three Kingdoms would unite, and he was not ready to engage them. But we cannot rest. Possession of the Ebon Eye is still uncertain, and we must continue to do our part. If the Shadow should claim his precious eye, then all we have sacrificed will be lost."

"Then we should abandon the Hill, and leave the Feng where he sits," said Sararth. "We should renew our efforts to seek Sahlohir."

"No," said Samiare, "There is little we can do to influence those who seek the Eye. Our faith must now be in our Gods, and our hope in Lady Ruegette; if she has done her part, then the Eye of Ebon will still be safe. For our measure, we will keep the Groll looking elsewhere by continuing to engage their forces." Samiare looked to the wall, and the long line of Alasdani soldiers filing past, and then back to Sararth upon his dark colored mare. "Take me to your Carand, Placent," she ordered. "And let us put an end to Rumsha's rule in the Wastes."

TRAVELLING UNDERGROUND WAS grueling work, but Ruegette had never been happier. Darimus gave his all to see them through, letting her heal and caring for her like he would not have before. And in the instances when they rested, she held him, and shared herself with him.

At the end of what she thought to be more than a week underground, she followed Darimus as they emerged onto a wide shelf overlooking a deep fissure in the rock. They had entered into a wide cavern, and other entrances dotted the sidewalls. Ahead, and above a rise of jutting stone, an inscription in Allarish was carved into the rock, and beneath it, two stone figures stood aside a bronze door. They were not the first to arrive, and the evidence that Groll had come before was plain to see; the door lay battered and open between the two figures, and the scuffmarks of many boots were ground into the grit that settled upon the rock.

"I think we have found it," said Ruegette, "but we are not the first." She drew forth her sword and started to move forward.

Before the door, Darimus stopped and read the symbols. "It's a warning," he said. "It speaks of guardians that cannot fall and is a notice to stay away."

Ruegette looked up at them as well, but the door was already battered down. She stepped past it to enter a room filled with many rows of ornately carved sarcophagi. Columns were spaced symmetrically to form wide corridors, and stone braziers, cold and unlit, lined the passages. Statues of Allarish figures were scattered throughout, and directly ahead, a lone pedestal of white stone stood prominently in the lane. A book, both thick and leather bound, lay upon the floor as if discarded, its pages bent under it as it lay. The room was more than a tomb, it was also a scene of great violence; spread across the entire chamber were the remains of Groll warriors, their bodies lay in twisted agony, their appearance horrifically withered.

Darimus came in from behind and stood beside her. His eyes were wide with astonishment as he surveyed the room. "I see it is than more a warning," he spoke, almost choking on the words as he said them. "Ruegette, perhaps we should not be here."

"It is a tomb," she said. "There are spirits here. We must take care not to disturb them, and we must not use our swords." She put her sword back at her side, and moved forward to pick up the book.

Darimus walked forward as well, putting away his sword as he passed. "Not use our swords?" he groaned. He started off down the corridor, but then came across something on the ground and reached down to take it. It was a fragment of stone partially etched with runes, one he had seen only once before, when he was at the burial site of Ilnydrifel the Shard Stealer. "*The Shard!*" he said astonished.

Ruegette looked up as Darimus spoke the words, but her eyes did not look on what he had found, instead her attention was drawn to a statue far past him; that of an Allarish woman sitting on a throne. The throne was turned sideways, and faced away from her, but the woman had her head turned and looked over an extended arm to meet her gaze. "Darimus!" she called, but even as she spoke the words, flames began to rise from the braziers and low howling moans came from places unseen.

Darimus stood frozen and looking on the statue with trepidation. Ruegette came forward to stand beside him. "Rue," he said. "What do we do?"

She looked about the room, and then at the almost glowing statue again. "I don't know," she said, "but we will do it together." She took hold of his hand and started to walk towards the statue of the sitting woman. The sitting figure made no movement, but never once did it appear to look at any but the two of them, and as she came to stand only paces from its outstretched hand, it glowed with a light of purest white. The moaning that preceded them began to grow in fervor, and in the darkest places of the tomb, luminous shapes began to form.

"I am Ruegette," she spoke with a noble pride in her tone. "A daughter of Tierinor and Princessa of the Eastern Citadel. Who or what are you?"

The reply came as a soft tone, spoken almost in song. It was single phrase in the ancient language.

She could not make out the words it spoke, but Darimus knew them. "She bids us to speak a word."

"A word?" said Ruegette, and it was then that she saw the resemblance between the woman upon the statue and the Allarish maiden she found laid in a tomb in far away Tierasol.

"She is Ellyndil," she said. "Her word is 'Yamoth'." As she spoke the word, the statue seemed to fade in splendor, and faintly the voice spoke again. Its words, she could not understand, but as they finished, the statue seemed to lose its illumination completely, and slowly the whole of it slid back to reveal a set of stairs leading down into darkness. The moans of the dead still continued, and the braziers still burned, but the fervor had subsided.

"She says she was the first," said Darimus. "And that more will follow. She delivers a warning as well. We should go no further."

"And we should not," said Ruegette. "We should leave while the Eye is still safe within."

"No," he said. "We cannot make assumptions about what is beyond. We must know that it will be safe. We must see it to be sure."

"It would be foolish," said Ruegette. "The guardians have done their work."

"But for how long?" said Darimus. "The Groll will not forget about this place. They will try again; they will try until they have it. We must know."

"I cannot guard this better," she said. "Can you?"

"No, I cannot," said Darimus. "But are you certain that you are the only one who knows that word? What if I told you that Ilnydrifel learned it as well? That it was written in the stone at his tomb."

As Darimus spoke, Ruegette recalled the Maygar that had invaded the temple of Miranae, and suddenly realized the things it may have learned. "You are right," she said. "We must know."

"It is not my wish," said Darimus. "But there is no other way. We will look, and then you can decide what to do."

She nodded and then was first to move down the stairs. As she descended, hot air rushed up to meet her, and from below a soft ebbing light glowed with a fiery red tint. Undeterred she proceeded forward until she came to the bottom and stood upon a wide ledge, high above a deep rock chasm. Steam and hot gasses rose from the fissure in waves of heat that were withering just to be near, and far below, a river of fire flowed rapidly under the mountain.

Before her was a narrow bridge made of chain and iron slats, and far across the chasm, upon a ledge similar to her own, a door of thick iron was pressed into the rock wall. The tall statue of an Allarish warrior, dressed in mail and wearing a great winged helm, stood before the bridge and at its side, it held a long spear.

Darimus went forward and put his hand upon one of the chain rails, but yanked it back in recoil; shaking it as it burned. "We cannot cross this," he winced, and he rubbed at his palm.

Ruegette stepped up to stand before the statue of the warrior and called out to it in a commanding voice. "We seek the Eye of Ebon!" A motion came from the statue that was almost imperceptible, a changing of its gaze, one that took away the blankness of its eyes and left them looking upon its caller, and then a voice spoke words at them that she could not understand in a deep and reverberating baritone.

"It's another word it seeks," said Darimus.

"Yes," said Ruegette. "And his word is 'Eomil,' for he is a warrior named Rafangil."

The statue raised up its spear and then lowered its end again upon the shelf with a thunderous clap, and as the sound of it reverberated throughout the cavern, the iron bridge began to hiss and steam. Becoming covered in a sizzling film that was evaporated off in a wispy haze, the bridge crackled with a deafening roar, and shook violently. The film lingered, seemingly unable to be consumed, and the bridge continued to strain against it, but soon the noise of it receded, and then it made no sound at all. It was then, when all was quiet, that the statue spoke again, but like the woman in the chair, its voice too was faded. Across the way, the iron door swung open with a squeak, and another dark tunnel was revealed.

Darimus tried the bridge again and found it to be cool to the touch. "Impossible," he said amazed. "It is now cool."

"What did he say?" asked Ruegette.

"He gave warning just like the first," said Darimus. "He bids us to consider what we do and turn away."

Darimus moved onto the bridge and started to cross, but Ruegette lingered still; she could not help but think the voices were right, and that perhaps to take the way ahead was worse than turning back. She watched Darimus, who went forward without even looking to see if she came, and again she knew her duty lay to the front. Giving one last look at the stolid stone warrior, she moved onto the bridge and crossed.

The tunnel went deep into the mountain and took them a great distance past the iron bridge before opening upon a large chamber of laid stone. There, water shimmered from within a recessed pool, and four round columns reached to a ceiling high above. Bronze braziers and rows of candles lined the walls, and beyond the pool, a large circle framed with Allarish sigils was carved into the stones of the floor. At the far end of the chamber a single statue stood like a somber judge, watching over all that came before him.

The statue was of an Allarish figure dressed in a long cloak with a wide belt cinching the carved fabric to its waist, and it wore a long sword that dangled to its feet. Its right hand took hold of the pommel, and its left was held up in an arcane gesture. Its face was narrow, and its angular eyes seemed to look right into the both of them.

Ruegette went with Darimus to stand within the sigil, and listened as he called out to announce his purpose, but in her heart, she was greatly troubled; she did not like what they were doing and was torn as to if she should continue further. The statue seemed to look at her in stern judgment and that was disturbing her as well, but as she stood deciding, a light began to glow from the statue's hand, its brightness increasing until it cast away all shadows within the room. When the words came, they were soft and melodic, much like the voice of the sitting woman.

Ruegette knew it wanted a word, but she could not speak it. Trembling, and with her heart pounding in her chest, she wavered. She wrestled with the choice before her, and questioned if it would serve any if she took down this gate. Finally, she turned to Darimus and shook her head. "I cannot," she said. "It is wrong."

Darimus gave a sigh and sank in his chest. He turned to her and looked long into her eyes, but she would not be swayed, and he lowered his head in resignation. "I understand," he said defeated. "If that is your choice—"

"Dar-Mis," spoke a voice in Marish that grated as much as startled. At the door stood a Groll warrior; he was of black skin and wore hard leather plates over thick muscles. A patch covered his left eye, and a large single-bladed axe was held tight in his hands. He did not come alone; Groll warriors began to fan out to his flanks, their ranks growing to more than twenty strong. The black Groll held up a single arrow and spat. "Everywhere I tracked, I found these in my warrior's bodies. Then I found the bow at the end of a tunnel filled with water. It has been a good hunt, but now it is over, and soon it will be Umgot the Foul-Tongue that will claim the Eye of Ebon."

Umgot issued his orders in his own tongue. "Take them both," he barked, "I will kill this 'Dar-mis' and we will pry the word from his woman's lips."

Darimus looked to Ruegette in hopelessness. "Can you fight?" he asked.

"I can," she said pulling forth her dark, slender blade.

"I really do love you, Ruegette of the Eastern Citadel."

"I know," she said. Then she stood beside Darimus and prepared for one last battle.

SAMIARE SAT ON the horse guided by Mirathue, and held her sword up like a beacon, letting its white flames cast their light over the battlefield. Before her, the armies of Alasdain and Marindor moved upon the blackened hill, and the Groll scattered before their might. Flames grew in the dark, the kicked over set fires of Groll archers, and a battle raged. Lines of Alasdani melee-men clashed with Groll warriors, while to their flanks, armored warhorses thundered over the soft ground with lances skewering in. The Groll were disorganized, and the combined might of Marish and Alasdani forces were overwhelming. It was not a battle she witnessed, but a slaughter.

Beyond the Blackened Hill, Marish forces moved onto the Hill of the Throne under the pennants of the Carand. The defenders formed a circle to contest them, but they were too few; the One Hill would fall, and any Groll not slain would be sent to scatter. Samiare watched from a distance. She was not needed in this battle. The assault was one laid out by the Marish Carand and the Alasdani Damar together. All she had to do was bring them together.

But it was still her victory. It was enough that she was there. The Groll feared the White Witch, she could see it in their faces as they looked on her and despaired. The flames of the White Sword in her hands were enough dispel their courage, and before her, and the armies she brought, they could only be consumed.

Mirathue stayed with her, and Janthro was on his mount near. In the field, she could see Sararth on his charger. He rode his heavy Corscan into a cluster of enemy Groll and held his blade high. Cleaving down, one fell as others scattered. He turned towards the Hill of the Throne where arrows, lit with fire, sailed and struck Groll defenders. The resistance of the Groll was growing thin. Kicking his horse again to motion, he set its path towards the throne itself, riding down into the gully before moving up the slope. The battle for the Hill was all but over, and it would all end soon.

Samiare had not expected that this fight would be the last, but she had thought it might be last for those who defended the Feng. Something had changed in the Wastes. The Feng had abandoned, and the throne sat empty. It was another they faced, Morgal the Skull Wearer. Somehow, Rumsha had slipped away, and it was a new Groll chieftain who stood to defend the Mor-hide throne. But the warriors of Morgal were falling and his army breaking apart. He would soon fall with them. In moments, his head on the end of a lance would make that plain.

A horn sounded in the night, a low groaning war horn. Its note, a signal to call the order, and she heard it plain; the Groll archers had been put to flight, and the Cavalry was set to turn; it was time to give up their slaughter and focus on the last that remained. Those that fled may escape this carnage, but on another day soon, they too would fall.

In the morning there would be a council. The Carand and the Damar would make new plans for war and lay them before her. She knew their course already. Rumsha had abandoned the throne and its reason seemed clear–the Eye of Ebon must be at hand. The old Feng would not be elsewhere when the Shadow came. Somewhere near must lie Sahlohir, and it would be there that the Feng waited. Somewhere, holed up within that cursed city, would be thousands more ready to fight at his word, and the contest for the Eye would be decided. She did not know where, but there were many Groll to question. They would soon learn its location.

RUEGETTE HELD HER sword in her strong hand, and pointed it low. A Groll with a studded mace was first to test her skill. He lunged in and she raised the point as she planted her feet; her sword jabbed him through the torso and he fell. Another charged forward and she cut him as well, slashing him open below his ribs and spilling out his entrails. A third brought his hooked sword down, and she stepped around it before lancing her sword up, piercing his head. She twisted her blade before jerking it out. She took wide steps back, favoring her weakened collar, but she still held more poise than those she faced.

Darimus did not fight with such skill as she, where she was a master, he was less refined. He bashed his way through their defenses and scored his hits by strength and force. The first he slew by overpowering its blade and splitting its head with an inelegant blow, the second he threw aside with a sweep of his arm before cutting into its spine.

The remaining Groll seemed not to care who fell, or how skilled the two seemed. Their numbers pushing them, they came forward as a mass and slowly forced the two champions back until at last they came to stand beneath the statue of Tolilzin, the mage. Darimus was valiant; he went before Ruegette with his sword before him, and she turned to guard his flank, but the Groll were too numerous. One lunged in from the right and Darimus wheeled to counter; beating down the weapon, he knocked the savage to the ground with a driving shoulder, but in doing so, he stepped away from Ruegette's guard. She tried to compensate, but was quickly engaged; She could not keep at his back. She saw him raise his blade to strike at one closest to him, but others began to swarm.

She gasped as she saw Darimus cut at his leg and tried to come to his aid. In a hasty effort, she swept past the wide head of a Groll axe and drove her blade into the ribs of one before her. She tugged at her sword, but it had become caught in the bone, and with the pain of her weakened shoulder, she could not wrench it free. A mailed fist ended her effort, striking her full across the face she was sent ringing to the floor.

She fell to her hands and knees, and tasted blood. Beside her fell the Groll with her sword still in its chest. Reacting only by instinct, she lunged for a long knife on its belt and grasped it as a heavy hand took her by the hair, and pulled. She was lifted to her feet by her own red strands where she turned in a fury and drove the wicked blade deep into the neck of the one who held her.

The dark Groll screamed, and fell showering blood as she jerked out the blade. Determined that it was better to be slain than taken, she turned upon the rest like a cornered animal and cried out with savage ferocity. But then she saw something emerge from the dark that made even she fall to her knees and surrender.

"Yes!" ranted Umgot the Foul-Tongue still standing near the entry. "Fall on your knees, mot, and know your suffering will be great." Umgot laughed with wicked glee, but he did not see what Ruegette saw, and as the tall Groll stood sick with mirth, a luminous grey shape took an almost corporeal form behind him.

The shape morphed into a ghastly visage of death and glowed like a spectral wisp in the darkened corridor beyond. In an instant, it lanced forward and passed effortlessly through the body of Umgot. Gasping helplessly as his breath was taken from him, Umgot fell to his knees and choked against seized lungs. Behind him more shapes took form, growing by the hundreds and bursting upon the room in a howling torrent.

A shriek rose from the Groll as the phantoms of Allarie dead descended upon them, and their screams curdled within the chamber. Desperately they flailed their weapons at the apparitions, but they could not rid themselves of the torment. Desperation turned to frenzy; Groll warriors scurried randomly, and weapons were swung wildly; in their panic more than one cut into those closest, and Groll blood quickly flecked the stones. Insanity followed, crumpling to the floor, and burying their heads in their hands, some began to gibber and others to foam, but nothing could free them—the apparitions swarmed like cold wraiths feeding upon their life's energy, and no axe or sword could drive them away.

For only heartbeats, Ruegette was free and she looked for Darimus. The Marish Captain lay only a few paces away, but he was slumped and cast in shadow; a sight that filled her with dread. Fear for him compelling her, she took to her feet and rushed forward; her hand still clinging to the Groll knife. As she moved, she felt the cold touch of ghostly hands; they bit into her flesh like icy tendrils and stole her strength. She fell, and before she could rise again, another came upon her; it was all she could do to just look on Darimus one more time before she could no longer find the will to move. The Groll knife clattered to the floor and she cried out, screaming at each life stealing touch until she passed into unconsciousness.

FOR THE EYE all was distorted. Vague images moved in a shimmering haze like blurry man-shaped shadows. At times there was a gleam of color or the face of one who peered within, and the Shadow hated them all.

The muffled sound of voices spoke from across distances; they were pleased that this would be his end. The Shadow was amused, for he was older than the Allarie, and eternity could not be too long a time for one such as he; the toils of mortals only brought him pleasure. Did they think a mere crystal cage could hold him?

They spoke their magic; the Shadow could feel it as the powers that once caused creation ebbed and pooled to their call. Prayers rose out against him, and the one he hated most, looked on—but this would not be a victory for any. The cage was weak, and any prison could be mastered.

The faith of these he would test. He flexed his will against the crystal, and slowly, like ice cracking to water, the surface gave. He was being moved; a void awaited; a darkness meant to hold him forever. Soon he was within, and a seal moved to decide his fate. One last reminder was needed.

In a darkness black as the pit from which he was spawned, the prison could not hold. He peered out; the Prince was there with the sword, and the wizard that sought so to vex him held a key. The key was being set into the recess of the seal; he saw it–all of it; its sigils and its shape, its depth and its function, and the Shadow knew; with but a touch of his will, enough to remain, he could make his own prison, and so break forever their hope.

The key was their hope, and so he would set himself hidden within their hope and shatter it forever. He reached out.

RUEGETTE WOKE WITH a start. The room was in darkness; there was nothing that stirred. She groped along the floor and found the cool edge of the Groll knife, and she took it in a steady grip. Her muscles ached with stiffness, and a coldness seeped through her. Her mind raced and suddenly she recalled the image of Darimus lost in shadow and was filled with dread. Crawling hurriedly upon the floor she went to where he should lay, but he was not upon the ground. She removed her pouch and shook to light a glow flask.

The room was a scene of great violence; the dead of Groll lay strewn about, their bodies contorted, and their visages dried and withered. Ruegette stood and surveyed; Darimus was not among them. Turning she looked on the statue of Tolilzin, its eyes were dark, and its countenance cold, but something else drew away her attention. No longer was there a ring of sigils carved into the floor before the great mage, but instead a spiraling stair descending into darkness.

Ruegette's heart sank in her chest–*it was opened*. Not even pausing to recover her sword, she took to the stairs and raced down. At the bottom, a long corridor stretched forth and beyond it an immense room loomed forebodingly. She ran the length of the long hall and flew into the chamber. The room was carved with symbols and painted with scenes from Allarish history; and before her, two sets of stairs twisted down from a wide platform. Above the platform, an arch made of stones was laid into the wall, and within its expanse lay a round stone glowing with sigils and glyphs. The round stone itself carved with a single niche to hold a triangular key.

She was not alone in the room; there was another who stood on the platform above. He was holding the Shard and pressing it against the seal. Within the frame of its lock, a shadowy image was forming, seemingly to complete what the Shard was missing.

"Darimus!" she screamed.

Upon the platform the Marish Captain leapt as if startled and stumbled back from the seal. He shook his head clear and turned to watch her as she came forward, but he drew forth his sword and pointed it at her as she bounded onto the stairs.

"Ruegette," he said. "I thought you were dead. When I used the Shard to drive back the spirits I came to your side, but you were so cold..."

He stopped on the stair. Darimus did not seem himself, there was a darkness to his features, and his sword made her uncertain. "Darimus," she said. "What are you doing?"

Darimus clutched at the Shard, holding it close to his body. He looked on it with the same wanting look that he so often held for her. "I knew the words," he said. "But not the order. I have a duty; I must claim the Eye for my Queen."

Ruegette was stunned. "No," she pleaded. "You must leave it. You must come with me from this place."

Darimus lowered the Shard and steadied his sword. "I cannot," he said. "I must live up to my oath and fulfill my obligation."

"If you love me, you will not," she said. She took another step forward, but Darimus's face grew fearful, and he pushed his sword at her.

"Stay back!" he warned. "I came for the Eye. I won't be stopped."

"I can't let you," she said with tears forming in her eyes. "Don't do this."

"You must leave me, Ruegette," said Darimus. "I cannot stop. I will take the Eye even if it means–"

"Would you?" she said, she put aside her knife and reached for Darimus as she walked towards him. Coming to the point of his sword, she let its blade press to her breast, and remained still. Darimus trembled as he wrestled with his choice and tears fell down his face. Then his sword dropped, and she flew into his arms.

"It will be okay," she said.

"I love you, Rue," he said. "I could not kill you. But it bids me–"

"Hush," she said. "I'm here. I will take you from this place."

"No!" Darimus screamed, finding new resolve, crushing the Shard in his grip. "I am sorry, I cannot leave without the Eye. My duty is to Marindor before it is to you."

Ruegette could not believe him. She pulled back in his arms and looked into his face. In it she did not see his love or compassion, only some form of insanity that had taken its grip. The darkness of shadow was in his veins, and his eyes grew black. Tears dropped from her eyes as she came realize; he was not the man she knew, something else entirely had come to rule within him.

"You cannot stop me," said Darimus almost ranting. "I know you are weakened. You must kill me first, and I know you cannot—just as I could not. I must take the Eye of Ebon. I must free it. Let us do it together."

Tears poured down Ruegette's face as Darimus made it plain. In her heart she knew he was right: he was too strong and she was still too weak. The only way to keep the Eye safe was to end his life. She trembled as the thought of it crushed her. "I love you," she said in a voice so faint she could just barely speak it, and then she turned her dagger behind his back, and plunged it in.

Darimus shoved her away, and she collapsed to her knees. He looked on her astonished, and his face went quickly pale. "Tierinor," he said faintly. "I don't understand." Then he fell on his knees and slumped forward. Ruegette could not bear it. She fell upon him with tears rushing down her checks, and holding him to her, she completely broke down, crying from a pain that went deeper than even she knew. Nothing to her, not even death, could be as tormenting.

Long after the room went dark, the halls silent, and the air still, did she think of anything else. She lowered Darimus' body to the floor and spoke at him pleading her sorrow to his dead ears. As he lolled from her arms, an object fell from him to clatter upon the stones. Ruegette heard it, its crisp sound grating on her like a terrible blight. Hardening her heart, and acting only out of duty, she slid her hand down along the flagstones, and groped for it in the dark. Her finger touched upon it, and she took it—the one object that had caused all this struggle and grief—*the Shard*. It was not a prize she wished for any longer; the Eye of Ebon was safe, but its cost had been too great.

WITHIN THE WASTES, the White Witch was near invincible; backed by the armies of Alasdain, and Marindor, and given to the counsel of Tierinor's finest fighting men, the Groll could not stand against her. Carried on a dark warhorse with Mirathue at the reins, Samiare rode at the head of near three thousand men, five hundred riding on metal clad chargers. Gone was the fear that Groll numbers could overwhelm, or that ambushes may wait in the dark. Her way through the Wastes was most direct, forward and through, and all with a sword of white flames held high above the field.

The rumors had abounded in the Groll camps: the approach of the Whar-Shumura was unstoppable. There were no more Groll champions to stand against her, no more Dahmor-ra to rally them, and no will among the Groll to fight. Her reputation had grown, and it alone sent the Groll into retreat. The woods under her power, she pressed for one last destination: Sahlohir, and the dark Feng that was within.

The ruined city lay within the cradle of two mountains at the end of a wide pass that had long since been cracked and broken. The city itself was only a sad memory of what it once had been; towers that once stood proudly within the backdrop of grey peaks, lay crumbled to the ground; halls and palaces, once lighting up the mountainside with their splendor, lay beneath the rock of age and weather; walls meant to keep safe those within, lay breached with gaping holes from long ago battles; and large iron gates that would have tested any Groll ram, lay worn and rusted. The city that would once have been among the greatest of the four lands was nothing more than a decayed ruin, broken and littered with the filth of Groll.

Samiare had come for one reason; somewhere beyond the ruined gate Ruegette fought to protect the Eye of Ebon, and she would not let her go alone into this den of evil. The Groll held the city; near two thousand set atop the ruined walls and more lay beyond, but as Mirathue trotted his steed forward to bring the Wardai before the host, not a one seemed proud enough to challenge her.

"He is here," said Mirathue into her ear. "The Feng has no where else to hide."

"Then let us put an end to his rule in the Wastes," said Samiare. She raised her sword to the wall. White flames pointing the way to battle and victory. Behind her four lines of archers made ready, warriors of both Marindor and Alasdain formed ranks, and knights in heavy armor steadied their barded warhorses; all of them waiting for her to give the command.

"Forward!" she screamed, "and bring down this stronghold of evil." Her language was unlike any heard in the four lands, but in a wondrous fashion, it was understood by all.

RUMSHA SAT ON the marble throne of the ancient palace. The warriors that once served Shargat the Shard Bearer now did his will, but they were not with him, nor were there any of his Dahmor-ra to do his bidding; all of them he had sent to defend the wall; all of them to kill this Whar-Shumura or die trying.

The Whar-Shumura... The bones told him nothing. Now that she had appeared, they revealed so precious little about her. As if her presence disturbed their portent. But she had appeared; she had bested his warriors whenever they met, and she would not be stopped, not until what the bones had spoken came to pass. But the bones also gave him hope, kept as she was from his gaze, he could still read the signs. This day would not be his last, and the struggle for the Eye of Ebon was far from over. Sahlohir was a wretched city; too much in the fancy of the Allar for the Feng's liking, but he had one task unfinished, and he would see it done before she came.

Amid the sounds of war spreading within the ruined city, and signaling the defeat of his forces, Rumsha heard the shambling sound of one warrior returning. Shargat the Shard Bearer stood at the opening to the marble throne room, his face gaunt and his pride broken, his eyes fixed on the bent-over form of the Feng.

"Come forward," spoke Rumsha holding up his staff, and sending an inky black tendril lancing forth to grab the defeated Shargat by the throat. Hissing with laughter, the Feng pulled the Shard Bearer to him, sliding him on his face across the debris scattered floor until he lay beneath the throne. The Feng gave a hiss and then dropped a small stone into the Shard-Bearer's view; the summoning stone Shargat had not used. "It seems we have much to settle, you and I," croaked the Feng. "A matter that I will find most forgivable after I have heard your gasps and choked out your life."

RUEGETTE WALLOWED IN sorrow. She could understand the need for her actions, and the requirements of her duty, but she could not forgive herself for what she did. Darimus fell because of his love for her, and she felt so terribly unworthy. It was cold in the tomb, but she did not wish to leave. For more than a day she stayed with him in the chamber, and even when she found the strength to stand, it was only to arrange for him a resting place.

Amid the rows of sarcophagi, she found one bare and within she placed the Marish Captain. Saying a prayer, and shedding many tears, she anointed his body, and as a final gesture she cut a strand of her hair and tied it as a ring about his finger. Before she left him to lay forever alone, she went to the Allarish Book of Lives Lost and added his name to its pages. It was painful for her to recount what she knew, but she felt compelled to write it all. When finally she left the tomb, she felt less than complete. To her it seemed as if she would always be where she was when he died; at his side and holding him.

It was light out when she emerged from the passages under the mountains, and it was a long way to Yeshale. She had seen the guardians reassume their role, and she carried the Shard, but she held no passion for her duty any longer. She was a soldier, she had given up a life for Tierinor before; she would do so again. With her hand on her dark sword, she began her descent to the forest floor. She may never be free of her sorrow, but she had the strength to press on.

SAMIARE STRODE THROUGH the ruined hall. Soldiers of Alasdain and Marindor marked the way as piles of Groll bodies lay throughout. Sahlohir was a ruin, but its throne still held.

She could hear the voices of the men, see the entrance they guarded, it was their will that it be she who entered and confronted the Feng. In the last remnant of hall that only a few strides could clear, a last guard spoke plainly. "He's in there."

Samiare entered the room. The throne remained, but Rumsha was not upon it. Instead, alone and misshapen, he waited on his knees before it, the only thing to live in the room. His arms were shorn off, and he held aloft his two bloody stumps in an open gesture as she came before him. On the floor at his side, his large skull staff lay broken, and near it, his own severed arms oozed inky blood upon the floor. Samiare stopped, and held her sword low, she could not understand his gesture, but the old Groll only smiled wide. "I surrender," he said.

Surrender...

The very word shook her.

Groll did not surrender.

She did not want to hear it, or even look on him. Her anger rose...

Did any care when it was she who was surrendered? When it was she who wanted it to end?

She held her sword, taking it up in both hands. She did not see him. She saw only something she hated. She raised her sword, and he lowered his head; her feelings drawing cold. Darkness surrounded him, lingering still from the powers he must have used to cut off his own arms. The Feng... One blow to end him, and all his dark power, and all he stood for. One blow to seal his fate. One blow to end this symbol of the Groll and satisfy her hate.

But he was helpless...he put his life in her hands...

She fought with herself, and her arms trembled. One more Groll, one more helpless Groll... She held her sword and looked down, willing him to take an action, to let it be right. *Did he not deserve his fate?* The music played, and she wanted it to command her, to strike, to kill...but again, its answer was always the same, to trust...to choose. To be in the light, or be forever in darkness...to be in darkness, and darkness was all she felt.

She closed her eyes. She made her choice. Her sword lowered, and her head cast down. His fate was deserved, but she would not give it to him. She would not become dark like him. She accepted his surrender. She would trust in the light.

YESHALE WAS NOT much of a village; only a few weathered buildings around the temple of Emshallet. In ages past more structures would have stood upon the sward, dwellings made of wood and brick, but now only empty patches of ground remained. The temple was still strong and proud; avoided by the Groll in their fear of the Deity of Light, it showed only the discoloration of age. Its thick walls and grand entry looked today as it had so many years ago.

Ruegette expected to find the young girl from Norvaine when she arrived, but she was not prepared for all that were with her. Gone were the fifty Tieran melee-men that came with her down the river, and gone as well was the ship that brought them. In their place was an army more than five hundred strong, and not only of Marindor, but of Alasdain as well. Ruegette saw a Marish Carand standing beside an Alasdani Damar, and both of them stepping aside for the passage of a young Wardai and the small band of Tieran soldiers who stood with her.

Samiare herself was changed; no longer did she wear a suit of mis-fitting chain, but an elegant suit of fine mail made in an Allarish fashion, and her manner was different; for the first time since she had known her, the young girl seemed comfortable in the company of those around her. Ruegette did not know what to think, but as she stood gawking, one of Tierinor came forward in a limp to greet her.

"Lady Ruegette," he said beaming. "We have been most eager for your safe return."

"You are Izarou are you not?" she asked. "Where is Captain Ambrue?"

"He was slain, milady," spoke Izarou. "Our ship was attacked shortly after you disembarked, and our journey through the Wastes has been perilous, but it was your Second who saw us to safety; she carried us through our first days, brought together an army and dealt defeat to the Groll. She made a prisoner of Rumsha the Feng, and scattered his forces into the woods. It is a long story, one befitting the Shal Comair and she should tell it."

Ruegette looked at Samiare with wonder. "A prisoner of the Feng?"

The girl smiled and bowed her head, then she spoke, not in the broken speech she once held, but with a command of Tieran that bore only a hint of her foreign accent. "We have sent scouts ahead," she said. "There are Marish ships to the south and the Carand has offered to deliver us to our home. A delegation from Alasdain wishes to board as well. It seems an old ally is ready to renew a forgotten friendship. And yes, the Feng has yielded to us."

Ruegette could not believe what she heard; she stood stunned before the small form of Samiare and was almost speechless. "It seems Zarue was right," she said. "You are a Wardai. You must tell me how you accomplished all of this."

Samiare smiled abashedly beneath Ruegette's apparent awe and blushed. Ruegette considered her for a moment longer and then remembered something she had. She pulled forth a crudely made charm of wood; that of a carved flower, cut on one corner, and attached to a leather string. "I found this," she said. "The man who wore it, I set to rest. I wished to give it to you when you were ready. You are ready. You should have it."

Samiare took the broken pendant and tears welled in her eyes as she looked upon it. She reached forward and embraced Ruegette who embraced her back; they had both lost much, and Ruegette could not begin to console either Samiare or herself, but perhaps they could grieve together. "Come," she said. "Let's us two Wardai go and explore the Wastes alone for a while."

EPILOGUE

DARK FIGURES SAT at the precipice of a deep pit. Hidden within the mountain, the crater emanated with dark energies that ebbed and flowed and washed all above with its radiance. None moved, gaunt figures that shown only in the negative light while the energy below writhed like a thing itself alive.

One stirred. Its head turned and looked away. Unmoving and unmoved, the others seemed not to take notice, but the one which stirred rose and turned away from the pit. "We are betrayed." Its words hissed out, though its grey ghastly visage seemed not speak. In the eyes of the others, not even a flicker of disturbance yet somehow they had all heard it.

Within the crater of the pit, darkness crackled, seeping past its walls like a cold breath. At its center, a dark figure could almost take shape. Itself a heart of blackness, to stand for an instant as energy cracked and be gone the next.

Above, the dark figures looked on, but the one that stirred had already left them.

~Continued in the Promise of Eternity~

SIGN UP FOR MY AUTHOR NEWSLETTER

Be the first to learn about P. Pherson Green's new releases and receive exclusive content for both readers and writers!

WWW.PPHERSONGREEN.COM

EXTRA SCENE

HIS CART, HIS prison, was pulled along the pitted and rocky lane by a beast not fit to ride. Men in gold helmets and lengthy red tabards, each with a spear in their hand, walked beside. He was chained, not by his hands, for he had none, but by his neck to boards of the wagon, while thick iron bars made the cage that held him.

Rumsha looked out and scowled. All of this over a Groll with no arms. All of this, as if he was their prize. But he had read the bones. He knew there was nothing they could do. He had seen his fate, and they were not his slayers.

Crowds lined the thin street where his carriage prison passed. People of the hated land come to see the captive, to see the Feng that had been brought low. He bore them in contempt and looked only into them to see how weak they all seemed. Men shouting as if they had done any of it. Women with scrunched up faces, gawking at the Groll—the monster spoken about but never seen, and children with wide eyes staring in wonder.

For only the shudder of his nerves, he sought to frighten them. He leapt for the bars until the chain at his neck stopped his motion, and outside the men winced back–fear–fear of one with no arms and only half their size.

But then he saw one who did not fear. An older girl with dark hair and ragged clothes and the filth of the streets upon her face and body. He stared at her, and she stared back, and then he felt it. The darkness hidden within. He began to laugh, loud and mocking, laughing at her and the crowds. Laughing at the very Gods themselves. She screamed and fell to her knees, and at that Rumsha only grinned. He spoke a word…"Witch!"

The girl looked on him, and then fell back. "No," she screamed. "Kill him…Kill him. He will bring the damned. He will bring back the damned."

Rumsha only smiled and looked on her as his cart moved ever forward, leaving her to become lost in the crowd.

BOOK 2
THE PROMISE OF
ETERNITY

"SHE'S IN THERE."

The voice came from one in the dark; a tall man who leaned on a crutch and bore only a single good leg; the other, only a carved wooden peg.

"I know."

The second voice was that of an older girl; she stood impatiently with her hand resting on the gold pommel a large sword.

"You don't have to." The man spoke again. "I can do it."

"No," said the girl. "I am her second. I will get her." Her voice carried just the hint of a foreign intonation.

The man gave a grunt, and then shifted his weight. "She won't come easy."

"No," the girl said. She went forward, the night air blowing cold against her face. "She won't."

The shadows of the darkened entrance could not hide her. Standing with eyes smoldering and a hand pressed to the golden hilt of her sword, she surveyed the room. It was a den of drunkenness and debauchery, the rank scent of stale mead permeating the air, the inhabitants, like a sea of bodies, moving under the red light of oil lamps; the sound of greedy merriment, somehow both indulgent and indifferent in its motions, mocking at its own lewdness. The one she sought could also not escape notice.

Wine spilled as the lady twirled and then fell, letting the arms of two who held only lust in their eyes hold her up. Laughter rose as one stroked her body, and then playfully she pushed him away. The other, she kissed, before pulling free, only to stumble again and fall against the roughhewn wooden bar. Drunk and unsteady, and with red hair spilling unkempt over her eyes, still this lady could never truly be caught unawares.

The presence of the girl could not be mistaken, and the lady scoffed. She took one last drink from her cup before standing up straight and raising it high. "Well, there she is, boys," Ruegette said at last. "Tierinor's finest hero. The newest Drothning of the Wastes—Samiare of the White Sword. She's come to collect me and to take me back to where I belong. Isn't that right, *Second*, I am to go with you?"

Samiare gave no reaction as the room fell silent and all eyes turned towards her. She kept her glare on the older Ruegette and spoke, a hint of a foreign inflection present in her dry tone. "Ruegette, your father—"

"Yes," said Ruegette. "My father." The lady took another swig from her cup before turning and walking back into the company of her evening suitors. "My father," she said loud and disdainfully. "I hear he wants to honor me—honor you." She paused to share words with one near her, and then laughing accepted his mouth on hers before turning her attention back to her unwanted guest. "Did you know," Ruegette said to her company, "that if my father had had his way, I would have been a dutiful wife to a stuffy lord in one of our sister nations, docile and placating and holding my tongue in all things between nations? How glorious that I should be his favorite now."

"Ruegette—" The girl spoke again, but the lady would not hear her.

"Sent you, has he?" Ruegette mocked. "Did he also send his warriors to escort me?"

"You know I have come alone," Samiare said. "This is not a place for you. I want you to come—"

"And what's wrong with a place like this?" Ruegette said as she coiled a ruffian in her arms and let her tongue glide over his face.

"Don't," said Samiare, taking a step further into the room. There was an uncomfortable shift from the crowd as she did, even a hint of menace.

"You want I should get rid of her?" said the one Ruegette embraced, his hand pulling at a knife at his belt.

"Oh, no," said Ruegette, caressing his face. "She would only kill you if you tried." She cradled his head as her attention turned. "Isn't that right, Samiare? Isn't that what you do? Leave 'em dead."

The eyes of the girl swept the room, her hand clutching at the gold hilt like it had no other home. "Will you come?" she said.

"Okay, boys," Ruegette announced. "Guess the party is over. I better go before she gets flustered. Would hate for things to turn…ugly." Ruegette stumbled away from those around her and crossed with a wobble to where Samiare stood waiting. Falling against the smaller form of her second and causing both of them to stumble, the red-haired Princessa of Eastern Citadel let out a laugh. "Guess we made an impression," she said. "Kill some of the bigger ones and people notice. The Battle of Two Rocks they are calling it."

Samiare half carried her friend, and gave a wry smile. "We have been good in battle together," she said. "I don't need anything else."

"You know they talk," said Ruegette. "Which one is greater? The Red Princessa, or the White Wardai. Which one should be the Second, and which one the Prime?"

"It is a foolish question," said Samiare. "I will always be second to you."

Ruegette gave a knowing laugh, and then left the den with Samiare as her guide.

~Find the rest of this tale at www.thewhiteswordsaga.com~

PRONUNCIATION GUIDE

As it happens that some of the names of the characters and places within the books of the White Sword Saga may prove difficult to pronounce, or have pronunciations may not seem obvious, this guide is provided to help with some that may prove tricky.

It should be noted, however, that some names may be pronounced in many different ways. Samiare, for example, travels to many foriegn lands, and encounters people with different languages and different dialects. It is unlikely they would all pronounce her name the same. She would likely answer to any close approximation.

Samiare: Say-mi-arr-ee
Ruegette: Rooz-zhette

Nechare: Neh-kar-ee
Zarue: Zah-roo

Adelle: Ah-dell
Ambrue: Am-brew
Avaugnol: Ah-vog-nul
Bajora: Bah-jor-ah
Darimus: Dare-ih-mus
Eklar de Mouge: Eck-lar de Mooje
Ellyndil: Ill-en-dill
Emshallet: Em-shaw-lett
Ereth: Ee-reth
Ginoux: Gin-noh
Glysandra: Gly-san-dra
Guryot: Grrr-yot
Huedrus: Hue-drus
Ifrangul: If-fran-gul
Ilnydrifel: Ill-nid-ri-fell
Izarou: Iz-za-roe
Janthro: Jan-throw
Karkella: Kar-kell-la

Kellenus: Kell-lay-nus
Krellus: Krell-lus
Kullis: Kull-iss
Leondis: Lee-on-dis
Lizelle: Liz-elle
Mavrou: Mav-roe
Miranae: Meer-ah-nay
Mirathue: Mir-ah-thew
Morgal: Mor-gahl
Murg: Merg
Mylindrifel: My-lin-dri-fel
Raefendal: Ray-fen-dahl
Raeshabel: Rae-sha-bell
Rafangil: Raff-an-gill
Rendid: Ren-deed
Rumsha: Rum-sha
Samael: Sam-may-el
Sararth: Sair-Arth

Shargat: Sharr-gatt
Shalee: Shah-lee
Shateel: Shah-teel
Stroja: Strow-jah
Saurul: Saw-rule
Tolilzin: Tall-lil-zin
Tokoron: Toke-or-ron
Tuz: Tuz
Umgot: Um-got

Aillsdale: Ails-dale
Alasdain: Alice-dane
Allarie: Ah-lahr-ee
Avanrill: Av-ven-rill
Carand: Kuh-rand
Chol-Junat: Chole Jun-ut
Dahmor-ra: Dah-mor-rah

Damar: Day-mar
Drisari: Drih-sar-ee
Durish: Durr-ish
Esilecolm: Eh-sile-lee-colm
Feng: Fang
Gorumgahl: Gore-um-gall
Meridel: Mare-ih-del
Mirneth: Mirh-neth
Sahlohir: Sal-low-here
Shal Comaire: Shall Cohm-air
Sharal: Sha-rahl
Sharin: Shar-in
Shuma-ra: Shoo-ma-rah
Tierasol: Tere-ah-sol
Wardai: War-die
Whar-Shumura: Ware-Shu-mor-ah
Yeshale: Yee-Shale

COMING SOON

The White Sword Saga

Book 1 - The Eye of Ebon
Book 2 - The Promise of Eternity
Book 3 - Wielder of the White Sword
Book 4 - Warriors of the Light
Book 5 - Way of the White Wardai

FROM THE AUTHOR

Dear Reader.

The writing of the Eye of Ebon was a labor of love for me, and it is to my great joy and honor that you have taken to time to read and enjoy this story. The Eye of Ebon, and the books that follow, is a tale that has taken me years to prepare, and some expense to produce. If you enjoyed this story, and would like to see others, please take some time to go and leave a review of this story on Amazon, or any place that it may be available for purchase. Your reviews help keep this story in front of others like you, allowing them an opportunity to enjoy it as well, and allowing me to continue to produce more stories in this story world and others.

As the author of this story, and with great humility, I wish to thank you for your time and attention in the reading of my story. Without you, this story could not come to life.

The QR code below will link you to where you can leave a review for this book on Amazon's web listing.

ABOUT THE AUTHOR

P. Pherson Green is the creator of the fantasy series, the White Sword Saga. He lives in Maryland, where he has been a lifelong resident, and has a successful career in IT. He is married, and has two children, and is a military veteran. He has several published works that have appeared in Daily Science Fiction, and the Sword Review, and can be found on Amazon. P. Pherson has a love of many large topics, including Fantasy, Religion, Philosophy, Politics, Science, History, and the Human Condition, which he tries to capture in his characters and stories. He shares many artistic talents, and has been writing his tales since the late 90's.